NAPA NOIR

PETER EICHSTAEDT

A WINE COUNTRY MYSTERY

WILDBLUE
PRESS

WildBluePress.com

NAPA NOIR published by:

WILDBLUE PRESS
P.O. Box 102440
Denver, Colorado 80250

ISBN 978-1-947290-63-1   Trade Paperback
ISBN 978-1-947290-62-4   eBook

Interior Formatting by Elijah Toten
www.totencreative.com

NAPA NOIR

PROLOGUE

Muffled shots broke the late morning stillness in the Northern California vineyard. Chao Ling dove to the ground, scrambled through a row of vines, leapt to his feet, and kept running.

A man with a pistol fixed with a silencer trotted after him, barrel held high.

Ling dove through another row of vines, and another, then crouched behind a post, his lungs aching.

Holding the weapon at arm's length, the gunman's eyes narrowed and he fired again, the bullet ripping through a cluster of the ripening grapes, splattering Ling's face with juice. He humped up the hillside vineyard, his chest heaving, and peered again through the leaves.

The gunman was nearly parallel to him, separated by four rows, aiming at him.

Ling ducked to his left as another *thunk* sounded. He cried out as his right thigh exploded with searing pain. He clutched his leg and tumbled to the ground, rolling onto his back. *The bastard is crazy! Why did I get involved with this idiot?* He looked up the row, searching for an escape. *Keep moving!* His leg on fire, he struggled to his feet and hobbled, blood soaking his pant leg. His left leg quivering with every step, he pulled out his cell phone. With shaky hands he tapped 9-1-1 and listened to the phone's buzzing ring.

"What's your emergency?" a dispatcher asked calmly.

"Someone's trying to kill me!" Ling shouted.

"Are you okay?" the dispatcher asked.

"I've been shot!"

"Tell me who and where you are, and what's going on."

"My name is Chao Ling," he yelled. "I'm at Morrison Creek Winery. It's Bernie Morrison. He's got a gun! He's trying to kill me!" Ling sucked in one breath after another, his body shaking.

"Can you get to a safe place?"

"What the fuck? That's what I'm trying to do!"

"Hold on." The line went silent for what seemed an eternity.

Ling peered across leafy vines as Morrison crawled through a row, rose, and took aim, firing again, the muffled shot ripping through the leaves. "Aw shit!"

The dispatcher came back on. "We have a unit in the area. I'm sending it now. You'll see it soon. Stay on the line and tell me what's happening."

Keeping his head low, Ling hobbled back down the slope and toward the winery, hoping the cops would get there before he'd be cut down. The phone slipped from his hand and fell to the dirt. He kept going.

Three rows separated him from Morrison, who kept moving, staying parallel to him. Blinding pain filled his head as two muffled shots sounded. Ling stumbled to the ground. He touched the side of his head and felt the wet warmth flowing from a gash in his scalp. His hand was bright red. He struggled to his feet at the edge of the vineyard, breathing heavily. His eyes stinging from sweat, his head on fire, he scanned the highway in front of the winery. A black-and-white cruiser, lights flashing, headed toward the vineyard.

Ling heard footsteps behind him and twisted around, his leg wobbly, and fell to the ground. His vision blurred, he wiped his eyes with bloody fingers, and squinted up at Morrison, standing over him, pistol pointed at his chest. "Don't!" Ling cried, staring at Morrison's bloodshot blue eyes, arms reaching up in appeal.

Morrison glanced to the winery entrance where the sheriff's cruiser swerved into the graveled parking lot and slid to a stop.

Ling saw two officers leap out and draw their weapons, crouching slightly. They shouted for Morrison to drop his gun.

Breathing heavily, Morrison returned his eyes to Ling and glared.

"No, no, don't!" Ling yelled. Three muffled shots slammed into his chest like iron fists. He wheezed a breath as the air crackled with the deputies' gunfire. Morrison's body shuddered, bullets staggering him backward and to the ground. Ling's world went dark.

CHAPTER 1

Dante Rath massaged the ache in his stomach. Heartburn flared from the black coffee he sipped, having devoured a foil-wrapped breakfast burrito at his desk. He leaned against the fraying pad of the low-backed office chair and re-read the memo from management. Consultants were reorganizing the newsroom. Early retirements and buyouts were coming, along with new beat assignments. He had been down this road before. He drew a deep breath and tossed the memo on one of the piles atop his desk. He yanked open a drawer, shook a couple of antacid tablets into his hand, and chewed them.

Dante crossed the newsroom to the drinking fountain and emptied his coffee mug, refilling it with cold water. He drank it down, refilled it, and looked out at the newsroom, empty but for a clerk with his feet up, reading the morning edition, and couple of section editors. Most reporters were on their beats. Dante wondered if he could survive another downsizing, or if he wanted to. He took a breath and returned to his desk.

At forty-four, he'd collected state and regional journalism awards. Three times his work had been submitted for the Pulitzer Prize as part of a team of investigative reporters at the *San Francisco Chronicle*. They won once for exposing a web of corruption around government contracts for private prisons. The stories had sparked a federal criminal investigation resulting in jail time for a state senator and the prisons' director. He ached to return to investigative reporting, but after reading the memo he knew his odds of doing it for his current employer, the *Santa Rosa Sun,* were in the negative numbers.

A call on a police scanner near the city desk caught his attention. A female voice called out a "ten-seventy-one" at the Morrison Creek Winery. Sirens wailed in the background. Then a "ten-forty-nine." Dante hurried over to the bank of scanners next to TV screens tuned soundlessly to local channels and listened closely to the calls. A ten-seventy-one was shots fired. *What the hell?* A ten-forty-nine meant a unit was proceeding to the scene. He sipped more water, his heart pounding.

The lights flickered on the Napa County Sheriff's Department band as more calls came. Another sheriff's unit was responding. The next transmissions were a ten-fifty-three and a ten-fifty-four. Person down, possible body.

Dante yanked the narrow notebook from his back pocket and jotted down the time, date, and ten-code numbers. It was nearly 11 a.m. and the crime beat reporter was out. Dante smiled as a shot of adrenaline pulsed through him. The story could be his and his alone. A shooting at the Morrison Creek Winery could salvage his sputtering career. It might even lead to … what? He didn't have time to think about it, or the personal problems he had with the winery owner. He hustled back to his desk, pulled on his corduroy sport coat and slipped the notebook into the outside pocket. Looking again at the management memo, he wadded it and tossed it into the wastebasket.

Dante wove among the desks in the crowded newsroom to the glass-walled office of his managing editor, Seth Jones. A veteran reporter and editor in his late sixties, he'd grown a little soft around the middle, but carried the extra pounds well. Jones wore hippie-styled wire-rimmed glasses, had bushy white hair, and loved murder stories even more than corruption scandals. "Did you hear that?" Dante asked, standing in the open door.

Jones looked up from his desk. "Yeah. What is it?"

"Shots fired at Morrison Creek Winery. Possible body. I'm going."

"The hell you are!" Jones barked, holding up a hand. "You're the wine editor. Let Hansen cover it."

Dante clenched his jaw, exhaled, and shook his head. "She's not here." Cathy Hansen was the newspaper's young cops, crime, and district court reporter. She'd been hired out of journalism grad school at UC Berkeley, his alma mater. She was the kind of person they wanted these days, tech savvy and a social media maven willing to work long hours for entry-level pay and who didn't talk back to her bosses. Nice girl, a good writer, but she was overly confident and naïve. She reminded him of himself at that age.

"I wrote about Morrison Creek a few weeks ago," Dante said. "Remember?"

"Yeah, I remember. What'd you call the wine? Horse piss or something?"

Dante swallowed and felt his face flush. "Not in those words. The guy who owns the place, Bernie Morrison, deserved it. He's selling box wine in bottles."

"He threatened to kill you if he ever saw you again."

"C'mon, Seth. Threats come with the territory."

"There's been a possible homicide at the winery of a man who said he hates you and the ground you walk on. Now you want to run over there and poke around? It probably has nothing to do with the wine."

"But maybe it does."

Jones leaned back in his chair behind the large oak desk, pulled off his glasses, and massaged the bridge of his nose. Dante knew Jones felt lucky to have his job. The *San Francisco Chronicle* had summarily dumped him years earlier after disbanding the investigative team Jones ran when the newspaper was sold and deflated to a husk of what it once was. Dante had worked for him then and had followed him to the *Santa Rosa Sun*.

"When are you going to accept the fact this newspaper can't afford a full-time investigative reporter?" Jones asked. "I went to bat for you, Dante. It's how you got the wine editor's job."

Dante looked out across the empty newsroom, waiting for the lecture to end. His job was to keep tabs on Northern California's billion-dollar wine industry. Spread a thick layer of happy talk over the endless acres of vines and proliferating wineries. Exposés were a thing of the past, a fact he refused to accept.

"Did you read the reorganization memo?" Jones asked, his voice low and conspiratorial.

"Of course," Dante said.

Jones glanced out into the newsroom and motioned for him to close the door.

After quietly closing the door, Dante settled into one of the straight-backed chairs facing Jones's desk. The burn flared again in his stomach. Closed door chats were never good.

"I want to give you a head's up," Jones said, mashing his lips together, struggling to find the words. "They're eliminating your job."

Dante swallowed hard. Not long after joining the *Sun*, he'd launched a wine column called "The Grapes of Rath," replacing a blandly named column, "Wine Country Week," telling Jones the column needed personality if anyone was going to read it.

"My wine column has been well-received," Dante said. "Wineries are calling us for a change, asking for their ads to be placed on the same page."

"I know," Jones said, holding his hands up defensively.

"I've put my heart into the wine beat," Dante said, his voice rising. "Earlier this year I helped organize the annual Symposium for Professional Wine Writers here in the Napa Valley. I read every wine book and magazine I can get my hands on. They're on my desk now, under all those winery press releases I get every freakin' day. I read all the wine blogs. The newspaper is even paying for me to get a wine certificate at the UC Davis! Now they want to cut the position?"

"Calm down."

"It's not like I needed to do any of this crap, you know," he continued. "I grew up right here in wine country. I helped my grandpa make what they used to call Dago red. Barrels of it, year after year. Long before anyone took California wine seriously."

"I know."

"I've been a good boy, you know," Dante said, not letting up. "When all those free cases of wine began showing up at my doorstep, I didn't keep them, did I? No. I donated them to charity auctions."

Jones shook his head and leaned back in his chair as Dante fell silent. "Done yet?"

He exhaled. "So, what the hell are they going to do with the job?"

"Slice 'n' dice. The wine business news will be handled by Thompson in the business section. The food and wine reviews will go to Donatello in the lifestyle section. Wine reviews will be freelanced by several of the self-styled wine critics who populate this region."

Dante's heart sank. He looked at the floor, then at Jones. "So now what?"

"Do I look like an employment agency?" Jones said.

"What about putting me on general assignment?" Dante said. "I've covered every kind of story there is, from obits to exposés."

Jones was unmoved.

"We won the Pulitzer, remember?" Dante said, trying to eke out a sympathetic smile.

"That's history," Jones said. "You know how the news business is these days. The only thing publishers want to know is what you've done for them today. Even if someone else quits in the next few weeks, you're not getting the job. According to the consultants, the staff is bloated." Jones exhaled noisily. "For what it's worth, you're not alone. After this reorganization, they're giving me a bonus and pushing me out the door."

The knot in Dante's stomach tightened, the heartburn smoldered. He felt his world slipping away—again. "So, how long do I have?"

"The consultant's report is due in a couple of week. It goes into effect a month or so later. So you have about six weeks."

"What the hell am I supposed to do?"

"You're one of the best investigative reporters around. Start looking. What's going on with your buddies at that nonprofit journalism outfit at UC Berkeley?"

Dante shook his head. "No openings. They've got problems, too. Nonprofits depend on grants. The grants come from rich people who don't like reporters writing about how they and their friends make all their damned money."

"The rich just get richer," Jones said with a groan.

Dante sat up and crossed his arms as a wry smile crossed his lips. "It's all the more reason for me to go out to the Morrison Creek Winery."

"It is?"

"There's more to this story than a dead body or two."

"How do you know?"

"I just know."

"I told you, Hansen is covering the story," Jones said.

"When you find her, tell her she can do the main crime story," Dante said. "I'll write a color sidebar with some history of the winery. It'll also give me something dramatic for my next column."

Jones sighed. "Okay. She and a photographer will meet you there. Help them out, will you?"

"Glad to be of service." Dante turned from the office and burst out of the newsroom and into the warmth of the late morning sun on the loading dock. He hurried down the steps, his mind reeling. In the parking lot, he pulled open the door of his aging dark green Mustang, a retro fastback coupe. Heat roiled from inside. The V-6 engine roared to life, settling into a soft rumble, enhanced by a hole in the muffler. He loved the sound. Much better than the putter of the mufflers punks installed on their rice rockets.

Dante swerved out of the parking lot, his tires squealing. He slammed through four of his five gears and merged into traffic, quickly hitting 70 mph as he headed south out of Santa Rosa on Highway 101, and found fifth gear. He avoided the two-lane State Route 12, knowing it would be clogged with SUVs, vans, and limousines loaded with wine drinkers in the hunt for their next winery amid the rolling hills of Sonoma County.

Yeah, the winery owner Bernie Morrison had threatened him all right. He'd expected nothing less from Morrison and knew he deserved it. Still, he had dismissed Morrison's death threats. If anything, Morrison should have been the one worried about him, after how Morrison had carried on with his late wife. Dante's stomach knotted and his heartburn returned. He was going 85 mph now, swallowed hard as he checked his rear view mirror for cops, and backed off the accelerator.

After Morrison's threats, he'd done what the newspaper management wanted. He talked to the police. The cops told him to take the threats seriously. He didn't. They also told him to consider buying a weapon. He didn't do that either.

If it were Morrison on the ground at the winery, Dante knew he'd have a hell of a story. Everything about Morrison was phony, even the name of his winery—"Morrison Creek." There was no such creek. Morrison made it up to sound rustic. Dante decided if he had only six more weeks as a *Sun* reporter, it was going to be six weeks no one would forget. He checked his rear view mirror for cops again and stepped on the accelerator.

CHAPTER 2

Dante wheeled onto the exit to State Route 116, and thirty minutes later turned off the Carneros Highway before reaching Napa and saw the sign he was looking for. He slowed and took the narrow paved road to the Morrison Creek Winery, a renovated barn nestled in a grove of trees just off the road. His pulse quickened at the sight of the emergency vehicles, police, and sheriff's units crowding the winery parking lot, lights flashing in the sunlight. He pulled over to the side of the road, stopped, and climbed out while checking for his notebook and pen. He drew a deep breath and told himself to calm down.

Yellow crime scene tape stretched across the parking lot entrance, but no cops guarded it. A few uniformed investigators clustered around a small table near the adjoining vineyard. Dante squinted at what looked like plastic baggies on the table. Evidence. His eyes fell on two bodies covered with sheets on the sparse grass near the vineyard. A couple of officers walked between the leafy vines, eyes to the ground.

A female voice called out his name. He wheeled to the sight of a woman in heels showing remarkable balance as she hurried toward him. She was Carmen Carelli, an attorney whose clientele included some of the best winemakers in the Napa and Sonoma Valleys and beyond. They'd had lunch not long ago, but nothing had come of it. Dante had wanted her to talk about a client, one of California's biggest winemakers. She'd been agreeable and polite, but had revealed little he didn't already know.

As she strode toward him, her dark hair fell over the shoulders of a gray pinstriped suit jacket. The plunging neckline of her ivory silk blouse revealed a glimpse of cleavage. She looked at him with dark, piercing eyes and knitted her brows, as if annoyed he was there.

"Chasing ambulances these days?" he asked.

"Hardly. One of the bodies over there was my client."

Dante caught his breath. "Who? Morrison?"

She shook her head. "No, the other one."

Dante glanced again to the vineyard and back. "So, one of the dead is Morrison?"

Carmen pressed her lips together. "It's what I've been told."

"By whom?"

"I have my sources, just like you do."

"So, what happened?"

"Ask the cops, Dante."

"You're not being helpful."

"What are you doing here?" she asked. "Crime isn't your thing, is it?"

"Some of the wine around here is criminal. Like Morrison's."

Carmen smiled. "That's funny."

"I mean it."

"I know you do. I read your column. You did a real number on him. Morrison was extremely upset. So was my client."

Dante didn't feel like going into it, not here anyway, and pulled the notebook from his pocket. He wanted to get a comment from Carmen before she disappeared into the crime scene.

"Who was your client?" he asked.

"Is this for the newspaper?"

"No, Carmen. It's for a comedy skit."

"That's why what you write makes me laugh."

"I'm glad you're amused." He held his pen, poised on his notebook. "So, if your client was upset about what I wrote, he must have been involved with the winery."

Carmen squinted at him in the sunlight, saying nothing.

"So, who was he?"

"You asked me already."

"You didn't answer."

Carmen exhaled, looked to the parking lot, and back at Dante. "You didn't get this from me," she said. "His name was Chao Ling."

"C-h-a-o…L-i-n-g," he said, jotting the name as he spelled it out. "What was Mr. Ling doing here?"

Carmen crossed her arms. "You *are* full of questions."

"Was Ling an investor in the winery? Or was he a customer?"

She tilted her head to the side. "Maybe he was both."

"Everyone dreams of owning a winery, don't they?"

"Not everyone."

"What else can you tell me about Ling?"

"Nothing. Attorney-client privilege."

"Carmen, the man's dead."

"Doesn't matter."

"You're being ridiculous."

"It's the rules. I follow them. He has assets. They need to be protected."

Dante waited for more, but she said nothing. He scratched his temple with his pen and looked off to the distant table where investigators were huddled. "If Ling had a financial interest in the winery, why would Morrison want to kill him?"

"We'd all like to know, wouldn't we?"

"It might be useful for you to talk to me about this, sooner rather than later."

"Useful to you, maybe."

"Rath!"

He turned as Cathy Hansen jogged toward him, with Nate Segura, the chief photographer, trailing, his camera bag bouncing on his hip. Two television station SUVs topped with broadcast dishes wheeled into the parking lot, spilling reporters and cameramen.

"What are you doing here?" Hansen asked. "This is my story."

Dante smiled calmly. "Glad you could make it."

Hansen wore her blond hair in bangs with the sides trimmed at her jawline. She wore a burgundy T-shirt tucked into her designer jeans under her tweedy sport coat. She scowled. "I'm serious."

"So am I," Dante said.

"So what the hell happened?" Segura asked.

Dante pointed toward the investigators and the bodies on the ground. "Two people dead."

"Can we get in there?"

He shook his head. "You'd better use a long lens, Nate."

With the arrival of Hansen and Segura, along with the television vehicles, a couple of deputies hurried to the crime scene tape, waving their hands for them to stay back.

"You're Ms. Carelli?" one of the deputies asked Carmen.

She glanced at her watch, the gold links of the wristband glittering against her light olive skin, and looked at Dante. "I gotta go. Call me sometime."

"Count on it," he said.

A deputy handed her a clipboard. "Here. Sign in."

She scribbled her signature, and the deputies lifted the tape for her.

"Why do you get to go in?" Dante asked.

She turned. "They called me. They want to talk to me about Ling."

Dante watched the sway of her hips as she strode into the winery, thinking about how he'd like to get to know her a lot better. He wondered why he hadn't done so already.

"Not fair," Hansen said with a whine.

Dante squinted at her. "She knows one of the dead. She's his attorney. And, she's part of the Carelli family, one of the oldest names in the California wine business."

"I know who the Carelli family is," Hansen said. "Who can I talk to here?"

"Hold on," Dante said, pulling out his phone and stepping away to talk. He came back and looked at Hansen. "I called a friend who's on the force. He's up there now. He's agreed to talk to us, but it has to be off the record."

"Okay," Hansen said. They watched Segura screw a monopod into the bottom of his camera, attach a 400 mm lens, and focus. He snapped a few frames and moved along the tape to get better angles.

A Napa County special investigator came down from the crime scene and paused on the other side of the tape. "Jake," Dante said, reaching out to shake his hand.

Jake Henshaw was a fortyish, muscled man with closely cropped hair. He wore a black fleece vest with "SHERIFF" emblazoned in yellow block letters across the back, an automatic pistol holstered at his waist. His jeans fell on tan desert boots. "Since when are you covering homicides?" Henshaw asked.

"People keep asking me that."

"And what do you say?"

"Not much. What happened here?"

"I'm really busy, in case you hadn't noticed."

Dante turned to Hansen. "Cathy Hansen, this is Investigator Jake Henshaw. She's the one who's covering this story for the *Sun*. Our photographer is Nate Segura."

Henshaw flexed his jaw muscle and looked around the crime scene, as if worried, and back at Hansen. "You can't quote me, okay?"

"No problem," she said with a smile. "Background. The sheriff's going to have a press conference in another thirty minutes."

"The man who owns the winery—" Henshaw began.

"Bernie Morrison," Dante blurted.

Henshaw scowled. "Apparently had some issues with the victim—"

"Chao Ling."

Henshaw scowled again. "We haven't released the names of the suspect or the victim."

"I just talked with the victim's attorney," Dante said. "Carmen Carelli. She's inside the winery now. I also know Morrison. I interviewed him a few weeks ago."

Henshaw looked irritated. "The victim, Chao Ling, was chased from the winery, into the vineyard, and shot. Five times. Once in the leg, once in the head, three in the chest."

"What about Morrison?" Dante asked.

Henshaw sighed. "When officers arrived, they found Morrison standing over Ling, who was still alive. Officers ordered Morrison to drop his weapon. He didn't. Instead, he fired three rounds into Ling."

Henshaw watched Hansen take notes.

"The deputies shot Morrison?" Hansen asked.

"They had no choice," Henshaw said.

"Two men gunned down in a vineyard," Dante said with a smile. "Can't make this stuff up." He watched Hansen finish her notes and look up.

"Do you think it was premeditated?" she asked.

"Hard to tell," Henshaw said. "But, yeah."

"Why?" Hansen asked.

"There was a silencer on the murder weapon," Henshaw said.

"What was the weapon?" she asked.

"A .22 caliber."

"It's what people use to hunt rabbits, I thought," Dante said.

"Pistols like the Walther are popular among a certain crowd," Henshaw said. "They're light and easy to use." He tilted his head from side to side, bones crackling in his thick neck. "Sorry. Gotta go."

"Thanks," Hansen said. She turned to Dante, her face sinking into a frown. "It's my story."

Dante lifted his hands and waved her off. "I know. I know."

CHAPTER 3

Three days later, the Napa County sheriff said the investigation was continuing, despite the fact both the suspect and victim were dead. No one was talking about a motive, which made Dante wonder. Two people shot dead in a vineyard and no one wants to know why?

The Napa Valley Vintners Association was unwilling to weigh in on the deaths, which did not surprise him. Bodies riddled with bullets and lying around vineyards were not what winemakers wanted to discuss in public. Nor was it what they wanted to read about, and to comment would only provoke more questions, the kind of questions Dante intended to answer—in print.

He had helped Hansen as much as he could, and her stories dominated the front page for the past few days. But the hard news edge of the story was gone, and Hansen was back to covering the routine stories of her beat: car accidents, burglaries, and assaults. It was time to dig a little deeper. Carmen Carelli was the best place to start. She'd sounded apprehensive on the phone, but agreed to meet him for dinner.

Arriving early, Dante elbowed his way to the restaurant bar, ordered a glass of wine, and took a swallow while keeping an eye on the parking lot. He recognized Carmen's Porsche when she wheeled into the parking lot. He greeted her near the door, guiding her through the noisy, upbeat crowd as they were shown to a glass-topped table on the outside patio. Whatever scent she wore was enticing. Dante reminded himself to stay focused. The pretext for this dinner was not romance, but information. His job was to get it.

The hostess dropped two menus on the table, flashed a fake smile, and disappeared. A busboy appeared and asked if they wanted water. "Because of the drought, we only serve water on demand."

"Please," Dante said, scanning the multi-page wine list. "This place has very good wines."

"Some are from my clients," Carmen said.

"Provided here, I'm sure, at a deeply discounted price," he said.

"Of course."

He pointed to one on the list. "What about this Italian Brunello? It's quite reasonably priced."

"It's a good one," Carmen said.

"You know it?"

"It's one of Ricardo's wineries. He gave me a case for my birthday this year."

"Ricardo, as in Ricardo Santos?" Dante asked, lifting his eyes from the wine list.

"Yes, of course," she said, perusing her menu.

In little more than a decade, Santos had become one of the major wine producers in the state. From the Santos Wine Company headquarters in the San Joaquin Valley, he lorded over tens of thousands of acres of vines and owned a handful of boutique wineries as well. But the bulk of his business was mass-produced, low-cost box wines called Santos Select. He'd once been fined for mislabeling wine, and the case put him on Carmen's client list. Dante had wanted to talk to her about Santos the time they'd met for lunch. Now she might talk.

"So, you're on a first-name basis?"

She looked up from her menu. "We have a professional relationship."

A waiter appeared at the table. "Good evening. My name is Brad. I'll be your server this evening. Can I get you started with some drinks?"

"We'll start with a bottle of wine."

"Certainly. Do you know what you'd like?"

Dante looked at Carmen. "Should we go right for the good stuff and get the Brunello favored by your good buddy, Ricardo?"

She shook her head. "Let's start with something lighter. He's not my buddy, by the way. He's my client."

"Okay." Dante scanned the wine list again. "How about we start with a bottle of this Rossese Di Albenga." He pointed to the item on the wine list.

"Good choice." The waiter spun and left.

"It's from Liguria, on the northern Italian coast," he said, returning to Carmen.

"You know Italian wines?" she asked.

"I spent some time with my mother's family in Italy. Near Spoleto, in central Italy."

"Lucky you."

"They own a winery. In Montefalco. I stayed for a season and learned the business."

"Italian style."

"I took the opportunity to travel. Northern Italy, Southern France, the Rhone Valley, Burgundy, Bordeaux, and the Loire."

"So you became a wine critic by drinking your way across Italy and France?"

"I'm not a wine critic. I'm a journalist who enjoys wine. I started writing my wine column out of necessity. I try to keep it about the business, not the nonsense usually written about wine. But sometimes I stray."

"Like what you wrote about Morrison Creek?"

"Yeah, well. There's more to the story. Anyway, the column has attracted a following."

He thought about his conversation with Jones at the office and was about to say the column would soon end, when Carmen said, "Ricardo reads it."

"He does?" Dante said, curious Santos would follow a local wine column.

"Yes. He told me so. I think you'd like him."

Dante straightened at the thought. "Do you think you could arrange an interview?"

She narrowed her eyes. "I suppose I could try."

"He's a recluse," Dante said.

"He's been burned by the press a few times," she said. "It would be a stretch to get him to talk."

"All the more reason for him to come out of his shell. Set the record straight, so to speak."

She shook her head. "He's a busy man. He's got affiliated offices in Rome, Madrid, and Mexico City."

"He's probably got Mexican business partners, maybe the Italian mafia, too."

"Why do you say that?"

"Anyone with money in Mexico is involved with the drug cartels. Same in Italy."

Her face flushed in annoyance. She drew a breath and exhaled. "It's a myth and you know it."

"Do I? The drug cartels make billions of dollars a year. What do they do with the money?"

"How would I know?" she said.

"Besides buying more drugs and paying their men to hunt and kill rival cartels, some of the money is washed through legitimate businesses," he said. "So why not wine?"

She shook her head in disgust.

"So where did Santos get all the money to make himself a leading player in the California wine business in such a short time?" he asked.

"Not all of his wineries are in the US. Some are in Italy, some in Spain. He's also in the olive oil business. He has olive presses in Spain and Italy, along with his wineries. Mexico, as you may or may not know, is starting to produce some very good wines now."

"Good-bye, tequila."

Carmen shook her head in annoyance. "The point is, Santos is an international businessman. Any number of international banks would loan him money. How does that make him a criminal?"

"He's rumored to be linked to the Aragon cartel."

"Carlos Aragon and his brother Miguel have businesses in the US. So what? It's not a crime."

Her response piqued Dante's curiosity.

The waiter brought their bottle of wine, showed it to them with a flourish, and pulled the cork. As he poured, Dante wondered why Carmen so readily defended Santos. Putting the thought aside, he lifted his glass for a toast. "*Centi anni!*"

"May you live a hundred years as well."

He rolled the wine around his mouth before swallowing. "Good. Very good." He looked at the glass thoughtfully. "Hints of *frutti di bosco,* but still dry."

She sipped. "I like it." She set the glass down.

After they ordered, he took another drink and leaned back. "Thanks for meeting with me."

"It's mostly because I'm afraid of what you might write about my clients."

"The live ones or the dead ones?"

"This conversation has to be off the record."

"What are you so worried about?"

Carmen wrinkled her nose, as if the question smelled badly. "What do you think? I'm taking a risk just meeting with you here."

"A risk? I don't think of myself as a risk."

"Meeting with a journalist? Are you serious?"

Dante dismissed the comment with a shake of his head. "I did a little research at the courthouse. You sued Morrison on behalf of Ling. Tried to take the winery from Morrison. What prompted the suit?"

She sipped from her wine, slowly putting her glass on the table. "Before I answer, I want to ask you something."

"Okay."

"You said there was more to the review you wrote about Morrison. What was it?"

He winced, reluctant to go into it.

She shifted in her seat. "Quid pro quo."

He sighed and returned her gaze. "You drive a hard bargain."

"I'm a lawyer."

"There's a rehab facility north of here, near Calistoga," he said.

"I'm familiar with it."

"My late wife, Nicole, was driving there one night to check herself in. She never made it."

She raised her eyebrows. "An accident?"

He drank from his wine, the memories of that agonizing night roiling in his head.

Carmen looked sympathetic, yet curious.

Dante cleared his throat, shifted in his chair, and continued. "It was about a year ago. She'd been visiting friends, or so I thought. She'd been drinking. It was raining. The car left the road at high speed." He drew a halting breath. "She was found by a driver who saw the car lights in the field, the car upside down. She was brought to the emergency room here in Santa Rosa."

"That's awful," Carmen said.

The bright glow of the red block-letter "Emergency" sign on the hospital wall, the glare of the blue-green fluorescent light in the ER, and the confusion and helplessness he'd felt that night were as strong as if it had just happened. It was 1 a.m. by the time they'd tracked him down and called. The emergency room was quiet. Too quiet. He'd asked to see Nicole immediately. Instead of showing him to Nicole, the nurse told him to wait. A doctor would talk to him.

"She died on the operating table," Dante said, his throat tight as he struggled to tamp down his roiling emotions. "Internal injuries, they said."

Carmen's eyes opened wide. "I'm so sorry."

"The emergency room doctor told me she was pregnant."
Dante's words hung in the air.

"You didn't know?"

He shook his head. "She never told me. That's why she was driving to the rehab facility, I think. She wanted to clean herself up to have the baby." He looked across the restaurant and back at Carmen. "I found her phone when I retrieved her effects from the wreck." He cleared his throat again. "It was filled with text messages."

She frowned, struggling to understand, and quietly asked, "An affair?"

His mind lost in the memories, Dante didn't answer.

"Did you know who?"

Dante swallowed hard. He could barely form the words. "Bernie Morrison."

Carmen sat back and looked at her wine glass, pondering the implications.

"He was texting her things like he couldn't wait until he held her in his arms again. It was such a bunch of bullshit." Dante swirled the wine in his glass and took another swallow, exhaling slowly. "Morrison had used her to worm his way into Napa wine society."

"How?"

"Nicole and her first husband once owned the Shady Oaks winery."

"I know the place," Carmen said. "The wine's pretty good. Small batches, high quality."

"Nicole's husband was stashing money in off-shore accounts rather than paying creditors."

Carmen shook her head in disgust.

"The banks eventually called in their loans, and when he couldn't pay, they threatened to foreclose on the winery. So he ran off to Mexico with one of the girls who worked there. The winery went on the market as part of the divorce settlement."

"It happens more than people like to admit," she said.

"So Bernie Morrison shows up, and with the help of some investors, he bought it."

"That's how they met?"

"That's how we met, too. I wrote a story about the sale. It was my first as the new wine editor."

"And you married her?"

"Nicole was waiting for the sale to become final. We had lunch. One thing led to another."

"Wait. I don't get it. So she was involved with Morrison as well?"

He shook his head. "Not initially. They knew each other because he was the managing partner for the new owners. She was very sociable and did a lot of volunteer work, like for the Napa Valley Arts Council. It hosts wine tastings for fundraisers. The wineries donate their wines, raffle off their best stuff—you know the drill."

"Yes. Good community relations," Carmen said. "My family has donated millions to the arts."

"Morrison was a charmer, you know, and professed a profound interest in the arts and that kind of thing."

Carmen smiled, recalling the man's good looks. "Tanned, thick white mane, trimmed goatee. Contagious smile. But still...."

"I blame myself. It's a hazard of the news business. Long hours, low pay. Nicole got lonely."

"So why do you do it?"

"I've been asking myself that a lot lately." He glanced at his wine and back at Carmen.

"So you and Morrison had some history," she said. "Interesting."

Dante sipped his wine. "After Nicole died, I lost track of Morrison until he resurfaced with his Morrison Creek Winery."

She narrowed her eyes again. "So you trashed Morrison's wines in your column out of revenge?"

Dante drew a deep breath. Yeah, he thought, and it had felt good, damned good. If revenge is a dish best served cold, this one had been delicious. But Nicole was dead. Had been for a while now and nothing would ever bring her back. Dante shook his head and tried to push down the feelings of regret. "The wine deserved to be trashed. Comparing them to Santos's box wines was accurate. Morrison's wines are very similar. I wouldn't be surprised if it was the same wine. Putting it in a bottle with a nice label does not make it good."

CHAPTER 4

The waiter returned with their dinners and the conversation paused as they pounced on the food. After devouring most of his entrée, Dante sat back and wiped his lips with the cloth napkin. He narrowed his eyes and cleared his throat. "So, what happened to Ling? Why was he killed?"

Carmen frowned and looked away. "It should never have happened."

"But it did."

"I really don't want to talk about it."

"Just help me fill in the blanks."

"Why?"

"Because you're a smart and attractive woman who believes in doing the right thing." As the words rolled off his tongue, Dante surprised himself. He let the words hang, unapologetic. Compliments never hurt.

"Really?" she asked with a smile and a glimmer in her eyes.

"Yes. Really," he said, convinced he meant it.

Her fork clinked on the plate. "Ling was a phenom in Silicon Valley. Started with Google, rising up through the ranks. He left to start his own company. Just a few years later, he sold it. He did well. Very, very well."

"It's nice to have clients who can pay their legal fees."

"He wanted to buy into a winery. Which is when he ran into Morrison."

"A lucky break for Morrison."

"Morrison was involved with a number of businesses—you know of one, Shady Oaks—

but he'd sold them. He was good at losing money, it appears, especially other people's money."

"I don't understand why a man as smart as Ling would go into business with Morrison."

"Both had dreams of making it big in Napa Valley wine. One had the money. The other had a winery."

"A marriage made in heaven."

"Hell is more like it."

"So there was a problem. What?"

Carmen sighed. "None of Ling's money ended up going into the winery."

Dante's mind raced. He reached for his glass and took a drink. "Where did it go?"

"It was supposed to go for winery upgrades and expansions, but they never happened. Ling came to me only after he realized he might never see a return on his investment. We sued Morrison, demanding the money or the winery assets."

Dante pondered what Morrison could have done with the money. He sensed the winery shooting was morphing into a story larger than a fight over an investment. "How much do you know about Morrison?"

Carmen looked at him and again hesitated. "Not much. Just what's in the lawsuit."

He drew a slow breath. Old habits were hard to break. When he'd first written about Morrison's purchase of Shady Oaks, he'd done an extensive search. Ling's lawsuit was not the first time Morrison had been sued. "He was from Ohio, Columbus, as a matter of fact," Dante said. "He'd been in the chemical business."

Carmen fell silent as he spoke, her face clouding, her eyes unfocused.

"Are you worried about something?" he asked.

"I still can't believe Ling is dead, though I guess I shouldn't be surprised," she said. "I mean, when Ling and I sued Morrison, I sensed he was a little … off."

"Just a little?"

"I obtained a concealed carry permit."

"You carry a gun?"

She nodded.

"Do you have it with you now?"

She nodded again, her eyes wide. "What about you?"

He tensed at the thought. "After Morrison threatened me, the cops asked if I had one. The implication was I ought to consider it."

"So do you?"

"No."

"It's not illegal."

"I know. But the problem is, if I had it, I might use it."

Carmen stared, lost in thought.

"You represent grape growers and wine makers, not criminals, yet you carry a weapon?"

"There's a lot of legal work in the wine industry," Carmen said. "And a lot of different characters."

"Like Morrison?"

"You can't be too careful."

He took a sip of wine and leaned back. "Or like Ricardo Santos?"

"Him?" she said, with a shake of her head. "He's not a danger. He's an asset. He keeps me on a retainer."

"The state fined him about $3 million a few years ago. He mislabeled about a million gallons of wine. Said it was Napa cabernet, but it wasn't. It was a zinfandel from the Central Valley or something."

"He paid the fine. End of story."

"There was the seventeen-year-old girl who died earlier this year working in one of his vineyards."

"It wasn't Ricardo's fault."

"It was his vineyard."

"That's not the whole story."

"I'm all ears."

"Ricardo hired contract labor. The contractor was supposed to provide food and water. He didn't."

"Your client, Ricardo, still bears responsibility."

"As it turns out, the girl was illegal."

"That's no reason for her to die."

Carmen dismissed his comment with a shake of her head, and turned to the busboy who reached for their plates. "May I take these?" he asked.

"Please," Dante said.

When the waiter returned with dessert menus, he asked, "Would either of you care for dessert?"

Carmen declined. "I'm not a dessert person, but if you want, go ahead."

Dante perused the price of after-dinner drinks. A prize-winning vintage port wine caught his eye, but the cost was out of his range. "Ah, I think I'll pass as well."

"I have a few bottles of Ricardo's Brunello," Carmen said, her voice soft, her gaze inviting. "I'm all about sharing."

Dante smiled and turned to the waiter. "In that case, bring the check."

Outside, he followed Carmen to her car, where she tugged open the door to the ivory Porsche 911 Carrera. He took her in his arms, kissing her deeply as she molded herself against him, only pausing to take a breath, as if coming up for air, diving again into the sensations. The second time, he looked around, suddenly self-conscious. "I'll follow you," he said, reluctantly releasing her.

CHAPTER 5

Dante awoke in the dark, his head pounding. Carmen lay beside him, sleeping on her stomach, her back exposed, her breath slow and soft, a pillow partially covering her head. The wine-soaked evening slowly came back to him.

The door to her Sonoma farmhouse had barely shut when they were wrapped in each other's arms, clutching and tugging each other's clothes. Carmen ached for him as much as he for her. They sank to her carpeted living room floor, their entwined bodies reaching a groaning, shuddering moment. Afterward, they'd opened a bottle of the Brunello, drained generous glasses, and headed to the bedroom.

Now his head hurt. He swung his legs over the side and stood unsteadily. He turned to gaze at her shapely body. It had been a while since he'd had such a sexual appetite. She'd awakened desire in him lying dormant for far too long. *Have I been that depressed?* Whatever it was, she had cured him.

He skirted the bed and stepped into the bathroom, lighted by a small nightlight casting the room in pale green. He found the medicine cabinet and a fumbled for a bottle of ibuprofen tablets. He shook two into his palm and was about to toss them in his mouth, but couldn't find a water glass. Easing the door open, he went back into the bedroom. He listened to Carmen's breathing and in the darkness exited the bedroom door, leaving it open only a crack.

In the kitchen, light from a distant street lamp reflected on the polished marble countertop. He found a glass in the cupboard, filled it at the tap and swallowed the pills. After downing a second glass of water, he headed back, but paused when his eyes fell on the door to an adjoining room.

He turned the handle and eased the door open. Her home office was dominated by a large desk with case files stacked at the sides and walls lined with built-in shelves filled with law books. He listened for movement from the bedroom. Silence. At the desk, he tugged the chain to a banker's lamp, flooding the desk with light. He squinted, waiting for his eyes to adjust, and focused. The Ling file was front and center. He flipped it open.

He leaned forward on one hand, using the other to massage his eyes awake. He scanned a few sheets of paper, turning each over, and reread the top page. It was a transcript of a witness interview by his friend, Napa Sheriff's Investigator Jake Henshaw of the Morrison Creek vineyard manager, a man named Gilberto Muñoz. He'd been at the Morrison Creek Winery when the shooting took place.

The police told Muñoz he could have an attorney present for the interrogation, and he had asked for Carmen Carelli, whose name he'd seen on a business card on Morrison's desk.

Dante shook his head to clear it, squinting to focus on the pages in front of him. Despite the ache, his mind raced as he scanned the pages. Carmen offered few objections to Henshaw's questions, unlike most lawyers who would try to protect their clients against self-incrimination. *Why?* Maybe she was as curious as the police as to what Muñoz knew. Muñoz answered questions grudgingly. Dante figured Muñoz didn't want be involved and feared being implicated.

He came to the critical question.

Henshaw: Why do you think Morrison killed Chao Ling?

Muñoz: He was angry with him.

Henshaw: Why would Morrison be angry at Ling?

Muñoz: Because of the grapes.

Henshaw: Because of what grapes?

Muñoz: Señor Ling was not happy because the grapes Morrison used did not come from the vineyards he said.

Henshaw: Where did the grapes come from?

Muñoz: From all over. Some from Lake County. Some from the Central Valley.

Henshaw: Can you be more specific?

Muñoz: St. Helena. Russian River. Lake County. In the Central Valley, it was from around Modesto, Madera. Places like that.

Henshaw: How did Morrison get those grapes?

Muñoz: He and Señor Grundy got them.

Henshaw: Who is Mr. Grundy?

Muñoz: Simon Grundy. He owns the Shady Oaks winery.

Dante thought about it. Morrison and his backers had purchased Shady Oaks from Nicole. But he no longer owned it. He'd sold out and moved on. Dante kept reading.

Henshaw: And, how did Mr. Grundy get those grapes?

Muñoz: Señor Grundy is in charge of the grape harvest at many places. The grapes are picked, put on trucks, and driven to the wineries.

It was a familiar scenario, Dante thought. People like Grundy, if they truly knew how to produce top-flight wines, were often hired to manage vineyards and make wine.

Henshaw: And then what?

Muñoz: Señor Grundy had the trucks stop along the way.

Henshaw: Stop where?

Muñoz: Sometimes at his winery. Sometimes at Señor Morrison's.

Henshaw: Shady Oaks and Morrison Creek?

Muñoz: Yes. We would unload one or two bins of grapes at his and Señor Morrison's wineries.

Henshaw: Those grapes were used to make wine?

Muñoz: Yes.

Henshaw: So Ling was upset?

Muñoz. Yes.

Dante stopped reading. Muñoz was making serious accusations. And he was inside the operation, so if anyone would know what was going on in the vineyards, it would be him. The winery Ling had financed was stealing grapes. The wine in the bottles was not what the labels stated. Dante had suspected as much when he wrote his review of Morrison's wine. Now he had proof.

His heart pounded as larger dimensions of the story took shape. The Napa Valley was one of hundreds of federally designated viticulture areas. The designation set the wine apart from the rest of California, if not the world. It meant grape growers and winemakers could charge higher prices if the grapes and wine had the Napa Valley designation. False labeling was a federal crime. If he was ethical, Ling would not tolerate it.

If the feds had found out, Ling and Morrison were out of business, their wine pulled from the shelves of stores across the country. They'd face fines, if not jail time. It had happened to people like Santos, who was a hell of a lot bigger than Morrison.

No wonder Ling had sued Morrison. Early on, Morrison must have convinced Ling his winery was a good investment, and he should get in on the ground floor. Then Ling learned the truth. If Morrison were caught, Ling's money would be lost along with his dream of being the owner of a notable winery. Ling would be liable as a co-conspirator. Ling must have blown a fuse. So what the hell had Morrison done with Ling's money? Ling obviously had wanted to know, and it cost him his life. Now, who was Grundy?

Dante felt a chill as he stood naked at Carmen's desk. He rubbed his arms and looked into the dark hallway. He heard movement in the bedroom. He jerked around. *Shit!* He yanked the chain on the banker's lamp and the room went dark. He let his eyes readjust, replaced the papers, and closed the file. He stepped from the office across the hallway to the bedroom door and quietly pushed it open.

A narrow strip of green light from the partially open bathroom door fell across the bedroom carpet. He slipped into the bed, took a deep breath, and tried to relax, his heart pounding. The toilet flushed, followed by water running in the sink. The bathroom door opened, casting a dim light on the bed.

"Where were you?" Carmen said with a sleepy voice as she crawled back under the sheets.

"I went to the kitchen to get a glass of water. Headache."

"There's ibuprofen in the cabinet," she said, sighing deeply. He listened to her breathing. She was asleep again. He sighed in the stillness, his mind buzzing.

A door slammed. Dante flinched, opened his eyes, and in the morning light looked at unfamiliar surroundings. He caught the scent Carmen wore the night before. He drew a breath and massaged his temples to ease the ache. The slam had come from the front room. He swung his legs over the side of the king-size bed and walked into the living room where he stood at partially-closed window blinds. He fingered the louvers open.

Dressed in bright pink running shorts, a gray hooded sweatshirt, and lime green shoes, Carmen was touching her toes in the graveled driveway at her ivy-covered farmhouse. The Carelli family mansion sat atop a large hill behind the house and overlooked the town of Sonoma and the large Carelli winery. She stood, extended her arms over her head, leaned to one side and then the other, and jogged down to the gate, which opened slowly. She trotted out of sight.

He let the blinds close and followed the scent of coffee to the kitchen. A large automatic espresso maker sat on the tile counter. Beside it was a hand-written note: "Help yourself to coffee. If you're not here when I return, I'll see you later." She'd added a smiley face and several x's and o's.

Finding a clean cup, he put it under the spigot and pushed the button. The machine clunked and whirred, grinding the beans, and dark brown espresso dribbled into the cup. With coffee in hand, he returned to Carmen's bedroom and stepped into the bathroom where he swallowed a two more ibuprofen tablets and took a quick shower to wake up. He toweled quickly and dressed.

On his way out, Dante paused in the hallway and glanced at the open door to Carmen's office. He went in and stood again at her desk. He flipped open the cover to the Ling case file and again scanned the Muñoz transcript. He turned on the copier/printer beside her desk, waited while it warmed up, copied the transcript, and replaced the original.

CHAPTER 6

Two hours later, Dante pushed open the door to the newsroom and glanced at the wall clock—9:55. A smile curled the corners of his mouth. *Last night at Carmen's? Yeah. It had been worth it in more ways than one.* He slipped off his coat, tapped the keyboard, and settled into his chair as the computer screen flicked to life. A yellow sticky note on his keyboard read, "See me," signed Jones.

Dante felt much better than when he'd awaken. He had returned to his condo after driving back from Sonoma. The stillness had been deafening, more so now after he'd spent a night with a woman for the first time in…how long? He couldn't say with precision, but it had been a long time. Memories of Nicole came swirling back, along with feelings of guilt he pushed from his mind. With his TV tuned to CNN, more for the noise than the news, he'd brewed coffee, checked his email, and headed to work.

Dante rapped his knuckles on Jones's open office door. Jones swiveled from his computer screen and looked at his watch. "Glad you could make it."

Dante was amazed at Jones, who after forty years in journalism, maintain a strict work ethic. "Well, you could always fire me, but that's already happened. What's up?"

"What I told you about the position is between us. Okay?" Jones said, his voice low. "Nothing will be official until the consultant's report is submitted."

"All right," Dante said, raising his hands. "I got it."

Jones settled back into his chair. "Thanks for helping Hansen, by the way."

"Always glad to be of service."

"You've been rather quiet. It's been four days since the murders, and if I know you like I think I do, you've been up to something. What?"

Dante tossed the Muñoz transcript on Jones's desk and settled into one of the straight-backed chairs.

Jones perused it. "What's this?"

"A transcript."

"I can see," Jones said. "Who's this guy Muñoz?"

"Gilberto Muñoz, the vineyard foreman. He was there at the time of the shooting. His people often work in the vineyard."

"A witness?" Jones asked.

"He ducked inside when the shooting began."

"Smart man."

"Muñoz told the police he figured Ling was killed because of what he knew."

"Which was?"

"Bernie Morrison and his partner, a man named Simon Grundy, were stealing grapes."

"How would he know?"

"His people are the ones who pick the grapes."

"So, what's it mean?"

"Ling was suing Morrison. If what Muñoz says is true, Ling must have sued to get his money back after he learned what Morrison was doing. He was afraid if the feds found out, they'd shut down the winery."

"Makes sense."

Dante scowled and thought. "If Ling could have proven Morrison was engaged in criminal activity, the courts could have jailed Morrison and given the winery to Ling."

"Maybe," Jones said. "Maybe not. By claiming Morrison was engaged in criminal activity, wouldn't that just bring the feds down on both their heads?"

"No," Dante said. "He'd have a strong case for being a victim of fraud. He could present himself as the good guy, trying to save his investment and the winery from ruin. "

"I don't blame the guy for wanting his money back," Jones said. "But if Morrison and his partner were stealing grapes, where did the money go?"

"Maybe there was something else going on," Dante said.

Jones cleared his throat. "Keep digging."

An hour later, Dante's Mustang rumbled as it slowed and turned onto the narrow road leading to the Morrison Creek winery. The police were gone, but the yellow crime scene tape still twisted in the breeze. The renovated barn with its landscaped front walk looked abandoned.

He parked, climbed out, walked down the graveled path from the parking area to the tasting room door, and tried the handle. It turned easily. *Unlocked?* He pushed the door open and slipped inside, closing the door behind him. He listened for voices, but heard none.

The exterior of the barn was rough wood paneling with carved and painted signs mounted on the sides. Morrison had continued the woody theme inside, with a tasting room bar and varnished picnic tables. Oak wine barrels rose from floor to ceiling along one side of the tasting tables, and two towering stainless steel maceration tanks gleamed against the back wall. *Nice, letting the customers feel close to the winemaking process.* Morrison Creek wine bottles, from whites to reds, still stood on the tasting tables. A few bottles, some open, some not, sat on the bar. A small operation, Dante thought, one Morrison could run with just a few people.

The odor of stale wine from the open wine bottles permeated the air. A carved sign on a door read "Office" in ornate, hand-painted script. The door was slightly ajar. He waited and listened. Still nothing.

He entered the office, scanned the room, and turned to shelves at his left piled with magazines, stacks of winery T-shirts and baseball caps, and a half-full wine rack. On impulse, he pulled a fat, glossy wine magazine from the pile. *Wine Spectator*. Dante flipped through the pages and put it back. There were a dozen back issues. He wondered if Morrison had dreamed he'd be featured in the magazine someday. Instead, Dante had savaged his wines. Too bad, he thought.

Dante went to the desk cluttered with papers—letters, bills, bank statements. On the wall behind it were photos of Morrison with friends and customers, he guessed, most with faces aglow from the glasses of wine they held. He leaned close to inspect one. Four men. Morrison with Ricardo Santos, he guessed. But the others? Dante looked closer. *The Aragon brothers?* Dante exhaled. *If I'm right, Morrison was keeping some dangerous company.*

A computer screen sat to the side, off and dark. Dante looked under the desk for the processing unit to turn it on. It was twisted around and the back had been removed. The hard drive was missing. Wires dangled, looking like the heart of the beast had been ripped out. *Had the police taken it? Or someone who didn't want the police to have it?*

A thumping sound outside made Dante jerk around. *A car door closing?* He couldn't be sure. He listened, but heard only his own breath. Dante went to the small office window and looked out. It gave him only a partial view of the parking lot. Seeing nothing, he turned back to the office. He tugged open a drawer in the four-drawer file cabinet beside the desk. It was jammed with file folders sprouting sheets of paper, a helter-skelter filing system that looked much like the desk. He pulled a fat file at random from the drawer, spilling papers to the floor when he opened it. He stooped to collect them, glancing at each as he replaced them. Receipts for grape purchases, each on letterhead stationary of vineyards and wineries around the region. He recognized the names. *Morrison was buying tons of grapes, but all for himself?*

"Can I help you?"

Dante froze, his heart in his throat as he turned and looked up at the source of the authoritative voice. A man in his mid-thirties, with a pudgy build and sandy brown hair, looked down at him. Dante swallowed hard, his mouth dry. "Uh, I suppose you can." He stood, leaving the file folder on the floor. "I'm Dante Rath, a reporter with the *Santa Rosa Sun*." He shoved out his hand for a shake.

The man scowled, face slightly flushed, hands on hips, ignoring the proffered hand. "What are you doing with that file folder?"

Dante felt his face grow warm, his heart sounding in his ears. "Uh, you could call it research. But ..." He smiled weakly, and squatting again to gather the remaining papers, he stuffed them into the folder, stood, and jammed the folder back into the drawer.

"But what?" The man's eyes darted around the office.

Dante retreated a step, unsure if the man was angry or afraid. "No one was here."

"So you just decided to come in?"

"Yeah, I guess," Dante said, now apprehensive.

"You came to the wrong damned place. There's nothing here. Get it? Nothing!"

The man seemed angry, as if he'd already rifled the place and knew there was nothing to find. Hoping to ease the tension, Dante blurted out a question. "Did you know Morrison?"

The man said nothing, and seemingly lost in thought, dropped his eyes to the floor. "It was a terrible thing he did."

"I think we agree on that."

Looking disgusted, the man ran his hand over his hair. "Chao Ling shouldn't have been shot down like an animal."

Dante expected to be chased out, but this guy was answering questions. Dante tried another. "So you knew Ling as well?"

The man licked his lips. "I liked Chao. He appreciated good wine."

"And, you are...?"

The man narrowed his eyes, not answering.

"I'm a reporter, not a cop."

"I know who you are. You're the guy who wrote that crap about Morrison Creek wines."

Dante swallowed hard, feeling vulnerable now. He glanced past the man to the door. If he had to, he could slug the guy and get by him. He drew a breath and tried another question. "Well, if you know wines, I think you'd agree with what I wrote."

The man's face flushed as he clenched his jaw. "I'm the winemaker here."

"Oh," Dante said, taking another step back. "Well, you know my name. What's yours?"

"My name is Grundy. Simon Grundy."

He recognized the name from the transcript. "We finally meet."

Grundy gave him a confused look.

Dante looked at the office door again. He could make it past Grundy in three steps.

Grundy twitched, as if deciding what to do.

Dante tried another question. "So, do you have any idea why Morrison would want to kill Ling?"

Grundy's eyes darted around the office, as if he was looking for something, and came back to Dante. "Ah, I'd say he was probably angry. Angry and afraid."

"Angry and afraid of what?"

Grundy glared at Dante. "What do you think? After what you wrote? The winery was finished. Kaput."

Dante shrugged and lifted his hands, palms up. "The wine has to stand on its own. I wrote what any knowledgeable critic would. I'm sure you'd agree."

A sigh escaped Grundy's lips before he spoke. "Okay, the wine's not great, but it's not bad. You didn't need to write what you did."

Dante felt somewhat vindicated now that Morrison's winemaker had acquiesced to his assessment, but Grundy hadn't answered his question. He cleared his throat. "So why did he shoot Ling?"

Grundy's eyes locked on Dante. "I already told the sheriff, I don't know."

"Doesn't help me, though."

It was Grundy's turn to shrug.

"How long had you known Morrison?"

Grundy sighed again, his shoulders slumping. "A few years, I guess. We met just after he arrived."

"So, you were friends?"

"Yeah," Grundy said. "We hit it off, mostly because we're both from Ohio."

Dante was about to pull his notebook out of pocket, but hesitated. He didn't want Grundy to stop giving up information. "Ohio? What brought you out here?"

"I grew up next to a vineyard in northeastern Ohio. They grow Concord grapes there. Sweet grapes. They're sold to Welch's for juice. I always wanted to run a winery, so I came out to Cal Davis and got a degree in winemaking."

"That's what you did for Morrison?"

Grundy drew a halting breath. "Bernie didn't know jack shit about wine except how to drink it and sell it."

"But you did."

"I was his business partner," he said. "It was a mistake."

"Mistake? Why?"

"It was hard to know what was going on with Bernie," Grundy said.

"Until it was too late?"

"Yeah."

"So you're a partner in this winery?"

Grundy crossed his arms. "No. Morrison paid me to oversee the winemaking here. I was his partner in a couple of his other businesses."

"Like what?"

"We started a small bottling company for the boutique wineries in the area."

"So you opened a bottling company, then what?" Dante asked.

Rather than answering, Grundy motioned to the tasting room and asked, "Do you want a glass of wine?"

"Sure." Anything to get out of the close quarters, Dante thought, even though Grundy seemed no longer a threat. Dante glanced at his watch. It was 11:30 a.m. *Not too early for a little hair of the dog.*

Dante followed Grundy into the tasting room where the winemaker slipped behind the bar like he owned the place, produced a couple of clean glasses, pulled the stopper from an opened bottle, and poured. Grundy took a deep drink, exhaled, and squinted.

"Is this the same wine I wrote about?" Dante asked, swirling the wine for a sniff.

"Yeah," Grundy said.

Dante took a sip, held it in his mouth, and looked around for a spit bucket. There wasn't one. He swallowed.

"Oh," Grundy said. "If we're going to talk, I want this off the record."

"Sure, if you prefer it."

Grundy took another drink, licking his lips. "Well, the bottling plant did all right."

"Just all right?" Dante asked. He swirled his wine. It was stale and tasted worse than he remembered.

"I mean, it generated cash flow."

"Always important for a business."

"It also led to other business deals."

"Like what?"

"Morrison and I bought a small bankrupt winery in Healdsburg."

"Which one?"

"Shady Oaks."

Dante twitched at the mention of the winery sold when Nicole and her first husband were divorcing. "I'm familiar with it."

Grundy smiled. "It's mine now."

"Now?"

"Bernie wanted to make it bigger. I didn't. Small production, high quality. It's the way to go. So I bought him out." Grundy took another big swallow and finished the glass. "Bernie used the money to buy this place. It was nothing but an old barn. Morrison leased it and the surrounding vineyard from a grape grower who lives a couple of miles away in a hundred-year-old farm house."

Dante glanced around the room. "He did a good job making it presentable."

"Bernie's problem was he wanted to make money fast. He didn't want to let his wine age. That's why it tastes so…"

Dante looked at him. "Young?"

Grundy took another drink. "Wine needs to age, to mature."

"Unless you treat it," Dante said.

"Speed up the aging process," Grundy said. "The science behind winemaking is fascinating."

Dante bristled at the thought of the additives used to doctor bad wine, all of which were approved by the federal government. The list was long. "So, Morrison sold his wine too soon?" Dante asked.

"Yeah. Morrison had a hard time waiting for wine to age and a hard time waiting for the money to flow in, so he approached me with another idea."

"Which was?"

"A lot of wineries belong to absentee owners."

"The kind of people who like to fly in from New York, Chicago, LA, and show off their winery to their rich friends," Dante said.

"Exactly."

"When there's nothing left to do but uncork the wine," Dante said.

"That's about the size of it. So Bernie and I formed a vineyard management company. He had the salesmanship, and I know grapes. Our business doubled every year."

"Where did Ling fit in?"

The tasting room door banged open. They both turned, stunned, as a couple of sheriff's deputies burst through the door, crouching with guns drawn. "Freeze!" one yelled.

Dante flinched at the sound of breaking glass. Grundy's wine glass lay in pieces in a puddle of wine. Grundy was slack-jawed, his hands up and open.

Dante put his glass on the bar and lifted his hands.

"What are you doing here, Rath?" Investigator Henshaw growled. "You're disturbing a crime scene. I can charge you right now."

"There was no one around, Jake. The door was open."

"It's a crime scene!" Henshaw said.

"My friend here and I were just talking," Dante said. "We were having a glass of wine and…."

Dante reached for his glass, but Henshaw barked, "Don't move! Keep your hands where I can see them!"

"Don't shoot, okay?" Grundy said, his voice wavering.

"Not unless I have to," Henshaw said.

The sunlight outside silhouetted a feminine figure in the doorway. Carmen Carelli strode into the room and stopped behind the deputies. They turned, still clutching their automatics.

"What the hell?" Henshaw said.

"Your timing couldn't be better," Dante said to Carmen. She wore fashionably high leather boots, a knee-length skirt, and a light silk blouse. Dante turned to Henshaw. "My attorney just arrived. Please direct all questions to her."

"What's going on?" Carmen asked, her eyes flitting from Henshaw to Dante and Grundy and back.

"These two men are trespassing on a crime scene," Henshaw said, staring at Dante and Grundy. "I'm taking them in."

"Were you?" Carmen asked, looking at Dante.

"I was talking with my friend here, Simon..." Dante said.

"I'm the winemaker here," he said. "Simon Grundy."

"See?" Dante said to Henshaw.

Carmen cleared her throat and stepped in front of the deputies. "Let's be reasonable, shall we?"

Henshaw looked her up and down, lowered his gun, and stepped back. He nodded to his partner. Both holstered their guns.

"There's been enough shooting around here," Carmen said.

Dante felt the tension drain from the back of his neck.

"Will Grundy here vouch for you?" Henshaw asked.

Dante turned to Grundy. "What do you say?"

"Sure."

"Good man," Dante said.

"As your attorney," Carmen said to Dante, "I'd advise you to vacate the premises before Deputy Henshaw changes his mind."

Dante glanced at Grundy. "I'm going to follow her advice. I suggest you do the same. We can talk later."

Dante, Grundy, and Carmen hurried from the tasting room to the parking lot. "You never did tell me what you're doing here," Dante said to Grundy.

"Just checking on the equipment," Grundy said, halting his walk toward a pickup Dante could now see was mostly hidden behind the renovated barn. "I need to know what's going to happen to this place. Morrison owed me money." He looked at Carmen. "Do you know?"

"The state can keep it locked up for evidence for years," Carmen said. "Until someone takes over the winery, that's probably what they'll do. Meanwhile, everything here will be considered critical to the investigation."

"They won't release it?" Grundy asked.

"Not until the case is closed," Carmen said. "The decision is up to the district attorney."

Grundy scowled and looked back at the tasting room. "This place needs to re-open, soon. There's wine inventory to be sold." Grundy looked desperate. "I just want what's mine."

"You're not the only one," Carmen said. "Chao Ling's estate still has a million dollars in equity here. A probate judge will decide who gets what."

"And there's Santos," Grundy added.

"Ricardo Santos?" Dante asked. "What's he got to do with this?"

"A silent partner," Grundy said.

Dante looked at Carmen. "Really?"

Carmen squinted in the sunlight.

"We should talk."

CHAPTER 7

It was nearly 1 p.m., the end of the lunch hour rush, when the waiter poured the chardonnay into oversized glasses on the patio table at Hurley's in downtown Napa. Dante had ordered the restaurant's own brand, which he knew was supplied by one of the area's better winemakers. He swirled the wine, sniffed, and sipped. "Hints of citrus with almonds. Nice finish. Very clean."

Carmen rolled her eyes.

"What?" Dante's mouth curled in a sly grin.

"Enough of the wine-speak."

"Lighten up," Dante said.

"I'm starving."

"Famished from an exhausting night, I'm sure," he said, his eyes locked on her.

Carmen smiled. "I went for a long run this morning."

"Oh, I see."

Carmen reached across the table and put her hand on his. "Yes, the night was good."

Pleased, Dante let the previous night's escapades play though his mind. He didn't want the memories to fade anytime soon.

It had been so long since he felt such an intimate connection. *Not since Nicole...* Dante felt a rush of emotion and memories about a time not so long ago when his life seemed to be coming together—a shot at real love and a second shot at his career. When the *Chronicle* dropped the investigative reporting team, Dante had felt disconnected, aimless. He dreaded looking for another job or a new line of work, like public relations. He didn't want to end up at a smaller newspaper with a lesser job and lower pay. He tried to drown his dilemma in a bottle. It didn't work.

Three months later, with his savings dwindling, his morale in the toilet, and no prospects on the horizon, Jones had called on a morning when Dante's head was throbbing from the night before.

"You interested in getting back into the game," Jones asked, "or are you going to keep feeling sorry for yourself?"

"Journalism's all I know," Dante said.

"Okay. What do you know about wine?"

Dante looked around his kitchen. The counter was littered with empty bottles of every sort, wine, whisky, beer. "A little," he said. "You'd be surprised."

Dante told him about his Italian grandfather's winemaking, and how he'd grown up around some of the older vineyards of Northern California. After the call, he'd cleaned himself up, driven to Santa Rosa, and become wine editor at the *Sun*. He'd barely unpacked when he met Nicole on his first story. They just clicked, fast. It was all new for him, but it felt right. With her death and all it revealed, he'd fallen into yet another deeper funk. He'd only recently begun to consider women in his life again. Sitting there with Carmen, he thought he might be ready, but not for anything serious. He caught her looking at him and tried to focus.

"Of all the people to come through the winery door this morning, you were the last one I expected," Dante said. "What were you doing there?"

Carmen's eyes narrowed. "Chao Ling's estate has assets to be protected. I told you. What were *you* doing there? I thought you had stories to write."

"I always have stories to write," he said, and fell silent, thinking about the Muñoz transcript he'd copied from her files. "I was in Morrison's office when Grundy showed up."

"That doesn't answer my question," Carmen said.

"Okay. I'm trying to dig a little deeper into the case. Research. It's what investigative reporters do."

"But you're the wine editor," Carmen said. When Dante didn't respond, she asked, "Well, what did you find?"

"Not much. But Grundy and I talked. He was more open than I expected."

"What did you talk about?"

"Nothing you probably don't already know."

"Maybe," Carmen said.

"So, what were *you* doing there?" Dante asked. "Were you going to rifle Morrison's office?"

"There are files in Morrison's office that might explain where Chao Ling's money went and maybe a whole lot more. The disposition of the winery will eventually be decided. I need to ensure Chao Ling's family gets compensated."

"So you wanted his files."

"Of course," Carmen said. "It's all going to be boxed up, sealed, and stored by the Napa district attorney. Once that happens, it'll be a nightmare to gain access."

"Don't you have an investigator who does that for you?"

"I did once. He became too expensive. If you ever want the job, let me know."

"I'll keep it in mind." Dante drank from his wine glass. "Tell me about Santos."

Carmen took a sip and exhaled slowly. "What can I say? He's got his fingers in a lot of pies."

"You didn't know he was involved in Morrison's winery?"

"No. I swear," she said, shaking her head with exaggerated motions.

"If Santos was involved with Morrison Creek Winery, it would explain why Morrison's wines taste just like the box wine Santos sells so successfully."

"What are you saying?" Carmen asked, her voice rising with irritation.

"Maybe Morrison was trying to pass off Santos's box wines as Napa Valley wines. Morrison was putting it in wine bottles, but it was still the same wine."

"You don't know that. Besides, you can't be objective, considering what you told me about him and your late wife."

"It works both ways, Carmen. You can't be objective about your client friend, Ricardo."

Carmen scowled and put down her glass, crossing her arms and leaning back in the chair. "You need to understand I represented Ricardo in only a couple of cases. I don't do *all* of his legal work. I'm just a local hire for him. He's got enough money to hire a team of international lawyers, if he wanted."

"Your cases were very important ones for Santos."

"They were. But if Ricardo had any serious dealings with Morrison and Grundy, it's news to me. I know nothing about any of that. It's the kind of thing you might find in Morrison's office."

"What about Ling? How exactly did he get involved with Morrison?"

"I don't know," Carmen said. "I already told you he came to me only when he was afraid he'd lost his money."

"What spooked him?"

"Did I tell you Morrison insisted Ling make his investment in cash?"

"What?" Dante said. "Ling gave Morrison a million dollars in *cash*?"

"In a large duffle bag."

"What does somebody do with that much cash?"

"Spend it, Dante. What else?"

"No, I mean physically. You just can't walk into Wells Fargo or the Bank of Napa or any other bank and deposit it without attracting attention."

"I know. The Bank Secrecy Act requires banks to report daily deposits of more than $10,000."

"It would be about a hundred trips to the bank. Who'd do that?"

"It's what Chao told me," Carmen said with a shrug.

"Morrison must have owed big money to someone like Santos or other people who might deal in large amounts of cash."

"What do you have against Santos?"

"Other than his cheap wines, nothing." Dante looked at his glass, thinking. "But seriously, why would Morrison want a million in cash?"

"How would I know?"

"The only people who deal in cash are the drug cartels. Santos is chummy with the Aragon brothers. Maybe Morrison was, too. Where there's smoke, there's fire."

Carmen sipped from her wine.

"What was Ling thinking when he agreed to deliver the cash?" Dante asked.

"Morrison told him he could buy grapes cheaper if he paid in cash."

Dante thought about the receipts he had seen in Morrison's file cabinet. "A man with that much cash could buy a lot of grapes from a lot of people. Santos got nailed for labeling his wine from the Napa Valley when it wasn't." He thought about it. *I was half-joking when I said the wine tasted like Santos's boxed label, but now it made sense.* "Maybe Morrison was doing that too."

Carmen dismissed the comment with a shake of her head. "Santos made an innocent mistake. He was misled. He used grapes he thought were from Napa Valley. They weren't. We appealed a lower court decision, and I argued Ricardo was a victim of fraud in this case, not the offender. He paid a reduced fine. End of story."

"A slap on the wrist for a man like Santos." Dante drained his glass. He doubted Carmen's defense of Santos, but he let it drop. He wanted to focus on Ling. "If there was no paper trail with the money, what was the basis of Ling's lawsuit against Morrison?"

"Morrison signed papers acknowledging Ling's investment and made him a principal in the business. It was the only leverage we had. If Morrison couldn't come up with the money, we asked the court to give the company to Ling."

"The fermenting tanks, aging barrels, and unsold wine."

"Yes. All the assets, including the lease for the converted barn and the vineyards around it."

"Morrison still refused?" Dante thought about what Grundy had said about Morrison being angry and afraid. *Angry enough to carry a loaded gun?*

"At the time of the shooting, Morrison was in violation of a court order, but he held off the court by promising he would come up with the money."

"How? Where would he get that much money?"

"I don't know."

"Maybe he tried to get it from Santos. He could borrow the money, using the unsold wine as collateral."

"I wouldn't know. Ling went to the winery that day because Morrison had promised he'd have some of the money ready for him."

"Instead, Ling collected a few bullets."

Carmen lowered her eyes to her glass and sipped.

Shaking his head, Dante reached for the bottle and refilled their glasses. "The more I learn of Morrison and Ling, the less I understand. Why would Ling be dumb enough to give Morrison a million dollars in cash?"

"I don't know," Carmen said.

Dante had known brilliant people who had absolutely no common sense. They possessed a keen intellect, but functioned in a bubble, not suspecting people were as devious as they often are. He felt sorry for Ling. The guy had been robbed and killed. Ling didn't deserve to die for being naive.

Carmen must have known Ling would never get his money back, not from a man like Morrison, he thought. Where had the money gone? Dante was hitting a wall. He glanced at Carmen again, who was scanning the menu. "You have no idea where Ling's money actually went?"

"I told you, there's no trail."

"What about Santos?"

Carmen sighed and looked at him. "Why would Santos be actively involved with Morrison, a small-time operator who had notions of making it big?" Carmen's voice was rising. "Why would Santos bother with a man like that? Morrison could have done anything with the money. Maybe he sent it out of state to pay bad debts we don't know about."

Dante clenched his jaw and exhaled. "You know Santos, you represented Ling, you knew Morrison. I can't believe you don't know."

Her eyes flared with anger. "What do you want me to do? Call up Santos and say, 'Hey, fess up. Tell me what happened to Ling's money?'" She looked away, then back at him with disgust. "You think Santos knows about this, but he probably doesn't. Don't be so suspicious. Santos is an international businessman. What he does is none of yours or anyone else's business."

"Unless he breaks the law."

"You're not a cop, Dante. You're not a judge or jury. You should know, mister journalist, people get in trouble when they make false accusations."

Dante swallowed hard. *Really? Is Carmen threatening me? She shouldn't be fighting me. She should be helping me. After last night? You act like this?* Dante's stomach soured. He drew a deep breath and frowned. "You made your point. Loud and clear."

CHAPTER 8

Dante was back in the newsroom by 3 p.m., hoping to brief Jones on what he'd learned. But Jones still had not returned from a late lunch with the publisher. Dante was uneasy about such long lunch meetings. Jones was not the kind of man to drink martinis at lunch, and neither was the editor-publisher, Oliver Ellsworth. They were cordial, but certainly not drinking buddies. Dante suspected the meeting was about business, to pore over details about the paper's future. Dante pushed the worries to the back of his mind, and feeling the momentum building on his investigation, left the newsroom again to find Simon Grundy. He wanted the man to open up like he had earlier at the Morrison Creek winery. Grundy was the best lead he'd uncovered so far.

Dante chewed over his conversation with Carmen as he headed north on 101 toward Healdsburg and the Shady Oaks winery. The tone had left Dante feeling ragged. The night before, she'd worked him for a long night of pleasure. Not that he regretted it. But after the lunch, he sensed she was toying with him. She'd revealed a streak of ruthlessness, an admirable trait for the legal profession, but he wondered if she was hiding something.

Carmen had been steadfast in her defense of Santos, insisting Santos was only a client, but acted like she would fall on her sword for him. *Is she defending her work for Santos, rather than the man himself? Why so vigorous a defense? Does she feel guilty about something she's done for him? Is it something she knows?*

The transcript he'd copied from her Ling file was extremely useful. *Had she planted it, knowing I might rifle her desk? If so, is she throwing me off course, or is she really helping me?* There was no other way to look at Muñoz as anything but another lead, if he could track the man down. He was there when the shooting happened, and he knew Morrison's business practices from the bottom up.

Passing one sprawling vineyard after another, the landscape reminded Dante of when he was twenty-two and first worked in his relatives' vineyard in central Italy. He'd arrived in Montefalco in the early summer, just after graduating from Berkeley. There was not a lot to do since the vineyard was mature, the vines in full leaf, and the young fruit hard and green. He was welcomed as the long-lost American cousin. When he saw the well-appointed, centuries-old villa surrounded by vineyards, he felt like the long-lost American country bumpkin.

Dante returned to America a changed man. The season with his Italian relatives gave him an appreciation for history and tradition—for authenticity. Living in a stone structure dating from the Middle Ages made him appreciate the past. Tilling the land, cultivating grapes, and making wine was a life's work that demanded care and love. It was not just another money-making scheme. It grated on him now to watch people come and go through the revolving door of the California wine world. For some, it was a calling, and he respected that. For those who could afford it, however, winemaking was but a temporary diversion, another jewel in their glittering crown of accomplishments until another gem caught their eye. For such people, Dante had little sympathy if their wines didn't measure up to his or other's standards.

Thirty minutes after leaving the newsroom, Dante wheeled into the Shady Oaks winery's parking lot populated by just a half-dozen cars. Shady Oaks was east of Heraldsburg and south of Geyserville, just off of State Road 128, and was housed in a two-story, stucco-and-tile structure with ivy creeping up the walls. Hopefully the tasting room would be quiet, he thought, enhancing his chances of finding and talking with Grundy. He parked and turned off the motor, slumped in his seat, and closed his eyes. It had been a summer day, about this time just a couple of years ago, when he first pulled into this parking lot.

He'd found Nicole in the winery's small office, packing boxes, taking files by the handful from drawers and dropping them into empty wine boxes. He'd been immediately taken by her girl-next-door good looks, her blond hair pulled into a pony tail, an unruly wisp of hair falling across her forehead. She was five-foot-six with an appealing figure. Dante never understood why her ex-husband had left her, but never complained about it.

Nicole had an open bottle of wine on her desk and a glass beside it. He remembered her pausing to wipe her forehead with the back of her hand, and smiling and thanking him for coming. She poured him a glass of wine, and she packed as they talked.

"It's the hardest thing I've ever done," she said, her blue eyes brimming with tears. She clutched thick office files and held them out to him. "This is more than just paper, you know. This is my life." She fell silent, continuing to stare. "What was *our* life. Do you know what it feels like to put it all in a box and haul it to recycling? Do you?"

Halfway through packing the box, Nicole said, "To hell with it." She turned to him and asked, "Are you hungry?"

They spent much of the afternoon in a quiet Healdsburg restaurant where she explained how her soon-to-be-ex-husband had fleeced their winery, skipped town for Mexico with his young girlfriend, and left Nicole to pick up the pieces. Dante had put down his pen and closed his notebook. The details were fascinating, but too personal and opinionated for his story. He felt sorry for her, and it showed in the story he wrote about the sale of the winery, portraying her as a courageous survivor. He wrapped the story around the theme of endings and beginnings.

Nicole had told him about the winery's new owner, a man named Bernie Morrison, and how she'd found him at just the right time. Dante contacted Morrison and interviewed him about a week before he took possession of Shady Oaks. Morrison had been effusive and optimistic, and Dante had left it at that. When the story came out, Nicole was elated. She invited Dante to dinner to celebrate. Dante accepted. Six months later they were married.

Dante brushed a trickle of sweat from his temple and climbed out of his Mustang, wondering how long he'd been sitting there daydreaming in the heat. He stepped onto sun-softened asphalt and shaded his eyes to survey the surrounding vineyards. He had always liked the place. Quiet, calm, and far from the boutique glitz of downtown Healdsburg. If I had a winery, he thought, it would be a one like this. Small, with nicely crafted wines.

He pulled open the tasting room door and paused to get his bearings. A polished wood bar ran along one wall. A handful of converted and refinished round oak wine barrels served as stand-up sipping tables. Large-paned windows admitted plenty of light, giving the place an airy feel and an excellent view of the vineyards. Floor-to-ceiling shelves stocked with a latticework wine rack of recent vintages covered the back wall. Round chrome racks offered a selection of T-shirts, caps, and fleece jackets embroidered with the winery's logo.

Dante walked to the wine bar where several couples were eagerly watching Grundy pour wine.

"Now this is our two-year-old petite syrah, aged in American oak," Grundy said. "It's one of our most popular. It's got a slight amount of cabernet franc in it to deepen the finish."

The tasters sipped, smiles spreading across their faces. "Very nice," said a man in his thirties, muscled arms straining the sleeves of his Hawaiian shirt. "Very nice indeed."

Grundy excused himself and stepped over to Dante. "You didn't waste any time."

"I was hoping we could continue our conversation from this morning."

"Why not?"

"Is there a place where we can talk? Privately?"

Grundy turned to a young woman washing glasses. "Marvee?"

The young woman looked up as Grundy pointed to the tasters. She wiped her hands, glancing at Dante with steely gray eyes. She had thick dark hair cut short and frosted with highlights. A small ring pierced one nostril. A tattoo on her face caught his eye. More tattoos decorated her slender forearms. She wore tight jeans and a T-shirt that hugged her contours.

Dante followed Grundy into the winery office where he took a seat at an antique rolltop desk and motioned for Dante to sit in the oak chair beside it.

"When the deputies arrived," Dante said, "we were talking about your business dealings with Morrison."

"Still off the record, right?"

"I'm taking notes," Dante said, flipping to a clean page. "If you knew Morrison couldn't be trusted, why did you continue to work with him?"

"I don't know, to tell you the truth," Grundy said. "I guess I liked the guy. He was always looking. He had a knack for finding new ventures. He was, for the most part, interesting to be around, even if he was irritating. Something was always coming down the road with Morrison. I'm not like that. I like to find one thing and make it work. I'll stick with it as long as I can."

"Morrison was interesting to be around?" Dante asked, raising an eyebrow. "Chao Ling might not agree."

Grundy looked at Dante, then said, "Morrison was always talking about the next big thing. Big for him, anyway. His excitement about new business ventures was infectious.

I tried to help him as much as I could. We worked together in this winery. When I bought him out, I knew he needed help getting his Morrison Creek wines up and running. Maybe it was a bad decision, but he always paid me. Up until the end, anyway."

"But you and he started a vineyard management business. It's called…MG Enology, I believe," Dante said, rifling back through his notebook for the name. "According to the State of California, it's a limited liability corporation."

Grundy said nothing.

"The business has a website, but it says the company is no longer accepting contracts. What happened?"

Grundy sighed. "The website was supposed to be taken down. We had to suspend operations. Bernie and I decided to focus on other things."

"What happened?"

"Like I said before, our business grew very quickly. But success has a way of catching up to you, if you can understand that."

"It's the kind of problem that most businesses would love to have."

"Maybe. It's one thing to have a lot of business," Grundy said. "It's another to actually do it well and manage it."

"There were legal claims against MG Enology."

Grundy's eyes darted around the room, finally returning to Dante. "You saw Bernie's office, right?"

"That's where you found me this morning."

"Some mess, huh?"

Dante nodded.

"That tells you something, doesn't it?"

"Morrison was disorganized," Dante said. *But you're not?* Grundy looked and acted like he could manage a business. So, why blame Morrison for his problems? Unless he was ducking his own responsibility. "You were partners."

Grundy drew a breath and exhaled slowly, looking at his desk as if it had a script sitting on it with the answers he needed. "Yeah, we were. But again, I trusted Bernie too much. It was a mistake. I told you." He looked at Dante, his eyes filled with regret.

Dante had no sympathy for him, but he could understand why Grundy might have trusted Morrison too much. It was because of Morrison's confident smile and believability, which he'd seen up close. "What else can you tell me about Morrison?"

"Like what?"

"Like his background."

"I never bothered to check. I didn't really care."

"If you had bothered to look, maybe you wouldn't have dealt with him."

"Why? What did he do?"

"He formed a company that manufactured a fungicide spray. Fungus is a big problem in damp climates, like parts of Ohio."

"He mentioned it. He said he sold the company at the just right time. He didn't want the daily grind of running a company. He was a startup kind of guy. But tell me. How do you know this?"

"It's my job to find out these things. I'm a journalist."

Dante's mind raced. It had been more than that. After Nicole's death, he'd tracked down Morrison's history and downloaded copies of the fraud complaints filed against him in federal district court in Ohio. There'd been an out-of-court settlement. The details were sealed. Dante assumed the investors wanted to avoid an extended court battle, especially if they thought the company and its product could be salvaged. So Dante sat on the information, waiting for the right moment to use it.

Morrison's history of fraud had made Dante suspicious of the Morrison Creek winery even before he tasted its wines. Dante didn't mention Morrison's background in the wine review because there was no need. But now Morrison had killed his primary investor, gone off the deep end, and been shot dead by the cops. Everything was fair game now.

Grundy looked at him, considering his words. "Morrison was an entrepreneur."

Muffled laughter came through the office door from the tasting room.

"The reality was quite different," Dante said. "Just ask his Ohio investors."

"Let me guess. They weren't happy?"

"Morrison's miracle fungus spray was bogus," Dante said. "It didn't remove the mold, it only covered it up."

"That would be a problem."

"The investors sued," Dante said.

"I imagine they would."

"But Morrison countersued. Rather than an extended legal battle and mounting legal fees, they paid Morrison an undisclosed settlement to get rid of him. Morrison walked away with some cash," Dante said.

"Interesting," Grundy said with a nod, then fell silent. He looked at Dante. "Sorry I can't be more helpful."

Helpful? Dante looked at his notebook, flipping through a few pages. He had nothing from Grundy but a few comments making him out to be a victim. Maybe he was. But Dante doubted it. He began to panic, thinking he'd reached a dead end. A thought came to him. "Do you know how Morrison met Chao Ling?"

Grundy scowled. "Ask Ling's family. They might know."

"Where might I find them?"

"I'm not sure," Grundy said, "but I believe the Ling family has a restaurant in Chinatown. Let me ask Marvee. I think she knows."

"Who?"

"The woman helping me at the bar." Grundy went to the door and motioned for her to come.

"What?" she asked, her shoulder against the door frame, her arms crossed. The snug jeans and T-shirt left little to the imagination. The face tattoo was a blue tiger, crawling down her temple onto her cheek. *Does it mean she's the type to pounce?* She eyed him and glanced at Grundy.

"Marvee, this is Dante Rath," Grundy said. "He's a reporter with the *Santa Rosa Sun*."

Keeping her arms crossed, she said, "Nice to meet you."

"He'd like to track down Chao Ling's family," Grundy said. "They own a restaurant in Chinatown, don't they?"

Marvee give him an indifferent stare. "The Ling Dynasty… something like that."

"Thanks," Dante said.

"Terrible what happened to Chao," Marvee said.

"You knew him?"

"A little." She gazed at Dante, her eyes unfocused as if daydreaming.

Dante was curious. "You knew Bernie Morrison as well?"

"Ah, yeah," she said, as if was common knowledge.

Dante looked to Grundy for an explanation.

"Marvee's been with us since when Morrison and I bought the place."

"The whole thing's nuts," she said. "I don't know what happened to Bernie. No one ever expected him to do such an awful thing. I certainly didn't!" She looked at the floor and back at Dante. "It's kinda scary." They fell silent, looking at each other. "I need to get back," she said. "I don't want to lose these people. They really like the wines."

"Go!" Grundy said with a wave.

She turned and disappeared.

"Ah, if that's all, I have to get back to work, too," Grundy said.

Dante lifted a hand for him to wait. "Do you have any idea why Morrison would have wanted to kill Ling?"

"You asked me already. I don't have a clue."

Dante wondered how that was possible. Still, he had a new lead.

At 5:30 p.m. Dante pulled into a parking place behind the newspaper building. His stomach knotted as he realized his regularly scheduled column was supposed to have been finished a couple of hours ago. "Damn," he muttered, and slapped the steering wheel. Intent on finding Grundy, he'd forgotten. A few minutes later he was at his desk, staring at his computer. As he signed on, a beep alerted him to a message on his screen. It was from Jones: "See me, now."

Dante rose, swallowed hard, and pushing his chair back, angled across the newsroom to Jones's office. The managing editor leaned back in his chair. "Need I remind you that in addition to being wine editor, you're supposed to be pursuing the vineyard murders? We need a follow-up story. A good one for the front page. And Hansen is busy with other things."

"I'm working on it."

"Not the answer I want to hear," Jones said.

"There's a lot of moving parts."

"Like what?"

Dante grabbed a chair and sat heavily. "Morrison was from Ohio. A failed businessman. He was sued over a bogus fungicide."

"You've got a whole lot of nothing," Jones said. "You'd better come up with a story angle, and soon."

"It may be with the man he killed."

"Chao Ling?"

"Morrison convinced Ling to invest in his winery," Dante said. "One million dollars. In cash."

"Are you serious?" Jones pulled off his glasses to massage the bridge of his nose.

"I'm going to put what I have in my column. Morrison was a Midwesterner who came west in search of California's new gold, the Napa Valley wines. He met IT genius Chao

Ling. But Morrison's past caught up to him, and he took Ling down with him."

"Sounds like a novel. Your column is supposed to be about the wine angle, not murder."

"Morrison's trail of broken dreams ended in vineyard shoot-out."

"This time," Jones said, "the title of your 'Grapes of Rath' column is all too true."

Deadlines were merciless things, and Dante's had long passed. Jones was gone, his office door closed, the room dark. A couple of night copy editors sat in the pale fluorescent light of the newsroom, eyes glued to their computer screens. Two other reporters, one of them Hansen, sat in the stillness, their fingers moving sporadically on their keyboards. Images of the talking heads of CNN and Fox News flickered across the flat-screen TVs hanging on the walls, the sound inaudible.

Dante couldn't count the number of evenings he'd spent in newsrooms. After twenty years? Maybe thousands. And for what? He had his awards. Maybe they'd bury them with him, he thought. It was all coming to an end. Too soon. Yeah, he'd miss it. He fought back his fears about the downsizing and tried to refocus on his column.

Jones liked the idea of this column enough that he'd slated it for the front page and a jump to an inside page. Not the normal place for a column, but it would boost Dante's exposure, Jones said, and more importantly, keep the story alive. Dante didn't argue.

One of the copy editors glared across the newsroom at Dante and lifted his hands, silently asking where the hell his column was. Dante considered raising his middle finger, but didn't.

He scanned the column one last time and tapped the send button. "You got it," he said to the copy editor. He slumped in his chair and felt drained. He tilted his head back and twisted his neck from side to side, the cartilage crackling, his shoulders cramped. He turned his computer off, donned his jacket, and headed out of the newsroom, anxious to get back to his condo and open a bottle of wine.

CHAPTER 9

The next morning, as Dante drove onto the Golden Gate Bridge, a bank of fog lingered over the Pacific side, bumping against the city's western hills. To his left, the sun sparkled on the bay, where a handful of sailboats tilted with the wind, cutting through choppy waves and whitecaps.

Ten minutes later, Dante shifted gears and the Mustang growled as it climbed into the public parking garage on Vallejo Street in the North Beach neighborhood. He locked his car door and hurried down the steps, glancing at the police station across the street.

He made his way past the City Lights Bookstore and turned onto Grant Street, intent on finding the Ling family restaurant in Chinatown. As he made his way past tourists, he paused at shop fronts where plucked and dried ducks hung above crates of black "century eggs" nestled in straw, all undoubtedly in violation of at least a dozen food safety laws.

He turned at a cross street and walked half a block, stopping at a restaurant where he saw a sign in Chinese and English that read "Ling Dynasty, Mandarin Food." The small restaurant looked familiar, though he couldn't remember when he'd ever been there before.

Inside, a counter ran from front to back with fixed low-backed stools, some occupied. The restaurant was painted pastel green and decorated with a large golden dragon that snaked across the wall. Large photos of Beijing and the Great Wall of China filled the otherwise empty wall spaces. The place was sparse, yet warm and efficient. The sounds and aromas of frying food wafted from the swinging doors of the kitchen and filled the restaurant. Six tables filled the middle and booths of padded red vinyl upholstery ran along the wall.

He glanced at his watch: It was just a few minutes before noon. He'd beaten the lunch crowd so he decided to eat, though he hadn't come for the food.

Dante stood at the cash register by the door, attended by a tall, attractive young Chinese woman. She looked to be in her mid-twenties, Dante guessed. She wore a sleeveless, red satin dress with a collar and ornate gold embroidery. She stepped from behind the register, clutching a menu.

"You can seat yourself at the counter or I can show you to a table."

Dante smiled. "I'll take a booth."

She stepped briskly to a booth where she put a menu on the table and turned to him.

"Can I get you something to drink?"

"Green tea."

"Right away."

Dante touched her arm. "Ah, I'm sorry to bother you. I'm a journalist from Santa Rosa. I'm looking into the death of a man named Chao Ling. Do you know him?"

"Chao?" the woman said, her eyes opening wide as if suddenly frightened.. "Yes. Of course," she said softly. "He was my brother."

Dante handed her his business card.

"You're a reporter?" she asked, then glanced around the restaurant.

"Yes. And you are?"

"Mei Ling."

Dante hadn't expected to find family so quickly and feared he'd scare her away. "Can I ask you a couple of questions?"

She thought for a second, bit her lower lip, and glanced toward the swinging kitchen door. "You'd better talk to my father."

"Okay. Where do I find him?"

"He's in the back, cooking. I'll get him."

"Give him the card." She was about to turn when Dante said, "He may know of my grandfather, Vincenzo Spoleti. He used to run a grocery store on the other side of Broadway, called Spoleti's." Dante hoped a neighborhood connection might prompt the man to talk.

"Maybe. It was before my time." She disappeared through swinging doors into the kitchen.

Dante perused the menu. He was hungry, having had little for breakfast, and his stomach was complaining. Asian chicken with oranges. Seared scallops. Stir-fried lemon chicken. Long-life noodle salad. He wondered about the link between a long life and noodles. He dismissed the idea. Zesty chicken. Sweet and sour pork. He settled on orange peel fried rice.

Mei reappeared with a small tray, a white porcelain teapot and a matching small cup. She put the tea on the table, along with his business card. "I'm sorry, but my father does not want to talk to you." She looked around, leaned close, and whispered. "Maybe I can help. What exactly do you want to know about Chao?"

Dante wondered why the secrecy, but played along and spoke softly. "How did he meet Bernie Morrison? And why did he invest in Morrison's winery?"

Mei opened her mouth, as if to answer, but closed it and frowned, her eyes glistening. "We just buried Chao yesterday."

He motioned to the empty seat across from him. "Sit down."

Mei blinked back tears and whispered again, "Not now. It's going to get busy."

"What about later?"

Mei looked over her shoulder toward the kitchen doors and back at him. "Do you know the Caffe Trieste?"

"One of my favorites."

"Meet me there. Three o'clock." She turned to leave.

"Wait!" he said, holding out his hand. "Can I order?"

"What would you like?"

He ordered the fried rice, and after she left, put his reporter's notebook on the table. He flipped through the pages, reviewing his notes, but his attention remained on Mei Ling. He followed her graceful and efficient moves from the front of the restaurant to the tables where she waited on customers, about half of whom were from the neighborhood and the rest looked like tourists who had ventured off Grant Street and down the side streets.

Mei worked the restaurant with an older woman, who also took orders and bussed tables. Dante guessed she was Mei's mother. He caught Mei glancing at him as she worked tables, moving between them and the cash register near the door.

Dante sat back when Mei returned and put a plate in front of him.

"Would you like more tea?"

"Please," he said, pushing the notebook aside as she hurried to the front counter where a group waited to be seated. He sank his fork into the mound of diced chicken and rice mixed with chopped orange peels. Dante's thoughts drifted to his mother, who lived in a large flat in the Marina district. He had a few hours to kill before meeting with Mei, so decided to pay her a visit.

Dante had eaten half of the fried rice by the time Mei brought him a fresh pot of green tea. She smiled, turned, and tended to another table. *She looks like she knows what she's doing in that tight red dress...* He forked the last of his fried rice and managed to catch Mei's glance, making a scribbling motion for the check. With a slight toss of her head, she indicated he could pay at the register. He took a last sip of tea and made his way to the front.

"Did you like your lunch?" she asked, without a hint of a smile.

"Yes, thank you." He caught the scent she was wearing, delicate and floral. "So," he said softly, "Caffe Trieste at three."

Mei looked over her shoulder, glanced back at him, and nodded.

CHAPTER 10

The drive was short from the hills of North Beach to the flats of the Marina District where Dante rang the doorbell to his mother's place. Antonia Rath lived in the second-floor apartment of an aging but comfortable building with a spectacular view stretching from the Bay Bridge in the east to the Golden Gate in the west.

Antonia's voice squawked over a small box by the front door coated with multiple layers of white paint. "Who is it?"

"It's me, Mama. Let me in."

The door buzzed and clicked open. He stepped inside, closed the door behind him, and took the stairs two steps at a time, pausing at the landing where his mother stood in the open door, her head tilted to the side, a smile on her face. She wore a red bandanna like a biker, covering her forehead and tied in the back, which kept her thick salt-and-pepper hair under control. She smelled of acrylic paint and patchouli oil. She'd rolled the sleeves of her paint-smudged shirt, a man's extra-large, Western-style denim with mother-of-pearl button snaps.

"*Caro mio*. How are you?" she asked, giving him a peck on the cheek.

"*Bene, Mama. Bene*," he said, using his limited Italian. "I had to be in the city, so…"

He followed her into the kitchen with the high, east-facing windows that made it bright and sunny most mornings. Overhead, potted plants hung in woven macramé slings dangling from hooks he'd screwed into the high ceiling years ago. Small potted cacti lined the sills. "Would you like an espresso? I made some earlier." She pointed to her angular Bialetti coffee maker sitting on the stove. "Do you want something to eat? I can warm some pasta."

Dante grunted noncommittally.

"You prefer wine? I have some in the fridge."

"It's a bit early, don't you think?"

She blinked and smiled. "What's wrong with a little buzz in the afternoon?" She took a puff on her gold metallic vaporizer and exhaled, filling the air with the acrid odor of marijuana.

"The time of day never has bothered you."

Antonia shook her head in dismay. "It's all relative." She took an open bottle of pinot grigio from her refrigerator, clunked it on her tile counter, and took two small wine glasses from her stippled glass door cabinets. She splashed wine into each and handed him one.

"An offer I can't refuse." He settled into one of the kitchen table chairs, a mismatched set she described as eclectic, and sipped. The sound of the Grateful Dead filtered into the kitchen. The ability to stream the quintessential California jam band's music twenty-four hours a day was how she justified paying for cable television, which she otherwise didn't watch or use. To Antonia, sitting down to watch cable news was nothing but a "bummer," a "downer" that often left her fuming. Whenever she watched the news she couldn't paint, she said.

She ignored his explanations it was the nature of the news beast. Privately, he didn't blame her, but he'd never admit it to her. News was "his thing," she said. She was right. He'd always been bored by the ordinary and the mundane, and fascinated by the odd, the ugly, the horrifying. Dante remembered smiling when his editor Jones had barked, "You've got to make people choke on their damned orange juice when they read the morning news." He thought about it each time he wrote a story.

"How's the back?" he asked, as the words to "A Touch of Grey" drifted into the kitchen. The song made him feel old.

He rubbed his chin, where he knew a little silver speckled his goatee.

"It's there," Antonia said with a shrug.

She had wrenched her back in the mid-1970s working their small family farm near Geyserville. She and Dante's father, Dieter, had left the city and settled on her family's ten acres during the back-to-the-earth movement. The land belonged to her father, Vincenzo Spoleti, who had used it for growing vegetables and grapes, and for making wine he and Antonia's mother sold in Spoleti's corner grocery in North Beach. Dante had been born in the old farmhouse, Antonia having shunned a trip to the hospital in favor of a home birth. He'd spent his earliest years there, and the first book he remembered reading was the *Whole Earth Catalog*.

When Dante was five, Antonia and Dieter were busted. Though they grew only organic vegetables, they also used the farm as a transfer and packaging point for marijuana coming out of the national forests across Northern California. Dieter was out of the country at the time of the bust, in South America, Antonia said. The farm was seized by federal agents. Dieter never returned. Antonia did some time in the state's women's prison, dubbed "Frontera," a word implying a new frontier for the inmates. She'd gotten out after thirteen months, for good behavior. She'd organized painting classes for the women inmates. The women had loved it. But the time she served had left her shaken. It was the state's only women's prison at the time, and there were hard-core criminals there, some on death row.

Dante had lived with his grandparents in their apartment above their store in North Beach where he'd helped his grandfather make wine in the basement. He had missed his mother, but remembered the time fondly.

Antonia's back pain was enough to justify monthly disability payments from the State of California, along with a medical marijuana permit. Not that she needed it. Good weed was not hard to find. Never had been if you were willing to pay top dollar for it.

Dante refocused on his mother. "How are art sales going?" he asked.

Antonia's eyes lit up.

"It's tourist season, you know. I can hardly keep Alex supplied."

Dante had never known her when she hadn't been painting. As she had often recounted to him in her many bouts of melancholia, art was how she and Dieter had met. It was May 7, 1967, and she'd been selling her surreal streetscapes of San Francisco at a street fair in Haight-Ashbury. The date and the story were burned into Dante's memory.

Now she sold through a gallery owned by Alex Tercero, a place with an airy storefront at the western end of Fisherman's Wharf. It was an ideal location on the path from the Wharf to Ghirardelli Square, just a block from the Buena Vista bar.

Antonia and Alex had been together for more than twenty years now. Tercero treated her well. Dante had no complaints there. As the owner of an art gallery and a boutique winery, he had a place in the affluent Pacific Heights neighborhood, drove a Jaguar sedan in the city and a Range Rover Sport when he was feeling adventurous for their weekends at his winery in the Russian River Valley. Tercero carried an aura of wealth, but it made Dante wonder. The man didn't make the kind of money he appeared to have from the gallery or his boutique winery, Alex Estates. Dante knew most art galleries were write-offs for their owners, a good thing to have come tax season, and he suspected it was true of Tercero.

Dante had searched online and found Tercero associated with the gallery, the winery, and memberships on the boards of a couple of nonprofits dedicated to supporting the arts— nothing else. It didn't add up. Still, Tercero was cultured, had a fine wine collection, and looked the part, with a thick head of white hair, a bronze cast to his face, and a trimmed white beard.

Antonia took a deep drag on her vape and exhaled, letting the thin smoke dissipate. "What've you been doing?" she asked. "You don't come by here often enough, you know."

"I'm looking into those vineyard murders in Napa."

"I read about it, but just the headlines. It's crazy."

"The shooter was a guy who owned the Morrison Creek winery. He killed his investor, a guy named Chao Ling."

"Ling? The name sounds familiar."

"His family owns a restaurant in Chinatown."

Antonia lifted her thinning eyes brows. "Oh, my God. The Ling family of the Ling Dynasty."

"You know it?" Dante asked.

"Of course. We ate there a lot when I was a kid. Old man Ling was friends with your grandfather, Vincenzo. The restaurant's been there for years. Just off Grant Street. A few blocks south of Broadway."

"I ate lunch there today. I went to talk to them about Chao."

Antonia took another deep drag. "Forget it. They won't talk. The only think you'll get from them is a good egg fu yung."

"You're right. The old man wouldn't talk, but the daughter will."

"Daughter?" Antonia's eyes crinkled in thought. "Let me see. If I recall, there was Chao and Mei."

"I'm going to meet with Mei later this afternoon."

"My God. I bet she's all grown up now."

"Yes, she's very good-looking."

"I haven't been by there in years. It looks the same, probably."

Dante now worried Mei might have second thoughts about an interview, get cold feet, and clam up. She could be a dead end. If so, then what? Since Tercero owned a winery, another possibility came to mind.

"Have you ever heard of a guy named Ricardo Santos?"

"Yes, of course. He's a friend of Alex's. Alex sold him a few of my paintings. He paid top dollar for them. Why?"

"He's a big player in the wine industry. His name keeps coming up. He might be involved, but I'm not sure how."

"In the shooting at the vineyard? You can't be serious."

"No, no," Dante said. "Nothing like that. It's just he had some business dealings with the shooter."

Antonia sighed deeply, looking worried. "You should talk to Alex. He knows Santos. But I'd tread lightly. Don't go messing with these people."

"What does that mean?"

"Just what I said. People with big money hate the press. They're very guarded about how they show up in print, especially if they're in the wine business."

"I've been writing about the wine industry for a few years now, Mama."

"When there's a lot of money at stake, well, people can get crazy. They do stupid things."

"Like shoot people."

"Yes. Like shoot people." Antonia drew again on her vape.

Dante thought about Morrison and Nicole and what he'd written about Morrison and his wine. Yeah. There was a lot of money at stake. Starting with Chao Ling's million dollars. There was more to this story. He could feel it.

"Just don't go stepping on people's toes for no good reason, Dante dear. That's what got Dieter and me in trouble."

"I know. You've told me." Dealing pot was small-time compared to what it is now, Antonia had said. She and his father had naively figured there was more than enough room in the drug business for everyone.

"We had product coming out of the northern forests," she said, repeating the story he'd heard many times. "At first it went well. Very well. What we didn't know was it was going *too* well. People started to notice, and some didn't like it."

Antonia got a faraway look in her eyes and fell silent. "Mama!" he said, trying to bring her back.

Her eyes refocused. "We were lucky they didn't kill us. It's what they do these days, just to send a message." She looked out the kitchen window at nothing in particular. "They got to Dieter. That's why you grew up without a father."

"You get melancholy when you're high, Mama. It's just half past two o'clock."

"So what?"

"Don't keep reliving the past, Mama. What's done is done. You have a good life. Why not enjoy it?"

Antonia looked at him with forlorn eyes. "Dieter couldn't come back. If he had, he'd still be in prison."

"You've told me this before." Dante dropped his eyes to the table. He knew his father had gone to South America, but his mother never talked about what happened to him. Maybe she didn't know. But, he knew she felt terribly guilty, thinking she was responsible for Dieter's disappearance, which had left him fatherless and her effectively a widow. It had left Dante to fantasize about his father breaking out of some prison, like Butch and Sundance, miraculously surviving.

Antonia's eyes glistened. She looked at her glass and brushed away tears. She refilled her glass and his. Dante glanced at his watch. "I need to get going." He swallowed the last of his wine and gazed at his mother. "Go back to your painting. Take your mind off the past. Okay?"

She reached across the table and held his hand in hers. "I'm sorry."

"Don't be. We both have things to do. I have a story to work on, which is why I came to the city in the first place. Your easel awaits."

"Next time, come for dinner." Antonia said. "Okay?"

"Okay, Mama."

CHAPTER 11

Dante checked his watch: 3:30 p.m. He sighed, thinking he'd been stood up by Mei. He decided to wait a few more minutes, his eyes hidden behind sunglasses as people hurried past on the sidewalk outside Caffe Trieste. A sleek motorcycle with two riders, both dressed in black leather, whizzed around the corner and made a sharp turn about half a block away. It returned and parked in front of the café.

The rear rider dismounted, lifted off her helmet, and glanced at Dante. It was Mei Ling, shaking her thick, dark hair out over the shoulders of her jacket. It fit her nicely and was cut at the waist, just short of her rivet-studded and belted leather pants, which she had tucked into her knee-high motorcycle boots. *No longer the China doll in the red satin dress.* Dante stared, amazed. She said something to the driver, another woman, who swung her leg up and off the street bike and pushed the street machine up onto a stand.

The driver removed her helmet and Dante was surprised to see Marvee, the woman who worked for Simon Grundy at Shady Oaks, the unmistakable blue-ink tiger crawling down her temple and onto her cheekbone. Marvee eyed Dante, silently sizing him up.

Dante waited as the two approached. Now he knew why Marvee had known the name of the Ling restaurant.

"Dante?" Mei asked, pulling off a glove and extending her hand. He shook it lightly and smiled. "Marvee, this is Dante, the reporter I told you about."

"We've met," Marvee said, her voice flat, as if she didn't really want to be there.

Do I turn her off for some reason? Dante couldn't tell.

"You have?" Mei frowned.

Dante looked at Mei. "At Shady Oaks the other day."

"Mei said she was meeting with a reporter," Marvee said. "I figured it was you."

"You figured right," Dante said. "So, you're a friend of Mei's?"

"Yeah. You could say that." Marvee shifted her weight to one hip, and tilted her head, a look of defiance on her face.

"Nice bike," he said.

"Thanks," Marvee said.

"You should take me for a spin some time."

"Maybe," she said, staring.

Dante motioned to the café door and followed them inside where they stopped at the counter. "What would you like?"

"Cappuccino for me," Mei said.

He looked at Marvee, who nodded.

"Three cappuccinos," Dante said to the barista. The loud clatter of cups and the hiss of the espresso machine drowned any chance for conversation. Marvee and Mei drifted to the back of the café to find an empty table.

Dante remembered how his Italian relatives had remarked with polite revulsion at the large containers of coffee carried around and consumed by Americans. The Italians, meanwhile, tossed back a demitasse of the thick espresso laced with sugar. Super-charged caffeine. No reason to linger.

The barista rattled the cappuccino cups to the counter. Dante paid and carried them to a corner table where Mei and Marvee had settled. They emptied packets of sugar into the thick milk foam and stirred their spoons.

"Thanks for meeting with me," Dante said, taking a sip.

"Sorry about my father," Mei said. "He's very traditional."

"Are you full-time at the restaurant?"

"It's a family business," Mei said. "We all pitch in."

"Are you planning to take over the restaurant one day?"

Mei's mouth opened slightly in surprise, as if the notion was shocking. "Not if I can help it. I'm getting an MBA."

"Where?"

"University of San Francisco."

"Do you like it?"

"It's a lot of work," Mei said, sipping her coffee and using a finger to wipe the foam from her upper lip. She wound a napkin around the finger.

"Sorry about your brother."

"Yeah, thanks." Mei said. "What did you want to know about him?"

"I'm trying to unravel what made Morrison want to kill him," Dante said.

Mei's eyes glazed over. She caught herself and blinked, used the small napkin to dab her eyes, and refocused. "It's hard because, well, he and I were very close. It was so senseless. Chao was a good person."

"Were you aware of his substantial investment in Morrison's winery?"

"I told him he was stupid."

"Like a good sister would," Dante said, glancing at Marvee sipping her coffee. He looked back at Mei.

"It was unsecured," Mei said. "He gave a stranger his money. No wonder he lost it."

"Did you know Morrison wanted the money in cash?" Dante asked.

"Yes!" Mei said, her voice rising, her hand slapping the table. "I couldn't believe it. I insisted Chao get his money back."

"The cash is what baffles me."

"My father was furious," Mei said.

"I don't blame him."

"My father adored Chao," Mei said. "Saw him as the hope for the Ling family."

"I'm told Chao was a high-tech genius," Dante said.

"He was extremely successful in internet technology. But he quit," Mei said with disgust.

"Maybe he wanted a more down-to-earth existence," Dante said. "Maybe he wanted to be a winemaker instead of a digital dynamo."

Mei's eyes watered. She used her napkin to wipe a tear.

Dante regretted the cynicism coloring his remark. "I'm sorry. I don't mean to put you through this if you don't want to talk about Chao."

Mei cleared her throat. "No worries. I'll do anything to help you figure out why Morrison killed him."

Dante drank from his coffee. "Why did Chao invest so much money with Morrison? I don't get it."

"Don't you see? Chao was smart, but he was naive," Mei said, sounding disgusted by her brother's lack of skepticism. "He thought he could invest his money in a random business, sit back, and let the money roll in."

"He thought it would be like the world of digital technology where you can make millions overnight," she said. "He was way too trusting. He'd lived inside the tech bubble for so long, he didn't understand how the real world works."

"Or doesn't work," Dante said. "So why a winery? It's not a very secure investment."

"What can I say?" Mei said. "He liked wine."

"You know what they say about the wine business?" Dante asked.

"What?"

"In order to make a small fortune in the wine business, you need to start with a large one," he said with a wry grin.

Mei smiled weakly. "That's good." She lifted her cup and sipped. "For Chao, it was the prestige. He wanted to be able to tell everyone he owned a high-end winery, one where the cheapest bottles sold for $100 each."

"And your father was against it?"

"Of course. He told Chao if he wanted to run a small business, he should take over the restaurant. But Chao wouldn't consider it. My father was completely against the winery, thought it was foolish. But in my father's eyes, Chao could do no wrong." Mei rolled her eyes, their sibling rivalry showing itself.

"He had other plans, obviously," Dante said.

"It wasn't the only thing," Mei said.

"What else?"

"His lifestyle."

"What do you mean?" Dante asked.

"Well, he never married," Mei said. "Didn't have any children."

Dante considered that. "Was he gay?"

Mei exchanged glances with Marvee. "You'd never know it to look at him."

"What do you mean?"

"To my parents, Chao was just a normal guy," Mei said.

"Did they know?"

"Chao kept telling them he just hadn't found the right girl. And, like always, they believed him."

Dante folded and unfolded his paper napkin, pondering the implications of this latest revelation. "Is that how he met Morrison?"

"Morrison liked the drag queen shows," Mei said.

"Was Chao a transvestite?"

"No." Mei said. "But Morrison may have been."

"Maybe your brother threatened to out Morrison," Dante said. "It might make Morrison want to kill him."

"That wasn't the reason!" Marvee blurted, breaking her glum silence.

Dante looked at Marvee. "Why not?" he asked. "If Chao was angry at Morrison, he'd try to hurt him somehow, sabotage his reputation."

"This is San Francisco," Marvee said. "No one cares. This is a gay city."

"You're right," Dante said.

Mei and Marvee looked at each other, then at Dante. "You're the one who trashed Bernie's wines in the newspaper," Marvee said. "Maybe you should think about that."

Dante glanced at her warily. "Why should *I* think about it?"

"He didn't deserve it," Marvee said.

"I guess we have a difference of opinion." Dante swirled the coffee in his cup and lifted his eyes. "You're suggesting my review of Morrison's wines triggered him to kill Chao?"

Marvee narrowed her eyes. "Bernie was at the end of his rope. He desperately needed help. He thought a good review might turn things around."

Dante swallowed and struggled to push his feelings of guilt aside. "From me?" Dante asked, incredulous at the thought. "Maybe Morrison had more enemies than some people think."

"Why do you say that?" Mei asked.

"He was stealing grapes," Dante said.

Marvee blinked, as if to say, so what? *She knows*, Dante thought.

"Morrison stole my brother's money and killed him," Mei said. "That's more important to me than anybody's grapes."

"Morrison used people," Marvee said. "It's the way he was."

Dante glanced at Marvee, waiting for her continue. "How do you know?"

"I just know," Marvee said. "Leave it at that."

"I'd rather not," Dante said.

"It was about the money," Mei insisted. "Morrison lied to Chao. Morrison said he needed the cash to expand and upgrade the winery. But nothing happened. The money disappeared."

"So Chao sued Morrison to get it back," Dante said. "I'm familiar with the lawsuit. But now Morrison is dead and the money is still gone. The only thing left is the winery."

"I'm talking with his lawyer about it tomorrow," Mei said, sipping from her coffee.

"Carmen Carelli," Dante said.

"You know her?" Mei asked.

"Yes, she's one of the top lawyers in wine country," Dante said. "Well respected, well connected. She's part of the Carelli wine family."

"He at least had the sense to get a good lawyer," Mei said. "My brother was brilliant. But his naivety sometimes made him do stupid things. I'm surprised he got as far as he did." The disgust had returned to her voice as Mei glanced at her watch. "Sorry. I have to go. Classes."

"How can I contact you?" Dante asked.

Mei handed him a restaurant business card and scribbled her cell phone number on the back. "Text me."

The two women stood and left, bulky helmets under their arms. Dante watched their leather-clad figures go out the door.

Traffic was stop and go as Dante approached the Golden Gate Bridge, having become part of the daily surge in commuter traffic headed north on Highway 101 to homes in the myriad communities in Marin Country, Santa Rosa, and parts north. Mei Ling's revelation her brother had been gay might lead to new possibilities, Dante thought, but Marvee was probably right. In the Bay Area, it was hardly worth noting. Yet Morrison was a Midwesterner. Maybe his sexuality was part of why he'd left Columbus, Ohio. Considering he'd had an affair with Nicole as well, he would have found it a lot easier to live as a bisexual in San Francisco. Dante swallowed hard, his throat now thick with worry. How promiscuous was Morrison? And with whom? How careful was he?

And how did Simon Grundy fit into the picture? Grundy had professed ignorance about Morrison's background. Dante had no reason to doubt Grundy was telling the truth. Grundy didn't need to know everything about Morrison's history as long as Morrison treated him honestly. And why wouldn't he? Morrison depended on Grundy for the expertise needed to make his wine.

Dante circled back to Morrison's abuse of Ling's money and trust. With Morrison's history of fraud and failure, he was undoubtedly jealous of Ling's success and envious of his money. Ling had what Morrison wanted, but Morrison lacked the wherewithal to achieve it. Morrison had quickly sensed Ling's weakness and had swooped in for the kill.

CHAPTER 12

The clock read 5:54 p.m. when Dante slumped into his desk chair in the newsroom. He was thankful he had no story or column to write. He felt empty, drained. He tilted his head back and twisted his neck from side to side, the cartilage crackling, his shoulders cramped. He knew exactly what he needed to do. He turned his computer off, donned his jacket, and headed out the newsroom.

Fifteen minutes later Dante pushed open the door to his health club and stepped into stale air that smelled of sweat, chlorine, and cleaning fluid. He found an open locker, shed his clothes, pulled on his shorts and T-shirt, and bent to tie his running shoes. He clicked the padlock shut on the locker door, reminding himself of the combination as he hustled out to the main exercise room.

He longed for a good workout, something he'd not done since the shooting at Morrison Creek Winery. Workouts cleared his mind, put the day behind him. Like Zen meditation. He climbed onto an empty running machine and stretched. He attributed his tight leg muscles to far too much sitting and the accumulated tensions from working the story. He bent to touch his toes, but settled for a good stretch from the back of his thighs to his calves and ankles. He pushed the start button and the treadmill began to move, then held the speed button down until he was trotting at a good pace.

Thirty minutes later Dante slowed the treadmill to a walk and pulled his ragged workout towel from the crossbar to wipe his face. He hit the stop button and stepped to the hardwood floor. *Yes! What I needed.* He looped the towel around his neck and navigated the weight machines, stopping at a long rack of free weights fronting a wall of mirrors. *Mirrors and workouts. They shame the shapeless into exercise and let the fitness freaks pose and flex.*

Sheriff investigator Jake Henshaw, who'd been at the vineyard crime scene days earlier, sat on a padded bench at the far end of the rack wearing a T-shirt stretched tightly across his chest. A couple of fat seventy-pound dumbells dangled from his heavily muscled arms. He alternately lifted the weights in arm curls, lips stretched tight in the strain, cheeks puffed out, eyes staring straight ahead, face red. He dropped the weights to the rubber floor mats with a resounding *thunk-thunk*. People turned to the sound. Henshaw caught Dante's eye in the mirror, nodded, and massaged his biceps as he prepared for another set.

Dante felt puny as he grabbed a couple of twenty-five-pounders, found an open bench, and began a set of arm curls. His arms strained against the weights, but warmed to the task. He moved through the repetitions until his muscles burned, rested a couple of minutes, and meandered to another angled bench where he hooked his knees over the padded restraints and did sit-ups.

He repeated the routine two more times and feeling tired, headed for the locker room where he shed all but his shorts and slipped on a pair of flip-flops. He refilled his water bottle, pulled open the frosted glass door, and stepped into the health club's dimly lighted sauna. He found an open spot on the upper bench and took a seat. He closed his eyes, tilted his head back, and waited for the heat to relax his muscles.

"Hello, stranger," said a throaty feminine voice.

Dante blinked open his eyes. Carmen sat in the corner, bringing a smile to his lips. "Hello yourself," he said.

Carmen's face was flush and moist. She wore a yellow elastic exercise bra, skimpy purple workout shorts, and her toenails were painted to match her shorts. Her taut thighs and supple skin glistened.

"I didn't know you belonged to the club," he said.

"I don't use it as much as I should," she said "How was your workout?"

"It's been a while," he said, and took a long drink of water. Three others in the sauna, their skin pink and glistening, rose and stepped out, leaving them alone. Dante scooped water onto the hot rocks, and it hissed and popped, filling the sauna with a blast of heat.

"Enough!" Carmen said.

Dante smiled. "Some like it hot."

"I suppose," she said, gulping from her water bottle. She brushed hair back from her face. "So, what have you found out about the murderous Mr. Morrison?" she asked.

Dante splashed water onto his forehead, letting it dribble down his face. He was reluctant to say anything, still stinging from her rebukes at their lunch two days earlier. She gave him a curious smile, and the possibility of another night with her came to Dante's mind. He took a drink from his water bottle. "You remember Donald Rumsfeld, the defense secretary under the former President Bush?"

"Don't tell me he's involved."

"No. Nothing like that." Dante sipped from his water. "Rumsfeld talked about things we know. He called them the 'known knowns.'"

"Never liked the guy."

"He also talked about the things we know we don't know. He called them the 'known unknowns.'" Dante took another sip of water. "Finally, there are the things we don't even know we don't know. He called them the 'unknown unknowns.'"

"Sounds like some weird mind game."

"Well, what I'm worried about are the unknown unknowns."

"Jesus, Dante. You're making my head hurt."

Dante smiled and sipped water, his skin beading with sweat.

"So what are you saying?" she asked.

"I'd prefer to explain myself over dinner and drinks."

Carmen worked her fingers through her thick hair, pushing it back from her face, and twisted it into a knot behind her head. She smiled. "Sure. I'm starving."

"How about Mexican food?" he said. "I have a taste for margaritas tonight. We should be able to get into Rosarita's."

"Great," she said. "I have to swing by my office to pick up a file. I'll meet you there, say, in thirty minutes?"

Dante smiled. "Okay," he said, the empty feeling now gone.

The door closed behind her. Dante slumped against the wall and dribbled more water over his forehead. Wiping it from his eyes, the door opened, and Henshaw stepped in and settled on the upper bench where Carmen had been. Dante smiled to himself. He'd wanted to call Henshaw for several days. This was better, much better.

"Good workout?" Dante asked.

"Always," Henshaw said, as if it was without question.

Scars crisscrossed Henshaw's knees, the marks of multiple surgeries. Dante felt bad for Henshaw, the scars visible reminders of how much the man had craved a football career. Dante wondered if arthritis had settled in his knees.

"What's the latest on the Morrison-Ling case?" Dante asked.

Henshaw looked straight ahead, as if he hadn't heard, then spoke to the cedar-paneled wall. "We're looking into it. What can I say?"

Anxious for any scrap of information, Dante tried to act disinterested. "Nothing much, huh?"

Henshaw leaned forward, his forearms on his thighs, his eyes on the black floor mat.

Dante sipped again from his water bottle. "Have you come up with a motive? Why would Morrison shoot his biggest investor?"

Henshaw looked again at the sauna wall. "None of it makes any sense, if you ask me," he said with disgust. He fell mute, as if he had nothing more to say. He rubbed his face as it began to grow pink, the heat taking effect. "How much do you know about Morrison?"

Dante swallowed, worried he'd not done enough digging. "Some. He's from Ohio. A couple of marriages ended in divorce. A lawsuit for fraud. He shows up in California."

Henshaw brushed away beading sweat.

What have I missed? On the day of the shooting, Dante had perused the extensive complaint Carmen had filed against Morrison on behalf of Ling, but the details had seemed convoluted and not immediately useful. "Morrison got a large investment from Ling—in cash. When Ling wanted the money back, Morrison didn't have it."

"Yeah, that's right," Henshaw said.

"But it doesn't seem to me like a reason to shoot someone."

Henshaw settled against the wall, his eyes unfocused, looking exhausted. "Sure it's a reason. Why wouldn't it be? Ling demanded Morrison return his million bucks, which Morrison no longer had, or lose his business. It would piss off Morrison big-time. It would piss off anyone."

"You're saying Morrison was at the end of his rope," Dante said.

"When you back a mad dog into a corner, it'll do anything to survive."

"But Morrison didn't survive," Dante said. "You guys shot him."

"What was the alternative?"

Dante thought about it and said, "So the case is closed?"

"As far as I'm concerned."

"What about the money?"

"What about it?" Henshaw asked. "We deal in murder cases, not financial crimes."

Dante didn't respond.

"Morrison's been on the radar screen for a while," Henshaw said with a sigh.

"The Napa County Sheriff's office?" Dante asked.

"The state and the feds, mostly," Henshaw said. "We didn't get involved until the shooting."

Dante mulled the implications. "Why? What was Morrison doing?"

"Mr. Morrison didn't think much about following the law. Any law."

"Like what?"

"Like getting a business license. Like zoning ordinances. Like paying taxes."

Dante had a sinking feeling. "How long has this been going on?"

"Longer than it should have," Henshaw said.

"How does someone get away with that?" Dante asked, the feeling deepening.

"You'd be amazed at what some people get away with," Henshaw said.

"Like what?"

"Morrison had a business partner."

"Simon Grundy," Dante said. "The guy I was talking to at the winery when you threatened to arrest us."

"I could have."

"But you didn't," Dante said.

"Morrison and Grundy had an interesting way of doing business," Henshaw said. "Have you talked to the TTB yet?"

"The feds? No. It's on my list."

"It'd be worth your time." Henshaw stepped down to the floor, leaned against the wall with both arms extended, one leg back, and stretched his calf muscles. "I'm outta here," he said, glancing at Dante. "Happy hunting."

Henshaw pushed open the sauna door and disappeared, leaving Dante alone in the heat, his mind buzzing.

Dante and Carmen settled into padded leather chairs at Rosarita's restaurant and ordered a couple of traditional margaritas. Still flushed from the workout and sauna, she looked as appealing as ever, even without her normally subdued make-up. She had slipped into a tight black T-shirt covered by an untucked blue blouse with rolled sleeves, snug jeans, and her pink running shoes, sans socks. Her thick hair was clasped behind her head and trailed down her back.

When the margaritas arrived, Dante licked the salt from the rim of his glass and savored the tart lemon-lime juice—a welcome change from wine. He considered the prospects for the night and lifted his glass. "*Saluté!*"

Carmen clinked her glass against his and drank.

He took a second swallow and scanned the menu, his eyes stopping on one item. "Look at this. 'Ricardo's Especial.' It's a combination plate."

Carmen looked up from her menu. "If you're hungry, you should order it."

"I might. Is it named after your client friend, Ricardo?"

Carmen wrinkled her nose. "You're obsessed by the man. It's probably named after the owner, or his brother, or someone."

"Maybe," Dante said, his mind reviewing the sauna conversation with Henshaw. "You know, the police have been watching Morrison for quite some time."

"So what?" Carmen returned to her menu.

"It seems," Dante said, "Morrison has been flouting federal, state, and local laws for quite a while."

"Old news, Dante."

"Maybe he was taking his cues from your friend, Ricardo?"

Carmen's eyes flared. "If Ricardo was linked with Morrison, he'd be stupid to let people know about it. There are consequences, especially now with what's happened."

"That's what worries me. Santos has tens of thousands of acres of vines. There's a lot someone could do with all of those acres of grapes."

"Look, Dante, the risk is too high for even big-time players to ignore the law. The wine industry is one of the most closely watched and highly regulated in the world."

She reached for her glass and drank. "Besides, the police have already talked to Santos."

"How do you know?"

"Ricardo called me when the police were at his offices. I was in on the interview."

Dante swallowed. "They grilled Santos about what he knew about Morrison?"

"Of course. I told Ricardo he didn't need to talk without a lawyer present. He did, but with me listening in on a conference call."

"Probably a good decision on his part," Dante said. "Otherwise, they'd be suspicious."

"They're more than suspicious."

"Did they get a search warrant?"

"No," Carmen said. "Why would they?"

"I don't know."

They ordered dinner, and soon the waiter placed guacamole and chips on the table.

"They say the avocado is the perfect food," Carmen said, scooping up a big bite of the freshly made dip.

"You believe it?" Dante asked.

"Of course, because it's true."

"It's a ploy by the avocado growers," he said.

"No, it's not," she said.

"Let me guess. Your pal Ricardo owns avocado farms."

"It wouldn't surprise me, but it doesn't mean…" Her voice trailed off. "You're very suspicious, and cynical, you know."

"Sometimes." He sipped his margarita.

Dante liked Carmen's instincts and her skeptical mind, but felt he was competing with her over every little thing. The back-and-forth tug of wills was trying. He looked at his margarita glass. Nearly empty, as was hers. It had gone down too quickly. He waved to the waiter and circled his finger in the air to order a couple more.

He gazed at her, wondering why the police had questioned Santos. Dante realized he probably sensed the same thing as the police: Santos was somehow linked to this case. What evidence did they have that he didn't? Morrison had killed a man. That wouldn't go away. What was Santos's relationship with Morrison? Maybe Ling had been a bigger problem to Morrison than anyone knew, big enough that Morrison felt compelled to kill him.

Dante hesitated to keep talking about Santos, but he didn't want to pass up this chance to pick her brain. "What do you know about Simon Grundy?"

"Grundy?" Carmen said, squinting as if struggling to remember.

Dante drew a short breath. "He's the guy I was talking with at Morrison's winery the other day."

"I know who he is. He was Morrison's business partner. He owns the Shady Oaks winery near Healdsburg. He made the wine for Morrison. A rising star in the winemaking world."

"He was very involved with Morrison," Dante said. "He and Morrison had a wine consulting business. MG Enology. Did Grundy come up in your conversations with Ling?"

"Of course. Ling knew Grundy, but as the winemaker. Trusted him. Respected him. It's all in the Ling lawsuit. Why are you so curious about Grundy now?"

"Winemakers are a competitive bunch," Dante said. "If they're good, they command huge salaries. Most end up owning wineries."

"They should," Carmen said. "The success or failure of a winery depends on the skill of the winemaker."

"Grundy was a newcomer, though."

"So what?" Carmen asked.

"It means he'd try harder."

"You're probably right," she said.

"Morrison left Ohio following lawsuits and a judgment against him," Dante said.

"I know."

"But Grundy went into business with Morrison anyway," he said.

"Wasn't such a good idea, was it?"

"There's more to Grundy's and Santos's dealings with Morrison than wine and winemaking," Dante said.

"Why do you think so?"

"Winemakers are like mother hens," Dante said. "They like to control the entire process, from growing the grapes to the harvest and the fermentation. They wait until the precise moment when they think the grapes are perfectly ripe before they're picked and thrown into the fermentation tanks and crushed."

"What's your point?"

"I don't get Grundy," he said. His stomach gurgled, anticipating the meal.

Carmen looked at him sympathetically, sipped from her margarita, and licked salt from her lips. He followed her tongue. "You want my take on Grundy?"

"That's why I asked," he said.

"He's a kid from Ohio. He wanted to make it in the California wine business. Just like Morrison. He and Morrison are, or were, birds of a feather. He may not talk or act like Morrison, but it's a fact."

"Really?" Dante asked.

"Just a hunch."

It was more than a hunch, Dante thought, and told himself to revisit the Ling lawsuit against Morrison. The waiter swirled up to the table with their dinners on a tray balanced on his shoulder. He gingerly set plates on the table, warned the plates were hot, and said, *"Buen apetito."* He eyed their nearly empty margarita glasses and pointed to them.

"Would you like another?" the waiter asked.

Dante and Carmen nodded in unison.

CHAPTER 13

Dante opened his eyes to the sound of running water in the bathroom. He was alone in bed, Carmen's bed, but her scent lingered. The alarm clock on her nightstand read 6:15. He groaned, sat up, and swung his legs over the side of the bed. He rubbed his face awake, stood, pulled on his pants, and bent to tie his shoes. He slipped into his shirt, tucked the tails into his pants, and looked at the mirror over Carmen's dresser to rake his fingers through his hair.

The aroma of fresh coffee hit him as he stepped into the kitchen. He took a cup from the cupboard, placed it under the spigot of the automatic espresso maker, and pressed the button, launching the machine into the frantic clunk, whirr, and grinding of beans. Dark, fresh coffee filled his cup. Leaning against the counter, foggy recollections of the night came to mind.

Carmen stepped into the kitchen carrying a cup of coffee and wearing her running shoes, shorts, and a light sweatshirt. "I see you found the coffee."

He groaned. "Hmmm. I did. Thanks."

Carmen raised the cup to her lips for a last swallow, rinsed it in the sink, and dried it with a hand towel. "I have a busy day ahead."

"Don't worry," Dante said with a voice not yet awake. "I'm leaving."

"I'm not trying to chase you out."

He sipped from his cup, savored the flavor, and leaned forward for a goodbye kiss. She gave him a peck on the cheek. *That's it?* Dismayed, he took a second swallow, emptied his coffee into the sink, and headed for the door. She was right behind him.

They stepped outside and Carmen closed the door. Standing in her driveway, she bent and stretched while Dante walked to his car. When he looked back at her, she held two fingers to her lips and blew him a kiss.

He smiled and settled behind the steering wheel of his Mustang, started it, and followed her to the end of the gravel drive where the gate swung open automatically. When he drove through, it closed behind him. He trailed her down the street to a paved running trail leading east of town and into the low rolling hills. He watched until she disappeared, drew a breath, and exhaled. Feeling empty, he turned and drove through Sonoma, heading back to Santa Rosa with the sun already promising another clear, warm California day.

Dante stepped into his modestly furnished condo and closed the door. It was virtually unchanged since when he and Nicole had lived there. After she died, he'd donated most of her possessions to Goodwill, returned her family keepsakes to her parents, but had left a few of her clothes still hanging in the closet. Framed photos of them together filled the spaces between the books he had accumulated over the years that filled the built-in shelves covering most of the living room wall. He picked up his favorite. It was their honeymoon in Hawaii, and they were each drinking fancy mai tais. They were sitting outside at the House Without a Key restaurant and bar at the Halekulani hotel. One mai tai had followed another, each decorated with a floating orchid. It had felt like a dream: the warm, moist air, the sunsets, the music, and hypnotic hula dancers. He replaced the photo on the shelf. It felt like another lifetime. Thoughts of Carmen crept into his mind. Yeah, he liked her, he liked her a lot. He put some coffee on to brew, showered, and changed.

He drove to the newspaper office with a full travel mug of hot coffee. It was after nine o'clock when he parked. His headache was beginning to fade. He walked into the newsroom holding his insulated mug and heard his name called just as he reached his desk. He draped his jacket over the back of his chair and settled into it as Jones crossed the newsroom, folded his arms across his chest, and leaned against Dante's desk.

"I need an update," Jones said. "Where do you go from here?"

"I'm working on it," Dante said, sipping his coffee. "Like I said before, there are a lot of moving parts."

"What happened to your leads about the theft of grapes, the false labeling of wine?"

"Still valid."

"Tell me more," Jones said.

"I'm sorting it out."

"C'mon, Dante. I'm fighting off our esteemed editor-publisher. You know how he feels about a wine editor who still thinks he's an investigative reporter. He's not happy about you running around wine country and not writing stories every day."

"Digging up dirt takes time."

"If you want to keep digging, you'd better feed me glowing reports on your progress."

Dante drank from his coffee. "I need to talk to the witness to the shooting. The guy named Muñoz."

"I thought you already did."

Dante shook his head. "Muñoz was a contract labor manager. He worked for both Morrison and Simon Grundy. He maintained their vineyards. Hired and supervised the people who pick the grapes."

"You told me," Jones said. "The foreman said Morrison wanted to kill Ling because Ling had discovered Morrison was using stolen grapes to make his wine. Grand theft. A violation of federal laws. Mislabeling. Blah, blah, blah. But is it a motive for murder?"

"I don't know," Dante said. "But depending on the extent of it, grape theft could have put Morrison behind bars, in addition to fines."

"I don't recall grape theft as being a big problem before. At least not that we've reported."

"Maybe the wineries don't want to admit it happens," Dante said.

"And the mislabeling of wine?"

"That's happened before. It draws big fines."

"And jail time?" Jones asked.

"Possibly."

"I just love how the rich people get punished," Jones said. "Pay a fine and draw a get-out-of-jail card." Jones adjusted his glasses. "The grape theft angle is a damned good story. Can you get Muñoz to talk?"

Dante swallowed hard and felt his headache returning. "Yes, I suppose."

Jones's expression became stern. "You suppose?" Jones let out an exasperated sigh. "Well, find this Muñoz character. Talk to him. Okay?"

"Of course."

"Do whatever you need to do to find him. Get it on the record. Let me know as soon as you do." Jones wheeled and strode back to his office.

Dante sipped more coffee. It burned in his still-empty stomach. *Now what?* He flicked on his computer and the screen came to life. One way to track down Muñoz would be through the Shady Oaks winery. But he'd have to go through Grundy. Muñoz had fingered Grundy and Morrison for serious crimes in the wine world: stealing grapes and false labeling. Muñoz was probably hiding, if not long gone. *Hell.* Muñoz could be hard to find, or not. If the cops had found and interviewed Muñoz, they'd probably also told him to stick around.

Grundy probably didn't know about the Muñoz interview with the Napa investigators. He wouldn't under normal circumstances. But this wasn't normal. Henshaw had already told Dante others had been looking into the business practices of Grundy and Morrison. That would be the feds, known as the Treasury Department's Alcohol and Tobacco Tax and Trade Bureau, commonly called the TTB in wine country. They wouldn't arrest Grundy based on Muñoz's word alone. The TTB probably had pile of information on Morrison and Grundy. After all, this was California wine country. This was Napa. *Of course, they'd be deep into it.* Dante realized he had a lot to do. First Muñoz, then the TTB.

CHAPTER 14

The noise level grew as the newsroom filled. Dante tried to ignore the personal chit chat around him and turned his thoughts to Grundy. Morrison's winemaker had to be worried. Grundy must know it would only be a matter of time before the feds caught up to him, if they hadn't already. Grundy could run, but running would only confirm his complicity in the grape theft scheme. No. Grundy would stay put. He could blame everything on Morrison. *Of course!* Grundy could claim Morrison led him astray. Morrison had a history of legal trouble. Grundy undoubtedly knew about all of those receipts for grape sales in Morrison's file cabinet. Grundy was clean, so far. Would federal agents buy that? Dante doubted it.

Grundy knew wine law far better than Morrison, so why would he knowingly commit wine crimes? If Grundy was desperate enough, he'd probably gone along with Morrison with very little prompting, like Carmen had said. Birds of a feather. Morrison may have enticed Grundy with the promises of riches and with only the slightest chances of being caught. *What was Grundy thinking?*

But first Dante needed to find Muñoz. Where did Muñoz live? Dante did a couple of online searches. There were a lot of people in the Bay Area with the name Muñoz, more than he'd imagined. He jotted down a couple of likely addresses and phone numbers and continued his search.

His attention was disturbed by the melodic ring of his cell phone. He looked at the caller ID and held the phone to his ear. "Mei Ling? What's going on?"

Her panicked voice came over the phone. "Chao's attorney! Carelli. She's been shot!"

"What? … Carelli's been shot?"

"Yes! Carelli!" Mei said, distraught.

"Where are you?"

"At her office."

"Sit tight. I'm close by! I'll be right there."

His heart pounding, his throat tight, Dante grabbed his sport coat and slipped it on as he bolted from the newsroom. *What the hell? How can this be happening?* He'd been with Carmen just hours earlier. *She can't be dead! It's impossible!*

Dante ran down Mendocino Avenue, his mind churning with possible scenarios. He darted left at Third Avenue and bolted into the street, dodging a couple of cars that braked to avoid hitting him, drawing angry shouts and honking horns. He cut between two parked cars and ran to the glass doors of the glass and stone building at Old Courthouse Square where Carmen kept her office.

Mei Ling pushed open the building's lobby door on her way out, her eyes wide with panic, her mouth open in fear. Dante grabbed her by the arms and barked, "Where are you going? Tell me what happened!"

"I don't know what happened!" she yelled.

"How do you know she's been shot?" Dante asked.

"I came for my appointment with her at ten this morning," she said. "Carelli's secretary was sitting at her desk, sobbing."

"And?"

"She said Carelli wouldn't be coming in, not today, not for a long while." Mei Ling searched his face, as if trying to find the right words. "She said joggers found her this morning. They thought she was dead. They called 911. They took her to the emergency room."

Dante ran through the events of the morning. "Did she say where she was found?"

"She's pretty upset," Mei said.

Dante wondered whether Carmen had something in her files so valuable and so dangerous that someone would try to kill her for it. "You said she's been taken to a hospital?"

"They operated on her," Mei said, fear in her voice.

Shit! Dante figured she'd been taken to the hospital in Sonoma, at least initially. His impulse was to rush there to be with her. But he wasn't family, and they'd probably not let him into post-op recovery. He could find out details from the cops on the scene and see her later. "I want to see where this happened. Let's go."

Dante didn't wait for Mei to object. He took her hand and led her back across the street and along the sidewalk to the newspaper parking lot. He opened his car for her, telling her to sit and wait while he checked on the latest chatter on the police scanner. Mei settled into the passenger seat, her eyes filled with fear and confusion.

His heart pounding, Dante darted into the newsroom where he dialed the police scanner to the Sonoma County Sheriff's Department frequency. *Carmen? Why, God? Why?* He heard references to the Montini Open Space Preserve, north of Sonoma, where units had responded to reports of a wounded jogger. He glanced around the newsroom. Jones was nowhere to be found. He pulled out his notebook and scrawled:

Carmen Carelli
shot near Sonoma.
While jogging.
-Dante

He ripped the sheet from the notebook, slapped it on Jones's desk, whirled, and left the newsroom.

He climbed behind the wheel and fired up the Mustang. Mei Ling looked at him with worried eyes. Myriad possibilities tumbled in his head as they rode. Start with what you know, he told himself. Was she shot because she represented Ling against Morrison? But Morrison was dead. So why was she shot? And by whom? Carmen must know something a client or lawsuit target didn't want revealed. Dante thought about the transcript with Muñoz and the theft of grapes. Carmen knew about the grape scheme. Muñoz had implicated both Morrison and Grundy. That left Grundy. Grundy a killer? Hardly. He glanced at Mei, who looked lost.

"What do you think happened?"

Mei turned her big eyes to him. "I have no idea. Chao should never have gotten involved with Morrison or the winery. I had a bad feeling about it from the first time he talked about it. When I met Morrison, my intuitions were confirmed. And when Chao told me he'd made the investment in cash, I was really angry at him."

"So you think Morrison killed Chao because of the money?"

"Of course!" Mei said, her voice rising. "What else could it be? Chao wanted his money back. That's why he went to Carelli."

"Do you think Carmen may have been shot because of the lawsuit?"

Mei frowned as she tried to form an answer. "Probably."

"But it would mean there are more people involved," Dante said.

"That's what I was thinking," she said.

"It could also mean there's more than money involved. Carmen represented a lot of people in the wine business," Dante said. "There could be many reasons why someone would try to kill her."

"Desperate people take desperate measures," Mei said.

Sadness welled inside him, like a fog rolling into the Bay. *Why Carmen?* He didn't have an answer. The memories hovered: her touch, her scent, her laughter, and her sighs. Shot? It was hard to believe.

He swallowed hard. He was fighting a losing battle to tamp down his roiling emotions. Carmen was the first woman he'd felt anything for ever since Nicole died. He'd written women off, not out of dislike, but because he didn't want to be bothered. He'd buried himself in his work. Until Carmen. Now she too could be gone.

Another thought made him pause: Was the shooting his fault? He swallowed hard again. Loss morphed into guilt. *Me? That's ridiculous! Or is it?* Was someone afraid of what Carmen might tell him and what he might print? Another client? But what could be so damaging they'd want to kill her?

Dante slowed, came to a stop, and parked on the shoulder outside the Montoni preserve behind a several squad cars. "We're here," he said, turning to Mei.

"You sure about this?" Mei asked.

"Don't worry," Dante said.

They climbed out and walked along the asphalt to what had been the narrow dirt road now serving as a trail into the nature preserve. They walked a couple of hundred yards up the slope between scrubby green trees, following the fresh tire tracks and footprints.

They stopped when uniformed deputies turned and, seeing them, waved them off. One of the deputies jogged down the slope toward them. "This is a crime scene!" the deputy said, waving his hands in the air for them to back off. "You have to leave."

Dante pulled his press card from his wallet and waved it high. "I'm with the *Santa Rosa Sun*."

The deputy just shook his head. "You have to leave. Now!"

Mei looked at Dante with worried eyes. "Let's go."

"No. We can stay. It's all right," Dante said, giving Mei's hand a squeeze.

She drew a deep breath and exhaled, trying to calm herself.

Dante held her hand and waited as the deputy approached.

"I said, move!" the deputy said, placing his hand on his holstered gun.

Frightened, Mei stumbled backward. Dante grabbed her arm and held her up. He glared at the deputy. "Don't do anything stupid, okay?"

"Move back down the road."

"All right!" Dante shouted, waving the deputy off as they headed back toward the car.

Ten minutes later Dante and Mei stood at the side of the paved road and watched a couple of crime scene investigators amble down the slope toward them. Among them was Jake Henshaw. Dante waved his notebook at Henshaw, who came over to them as the other investigator returned to his vehicle.

"Out of your jurisdiction, isn't it?" Dante asked.

Henshaw scratched his head distractedly. "Not really. We cooperate with Sonoma County and anyone else who asks for our help."

"Carmen Carelli represented Chao Ling, the man Morrison killed," Dante said.

"That's why I'm here," Henshaw said.

"How was she shot?"

"Don't quote me," Henshaw said under his breath, leaning in close. "Leg shot. And a small head wound. It looked worse than it was."

"She's going to be okay?" Dante asked.

"The medics said the leg shot was just a flesh wound," Henshaw said. "No major damage."

The knot in Dante's stomach tightened despite the relatively good news. Three people shot in wine country in less than two weeks. This one was close, too close for comfort.

"But she's a tough cookie," Henshaw said.

"What do you mean?"

"Carelli got a few shots off."

"You're kidding?" Dante said.

Henshaw frowned. "No, I'm not."

"Carmen had a concealed carry permit," Dante said, remembering what she'd told him, but wondering where she carried it in her jogging clothes.

"She had the weapon with her," Henshaw said. "It looks like her assailant shot a couple of times. Carelli went down, rolled over, pulled her gun, and got off three rounds."

"Three?"

"We have the casings," Henshaw said.

"But she didn't hit anything?"

"We didn't find any blood traces."

"Nothing?"

Henshaw shook his head. "It's tough to hit a target when you've been shot, and are on the ground and on your back."

"Not like Hollywood, you're saying?"

"No, it's not," Henshaw said.

"Anything else?"

Henshaw nodded. "Motorcycle tracks."

Dante drew a deep breath, squinted, and glanced at Mei. She looked worried. He turned back at Henshaw and said, "Thanks."

Mei looked at the passing countryside as they drove back to Santa Rosa.

"Did you ever meet Carmen?" Dante asked, breaking the silence.

Mei squinted at him. "Never. Chao talked about her. Said he liked her."

"I like her, too." Dante cleared his throat. "Who would do this?"

Mei glanced at him, returned her gaze to the road. "I don't know. I really don't."

"My friend Henshaw said they found motorcycle tracks."

"I heard," Mei said softly.

"Would Marvee have anything against Carmen?"

Mei turned and glared. "What? Why would you say that?"

"Marvee rides a motorcycle."

"I can't believe you." Mei said. "She'd never do something so violent."

"How do you know?"

"You don't even know her," Mei cried. "I do!"

"Carmen was worried about something or someone," Dante said. "She carries a gun."

"I can't imagine who," Mei said, her eyes on the highway.

"She did what she could to pressure Morrison into returning the money to Chao," he said.

"But Chao didn't get his money back," Mei said. "That's why I went to see her."

"There was no money to get," Dante said. "It was gone."

"So you're telling me there was no point in my visiting her?" Mei asked. "There was nothing she could do?"

"Actually, there was," Dante said. "She put together a good case against Morrison. It included Grundy. They were in the middle of a lot of grape and wine fraud."

"Was Chao involved?"

"I don't know, but I don't think so," Dante said. "He seemed to be a straight shooter."

"He was," Mei said. "That was his problem. He was too honest."

Dante glanced at Mei. "Maybe you're right."

They rode the rest of the way in silence. Dante stopped beside Mei's car, which was parked at Carmen's office building. She climbed out and glared at Dante through the open door. "You can just forget any thoughts about Marvee being involved," Mei said. "I want to find out why my brother was killed as much as anyone. But you're way off base with Marvee." She slammed the car door.

Five minutes later, Dante stood at Jones's desk, explaining how he'd learned of the shooting and why he was at a crime scene first, again, instead of Hansen. "Mei Ling. The sister of Chao Ling, the man Morrison shot," he said. "She was supposed to meet with Carmen Carelli this morning."

"What about?" Jones asked.

"About getting her brother's money back," Dante said. "That's how she learned Carelli was shot."

"Who found Carelli?" Jones asked.

"A couple of joggers," Dante said. "They called 911."

"Any witnesses?" Jones asked.

"One of the investigators told me Carelli got off three shots of her own."

"Nasty business," Jones said. "Who'd want to kill her?"

"I need to find out."

"Any leads?" Jones asked.

"This guy Muñoz," Dante said. "He could be the key."

"First you need to work with Hansen on the Carelli shooting story," Jones said. "Give her your notes from the crime scene." He turned back to his computer screen.

After sitting with Hansen and going over his notes, Dante called the Sonoma hospital where police said Carmen had been taken. Dante didn't identify himself as news media, but as a friend. She'd been transferred from post-op recovery to a private room, the nurses said. The next day, she'd be up and alert. He could visit her then. He asked about a prognosis for recovery, and they said it was all but assured. Nothing vital had been damaged. The shot had missed the femoral artery, but it had gouged a hole in her thigh. She'd been very lucky, they said.

Dante returned to his condo late. The silence was oppressive. He'd never felt so alone, even though Nicole remained a presence in every room. He wondered why he hadn't moved, chosen a new place to live and start over. He emitted a rueful chuckle. The answer was simple; he'd been too lazy. Now there was Carmen, confined to a hospital bed with bullet wounds. *What the hell? Why is it every woman I get close to gets hurt? I'm bad karma walking.* He opened a bottle of wine, sprawled on the couch, clicked on ESPN, and ruminated about the shooting.

Sure, Carmen could be abrasive, but he dismissed it as a hazard of her profession. She knew what she wanted, and she went after it. Maybe that was her problem. He wondered what Carmen had done or known that someone would leave her shot and bleeding on a rural jogging path. Dante took a deep drink of the wine he'd poured. It was from the Spoleti family's vineyard in Montefalco. Made exclusively from the region's unique Sagrantino grapes growing in the family's vineyards, the wine was big and bold, very dry, and had an earthiness recalling the time he'd spent there. The wine reminded him of Carmen. Assertive. No-nonsense. He smiled as he remembered her once saying she could not imagine herself stomping grapes with her bare feet and having lots of babies. Neither could he.

CHAPTER 15

The next morning, Dante took the Richmond Bridge across the North Bay and drove on the East Shore Freeway past Berkeley and into Oakland.

Gilberto Muñoz lived in the Fruitvale neighborhood. He'd found the man's address on the transcript of the interview Muñoz had given investigators. Dante knew about the neighborhood from his work as an intern for the *Oakland Tribune* while studying at Berkeley. The internship had led to a full-time job at the same newspaper, his first after college. Like all cub reporters, he began by covering the cops and courts, tracking crime and criminals throughout Oakland.

Fruitvale was not a place he'd go unless he had to. Homes in various states of repair were sandwiched between nameless warehouses surrounded by high chain-link fences. Not at all like the bucolic luxury of the Napa Valley wine country where Muñoz worked his crews.

Fruitvale was just off of I-880, a neighborhood between the highway and a tidal canal separating the mainland from Alameda Island, a densely suburbanized piece of land remarkable for nothing Dante could remember. He passed by the address Muñoz had given him, but didn't see the dark gray pickup truck Muñoz said would be parked out front.

Dante checked his watch. He was early. He took Park Street over to the Alameda neighborhood to look around. The streets were populated with auto repair and body shops, the kind of places where the Bay Area's thriving drug trade could conduct business largely unnoticed. Cars, trucks, and vans with drugs packed into specially fabricated compartments carried their contraband from Mexico across the US border and rolled north on I-5 to chop shops. They'd pull in, no one giving a second look, empty their loads, and be gone, cash in hand.

He hit redial on his phone to call Muñoz again. Muñoz answered with, "*Si, digame.*" Yes, speak to me.

"Gilberto? It's Dante."

"I'm on my way. Meet you there."

About ten minutes later, Dante turned the corner, but the Dodge Ram still wasn't there. Dante made a U-turn and parked at the chain-link fence surrounding the lot beside Muñoz's house. The lot was concrete and cluttered with agricultural equipment. A six-foot-high chain-link fence was topped by curled razor wire.

Dante climbed out to wait and surveyed the street.

Muñoz lived in a faded pink house with green trim, fronted by a waist-high, chain-link fence with a gate opening to a short front yard. Wide wooden steps rose to a high porch. Below the porch, on the ground level, was a converted garage.

Dante jerked around to the sound of footsteps. A couple of gangbangers. Bandanas covered their foreheads, sunglasses concealed their eyes. One was short and thin and wore a silver and black Oakland Raiders sports jacket, his hand hidden inside. *Holding a gun!* The other wore an undershirt and jeans, his arms covered with tattoos crawling up his neck. A flat-brimmed baseball cap was perched sideways on top of his bandana-wrapped skull. More footfalls made him whirl back around. A third gangbanger wore a loose hoodie, his face obscured.

Dante froze, his heart pounding. He lifted his hands.

The one wearing the silvery jacket had a wispy mustache and goatee and kept his hand buried inside the jacket.

Dante backed against the fence, his blood running cold. Now he remembered why Muñoz's street address had sounded familiar. The notorious East Seventh Locos controlled this part of Oakland. He was on East Seventh Street.

The one with the tattoos grabbed Dante by his shirt, pulled him from the fence, and shoved him backward into the arms of the man with the hoodie, who twisted Dante's arm behind his back and slammed his face against the fence, mashing his nose and banging his chin. Dante groaned, his face flaring with pain, his shoulder wrenched, but didn't struggle as they kicked his legs wide apart. Dante froze at the feel of the hard, cold steel of a pistol against the back of his head.

"I'm a journalist," Dante wheezed. "I'm here to talk to Gilberto Muñoz."

"Fuck you, asshole," the first one said, jabbing the gun barrel hard.

A horn honked three times. Truck tires squealed to a stop.

Dante twisted around to see Muñoz lean out his truck window and wave. "*Esta bien!*" he shouted angrily. It was an order to stand down, not a suggestion.

The gangbangers released Dante and stood back. Dante touched his chin and nose. They stung. His fingers were bloody.

Muñoz climbed down from his truck. A smudged baseball cap was fitted snugly on his head of thick salt-and-pepper hair. Dark, piercing eyes were set in a leathery face. A round belly presided over a glittering rodeo belt buckle. Muñoz glared at the three gangbangers and spoke to them in rapid, clipped Spanish.

Dante looked at the gangbangers. The gun was gone, tucked again in the gangbanger's waistband and hidden by the jacket.

"It's okay," Muñoz said, narrowing his eyes, looking worried Dante was hurt.

A taller and leaner version of Muñoz stood near the truck, a man with dark eyes set in a deeply lined, coppery face. Hair curled out from under his straw cowboy hat as he palmed his thick, salt-and-pepper fu-manchu mustache.

Jittery from the confrontation, Dante followed Muñoz to where they were joined by the other man. Muñoz opened the gate and directed Dante up the stairs and to the porch. At the top step, Dante turned. The gangbangers were walking back across the street.

"Don't worry about them," Muñoz said. "They won't bother you anymore."

Inside, Muñoz motioned for Dante to sit on a large couch covered with brightly colored woven blankets, but Dante stood, unnerved, dabbing at his bloodied chin. Muñoz pointed down the hall. "*El baño, aya.*" The bathroom is there.

Dante closed the door to the bathroom and mugged in the mirror. *What the hell have I gotten myself into?* Blood smudged his mustache and goatee. He rinsed his nose and chin and pressed tissue against the scrapes to stop the bleeding.

Dante returned to the living room where the aroma of fresh brewed coffee wafted from the kitchen. The second man was seated now, flanked by two children, who Dante guessed were Muñoz's grandchildren. The two children each shuffled their feet and twitching slightly as they leaned against the padded arms of the chair. They looked at Dante like he was a zoo animal. He offered them an uncomfortable smile as he remained standing, dabbing his chin with a tissue.

The man talked quietly to the children, leaving Dante to peruse the walls. A loosely woven tapestry depicted Jesus on the cross, a crown of thorns, forehead dripping blood, face upturned and bathed in moonlight, eyes mournful. Beside the tapestry were framed photos of Pope John Paul II and Pope Francis. Black enamel and straw inlay crosses of various sizes surrounded a large, carved rosewood crucifix with Jesus wearing his crown of thorns. A sparkling red sombrero completed the wall.

Dante respected religious passion, but didn't share it. He glanced through the front windows, framed by heavy curtains, to where the gangbangers lingered across the street, leaning against their lowrider. Maybe religious passion came from praying to be free of people like the ones out there. He turned as Muñoz reappeared.

"Who were they?" Dante asked, pointing out the window to the street.

Muñoz offered him a guilty look. "In this neighborhood, it's important to watch each other's backs." He looked to the other man and said, "This is Luís Rocha. He's a truck driver. He works for me. I wanted him to talk to you."

Dante stepped forward and shook Rocha's hand.

Muñoz again motioned Dante to the couch. "Have a seat."

"So you know them?" Dante asked, ignoring Muñoz's request for him to sit, instead moving close to the front window to check on the gangbangers. They were smoking a joint, passing it among themselves, waiting and looking at nothing in particular. The Seventh Street neighborhood watch.

"We have an agreement. They help me. And I help them."

"You help them?"

"They work for me during the harvest season. Like Luís here."

Looking at his grandchildren with a big smile, Muñoz announced, "*Mis nietos.*" A stout woman emerged from the kitchen. He introduced her as his wife, Maria. A broad smile spread across her round face, her soft eyes sparkling, her graying hair pulled into a braided pony tail trailing down her back. "Would you like coffee?" Maria asked, as if all was fine with the world.

"Yes," Dante said, though the last thing he needed was more coffee.

"Leave poor Luís alone," Maria said to the grandchildren, who didn't move. She looked at Muñoz, then disappeared into the kitchen.

"Shoo!" Muñoz said, waving for them to leave. "Do what your *nana* says." Muñoz clapped his hands. "Go to your room and play." The young boy and girl reluctantly moved.

Muñoz took a seat on the couch and Dante joined him. Maria returned with a mug of coffee for Rocha and another that she put on the coffee table for Dante. "I hope you like Mexican coffee," she said.

"Yes, of course," Dante said.

"Do you need cream and sugar?"

"No, thanks." He lifted the cup and took a drink. "Dark and strong. Just the way I like it."

"I'll let you talk," Maria said, and returned to the kitchen.

Dante found his notebook and pen. "Thanks for meeting with me," he said, trying to collect his thoughts, glancing at both men.

Muñoz took the cap from his head and twirled it in his fingers.

Rocha settled deeper into his chair.

"I'm surprised you would," Dante said to Muñoz, "considering the information you gave the investigators about the shooting."

"I had to tell them what I saw, what I know," Muñoz said.

"Aren't you worried?"

"Why should I be?" Muñoz said with a frown.

"Morrison is dead. And what you told the police about Simon Grundy could put him behind bars. If you get a reputation for making trouble, you and your people could be out of work."

Muñoz frowned. "Grundy is the one who should be worried. Not me. Is that what you wanted to ask me about?"

Dante shook his head. "How long have Grundy and Morrison been stealing grapes?"

"I don't know," Muñoz said with a shrug. "I can't say."

"When did you first notice it?"

"One day I got a text message from Luís," he said, glancing at Rocha. "He was driving one of the trucks. Grundy told him to drop two *contenedores* of grapes at Morrison's winery."

"Two containers?" Dante said. "About three tons. A lot of grapes."

"The grapes were supposed to go to another winery, not Morrison's," Muñoz said.

"How do you know?" Dante asked.

"Grundy and Morrison managed several vineyards," Muñoz said. "At harvest time, he'd tell me how many pickers he needed, where he needed them, and when. Once the grapes were picked, we'd load the container bins of grapes on the trucks with a forklift."

"Then what?" Dante asked.

"One day Luís was given an envelope," Muñoz said. "Inside was a note telling him to drive to Morrison's winery."

"What's wrong with that?" Dante asked.

"The grapes were supposed to go to a different winery," Muñoz said.

"What did you do?"

"I met Luís at Morrison's winery," Muñoz said. "I wanted to see what was happening."

"The container bins are labeled, right?" Dante asked. "Each has a tag with the vineyard where the grapes were picked, the weight, and the date."

"After Luís arrived at Morrison's place with the grapes, I checked the tags on the containers," Muñoz said. "The tags said the grapes were from the Napa Valley, but they weren't."

"Where were they from?" Dante asked.

"Red Hills."

"In Lake County," Dante said, tapping his pen on his notebook. "It's illegal, but who's going to know the difference?"

Dante looked at Rocha, who sat quietly, and asked. "Is that right?"

Rocha had large eyes, one of which was perpetually half closed, giving him a cynical, slightly sinister gaze. He said nothing.

Dante glanced at Muñoz, who now looked apprehensive, and asked, "So what did you do?"

"I called Ricardo Santos," Muñoz said. "Those grapes belonged to him. Grundy managed the vineyards in Lake County that belong to Santos. I wanted to know what was happening."

Dante glanced at his notebook, his mind churning. Grundy must have figured Santos would never know. After all, Santos produced millions of gallons of wine a year. He looked back at Muñoz. "What did Santos say?"

"He thanked me for telling him," Muñoz said.

"Maybe Morrison had a deal with Santos and bought them?" Dante said.

"*Si. Es posible*," Muñoz said. "But why would he sell only a couple containers to Morrison? Why not an entire load?"

"Good point."

"I also saw trucks loaded with grapes my people picked that stopped at Grundy's winery" Muñoz said. "They unloaded grapes there, too. The grapes from another Santos vineyard."

"Grundy and Morrison were both doing it?" Dante asked.

Muñoz nodded.

"Maybe that's how Morrison and Grundy were getting their best grapes?" Dante asked.

"*Es posible*," Muñoz said, nodding.

"And Santos did nothing?" Dante asked.

"He likes to take care of things by himself." Muñoz glanced at Rocha.

Dante puzzled at the comment and looked at Rocha, who sat straight-faced, hoping to discern a reaction. Nothing. If Santos had retaliated, Dante suspected, Muñoz had not been involved. "How long have you known Grundy and Morrison?"

"Since when Grundy started to work for Santos," Muñoz said.

"So later when Grundy and Morrison opened their own winery, they contacted you?" Dante asked.

"Anyone who needs pickers and drivers, I can help them out," Muñoz said.

"How long have you worked for Grundy?" Dante asked.

"A few years."

Dante asked, "Did Morrison owe you money?"

Muñoz glanced out the front window and sighed. "Morrison owed everyone money."

"What about Simon Grundy?" Dante asked. "Does he owe you money as well?"

Muñoz shrugged.

Dante took it as a yes. He saw how tough the business had become for wineries lacking capital. As small-time operators, Morrison and Grundy needed to sell their previous years' vintages to have the cash to pay pickers each fall harvest. Muñoz in turn needed cash to pay his people. People like Muñoz didn't work on credit.

"Aren't more and more wineries going to mechanical harvesting?" Dante asked.

"Yes," Muñoz said, "but many of the people in Napa and Sonoma still prefer to hand pick the grapes."

"It's more expensive, isn't it?"

"Hand picking is better because the grapes are not damaged," Muñoz said. "My pickers are experienced. They don't hurt the grapes."

Dante cleared his throat. Grapes for the lighter wines had to be picked carefully, which could only be done by hand. The harvesting machines used whirling wands to knock the grapes off the stems. They were fast and efficient, but the thin-skinned grapes were easily smashed and oozed juice before they reached the fermenting tanks. Boutique winemakers dreaded the machines. Grundy knew about this, as did Morrison. But did either of them care?

"What about people in the Central Valley?" Dante asked.

"They like machines better," Muñoz said.

"Because harvesting is faster and cheaper."

Muñoz only nodded again, as if it was obvious.

"What about Santos?" Dante asked. "Does he use manual labor?"

"*Si*. We help him take care of his vineyards all year long."

"Do you pick grapes for him?"

"It depends," Muñoz said. "His small vineyards in the north, yes. But Señor Santos has many vineyards. He keeps my people busy most of the year."

Dante exhaled and looked at his notebook. Muñoz knew more than he was willing to talk about. Dante sensed Muñoz was a dam, holding back a wall of information. Dante wanted to open the floodgates. Muñoz worked for many other winery owners. But if he revealed all he knew, neither he nor his people would ever work again. And Santos was among the biggest and not a man to cross. Dante knew he had more digging to do. He dropped his pen on his notebook and sat back in the couch. He thanked Muñoz and Rocha for meeting with him. Muñoz apologized for the gangbangers. It was Dante's turn to shrug. Dante's coffee was now cold, but he finished it off, thanked them both, and left.

Outside, the three gangbangers sat in their low-slung customized 1975 Chevrolet Impala. They watched Dante climb into his Mustang, make a U-turn in the street, and head for the interstate.

CHAPTER 16

Dante gunned his Mustang back north on I-880 past Berkeley. To his left, the tidal flats of the East Bay stretched like stippled glass to the west where the Golden Gate Bridge was etched on the horizon. To the north, white steel petroleum storage tanks sat near the shore, making Dante wonder what kind of environmental disaster awaited the next big quake.

He remembered October 17, 1989, when he'd first felt the ground shake. He was on the staff of the *Daily Californian*, the student newspaper at UC Berkeley. His thoughts had raced: *Maybe it's the big one—the earthquake everyone fears!* At the time, the Bay Area was buzzing with baseball. The Oakland Athletics were playing the San Francisco Giants in the World Series. The Battle of the Bay. At 5:30 p.m., the ground shook. Buildings collapsed, a section of the Bay Bridge fell, and long stretches of I-880 along the East Bay crumpled, like a discarded ribbon of asphalt.

He'd been among the first to the devastation along the busy interstate. Motorists were crushed in their cars when the upper deck of the freeway dropped onto the lower. Survivors staggered from their cars, eyes wide with fear, mouths agape, stunned and confused. His first big news story. He walked up to the lucky ones and asked, "What happened?"

Throughout the evening and into the next day, Dante fed names and quotes to the Associated Press, the *San Francisco Chronicle*, the *Oakland Tribune*—anyone who'd take his material. He'd been in the zone, a news-gathering machine. Later, when people asked if he had been scared, he said, no. *Why would I be? I was doing my job.*

Dante remembered the day clearly, what he saw, and how he felt. *I'm a different man, now. Or am I?* He shook the thought from his mind and focused on Gilberto Muñoz and Luís Rocha. Muñoz was not the only go-to man for grape pickers and truckers at harvest time. There were many others. Still, Muñoz's confirmation of stolen grapes could be the tip of the iceberg.

He glanced to the passenger seat where he'd tossed the canvas briefcase. It held a pile of court documents he'd copied at the Napa courthouse the day of shooting. He'd scanned them quickly, but had not scoured them for details. It was time.

Thirty minutes later he turned off of First Street and onto McKinstry Street in Napa and parked. He locked his car with a beep of his keychain and shaded his eyes from the afternoon sun as he glanced at the white lettering, "Burgers, Shakes, Fries," set against the red-trimmed awning. Gott's Roadside was one of his favorite eateries. Besides serving one of the best burgers in the Bay Area, he could grab glass of wine or two. Life was good, he thought, as his empty stomach growled in anticipation.

Dante ordered a green chili cheeseburger in honor of his friends on the street outside of Muñoz's house, a side of sweet potato fries, and a half-bottle of a Napa Valley cabernet sauvignon. He touched his chin. Still sore, but it had scabbed over. As had his nose. *Assholes.* The incident confirmed his thoughts about the American melting pot. Whites, blacks, and browns marked boundaries around their turf, drew their guns, and fired at will. Now states were approving open-carry laws. *The American dream, gone in a blaze of gunfire.*

He settled into a corner table, nibbled on the fries, and poured himself a glass of wine. He pulled the file folder from his briefcase and set it beside his plate, and bit deeply into the burger as he opened the folder and scanned the first page.

Dante suspected Grundy and Morrison could never afford to buy Napa Valley or even Lake County grapes, which was probably why they stole them. They could make blends using them and grapes from all over California, north, south or central. Few wine drinkers would know the difference as long as the taste approximated what they expected from a Napa Valley cabernet. The physical appearance of the grapes was equally useless. A cluster of cabernet or merlot grapes from one vineyard looked just like those from another.

Laboratory tests existed that could identify the origin of a grape, but were expensive, complicated, and imprecise. Except for the winemaker, few would ever know a bottle labeled as Napa Valley wine was made with only fifteen, twenty-five, thirty-five, or forty-five percent of grapes grown in the Napa Valley rather than the required eighty-five percent.

Grapes grown in the Central Valley were vastly cheaper than the ones grown in Napa and Sonoma valleys, or even Lake County. Morrison and Grundy pilfered the grapes, he believed, because they could. Play with the big boys. Make and sell top-of-the-line California wine, even if only a small percentage of the wine was what they claimed.

Dante knew it would be easy to mix, match, and move grapes around in the chaos of harvest. Grapes had to be picked during a tight timeframe. A lot had to be done quickly. It was the time of year when people like Muñoz and his pickers became the most important people in Northern California wine country. No pickers, no grapes—no grapes, no wine. For a couple of months each year, Muñoz could name his price, and did. He and his crews were golden.

But with mechanical pickers, the story was different. Grapes could be harvested at night, all night. Under the cover of darkness, grapes were dumped into bins, and the bins were tagged and loaded onto trucks. The trucks moved around the valley at all hours. Dante smiled to himself. The perfect opportunity for a sleight of hand.

But how much did Ling know? Morrison would not have admitted he and Grundy were using stolen grapes. Had Ling been at the winery during a harvest? Possibly. But if Ling was like most investors, he preferred to enjoy the fruits of the labor, not the labor itself. The grapes were undoubtedly dropped at the winery in the middle of the night when only Morrison was there, making it easy to change or alter a bin tag. If Ling knew, would he have threatened Morrison over it?

After reading a couple of pages, Dante pulled out his highlighters and his red pen. The pieces of the puzzle seemed to be jumping off the pages as he read. Everything he needed was in front of him, on the page, in black and white! *Damn! Why didn't I read this earlier?* Names, dates, and places. Dante dove in, marking phrases, highlighting sections, and jotting asterisks, stars, and question marks in the margins.

Finished, he lifted his head and drew a deep breath. His head ached, his neck muscles were sore, and his neck bones creaked. The wine bottle was empty. He scanned the restaurant. Just a few customers lingered. He glanced at his watch. It was 3 p.m. He'd been at it for nearly two hours. He considered another half-bottle of wine, but rejected the idea. It would be a long night of sorting through his notes, but his stomach was full. He'd be all right.

He fired up the Mustang and headed out of Napa, where he picked up the 101 Freeway in Petaluma and headed north toward Santa Rosa. Playing a shell game with grapes was just one of the sleights of hand he found. The case Carmen had filed against Morrison, Grundy, and their MG Enology vineyard management company read like a criminal's guide to Napa Valley winemaking. The source of many key details was a team of investigators at the Department of Treasury's TTB, the people who enforce the Byzantine rules governing each federally designated American Viticultural Area.

In September of the year before, the bureau claimed MG Enology sold grapes it claimed were Napa Valley cabernet sauvignon—about 15,000 pounds worth—to several wineries, including Santos Wine Company. The wine actually came from a sprawling vineyard in the East Bay at the northern edge of the Central Valley. MG Enology had sold the bulk of the grapes, about 5,000 pounds each, to two other wineries, Triumphant Wines and Attica Hill Cellars, among the most prestigious in the Napa Valley.

The TTB agents had contacted Santos and informed him he'd sold several thousand bottles of wine illegally because it was mislabeled. The label read Napa Valley cabernet sauvignon, the TTB said, while it was actually a blend of mostly merlot grapes. Because Santos didn't spend a lot of time aging his wines, most of it was already packaged and sold or still sitting on the shelves of liquor stores. Santos had to recall all of the wine and pay a $3 million fine. Dante had written about it, just one of the legal proceedings for which Carmen had represented Santos.

Why had Santos not sued Morrison, Grundy, and MG Enology to get his money back? Oh, of course, Dante thought, Santos wouldn't sue if he was somehow involved in the scheme. A suit against MG Enology would bring more attention to the activities of Morrison and Grundy, possibly leading to more investigations uncovering more problems.

What had been done with the recalled wine? About 300 cases of Santos's wine, Dante had read, had been sold to the BevMo chain of liquor stores. If all of that wine was returned, what was to prevent Santos from relabeling the wine, or putting it in boxes and reselling it? He easily could have recovered some of his losses, perhaps even made a profit.

This was all his own speculation. Dante had no proof Santos was involved.

As he read the details of MG Enology's many sleights of hand, he struggled to figure out who had ratted out the company. He thought about his interview with Muñoz earlier in the day, and the answer came to him.

Morrison and Grundy had been playing a shell game with all of their clients at each stage in the winemaking process. Grundy and Morrison each had their own wineries, which gave them legitimacy. Grundy especially had an unblemished reputation as a vineyard manager and winemaker. This allowed MG Enology to conduct business largely under gentlemen's agreements. Dante envisioned the smiles, the verbal contracts with wine growers to buy the grapes. On the surface, it would all look clean and easy. Handshakes sealed the deals. But on the critical day when the grapes were picked, things would change.

Dante marveled at the simplicity. He remembered what Muñoz and Rocha had said. With the harvest underway, the grape grower was handed a sealed envelope to be given to the truck driver once the grapes were loaded. The instructions told the driver where to take the grapes.

If the growers dared to open the envelopes, Grundy and Morrison warned them they would not be paid and their grapes would not be accepted at the destination. They claimed the envelope contained only proprietary business information. Anxious to get their money, the growers wouldn't complain. Grundy and Morrison also insisted, when and where possible, only they, not the growers or the truckers, filled out the identification tags for the bins.

MG Enology easily falsified the origin of the grapes, the variety, and the weight, Dante realized. With a bin labeled with less weight than it actually contained, they unloaded a portion of the grapes at their own wineries. Once the remaining grapes arrived at the final destination, the under-recorded bin weight would be correct.

The harvested grapes were de-stemmed and dumped into the large fermentation tanks to be macerated and left to ferment. The floating pulp and skins would be stirred and pushed to the bottom and left to rise again. Four weeks later, the wine would be drained and transferred into oak casks for aging. What had preceded the aging wine no longer mattered, and, for the most part, no one cared.

Dante appreciated the ingenuity. It was the perfect shell game. But it had collapsed.

Morrison and Grundy had gotten sloppy. Too many people were left dangling, unpaid for too long. Money promptly paid kept the growers and truckers quiet, along with the threat of being implicated themselves. But when the money didn't arrive, the growers and truckers grew anxious and angry. They went to the feds.

This was why Morrison needed Ling, Dante realized. Morrison had needed Ling's $1 million in cash. It would also explain why there were piles of cash receipts. Grundy and Morrison were buying the grapes with cash and giving hand-written receipts stating whatever they wanted. As long as money was coming into one end of the pipeline, it could flow out the other. But when the money dried up, the feds arrived.

How to put it all in a story for the newspaper? Dante's stomach gurgled.

Convincing people to spend big bucks on wine meant they had to believe what they were buying was rare and special. When it came to wine, there was no way to know if it was truly what the makers claimed it to be. It was based on trust that everyone along the way was saying and doing the right thing. But if they weren't? Dante chuckled to himself. He wondered why Grundy hadn't already been killed.

Grundy had been ill-at-ease on both of the occasions when they'd met. He answered Dante's questions with only the briefest of answers. Claimed he didn't know much about Morrison's background. He complained about how bad Morrison was as a business partner. Now Dante realized he, too, had been misled by Grundy.

Dante sauntered into the newsroom, unsure of what to tell Jones about his visit with Muñoz and Rocha, how to explain the scabs on his nose and chin, and still worse, what he was going to write.

"How did it go?" Jones shouted across the newsroom, waving and pointing to the clock: 3:55 p.m. Dante slipped out of his jacket and draped it over his shoulder as he stepped into Jones's office.

Jones's jaw dropped when he saw Dante. "What the hell…?"

"I had an unexpected encounter with the Seventh Street Locos."

"Who?"

"It's a gang. In Oakland."

"My God, Dante."

"Don't worry. Just a couple of scratches."

"What were you doing in Oakland?"

"I found Muñoz."

"Good! I have a news meeting in five damned minutes! What do you have?" Jones said.

"It's complicated."

Jones flushed, his lips thinned, and a strange smile spread across his face. "Life is complicated," he said in a low growl. "But your job is to make it simple for our readers. It begins with me. *Capeesh*?"

Deadline time. Once Jones assembled all of the day's stories and figured out where they would go in the next morning's newspaper, he again would be reasonable. "Okay. In a nutshell, Morrison and his partner, the guy I told you about named Simon Grundy, have been scamming the wine biz for the past several years by mislabeling wine, selling cheap wine at high prices, stealing grapes, falsifying reports, evading taxes. You name it, they did it."

Jones's eyes opened wide. "We already talked about this."

"Muñoz confirmed just about everything in the Ling case files. I spent the afternoon combing through it all, just to make sure. There's way too much material here for a daily story. I need time to sort through it all."

Jones looked exasperated, sighed deeply, and glanced again at the clock. "Okay. I don't have any time talk right now. We'll have to make do with what news we have for today. Start outlining what you have. It better be good. We have a meeting with Ellsworth tomorrow."

Dante swallowed. His stomach knotted. Dante was nervous around Ellsworth, the editor and publisher, not because the man possessed any overwhelming talent, but because he carried a sense of privilege that came with his blue-blood background. Ellsworth counted the Kennedy clan among his family's circle of friends. He stood a full six-foot-three, was clean-shaven, and had steely blue eyes, a ruddy complexion, and a head of thick, graying hair. Dante hated feeling intimidated and avoided the man as much as possible.

"I'm going to talk to some of the people Grundy and Morrison ripped off," Dante said.

"That ought to be fun," Jones said.

"Some had to eat tens of thousands of dollars," Dante said. "It's not the kind of thing most people want to admit, let alone talk about."

"Or see in print," Jones said.

Dante smiled weakly and headed for his desk.

CHAPTER 17

Dante sat heavily into his desk chair and looked at the clock. 4:10 p.m. The end of his day was still hours away. He flicked on his computer and watched it come to life. He pulled the files from his briefcase and put them beside his computer. Carmen had collected this material about the workings of Morrison, Grundy, and their MG Enology company and made it part of her lawsuit. He thought about Carmen lying in the hospital bed. Who had tried to kill her and why? Dante leaned back, laced his fingers behind his head, closed his eyes, and mentally combed through the details of what he'd read. *What am I missing? Why would someone want to kill Carmen?* Nothing came to mind. He sat up, opened his eyes and focused. *Keep pushing, keep stirring the pot.*

One of the victims of MG Enology's grape scam was the Triumphant winery, a thriving enterprise near the town of Napa. Dante opened up the winery's website, which proclaimed it was more than a winery, it was also a spa, a place to rejuvenate body and spirit. High-resolution photos depicted rolling hills covered with vineyards stretching into the distance, close-ups of grapes on the vine, the orange light of a sunset glinting off wine bottles and glasses. Images of Greco-Roman columns beside a vineyard implied a Bacchanalian experience.

He clicked on the purchasing choices. The base price for a bottle was $25. It was a blend of red varietals, but you'd never know it from the description. Rather, it was a "perfect complement" for a visit to the winery and spa, sounding more like an elixir of the gods than an alcoholic beverage.

Triumphant was run by a family with roots in Midwest, and the winery had been in the business for more than twenty-five years. Yet they'd been swindled by Morrison and Grundy. Dante found a name, a number, and dialed.

A pleasant-sounding young woman answered. She had an enthusiastic voice suggesting Dante had reached a resident of the Promised Land whose joy could barely be contained. She sounded as if his call had put him on the precipice of a life-changing event, which would of course be a visit to the spa or lightening his wallet with a purchase of their wine.

When Dante finished explaining what he wanted, she sounded deflated and said he needed to speak to Max. Was there anything else she could do for him? Dante thought of a few lewd responses, but said, "No thanks." Then he was listening to Mozart.

From the website, he learned "Max" was Maximilian, the son of the owner, Milton Hartmann and his wife, Cheryl, who were from Oklahoma and Michigan respectively. They'd each migrated separately to Southern California in the early 1980s. Milton played bass guitar, and had hooked up with an LA-based heavy metal band called Scourge. They'd produced a couple of screaming, head-banging, guitar-smashing albums and had gone on a global tour. The band eventually disintegrated and faded into oblivion.

Dante remembered the music was something only disaffected teenagers could like. Milton's stage name had been Dirt Dawg. There'd been tabloid stories about the band's drug abuse and recurring rehab episodes. He chuckled at Milton's website bio, which described his musical career as one of the "bright lights in the LA constellation of rock stars."

Cheryl had come from an upscale neighborhood of Detroit. The website noted she was the daughter of a former executive with General Motors and had pursued an acting career in LA. A quick view of her filmography revealed parts in a few low-budget films featuring chainsaws and a couple of minor roles in daytime soaps. Dante mused there might have been an unlisted blue movie or two.

The "About Us" pull-down menu contained references to Christian values being the guiding principles of the winery and spa. After a debauched and drug-addled existence, apparently Milton had found God and Cheryl and turned his life around, perhaps not in that order. Dante suspected her daddy's General Motors money had probably helped open the winery.

Grundy and Morrison must have connected with their fellow Midwesterners to convince the Hartmann family they should buy their grapes. The business dealings were not a surprise. The Hartmanns had what both Grundy and Morrison craved: a thriving wine business in the heart of wine country.

The Mozart music ended when a man's voice said, "This is Max."

Dante explained he was writing about the deaths of Morrison and Ling.

"Well, I'm glad you're doing that," Hartmann said. "You know, when I read a couple of weeks ago Morrison had been killed by police, it just didn't surprise me."

"It didn't?"

"In fact, I was relieved."

"Relieved? Why?"

Hartmann hesitated. "Don't quote me, okay?"

Dante hesitated. "Well, all right. But that's a, well, curious thing to say."

"Let's just leave it."

Dante's stomach soured. *C'mon. I need something I can use.*

"Why were you relieved?"

"I'd rather not go into it," Hartmann said.

"You'd rather not go into it?" Dante said.

"I really can't explain. I shouldn't have said it."

"You had some business dealings with the late Bernie Morrison and his partner, Simon Grundy, doing business as MG Enology," Dante said.

"I really can't talk about it, to you or anyone."

Dante let the comment hang in the air, wondering what to say next.

"Is there anything else I can do for you?" Hartmann asked.

Max was nervous, but polite. Sometimes people would simply shout, "Go to hell!" and hang up. Dante sensed he could push Max a little more. If he was smart, he would know it was better for him to talk than not. If Triumphant had a "no comment" when asked about having bottled and sold a low-grade merlot or a zinfandel wine as a Napa cabernet, it would leave a cloud of doubt hanging over the winery.

"According to the material I have," Dante said in a slow, methodical voice, "in the fall of 2014, Triumphant purchased a rather large allotment of grapes from MG Enology. The wine was sold as Napa Valley cabernet. In fact, however, the grapes were not from the Napa Valley, but from elsewhere, and the grape varietal is still uncertain, but probably was a zinfandel."

"Where did you get that information?"

Dante smiled to himself. Max wasn't going to hang up. "I'm reading from documents in a lawsuit against MG Enology on file at the Napa County Courthouse. The particular purchase I mentioned is noted in a separate complaint filed by the federal Alcohol, Tobacco Tax and Trade Bureau."

Max was silent.

"The misidentified wine must have caused you problems," Dante said, doing his best to sound sympathetic.

Max sighed audibly.

"It amounts to about several thousand bottles of wine, or about three hundred cases," Dante said. "Did you have to recall the wine?"

Max groaned and said, "You know, that was a very difficult time for us here. Thankfully, we got through it. We're okay now. Knock on wood. Is there anything else?"

"What did you do with the wine?" Dante asked. "Did you re-label and resell it?"

"Like I said, it was a very difficult time," Max said. "It's in the past and where I'd like to leave it."

"What did all of the misidentified wine cost you, in terms of time and money?"

"I really couldn't tell you," Max said.

Dante waited.

Max was silent.

"Triumphant has an excellent reputation," Dante said. "You must have been worried."

"We stand behind the quality of all of our wine," Max said. "Now, look, I really have to go. If you want anything further, you'll have to call our attorney."

Dante scribbled down the quote. "Who is that?"

Max gave him a name. "Lots of luck with your story. I look forward to reading it." The line went dead.

Max Hartmann was not helpful, but admitted his company was defrauded by Morrison and Grundy, without divulging the details, which Dante already possessed. Max said the company stood behind the quality of its wines. He could use the quote. Dante leaned back and got ready to make another call, this time to the Attica Hill Cellars.

Dante found the Attica Hill website and clicked on a short video. The winery didn't have acres and acres of vines and instead purchased grapes from growers from all over Northern California. Dante liked that. Focus on the wines, not the grape-growing. This undoubtedly was how Attica Hill had hooked up with Grundy and Morrison. The winery's least expensive wine was a chardonnay listed at $28. The list topped out with a cabernet at $125 a bottle.

Dante called the main number and was told he had to talk with the owner, Sam Attica. He was put on hold and left to listen to a throaty, alluring female voice tell him about the winery's current offerings, as if it were a proposition for unending pleasures. As he listened, he perused the winery's website.

The wine descriptions were overtly sexy, being "voluptuous" with a "sweet core" and having "penetrating aromas," all in a "well-integrated package" that was "long and smooth."

"Hal-oohh," a mature male voice said, interrupting the recording, his tone suggesting a friendly but hassled speaker.

"Is this Sam Attica?" Dante asked.

"Yes, it is. What can I do for you?"

Dante explained himself and the reason for his call.

"I can't say I feel sorry for the man," Attica said about Morrison's demise.

"Why not?"

"Well, if you've done your homework, you know why," Attica said.

"The grapes you bought from him were a problem."

"That's right," Attica said.

"What happened when you discovered the grapes you bought from Morrison were not what you thought?"

"Can we talk off the record?" Attica asked.

"How about we talk on the record, but I won't identify you," Dante said. "I'll just refer to you as a California winemaker who had business dealings with Morrison, Grundy, and MG Enology."

Attica sighed noisily. "Okay. But if I see my name in print, I'll come after you, the paper, and anyone else I can get my hands on."

"Your name will not appear in print," Dante said. "Okay?"

"Just so we're clear."

"We're clear." Dante took a breath. "So, when did you first find out the grapes were not what you thought?"

"I didn't know anything was wrong until this guy named E.J. showed up."

"Who's E.J.?" Dante said.

"E.J. Edwards. He's an agent with TTB. You know what that is?"

"Of course," Dante said. "Do you have his number?"

"Sure. Hold on. I got his card here."

Dante jotted the number as Attica read it aloud, then asked, "So what did E.J. tell you?"

"He laid it all out for me," Attica said. "Told me my cabernet grapes from Napa were probably zinfandel from the Central Valley."

"So, how did you feel when you learned that?"

"I wanted to kill the son of a bitch," Attica said.

"Did you ever see the grapes?" Dante asked.

"I did, but most people can't tell the difference between a zinfandel grape cluster or a merlot or malbec or a cabernet. I know I can't."

"Me neither," Dante said, again trying to be sympathetic. "Most look the same, but some are clearly different, like a chardonnay and a pinot noir."

"I know," Attica said. "Grapes are smaller, lighter or darker color, that kind of thing."

"So you didn't notice anything strange?"

"No, but my winemaker did."

"How so?" Dante asked.

"You know," Attica said, "once the wine is fermented, it's ready to be tasted."

"Before you age it in oak barrels."

"So, my winemaker sampled it and gave me a taste," Attica said. "It was a little off. But, hey, every grape is different. Every vineyard is different. Every year is different."

"The *terroir*," Dante said, using the French winemaking term.

"The soil, the climate, all of what can affect the taste and quality of wine. It's what we all want to recognize and appreciate."

"Rather than standardization," Dante said.

"Standardization is fine," Attica said, "but that's not what we sell here at Attica Hill Cellars."

"So what happened when you found out you had bad grapes?" Dante asked.

"The grapes weren't *bad*. They just weren't cabernet. But I was pissed."

"The wine wasn't bad?"

"No. It wasn't bad at all. It was just…"

"Not what you thought it was," Dante said.

"And I had this federal agent sitting in front of me…"

"E.J."

"He's telling me I'm breaking all kinds of laws by selling a bottle of this Attica Hill cabernet as a Napa Valley wine when it's probably a Central Valley zin," Attica said.

"Which you were," Dante said.

"It wasn't my fault!" Attica said, sounding aggravated. "I'd been, or we, all of us at this winery, had been swindled. E.J. tried to make me feel better by telling me I wasn't the only one."

"Did it help?"

"Hell, no."

"Okay," Dante said. "You buy ten tons of grapes. You crush it, ferment it, age it, and bottle it. You sell it. Then what?"

"We didn't sell it," Attica said.

"You didn't?"

"It was still in oak barrels, aging."

"Lucky you," Dante said.

"Lucky? I wouldn't say that. But yeah, we age all of our wines at least a couple of years. We barrel sample our wines, and when my winemaker and other members of the staff think the wine's ready to go, we bottle it."

"So the misidentified wine was still in-house?" Dante asked.

"Each barrel is well marked, so we knew exactly what we had, how much, and where it was," Attica said.

"What did you do?"

"We had enough for about 5,000 bottles," Attica said. "Four hundred cases, give or take. We sampled it and decided it was about as good as it was going to get. As best as we could tell, it was a zinfandel. As you know, it blends well. So, we came up with a blend from other grape varietals and called it Attica Hill Red."

"How did it sell?"

"Very well," Attica said. "We made it very affordable, and it flew out the door."

"Was it profitable?" Dante asked. "I ask because you must have paid premium prices for what you thought was Napa Valley cabernet."

"Profitable?" Attica said. "We were hoping to sell it for about a hundred dollars or more per bottle. But that was clearly impossible."

"But you sidestepped legal troubles," Dante said.

"Legal beagles would have been the only ones to make money out of the mess," Attica said. "If the wine would have hit the market as a cabernet, and we'd been forced to pull it back, the damage to our reputation would have been irreversible. It would have cost us more than the legal fees."

"I can imagine."

"A good reputation is not something you can put a price on," Attica said.

"If the feds had all of this information on Morrison and Grundy," Dante asked, "why didn't they just arrest them?"

"I wondered that myself," Attica said. "I wanted to know why they would go after me when I was a victim, not a criminal."

Dante hesitated to answer. "I don't know. What do you think?"

"I think the powers that be in this state don't want the feds running around arresting people in wine country," Attica said.

"They don't?"

"Think about it," Attica said. "What are the two things people around the world think about when you mention California?"

"Ahhh, I'd say Hollywood," Dante said. "And number two is probably the Golden Gate Bridge."

"Yeah, but Northern California wine country and the Napa and Sonoma valleys gotta be up there too," Attica said. "What's going to happen to the wine business if the feds are running around arresting winemakers and forcing them to pull their products off the shelves?"

"Good point," Dante said. "So, you're saying the feds are under pressure to keep things quiet. Enforce the law, but do it judiciously."

"It's the damned reality, man!" Attica said, exasperated.

Dante typed Attica's comments on his computer as he formed another question. "But how do you explain the fact Ricardo Santos was forced to pay a $3 million fine? The fine was neither small nor was it a secret."

"Santos was supposed to be an example to others," Attica said. "He was being slapped around by the locals."

"Because he's not exactly the Napa Valley type?" Dante asked. "He runs around telling everyone Napa and Sonoma wine is overpriced."

"He sells a cheap product," Attica said. "He sells a blended, standardized wine. These days there are many high-tech processes to convert fermented grape juice you wouldn't drink yourself into a saleable product. Santos uses all of them."

"People like knowing what they're getting when they buy a bottle of wine," Dante said.

"Of course they do," Attica said. "It's like buying a Ford or Chevy. It's dependable, has a reasonable price, and gets you where you want to go. But that's not what the vintners of Northern California are trying to sell."

"They are selling Mercedes Benz," Dante said.

"Trying to, anyway."

Dante took a deep breath. "Thanks."

"No problem. Just don't use my name."

Dante thanked Attica and hung up, massaging his burning eyes. He read over his notes, saved them to his computer, and glanced at the wall clock. It was nearly six o'clock. He looked at his notes and decided he'd leave writing the story for the next day. He needed to be fresh.

He had one pressing desire, and it was to see Carmen.

CHAPTER 18

An hour later, Dante stopped at the main reception desk at the Sonoma hospital, gave his name, and, saying he was a friend, asked to see Carmen Carelli. The woman behind the desk looked at the clock, told him visiting hours would end at 8 p.m., and gave him the room number. He strode down the corridor to the slightly open door, and not hearing a conversation, eased the door open and stepped into Carmen's room.

She was asleep. The mechanical bed was raised so she was partially sitting up. Her head was to the side, her mouth slightly open, her breath rhythmic. Dante's heart sank. He wanted to take her in his arms, as if he could make her well and whole. Guilt gurgled up inside him, like a swirling mist, clouding his mind. Had he somehow been the cause of the attack?

He remembered her words from their dinner on the night they'd first slept together. She was taking a risk just meeting with him. Dante had scoffed at the suggestion. He had never considered himself a risk to anyone, except to those he was investigating. A risk to Carmen? He began to wonder. What did she know?

There was a bigger question he needed to answer for himself. *What are you doing? You lost Nicole, in part because of your job. Now you could lose Carmen, and all because a story—a story you're following because you don't know when to stop. So what are you doing?*

Carmen opened her eyes and slowly focused. As she recognized him, her eyes brightened.

"Took you long enough," she said.

Dante smiled weakly. "Yeah, well, your family has been here ever since the shooting. I figured they were enough."

Carmen smiled. "It was. But it's still good to see you. Thanks for coming."

"How are you feeling?"

Her eyes drifted and floated back to him. "They've got me pretty doped up. I can't feel a thing."

"It's probably for the best," Dante said. "They want to make sure you stabilize."

"I'm more than stabilized. I'm nearly flat-lined."

Dante smiled. "Not quite. So, what happened?"

She touched the white gauze bandage encircling her head. Then he noticed her thick, long hair was gone. Her head was shaved.

"Your hair. What happened?"

"My God, you're so observant," she said.

Dante felt his face flush. "I…ah…well, seeing you with your head wrapped …."

"Shocking, isn't it?" Carmen looked worried.

"Not really. I kinda like it," Dante said. "You could add an eye patch, put on a three-corner hat, and try out for the next 'Pirates of the Caribbean' movie."

Carmen frowned. "Not funny."

"Don't worry. Hair grows back. Even when you're dead."

"That's encouraging!" Carmen said. "You don't think it looks awful?"

"No," Dante said.

"They said they needed to cut it all off," Carmen said. "Infection is not something you want to play around with."

"Especially a head wound. You wouldn't want brain rot to set in."

"You're so encouraging," Carmen said, knitting her eyebrows.

"So tell me what happened."

"You don't know?"

"The police can't tell it like you can," Dante said. "All I know is you went jogging and were shot. Twice."

Carmen winced at the memory. "All I remember clearly is the jogging. You know how it is. You get into the zone. It's meditation for me. There was a shot. The first grazed my head." She lightly touched the bandage. "It burned, as if someone held a red hot poker to my head." Carmen's eyes were angry, fearful. "I stumbled and stopped. It hurt like hell. I put my hand to it. I could feel the gash. It stung. Badly. My hand was covered with blood."

"They were aiming at your head?"

Carmen's eyes lost focus. "They missed, fortunately," she said, lost in her memory. "I was hit by the second shot. My thigh. Went right through."

Dante squirmed at the descriptions. "It must have hurt."

"It knocked me down. My whole right leg was on fire. It went numb."

"But you still were able to shoot back."

"Yeah. Because I'm right-handed," Carmen said.

"But you were on the ground."

"Well, the shot spun me around and I fell on my shoulder. It felt like…I've never experienced pain like that." Her eyes went unfocused again.

Dante waited for her to continue.

"I lay there on the ground looking up at the sky, stunned, unable to think," she said. "I remembered I had a gun with me."

"A shoulder holster?"

"It's like a snug T-shirt," Carmen said. "A fabric holster attaches right here with Velcro." She pointed to the lower rib cage on her left side.

"So, you pulled the gun and fired."

"Of course. Through the pain, I remembered seeing something or someone in the trees closer to the road, where the shots came from."

"So you fired."

"Well, yeah!" Carmen said. "I wasn't going to just lay there! Both my hands and arms worked fine. I didn't want whoever it was running up to me and finishing me off with another shot to the head."

"You scared them off," Dante said.

"I guess. The firing stopped."

"Then what?"

"I heard a motorcycle start up."

Dante waited, then said, "You're lucky the shooter was a bad shot."

"Maybe the shooter was a good shot. I was running, after all. They still hit me. Twice."

"Yeah, that's not an easy shot," Dante said. "What was the caliber of the bullet?"

"A .22," Carmen said. "You can buy adapters with sights and silencers. A pistol becomes a rifle."

"Who do you think did it?" Dante asked.

"I don't know," she said. "They were in the shadows."

"They? There was more than one?"

"No. I don't know. I don't think so. The shooter's head was covered. Probably a balaclava."

"I was told there were motorcycle tracks," Dante said. "The person could have been dressed in leathers."

"Makes sense."

"I still can't believe you carry a weapon."

"It saved my life, Dante."

"You missed your target, unfortunately."

"But I scared them off," she said. "Whoever was shooting didn't expect me to return fire."

"I'm impressed. Where did you learn to handle a gun?"

"I told you I never wanted to grow up squishing grapes with my bare feet and having babies?"

"Yes, you did."

"I studied criminal justice at Sonoma State."

"Okay," Dante said. "Then law school?"

"Yes, but along the way—"

"You learned how to shoot a gun," Dante said.

"I dated a few cops," Carmen said.

"That explains some things," Dante said. "So when can you get out?"

"Soon," she said. "They sewed up my scalp. Said the wound should heal nicely. But I may need some cosmetic surgery to remove the scar. It'll eventually be covered with hair. The shot to my leg is just a matter of healing now."

"It's going to curtail your jogging."

"For a while." She looked at him and smiled.

"I'd better let you rest."

"Don't leave," she said.

"Are you sure?"

"Not before you give me a kiss."

Dante rose and bent over her, kissing her gently on the lips. She slipped her right hand around the back of his neck, and pulled him close again, kissing him deeply. When her hand fell away, Dante stood and smiled. "Something to remember."

Carmen's eyes were half closed. "Hmmm. That was nice."

"In a few days, you'll be out," Dante said. "Who's going to take care of you?"

"Don't worry about it. I have family just up the hill. Remember?"

"I'll be by anyway," Dante said. "Very soon."

She narrowed her eyes and focused. "You're a nice guy. Did I ever tell you?"

Dante kissed her again and said, "I'll see you later. Okay?"

Carmen waved weakly. "Bye."

CHAPTER 19

The next morning, Oliver Ellsworth, the *Sun* editor and publisher, bent forward over his broad desk and perused Dante's story outline. Jones and Dante sat facing the desk, having settled into a couple of leather wingback chairs that gave the office an Old World feel. Ellsworth cleared his throat a couple of times and twitched. Anxiety clouded the air, Dante attributing Ellsworth's unease to the fact there was too much nastiness in wine country and it was on the front page almost every day. It left the impression that Northern California was a free-fire zone. Ellsworth was getting nervous.

Ellsworth was the namesake of his distant ancestor, one of America's founding fathers. He'd arrived from New York to manage the *Sun* when it was owned by a national chain operated by a prestigious New York newspaper. As Internet news providers siphoned advertising dollars from the world of print journalism, the smaller newspapers in the chain, including the *Sun*, had been scraped from the hull of the mother ship like useless barnacles. The move consolidated the corporate balance sheets. Ellsworth had stayed on, realizing he could do a lot worse than making Northern California his home.

Jones broke the malingering silence, speaking with a low monotone, detailing Dante's progress. Dante listened with feigned interest as he glanced at the office walls covered with framed photos of Ellsworth's exploits: a safari in Africa, a trek up Mount Kilimanjaro, white-water rafting in the Grand Canyon, scaling Mount Denali in Alaska, and skiing in the French Alps. Ellsworth let it be known he was preparing for an attempt on Mount Everest.

Ellsworth listened as Jones hit the highlights: the Carelli shooting pointed to a hit man. That meant a criminal conspiracy and/or organized crime. "The bottom line is there's a lot more here than meets the eye," Jones said.

Ellsworth settled back into his padded high-backed chair, rolled a fat Mont Blanc pen in his fingers, and narrowed his eyes. "The more we play these events on the front page, the more nervous the wine community gets. I'm surprised the Napa Valley Grape Growers haven't called me to complain."

"The story is hot," Jones said. "They're just going to have to deal with it."

Ellsworth placed the pen to the side of his desk pad and massaged his eyes, as if trying to stay awake. "You know they about had a heart attack over the way we covered those black ladies being tossed off the wine train. The train operators got their lily-white asses sued, which they deserved. But that's peanuts compared to this. What do you think is going on, Dante? You're in the middle of it."

"I think the wine growers ought to be scared."

"Scared?" Ellsworth said. "Why?"

"The federal government has been tracking and documenting illegal activity in the wine business over the past few years. I have a feeling this is only the tip of the iceberg."

"And you think it's all related to these shootings?"

Dante swallowed. He wasn't sure, but felt compelled to answer. "Yes, I do. The illegal activity provides a motive for murder."

"Like what kind of illegal activity?"

Pointing to the outline on Ellsworth's desk, Dante said, "Grape theft. Buying and selling grapes that aren't what people say they are. Mislabeling of wine. Squandered investments. All kinds of things."

"You have it all documented?" Ellsworth asked.

"Of course," Dante said, as if it were without question.

"How widespread is it?" he asked.

Dante did his best to sound confident, knowing if he faltered, Ellsworth could pull the plug and kill the investigation. "It centered around two men, Bernie Morrison, the man who was killed by the police after he shot and killed his investor, a guy named Chao Ling."

"We know." Ellsworth frowned, looking studious and intent. "Go on."

"Morrison's partner is a man named Simon Grundy, who owns and operates the Shady Oaks winery in northern Sonoma County. The two had a wine management company, MG Enology. They figured out how to scam the system. And they did it well."

"So, if the feds have all this evidence, why haven't they acted on it?" Ellsworth asked.

"I've wondered that myself," Jones said.

"They have," Dante said. "But they keep it all quiet."

"How?" Ellsworth asked.

"They let the winemakers know what they have before they file charges. They let the wineries fix the problem before it becomes a public scandal."

"Fix the problem? How?"

"By letting the winemakers pull back the wine before it's sold," Dante said, "no laws are violated."

"Pressure from inside the wine industry," Jones said. "It's the only explanation."

"What do the feds say?" Ellsworth asked.

"I haven't talked to them yet. But they're next."

Ellsworth frowned, lost in thought. He picked up the pen, twirled it in his fingers, and looked at Dante. "So how does all of this grape fraud explain why Morrison killed his biggest investor. Or does it? And why would someone try to kill the attorney, Carmen Carelli?"

Dante's stomach tightened. "Well, I don't know yet. I'm working on it."

Ellsworth scowled and again twirled the pen. Dante's answer was not what he wanted to hear. There was nothing else Dante could say.

"Okay," Ellsworth said with an exasperated sigh. "Keep me informed." He tapped his thick pen on the desk pad. "You know we have to be damned sure about everything we print. Wine is the lifeblood of Northern California. The grape growers are on edge. We need to remember we're part of the community."

Jones turned to Dante, who clenched his jaw and swallowed hard.

"I know you've done a lot of good work on this story," Ellsworth continued. "But we really need to be cautious. We live or die on advertising. It's down, as you know. If we erode our community support any more, well, we'll all be looking for jobs."

Dante groaned, looked out the window, then back at Jones and Ellsworth. "Two killed and one shot in less than two weeks," he said. "It's not the kind thing easily swept under the carpet."

Ellsworth grimaced. "One slip-up, one mistake, and they're on us like hyenas on a fresh kill."

Dante liked the analogy. He stood and followed Jones out of the office.

CHAPTER 20

Fifteen minutes before noon, Dante waited at the street-level door to his mother's apartment. The buzz and click of the automatic door opener made Dante flinch. He was on edge. He took a deep breath and scaled the stairs two steps at a time. She greeted him at the top.

The faint odor of marijuana filled the air. Antonia had been using her vape to full effect. Her denim shirt was dabbed with fresh paint marks. She brushed her hair back with a wrist, a painting trowel in her hand, coated with luminescent blue. "This is a pleasant surprise."

"I left a message on your phone saying I was coming."

"It's still a surprise."

"You didn't respond," Dante said.

"I'm painting."

"The point of having a cell phone is to keep it with you so you don't miss a call."

"A cell phone is nothing more than a dog collar," Antonia said. "If you want to wear one around your neck, be my guest. Woof, woof. I'm not going to. They have off buttons, dear." Antonia forced a wide smile.

"Hmm. So, you're painting."

"It's what painters do." Antonia led him to her studio room. The canvas was a wide horizontal seascape. Blue sky, rolling foamy waves washing onto a flat shoreline. Strands of long brown seaweed bunched in the foreground, seagulls and pelicans sailing overhead.

"Nice," he said. "I can almost smell the salt air."

Antonia squinted and looked at him skeptically. "That's the paint you're smelling."

"I made us a reservation for lunch. At your favorite place around the corner. I didn't think you'd object."

"Of course not!" Antonia scraped the paint from her trowel and shed her shirt. "You know me too well, my dear. Do you mind if I call Alex? I told him you wanted to talk to him. He'd love to meet us there."

"Sure," Dante said. "If he's willing to let me pick his brain."

They were soon seated in an Asian-French fusion restaurant just a block or so away from Antonia's apartment. Dante liked the place because it was close, unpretentious, and had a reasonably priced seafood and a good wine list. He ordered a bottle of Corsican rosé, a Domaine Vetriccie, a light Mediterranean wine just a year old.

"Oh, this is nice," Antonia said, sipping from her glass.

Dante took a drink as well, letting the wine linger on his tongue. "I thought it might be a little too fruity, but it has a nice clean finish."

Antonia blinked. "You and your wine talk."

"I'm supposed to be a wine writer, Mama. That's why I'm going to Sacramento."

"So what's in Sacramento?" she asked.

"The TTB."

"Is that a disease?" she said.

"It's the federal agency regulating the wine industry," Dante said.

"It has something to do with the murders?" Antonia said, looking confused.

"I think so."

"What about that woman lawyer?" she asked. "Who tried to kill her?"

"I don't know. I just think …." Dante followed Antonia's eyes as she looked to the entrance and to her companion and gallery owner Alex Tercero. He wore loafers, jeans, a black T-shirt under a tan linen sport coat, and crossed the restaurant quickly to their table. He pulled a bentwood chair out to sit, but first reached out to shake Dante's hand before settling into it.

"Good to see you again, Dante," Tercero said. "Antonia said you were two were having lunch and you wanted to talk."

"Glad you could join us," Dante said.

"We haven't ordered yet," Antonia said.

"But I see you didn't wait to order the important stuff," Tercero said, glancing at the wine. A waiter handed Tercero a menu and a wine glass. "Antonia said you had questions about my friend Ricardo."

Dante glanced at Antonia, who smiled warmly at Tercero, who was as self-assured as ever. The man possessed an unassuming personality that made him easy to like, and Dante guessed it was why he did well in the gallery business. Beneath his casual exterior, Dante sensed he was all business.

"I'd like to know more about the extent of Santos's business interests," Dante said.

Tercero opened his eyes wide. "Well, he has businesses around the world."

"Wineries in Mexico, Spain, Italy, and here now," Dante said. "Olive groves in Spain and Italy as well."

Tercero casually scratched his trimmed, white beard. "You know about as much as I do. Tell me, why are you so interested in Santos?"

"Just a feeling," Dante said. "He and his Santos Wine Company are among the biggest players on the California wine scene. It's amazing what he's been able to accomplish in just four or five years."

Tercero furrowed his brow. "Actually, he's been doing business in the U.S. and California for about a dozen years."

"That long?" Dante said. "He's considered one of the newcomers to the California wine business."

"Yes, well, people's perceptions can't be helped," Tercero said.

"So you've done business with him?" Dante asked.

"I sold him a couple of your mother's paintings," Tercero said with a broad smile. "I suppose that counts." He lifted his glass to Antonia and drank.

Dante sipped his wine and said, "It does. Anything else?"

Tercero reached for the bottle, refilling Antonia's glass, Dante's, and his own, watching the last few drops fall. He turned to catch the eye of the waiter and wiggled the empty bottle, ordering another. "I'm in the wine business myself as you know. Your mother and I are the ones who introduced Ricardo to the world of California wine."

"I'd almost forgotten!" Antonia said with shake of her head.

"You brought Santos here?" Dante said, surprised.

Tercero raised his hands in a gesture of innocence. "Ricardo was dying to buy into the California wine business. I simply provided him with an opportunity."

"How?" Dante asked.

"No mystery to it," Tercero said. "There's a lot of overlap in the worlds of art and wine."

"How did you meet Santos?" Dante asked.

Tercero sighed, as if it was a long story. "It was in Spain." He looked at Antonia. "Antonia and I were in Madrid visiting the Prado and Reina Sofia museums."

"To see Picasso's 'Guernica,'" Dante said.

"There's a lot more to the museum than Picasso," Antonia said.

"I know," Dante said, "but—"

"We decided to go north and spend a few days in La Rioja wine country," Tercero said, interrupting. "We were visiting the Santos family winery, which also has an excellent restaurant and a small hotel. We decided to stay."

"When was that?" Dante asked.

Tercero looked at Antonia.

"When we visited the Spoleti family," Antonia said. "So maybe ten or twelve years ago."

"We met Ricardo, who showed us where we could find a well-known local artist's studio," Tercero said. "I ended up representing the man, a fine Spanish painter named Juan Moreno."

"I've seen his work at your gallery," Dante said.

"You can't miss it," Tercero said." He's a contemporary abstract painter, large canvases, bright colors, bold strokes."

The waiter arrived with the second bottle of wine, pulled the cork, and poured, then asked if they'd like to order. Dante selected the seared scallops. Antonia chose the crab salad, and Tercero asked for the grilled prawns from the Sea of Cortez.

"So, you met Santos at his winery in Spain?" Dante said.

"A couple of months later, he was doing some business in Mexico City and flew up to San Francisco," Tercero said. "I'd found a few wine properties for sale. There's always something on the market if you're willing to pay."

"So you introduced Santos to the California wine business."

"A number of very attractive vineyards were for sale. I ended up going into business with him."

"Partners in a winery?"

"Man cannot live by art alone," Tercero said.

"Alex Estates wine is considered one of the best in the Russian River," Antonia said.

"Okay," Dante said.

"It's where we sometimes spend the weekend," Antonia said. "Such a wonderful place and just a short drive away." She narrowed her eyes. "Of course, only when Alex can tear himself away from his *other* girlfriends."

Tercero flushed slightly, deepening his ruddy complexion.

"I only have eyes for you, dear," Tercero said, patting her hand and smiling. He cleared his throat and turned to Dante. "We produce small batches. I bottle several thousand cases a year. It's only about half of the grapes I own. The rest I sell."

"It sits on a hill and overlooks about 120 acres of grapes," Antonia said. "You should come."

"How about this weekend?" Tercero asked, sounding insistent.

Dante's stomach knotted. "I wouldn't want to disturb you."

"Don't be ridiculous," Antonia said. "It's just a short drive from Santa Rosa. Not far from the old family farm."

"Near Geyserville?" Dante asked.

"I'll send directions, if you need them," Tercero said, turning as a waiter placed their food on the table.

Dante cut into this scallops, his mind racing. Tercero was deep in the wine business and had done business with Santos. Chances were good if Tercero was selling grapes as well as making his own wine, he'd had contact with Morrison and Grundy. Dante also doubted Tercero's connection with Santos was as casual as he made it seem. "You're familiar with the murders in the Napa area?" Dante asked Tercero.

Tercero dabbed his mouth with his napkin. "Terrible what happened to that Carelli woman. I'm glad she's okay."

"Did you know her?" Dante asked.

"We've met," Tercero said. "She's done some legal work for Ricardo."

"Did you also know Bernie Morrison and Simon Grundy?" Dante asked.

"By reputation."

"They were buying and selling grapes in addition to running their own wineries," Dante said. "You never had any dealings with them?"

"The grapes I don't use in my own winemaking are under contract for the next several years," Tercero said.

"They're in high demand," Antonia said. "They command top prices."

Tercero cut into another shrimp and chewed. "Actually, most of the grapes grown in Northern California are under contract each year."

"What about Santos?" Dante asked. "What were his dealings with Morrison and Grundy?"

Tercero shrugged and said, "You'll have to ask him."

"Grundy worked for Santos before going out on his own as a contract vineyard manager and winemaker," Dante said. "Was Santos a partner with Morrison and Grundy?"

"It's conceivable," Tercero said. "Ricardo is a very aggressive businessman. He's always looking for a new venture." He reached for his wine and drank.

Dante waited for Tercero to continue, but he poked a prawn with his fork, pried off the shell, and ate it.

"For Santos to come to the US and buy a handful of wine properties required money," Dante said. "A lot of money. How does a man like Santos do that?"

Tercero frowned. "Ricardo could easily borrow money from any number of banks around the world, based on his existing holdings. I don't think it's fair to assume otherwise."

"Maybe," Dante said, "but it took substantial resources to become one of the biggest wine sellers in the state in such a short time."

"There are two ways to make money in the wine business," Tercero said. "One is sell a lot of wine at a low price. The other is to sell a small amount of wine at a high price."

"I get that," Dante said.

"Most of the boutique winery owners in Northern California, like me, prefer to keep things small," Tercero said.

"And hold your cards close to the vest," Dante said.

"Yes," Tercero said. "When people like Ricardo go big, they step into the public spotlight. They're more visible than most people want to be."

"People like you," Dante said.

"As a gallery owner and a winemaker, I need to be somewhat public," Tercero said. "But I try to keep it at a minimum."

"Not like Santos," Dante said.

"People like Ricardo can become a target," Tercero said.

"Santos has both big and small wineries," Dante said. "He's playing both sides of the game."

"And why not?" Tercero asked. "He likes a glass of fine wine as much as the next guy."

Dante ate the last of his scallops. "I'm meeting with agents from the TTB later today."

"Our friends in the federal government," Tercero said.

"They've been following Morrison and Grundy for a long time," Dante said.

"Not surprising," Tercero said.

"Fraudulent buying and selling of grapes," Dante said.

"Stealing is the rumor," Tercero said.

Tercero knows! "It's not a rumor," Dante said. "They left a trail of very angry people. One of them may have been Santos. I've been told grapes from the vineyards Grundy managed for Santos and others ended up in places they shouldn't have been. They caused a lot of problems."

"It's no wonder such people often end up dead, is it?" Tercero said.

Dante swallowed hard.

Tercero stabbed his last prawn with a fork, pried off the shell, and ate it.

CHAPTER 21

By the time Dante reached Vacaville on his drive to Sacramento, he felt like he was in another country. The cool ocean breezes rippling the water of San Francisco Bay were a distant memory, replaced by shimmering heat waves rising from the baked concrete of I-80. The land was wide and flat, parched fields interspersed with orchards of almond and walnut trees.

It was yet another world where Alex Tercero lived, Dante thought. Dante slapped the steering wheel in disgust. Tercero had been connected with Santos since day one, had brought him into the country. He'd been a business partner of Santos at one point, and could still be. He knew about Grundy, about Morrison, and Carelli. And what else? Yeah, Dante would be at Tercero's place this weekend. How could he pass that up?

But what did his mother know? Not much he guessed. She tuned out the news, sipped wine, and dragged on her vape. Tercero was her guardian against the all-too-ugly realities of the world, a rich boyfriend who sold her paintings for top dollar and with whom she spent her weekends at his wine estate. All she had to do was focus on her canvases. Why not?

When Dante's father, Dieter, had disappeared, his mother had become his world. When she'd been in prison, he'd lived with his grandparents and had become close to them. They were gone now, and their loss had left a hole in his heart; he would miss them until the day he died. In high school, and more when he was in college, he'd come to pity Antonia for her indulgences in wine and weed.

But now he was gaining a newfound respect for what she was doing. She'd made her peace with the world and was comfortable in her niche, its air perfumed with the scent of patchouli oil, acrylic paints, and weed. *Not so bad, all things considered. Okay, but is that where I'm headed, too?*

Dante still felt light-headed from the wine he'd had at lunch and needed to refocus, keep his eyes on the road and his mind on the story. Why had Morrison killed Ling? Was it just about the money? That was the obvious answer. *So why am I nagged by doubt? Is it just too simple? Why make it more complicated than it is?*

Morrison had taken Ling's money and squandered it. Ling had found out about the shell game Morrison and Grundy were playing with grapes and used it to pressure Morrison to get his money back. Only Morrison didn't have it.

Was money alone enough of a reason for Morrison to kill Ling? *Why not? But why had Carmen been attacked? Because she represented Ling? But Morrison was already dead, so it meant someone else was involved.* Dante had wanted to ask Carmen about all of this at the hospital, but had not wanted to press her too hard. He wondered now if she'd ever tell him.

Ninety minutes later, Dante pushed opened the thick glass door to the federal office building on Capitol Mall in downtown Sacramento, gave the receptionist his name, and asked for agent E. J. Edwards. Fifteen minutes later, Dante sat in the TTB conference room with Edwards and another agent, Thomas White. Edwards was overweight, had a full and florid face, and wore his shirt with an open collar and loose tie. His brown hair was cut high and tight, which only emphasized his thick neck and sloping shoulders.

Thomas White was a tall black man who wore a blue shirt with a crisp white collar, a gray sport coat, and a gold silk tie. He had a shaved head and complexion the color of coffee with cream. After they exchanged business cards, Edwards and White looked at Dante. "What can we do for you?" White asked.

Dante took a selection of documents from his canvas briefcase and pushed them across the table. The agents glanced at the papers, saying nothing.

"These are detailed dossiers compiled by your office," Dante said, "about the violations of federal laws governing the identification and sale of wine grapes and wine by the late Bernie Morrison and his partner, Simon Grundy. They did business together as MG Enology. They cut a rather wide swath across wine country."

"Where did you get those?" Edwards asked.

"They're part of a lawsuit filed against Morrison."

"So, what would you like to know?" White asked.

"Why you didn't file charges against them if you knew of all of these violations?" Dante said.

White and Edwards looked at each other and back at Dante.

Edwards cleared his throat and said, "Our job is to enforce the laws. To do that may not require placing people under arrest every time we find a violation."

"If we did, we'd be taking people to the slammer every day," White said.

"Two people have been killed and a third, attorney Carmen Carelli, nearly killed in a matter of weeks," Dante said.

Edwards sighed and rubbed his eyes with his knuckles. "You're talking to the wrong people. If you want to find out about what's going on with those murders, you need to talk to criminal investigators."

"That's not us," White said, tapping the table as if the conversation was over.

Dante's stomach knotted. "You have documented more than enough illegal activity to put the perpetrators in jail. Yet there've been no arrests."

"I beg to differ," White said. "In the past, the violations we've uncovered have drawn significant fines and penalties."

"You're talking about Ricardo Santos?" Dante asked.

"Yes," White said. "Millions of dollars in fines is not insignificant."

"A lot of people have been screwed out of a lot of money by Morrison and Grundy," Dante said. "Money is a motive for murder."

Edwards shook his head, disagreeing. "Morrison was killed by the police. And whoever tried to kill Ms. Carelli is unknown."

"We already told you we don't investigate murders," White said.

"You're cooperating with investigators, I assume," Dante said.

"Of course," White said. "It goes without saying."

Dante exhaled and dropped his pen on his notebook. "You're part of the Treasury Department."

The agents nodded, but said nothing.

"Your department tracks international money laundering, funding of terrorism, that kind of thing, correct?" Dante asked.

"It's handled by the Financial Action Task Force on Money Laundering," White said.

"There's a lot of money moving in and out of the wine business," Dante said. "Big money."

"We know," Edwards said.

"What are you saying?" White asked.

"Santos is known to associate with the Aragon brothers."

White glanced at Edwards before answering. "The Sonora Cartel."

Dante waited for more, but Edwards and White only looked at each other again.

Edwards pointed to Dante's notebook. "Put your pen down. Close it."

"Okay." Dante clicked his pen closed and put the notebook in his pocket.

"This is deep background only," Edwards said. "If you identify us in any way as the source of any of the information we're about to give you, we will deny ever having met or talked with you."

Dante looked at each of them. "Okay. I get it."

"That would be only the first step we can take to discredit your work," White said. "Do I make myself clear?"

Dante's stomach knotted.

"So, what are you going to do with it?" Jones asked.

Dante said nothing as he waited for Jones to fill his coffee cup from the bulky thermoses at the 4th Street Deli, which was around the corner from the newspaper office. Jones pressed the lid onto his cup and paid for the coffees at the cash register. They settled into chairs at one of the black wire mesh tables just outside the door.

"I'm not sure," Dante said, ignoring the street noise. "It was all on background. It's not like I'm going to call up either Santos or the Aragon brothers and ask them to admit to laundering drug cartel money through the wine industry."

Jones laughed. "Why not?"

Dante pried the plastic lid from his cup to let the coffee cool. He'd seen the gruesome photos of Mexican drug cartel beheadings, mutilations, and hangings. The gore was beyond comprehension. What drives people to do such things? Even wild animals don't kill and mutilate their own kind. It was hell. The devil's playground.

"Proving links to the drug cartels is not easy," Dante said. "First you have to show the money being invested in the wine industry is drug money. Tough to do unless you can track drug transactions, which are done in cash. The cash is deposited in foreign banks and moved into legitimate businesses."

"Like the wine industry," Jones said.

"Maybe, but it's just one of many methods."

"Well, at least you know the feds are watching," Jones said.

"And Santos probably does, too."

"So, he's extra careful," Jones said.

"If he's smart, which he is."

"Where does this leave the story?" Jones asked.

"I think Santos is involved."

"Why?" Jones asked. "This started with Morrison killing Ling and being gunned down by the Napa County deputies. Then Carmen Carelli was shot."

Dante sipped coffee. "Whoever went after Carelli may have been a professional. It would mean someone with money and underworld connections hired a contract killer."

"But they missed," Jones said. "You can't be a professional killer if you miss. It also doesn't explain Morrison and Ling."

"You're right. It doesn't."

"So why Carelli? What's the motive?" Jones asked. "She didn't steal grapes."

"Carelli is the one who got in touch with the feds," Dante said. "She was able to include the grape theft and fraud in her lawsuit against Morrison."

"That was about Morrison and Grundy, not Carelli."

"Carelli represented Santos on several sensitive cases," Dante said. "She knows a lot, I'm sure, and it could have been a problem."

"You mean, if she knew something Santos didn't want exposed," Jones said.

"It probably didn't help that I've been seeing her."

Jones squinted, surprised. "How long?"

Dante swallowed as his guilt simmered. "Not long."

"You think someone tried to kill her because of you?" Jones asked.

"If Santos was worried about Carelli," Dante said, "her seeing me didn't help."

"Who tries to kill their attorney?" Jones asked. "Why not just fire them?"

"The Mexican drug cartels kill for a lot less."

"What about Morrison and Ling?" Jones asked. "We still don't know what made Morrison want to kill him."

"Whatever Ling knew, and I think it was the grape theft and fraud, he tried to use it as leverage against Morrison," Dante said. "And he died for it."

Jones focused on the lid to his coffee, then looked at Dante. "Do you think Santos was involved in the grape theft and fraud?"

"Santos may have sold Central Valley grapes to Morrison and Grundy, who sold the grapes as being from the Napa Valley. If Santos knew what they were doing, he could hold it over their heads, use the info to control them, keep them in line."

"So they wouldn't dare rat him out," Jones said. "But why would Morrison and Grundy turn around and steal grapes from Santos? It's stupid and dangerous."

"Out of spite," Dante said, and sipped his coffee. "Muñoz said he told Santos about his grapes being diverted to Morrison and Grundy's wineries. But Santos didn't do anything about it."

"Santos wouldn't if he was part of their game," Jones said.

"There's more at play here," Dante said.

"You'd better figure it out fast," Jones said. "Ellsworth is getting antsy."

CHAPTER 22

It was nearly 11 a.m. the next day when Dante drove his Mustang along a twisting, leafy lane in Healdsburg, looking from his notebook to the house numbers. He was searching for Bernie Morrison's house and was going on nothing more than a hunch and a growing sense of desperation.

Dante knew he ought to go back and pick up where he'd left off rifling Morrison's office files. But he didn't want to risk another confrontation with Henshaw or any other deputies. Dante knew he could have been charged with tampering with evidence and had been lucky once. He didn't want to tempt fate a second time.

Morrison's house held other possibilities, however. It wouldn't be part of a crime scene and should be empty, quiet as a tomb. He'd scribbled the address in his notebook, and he glanced from it to house numbers as he drove up a narrow and curving asphalt road. The lack of curbs lent a laid-back, country feel to the neighborhood. He pulled into a short driveway fronting a small garage and stopped. He climbed out, shut the door, and looked around. The street and house were quiet.

Dante looked up at the two-level house built onto the side of a steep hill. It was the kind of modest, yet pricey house where people with money would live and pretend they were just plain folks. He noticed a motorcycle partially hidden in brush behind the steep, wooden stairway. It was protected by a dusty gray cover and looked like it hadn't been moved for days.

Dante pushed the brush aside and lifted the bottom of the cover. The motorcycle was dark black, making him pause.

He retreated a step to look at it, replaced the cover, then climbed the stairs to the landing at the front door. Silence. Not seeing a doorbell, he knocked firmly. The door swung open. Was someone else inside? He scanned the interior. The house seemed empty. Dante stepped in, but left the door slightly ajar. "Hello," he called out, listening for a response. Silence.

The living room was spacious, with leather couches, oriental rugs on the hardwood floor, and Buddha statues on corner shelves. A large, framed circular Zen-like work of brush calligraphy dominated one wall. Whoever lived here wanted to be seen as a practitioner of an enlightened lifestyle. Dante chuckled at the thought of Morrison being spiritual and wondered if he was in the right house.

Dante stepped toward the galley-style kitchen with tile counters and a stainless steel sink. A floor-to-ceiling wine rack was partially full. Dante pulled a bottle and examined the label: Morrison Creek. It must be the right house. Dante moved through the living room and to a back porch. A sliding glass door opened to a covered porch facing a tangle of vegetation growing up a steep hillside.

From the opened doorway, he gasped at the sight of a young woman, naked except for a string bikini bottom, looking at him upside down. She was in a yoga pose, the chakrasana position, her back arched high and her legs and arms fully extended with only her feet and hands on a yoga mat. Ear buds were stuck in her ears from the small iPod tucked into her bikini bottom. Her upside-down eyes opened wide, and her face twisted into a snarl.

She screamed, eyes wild and crazed, and kicked her feet up into the air. Pushing with her arms, she cartwheeled toward him and landed her on her feet. She was slightly crouched, her legs spread and taut, her fists balled, with one arm held out toward him and the other close to her shoulder. Dante stood slack-jawed at the sight of her agile body coming at him so fast. He couldn't get a good look at her face before she emitted a karate shout and slammed a foot into his chest.

Pain exploded as he lost his breath and tumbled backward into the living room, sprawled on his back. With another shout, she was on his chest, her knees straddling him, her left hand clutching his windpipe and squeezing, the fingers of her right hand grasping his ear and her thumb pressing on his left eye.

"You'd better have a damned good explanation for what the FUCK you're doing in MY house," she screamed, "or I'm going to rip your fucking eye out!"

Dante choked and gasped, "Stop! Stop!"

She squeezed his windpipe.

Dante gagged. "Stop it," he croaked. "Let me talk."

The woman released her thumb slightly, but still held it in position.

"I'm a reporter … I'm with the *Santa Rosa Sun*."

"Don't you know how to knock?" she yelled.

"I did," Dante said. "The door was open."

"So you just fucking walked in?"

"I called out. No one answered."

She released the grip on his throat, sat up straight, and yanked out her ear buds.

Dante gasped and wheezed, sucking in a couple more breaths. He eyed her more closely, taking in her tattoos, the sparkling stud in one nostril, and her spiky blond-tipped dark hair... He knew her!

The tiger was there, creeping from her right temple to her right cheekbone, wrapped around her blazing right eye. It was Marvee, the girl from Grundy's winery and Mei Ling's friend. A vine with purple grapes and green and reddish leaves tracked up her arm to the base of her neck.

"I know you," he said. "You're Marvee. We've met. Twice."

"And I know you," she said. "You're the reporter who's been writing all of the stories about Ling and Morrison."

"Dante. Dante Rath. I was at Shady Oaks a week ago."

Marvee frowned. "And at the Caffe Triest. I remember. So, what the fuck are you doing here?"

"Are you always this hostile?" Dante asked.

"Who wouldn't be?" she said. "Two people I know died recently. And a strange man walks into my house. What the fuck?"

"Sorry. Didn't mean to upset you."

She sighed noisily.

His gaze fell from her face to her bare breasts and her hips and thighs straddling him. He smiled and chuckled at the absurdity of the situation.

"What's so funny?" she asked.

"Ah…Do you always dress like this?"

She flushed and crossed her arms to cover her breasts. "When I do yoga. But it's none of your God-damned business." Her face again fell into a frown.

"Are you going to let me up?" Dante asked.

"All right." She rose, stepped over him and quickly turned away.

"Put a shirt on, please."

"Am I turning you on?" she said, looking over her shoulder with a suggestive smile.

Dante got up, took a deep breath and massaged his chest. *Hell, yes.* He watched Marvee patter onto the rear deck, grab a bright yellow cotton T-shirt, and pull it on. She skipped back into the living room, where Dante settled onto a couch. The T-shirt fit snuggly, stopping just above her navel, surrounded by a curling tattoo and pierced by a small, gold ring. She slipped onto a padded chair to the right of the couch, and tucked her legs under her.

"This is supposed to be Bernie Morrison's house," Dante said.

"It is," she said.

"So, what are you doing here?" he asked.

"What the hell are YOU doing here?" she said.

"I told you before," Dante said. "I'm researching the Morrison and Ling murders. How in the world did you end up here?"

"I live here," she said.

"You lived with Bernie Morrison?" he asked. "Odd you never mentioned it when we talked at the Caffe Trieste." *Mei Ling knows her brother's killer was her friend's roommate!* Dante's mind reeled as he reconsidered the relationships he thought he understood.

Marvee rolled her eyes and looked out the window. "It's not like we were boyfriend and girlfriend. We were roommates. We shared this house. I have my bedroom. He had his."

Dante looked at her, waiting for more.

"He let me stay here in exchange for keeping the place neat and clean."

Dante barely heard her response. *Could Mei Ling have been visiting Marvee when Chao was hanging out with Morrison? If so, then…?* He refocused on Marvee. What did she say?

"For keeping the place clean?" he asked. "How did it work out?"

"Okay, I guess."

"Sweet deal, I'd say," Dante said. "How did you land it?"

"I met Bernie when he was partners with Simon."

"Simon Grundy?"

"Yes," Marvee said. "A few years back. At Shady Oaks."

"You've known Grundy a while?" he asked.

"We met at wine school," she said.

"Wine school?" Dante asked, massaging the ache in his chest.

"UC Davis. The viticulture program. We took classes together."

Dante waited for her to continue.

"Why are you looking at me like that?" she said. "I went to college. It's not like I'm stupid."

"Who said you were?" Dante asked.

"I had to drop out," she said.

"Why?"

"No money," she said. "Had to get a job."

"So Grundy hired you?"

"Hmmm," Marvee said.

"What did you think of Morrison?" Dante asked.

"He had his moments."

"Meaning what?" Dante said.

"He could be a nice guy, when he wanted," she said. "He could also be an asshole."

Dante thought about her comments and about the timing of Marvee's employment at Shady Oaks winery. "Did you know the former owner of Shady Oaks? A woman named Nicole Anderson?"

Marvee eyed him. "Sure. Nicole. She was over here sometimes."

Dante winced at the thought. *How was that possible?* "A lot?"

"I was working long hours," she said. "But I knew she was here."

"What did you know about her?"

"She sold the winery to Bernie and Grundy," Marvee said. "She and Bernie became friends. She was married, I know. She died. In a car accident."

The words punched him in the gut. Dante drew a deep breath and slowly exhaled. "She was my wife."

Silence hung in the air. "Oh. Sorry. I didn't know," she said.

"It's all right. She's gone." Dante swallowed hard. His throat was dry. He forced himself to refocus. "Why do you think Morrison killed Chao Ling?"

Marvee scrunched her face. "The cops asked me that. But I don't know. Maybe it was over money."

"Did Morrison ever complain about Ling?" he asked.

"Not really," Marvee said. "I knew Chao was an investor. Bernie never confided in me about the business. He kept most things to himself. He was gone a lot. Working or whatever. When it was slow, he'd disappear into the city."

"Where he met Ling," Dante said.

"I guess. One day he just showed up with Chao."

"Chao was here a lot?" Dante asked.

"Sometimes. Weekends usually. They'd hang out at the winery."

"Which is where you met Mei Ling?" Dante asked.

"Uh huh. Mei likes wine as much or more than Chao. She'd come out here on the weekends with him. We had really good times. Still do, as a matter of fact." Marvee jumped up and went to the kitchen. "Would you like a glass of wine?"

Dante looked at her in surprise. "You were going to kill me a few minutes ago. Now you're offering me wine?"

"After yoga, a little wine helps me relax. You scared me. And, if we're going to be talking for a while…"

"You're very health conscious," Dante said. "Yoga and wine."

Marvee rolled her eyes. "Do you want wine, or not?"

"Yes. I'm parched."

Marvee deftly pulled a cork from a bottle, gurgled white wine into two glasses, and handed one to Dante before settling into a padded cane chair facing him.

Dante lifted his glass in a silent toast and sipped. "You have no idea why Morrison would want to kill Ling?"

"Maybe it was the formula."

"The formula?" Dante asked. "What are you talking about?"

"He was working on a spray to treat grape vines."

"An insecticide?" Dante asked.

"Could be."

"What do you know about insects?" Dante asked.

"They're like men."

"Sounds like a sci-fi movie," Dante said.

"It's true. Really," Marvee said.

"Men are like insects?"

"Uh, yeah."

"You've had bad times with men?" he asked.

"Maybe." Marvee sipped and cast her eyes around, then pattered into the kitchen, grabbed the wine bottle, and skipped back to the couch, refilling their glasses. She put the bottle on the coffee table and sat beside Dante. He caught her scent as she held out her glass in another toast.

"Here's to grapes," he said. They clinked glasses and drank. Dante rolled the wine around his tongue and swallowed. "It's a chardonnay, but doesn't taste like it's from Napa."

"Why not?" she asked.

"The Central Valley grapes are a bit more... acidic," Dante said. "The Napa chardonnays are more fruity and oaky."

Marvee smiled. "Well, you are a wine critic!"

"Grundy made this?"

"Simon made Bernie's wine, so, yeah," she said. "You could say it's his wine."

"It's drinkable." Dante grabbed the bottle and examined the label. "It says it's a Napa Valley wine."

"It is, more or less," she said. "Morrison got his grapes from all over."

"From all over where?" he asked.

"The Central Valley, local vineyards, anywhere he could."

"That's illegal, you know," he said, "if the grapes aren't actually from the Napa Valley."

"I suppose," she said. "But who's to know?"

"Do you know where in the Central Valley he got the grapes?"

"Do you know Ricardo Santos?" Marvee asked.

"Of course, but we've never met." Dante drank some wine. "Tell me about Morrison's vine treatment project."

"Why are you interested?"

"Before he came to California, Morrison developed a spray to fight fungus. He was sued over it. I think it's why he came to California."

"Everybody's running from something," she said.

"Are you?" he asked.

CHAPTER 23

Sitting next to Dante on the couch, Marvee considered his question. She narrowed her eyes, but said nothing.

Dante rubbed his sore chest, wincing as he touched the spot where her kick connected. "Are you a martial arts fanatic?"

"Are you a wine fanatic?" she replied.

"No. I just like wine."

"I like yoga and martial arts because they help me attune my mind and my body."

"Attune them to what?" Dante asked.

"It's a matter of being clear about what you want to do."

"Like being an acrobat?"

"C'mon. I'll show you." Marvee jumped up, grabbed Dante's hand, and tugged him to the porch where her yoga mat remained on the floor. She rolled it up and put it in the corner. "Take off your socks and shoes."

"Why?"

"So you don't slip and hurt yourself," she said.

Dante bent down, pulled off his shoes and socks, and tugged his shirt tails from his pants.

Marvee faced him, striking a karate pose. "Stand like this. Feet apart, one foot in front of the other. Balanced weight. Hands up."

Dante moved, crouched slightly, and raised his arms.

"Now, put your weight on your back foot, and raise your front foot off the ground."

Dante did, struggling to keep his balance.

"Now, kick out your front foot like this." Marvee tilted back, twisted slightly, and snapped her foot out and back, her heel within inches of Dante's chin. She stepped back and exhaled. "Now you try."

Dante made a timid and awkward kick.

"Again, this time a little stronger," she said.

Dante extended his hands out to his sides for balance and kicked aggressively.

"That's better. Now, come at me."

Dante hesitated, but took a deep breath. "I don't want to hurt you."

Marvee motioned him forward. "C'mon. You can't hurt me."

"I can't?"

She shook her head.

Dante stutter-stepped toward her, twisted and kicked.

Marvee swung her forearm to the side, knocked Dante's kick away, and pivoted on her back leg, slamming her heel into Dante's chest again, knocking him backward to the floor.

Dante felt like he was dying. He clutched his chest and gasped for air. She had knocked the wind out of him.

Marvee leapt on him with a full-body press and held his head in her hands, genuine concern on her face. "I'm sorry! Are you okay?"

Dante groaned. He drew several halting breaths as his diaphragm began to work again.

"Let me make it up to you," Marvee said, looking into Dante's eyes. She gave him a lingering, wet kiss.

Dante gazed into her gray eyes.

She moved on him as a slight smile crept across her face.

His desire for her stirred.

She bent forward and gave him another deep kiss, her tongue probing his mouth. She withdrew and slowly sat up.

Dante's desire became increasingly apparent. *Don't stop now!*

Marvee looked down at him, her eyes half closed and dreamy. Her fingers caressed his cheek and neck. Marvee's eyes blinked, as if returning from far away. She rose to her feet and scowled. "You'd better go."

Dante drew a breath and sat upright. He puzzled over her mood swing. She was adrift, he sensed, maybe because of Morrison's and Ling's deaths. Despite how she may have felt about Morrison, she'd been left alone in a house where a dead man's things were everywhere. He exhaled slowly and rubbed his aching chest. He shook his head. "Are you angry about something?"

"Didn't you hear me? This is my house. I think you should go. Okay?"

"I'm not done yet," Dante said.

She lifted her eyebrows and said, "What? I think you are."

"If this is Morrison's house, I want to look around a little bit. Where's his room?"

Marvee raked fingers through her hair. "Too late. The cops were already here."

"I still want to see it."

"Okay. But after, you go."

Marvee pattered across the wood floor in her bare feet, grabbing her wine glass on the way. Dante got to his feet and followed.

Morrison's king-sized bed filled much of the bedroom. It was neatly made. "At least Morrison wasn't a slob."

"He was a total slob," Marvee said. "You wouldn't believe."

"I forgot. It's why he let you stay here."

"After the police left, I changed the sheets, made the bed, straightened up." She put her wine glass on the nightstand, bounded onto the bed, and sitting upright with her legs crossed, ran her fingers across the bedcovers.

"What about Morrison's family?" Dante asked. "Have they called?"

"They haven't talked to me. Why do you ask?"

"His family might want his personal effects."

"There's not much except for his CD collection, that computer, and the furniture."

"What are you going to do now? Stay here?" Dante asked.

"I don't know," she said, shaking her head. "I'll stay here as long as I can. I really like this place. But it's not mine. I can't even think of buying it."

Dante scanned the bedroom. In one corner was a floor-to-ceiling narrow shelf of compact discs. He pulled a few of the CDs and DVDs from the rack and shuffled through them. Movies, music, and video games. On the shelf below, however, Dante found an extensive collection of gay porn. About fifty discs in all, he guessed. He showed a couple to Marvee.

"What can I say?" she said. "Bernie liked to lie in bed and watch movies."

Dante grunted an acknowledgement, replaced the discs, and turned to a built-in desk and shelves covering the wall opposite the bed. A flat-screen TV dominated the wall above a computer screen on a desk. Below the desk was a computer processor.

"The cops took the hard drive," Marvee said.

"Why?" Dante asked. "There's no one alive to be charged in the murder. What's to investigate?"

"So remind me why you're here," she asked.

"I want to know why Morrison killed Ling."

Marvee pursed her lips. "Hmm. You don't think it was the money?"

"Maybe. But who kills their biggest investor? Especially if they're in a relationship."

"Shit happens, you know."

Dante took a seat at the desk. He absentmindedly tapped the keyboard. "I wonder what was on it." Dante glanced at a pile of envelopes beside the keyboard. "What's this?" he asked, picking up the pile.

Marvee looked over to the desk. "It's his mail."

"The cops didn't take it?"

"It came after they left," she said.

Dante sorted through it, stopping at one envelope. "This is interesting."

"What is it?"

"A letter from the State Office of Environmental Health Hazard Assessment."

"The office of what?" she asked.

"Proposition 65," Dante said.

"What's that?"

"Prop 65 requires all potentially toxic materials to be identified on product labels," he said.

"Rad."

"The chemical industry hates it."

"Of course they would," Marvee said. "If you have to say your product is hazardous, you're screwed."

"You got it."

"So what's the letter say?" she asked.

Dante tore open the envelope and scanned the letter. "Hmmm."

Across the top were the words, "thiophanate-methyl," followed by column headings: Identification, Toxicity, Use, Water Pollution Potential, Ecological Toxicity, and Regulatory Information. Below each were symbols, including several skull-and-crossbones images.

"Look at this," Dante said, showing her the letter.

"What is it?" Marvee said, jumping from the bed to look over his shoulder.

"A toxicology report." Dante studied it. "It calls the chemical a 'PAN Bad Actor,' whatever that is. The acute toxicity level is slight, but the chemical is a carcinogen…a likely pollutant of groundwater."

"Sounds awful," Marvee said. She took the letter from him and continued to read it. "It also says the chemical is a 'developmental or reproductive toxin' but the information is incomplete about it being an 'endocrine disruptor.'"

He gave Marvee a confused glance. "Does that make any sense to you?"

"Actually, it does," she said. "It's saying the chemical compound can mess up your hormones."

"How do you know?"

"I'm not completely stupid," she said, glaring and grabbing the pages from him. "See? I'm right," she said, pointing. "Here at the bottom." She read aloud. "These disruptions can cause cancerous tumors, birth defects, and other developmental disorders." She looked at him lost in thought.

"What the hell is a PAN Bad Actor?" Dante asked, taking the letter back from her.

Marvee disappeared from the bedroom as Dante continued to read. She returned holding her smartphone and showed him the screen. "P-A-N is the Pesticide Action Network. It calls a chemical a bad actor if it's toxic in any of those categories. What is it again?"

"Thio…phanate…methyl," Dante said, as Marvee tapped the words into her phone.

"It says exposure causes skin problems, itching, redness, swelling, dryness, and hyper-sensitized skin."

Dante continued to read the letter. "It says there is no known immediate first aid for thiophanate-methyl poisoning, and it recommends going to the hospital." Dante thought about it. "It's poisonous. The only reason Morrison and Grundy would be working with such a chemical is because they were developing a pesticide or something."

"It's kinda removed from winemaking," Marvee said.

"Not really," Dante said. "Ever heard of Pierce's disease?"

"Of course," Marvee said. "It kills grape vines."

"It almost wiped out vineyards across Southern California," he said. "Just about killed the wine business down there."

Marvee frowned. "How do you stop it?"

"I don't know. But I know wine growers are damned worried."

"Of course. The winemakers would want to wipe out the disease," Marvee said.

"An insecticide that could be used on grape vines," Dante said. "But this says the key ingredient is toxic." Dante read on. "It also says agricultural workers exposed to the insecticide have the most risk." Dante looked up from the letter and at Marvee. "Probably because it's concentrated in the spray."

"An insecticide to control Pierce's disease would be a valuable thing," Marvee said.

"Not if it kills people," Dante said. "I need to find someone who knows about this stuff."

"Professor Brickman."

Dante frowned. "Who?"

"UC Davis wine school. He knows everything about wine."

"Let's go." Dante said, glancing at his watch. "We'll call him on the way."

"I'm going too?" Marvee asked, wide-eyed.

"Do you know him or not?"

"Yes, well, sort of," she said.

"Do you have anything better to do?"

"I'm off today," Marvee said. "So I guess not."

CHAPTER 24

Slumped in the passenger seat of the Mustang and sipping water from a small plastic bottle, Marvee watched the passing landscape as Dante drove east on I-80.

"How did you get a name like Marvee?" Dante asked. "Is it French?"

"It's short for Marvelous. Marvelous McGregor."

"Are you serious?"

Marvee scowled. "Screw you."

Dante glanced at her and scowled.

Marvee muttered, "Men."

"What are you so grumpy about?" Dante asked.

Marvee exhaled.

"Your mother must have been an optimist," he said.

"What are you saying?"

"She thought highly of you."

"My mother didn't name me," Marvee said. "I changed my name."

"What was it before?"

"Alice."

"Alice?" he asked.

"She named me after the movie, *Alice Doesn't Live Here Anymore*."

"I've heard of it," he said. "But remind me about the story."

"It's about a woman who wants to be a singer," Marvee said. "She's from Socorro, New Mexico, and tries to go to Los Angeles. She never makes it and ends up working in a restaurant in Tucson. It starred Kris Kristofferson. He was kinda cute."

"Okay."

"The movie could have been about my mother," Marvee said. "She left New Mexico after she had me and moved to Southern California. She wanted to be an actress."

"How'd she do?"

Marvee looked at him, lost in thought.

"Is she still alive?"

"She died," Marvee said softly.

"I'm sorry. It must have been hard."

Marvee looked at him with glassy eyes and blinked. She drew a deep breath. "It was a relief, actually. The suffering ended." Marvee fell silent. "It's in the past. Let's leave it there."

Dante sensed more to the story, much of it raw and painful, and decided not to push it. "So you changed your name?"

"Hmmmm," she said.

"A break from the past?" he asked.

"You could say that."

"When did you get the tattoos?" he asked.

"I got my first when I was sixteen."

"What about the one on your back?" He'd seen it when she'd turned her back to him, a detailed depiction of two large red cranes on a pine branch, one taking flight and another balanced on one leg. The tattoos had been done by a skilled artist and ran from her lower back nearly to the base of her neck.

"I just liked the red cranes. They looked wild and exotic to me."

"They're revered in Japan and China," he said. "They're endangered."

"When I learned about them, I loved them even more." Marvee looked at the passing brown landscape. "They symbolize good fortune and a long life, neither of which my mother had."

"And you do?"

"I think about the cranes," Marvee said. "They're part of my training and my practice."

"Practice? Your karate, or whatever it is?"

"Mindfulness," she said.

"A lot of people are into that lately," he said. "It's a good thing, I suppose."

"It helps me relax. It helped me deal with Bernie and Chao dying."

Dante cleared his throat. "So…McGregor. You're part Irish?"

"No. McGregor is a Scottish name. My father's a redhead. Fancies himself a cowboy. He lives in Ruidoso."

"Where's that?" he asked.

"New Mexico."

"But he's not really a cowboy?"

"He works at the horse track there," she said. "When it's slow, he's a dealer at the Apache casino."

"And your mother?"

"Maggie Montoya. She was from Albuquerque, part Mescalero Apache and part Mexican."

"That's how you got your black hair," he said. It would also explain her cinnamon complexion and gray eyes.

She pulled up the sleeve to her T-shirt and pointed to the intricate dream catcher tattoo on her upper left arm. "It's why I got this one."

"To catch the bad dreams," Dante said. "Does it work?"

"I don't know."

"What about the one on your stomach?" he asked.

"This?" She pointed to a floral and vine design curling across her lower stomach to her navel and disappearing into her pants. She looked at him. "I just liked this one."

"You figured since you had the others, one more wouldn't hurt," he said.

She wrinkled her nose. "What do you think? Do you like them?"

Dante gazed at her. "What's not to like?"

Marvee smiled.

"So, if your mother named you after that movie, you're about thirty, thirty-five?"

"Close."

"Any kids?"

Marvee turned angrily and snapped. "Am I supposed to? What is this? An interrogation?"

"It's called conversation," Dante said.

"What do you want to know for?"

"Just curious."

"I don't. Okay? It's your turn to talk."

Dante told her about growing up in the Bay Area, of his Italian relatives, his absented Swiss-born father, his artist mother.

"Any kids?" she asked, drawing out the word, *kids*.

Dante told her about learning Nicole was pregnant after she died in the emergency room. "You could'a been a father," Marvee said.

Dante swallowed hard and said nothing.

Marvee pointed to the overhead highway sign for the turnoff to UC Davis. "Take this exit," she said.

Dante angled off the interstate.

CHAPTER 25

Heading down a sidewalk flanked by a thick lawn, Dante and Marvee hurried toward a modern, multistory building. "Here we are," Dante said, looking at a sign. "The Mondavi Institute for Wine."

"Winemakers rule!" Marvee said, thrusting a fist into the air.

Dante rolled his eyes.

Professor Harold Brickman was in his sixties, of average height, with the soft round features of a comfortable academic, and thinning white hair. He adjusted his tortoise-shell glasses on his thick nose. "So you're the reporter with the *Santa Rosa Sun* newspaper?" he said to Dante.

Dante handed Brickman his card.

"Well, what can I do for you?" Brickman asked.

"We're...or I'm researching the circumstances surrounding the shootings in Napa of several people over the past few weeks, two of whom died," Dante said.

"The guy who shot his partner in the vineyard?"

"Yes," Dante said.

"What a terrible tragedy," Brickman said. "Shocking, actually. The wine industry isn't supposed to be violent. What happened?"

"The owner killed his primary investor," Dante said.

Brickman pulled off his glasses, fished a handkerchief from his back pocket, and cleaned the lenses. "Money's at the core of most disputes."

"They weren't the only ones. There was an attorney who was shot," Dante said. "Carmen Carelli, part of the Carelli wine family. She represented the investor, Chao Ling, in a suit against Bernie Morrison, the man who killed Ling and who was killed by the police. Morrison was a business partner with Simon Grundy."

"Simon Grundy!" Brickman said. "I know him, as well as the Carelli family. They're benefactors of the wine school here."

"Simon was a student here," Dante said. "As was Marvee here."

"I know," Brickman said. "It's why I agreed to meet on short notice. Simon was a natural. At the top of his class. I expected him to do well, and he did. I got him his first job out of the wine school."

"It was for the Santos Wine Company," Dante said. "You know Ricardo Santos?"

"Who doesn't?"

"He's not exactly a household name," Dante said.

"In the California wine business he is," Brickman said.

"I suppose so," Dante said. "Grundy became a winemaker and vineyard manager for a number of wineries in the region. The federal agency overseeing the wine industry—"

"The TTB," Brickman said.

"Yes. The TTB has been looking into Morrison and Grundy's business practices."

"Is Simon in trouble?" Brickman asked.

"It would appear so," Dante said. "He's been investigated."

"Can you tell me about it?"

"He's been buying and selling grapes, falsifying harvest records, shipments, grape types, among other things."

Brickman dropped his eyes to the floor. "That is a problem." His gaze floated from Dante to Marvee and the curves of her tight-fitting T-shirt.

"He did most of the work through a company he'd formed with Morrison," Dante said. "MG Enology."

"It sounds to me like you already have a lot of information," Brickman said. "What do you need from me?"

Dante reached into his briefcase, pulled out a file folder, and took a double sheet of paper from it. "Morrison recently received this letter from the agency that administers and enforces Proposition 65."

Dante handed the letter to Brickman, who sat back and adjusted his glasses to read it. "This does not surprise me," Brickman said.

"Could you explain what the product is and the chemical?"

"It's an insecticide, I would guess. Probably still experimental. It could be used to control the glassy-winged sharpshooter."

"The insect that spreads Pierce's disease?" Dante said.

"Yes," Brickman said. "The disease is native to the southeastern US and northern Mexico. But now it's global. It has spread from Central and North America to South America, and now it's infecting olive trees in southern Italy. The Europeans are very worried, as they should be."

"Italy?" Dante asked, and thought about the implications for his own relatives.

"We're not sure how," Brickman said, "but we think it may have been carried there on fruit imported from South America."

"Fruit?" Dante asked. "The Italians grow most of their own fruit."

"Not all of it," Brickman said. "They import some. The insect seems to like citrus. Research indicates it lays its eggs on fruit or may just attach itself to fruit."

"So the insect hitched a ride on Central and South American fruit sold to Europe?"

Brickman pulled his glasses off to rub his face. "How much do you know about Pierce's disease?"

"It's bad for grapes and the wine industry."

Brickman took a breath and sighed. "It's a bacteria that kills grape vines. The disease is named after Newton B.

Pierce, the man who first identified it in 1892. He found it on grapes near Anaheim."

"There was a big infestation in Southern California about twenty years ago, right?" Dante asked.

"Temecula. In 1996," Brickman said. "In just several years, the disease wiped out most of the vineyards."

"The community is between San Diego and LA," Dante said. "But as far as I know, the wineries have recovered and are doing well."

"Doing well?" Brickman said. "Maybe. But it wasn't easy."

"Why not?"

"Well, you have to rip out all of the infected vines and start over."

"Replant everything?" Dante asked.

"It's a huge expense," Brickman said. "Pull out all of the infected vines, destroy them, and replant. Start from scratch."

Dante jotted notes. "I know it takes three to five years for the vines to mature and produce grapes."

"Exactly," Brickman said. "Planting and growing a vineyard requires time-consuming labor and enormous expense. And it means at least three years of little or no wine production."

"No wonder the growers are scared shitless of the disease," Dante said.

"I wouldn't say scared, but they're, well…extremely vigilant. If the disease gets out of control, the California wine industry could be devastated."

"Why can't the infected vines be treated?" Marvee asked.

"There's nothing to be done once the vines are infected," Brickman said. "The winemakers just have to start over."

"So," Dante said, "they're focused on the insect that spreads the disease."

"Yes," Brickman said. "It's the most effective treatment we have. The disease occurs naturally in many parts of California, including the Napa and Sonoma Valleys. The sharpshooter is found in most areas of the state. The agricultural agencies have done a good job keeping the insect under control, but it's not easy."

"Why not?"

"In addition to fruit, the insect eggs are found on popular landscaping plants, like crape myrtle," Brickman said. "These plants are grown in nurseries in Southern California."

"Which is where the insect is most prevalent," Dante said.

"The plants are shipped throughout California and out-of-state," Brickman said.

"So the disease is spread by people trying to make their property look good?" Marvee asked.

"Each nursery plant has to be treated with a mild insecticide to ward off the sharpshooter," Brickman said.

"And it's enough to keep the sharpshooter under control?"

"Because of the California drought, the sharpshooter has come back stronger than ever," Brickman said. "Especially in the south, where it's been the driest."

"The wineries across Southern California could be at risk, yet again?" Dante asked.

"Cool, wet, foggy weather in Northern California helps keep the sharpshooter under control," Brickman continued. "If it rains a lot, the sharpshooter can't move around as well and feed. If it goes several days without eating, it dies. Because it's been dry for several years now, all over California, the sharpshooter population has exploded."

Dante jotted notes.

"Like I said, there's no known cure once a vine is infected," Brickman said.

"Considering the size of the California wine business, and the science community here," Dante said, "you'd think the problem would have been solved already."

"The problem is being attacked in a number of ways. The focus has been on the bacteria the insect carries. It's called *xylella fastidiosa*."

"Sounds freaky," Marvee said.

Brickman glanced at Marvee again and continued. "Once a vine is infected with the bacteria, the vine produces a gel to fight it. Like when a tree oozes sap to surround and kill insects that burrow into it."

"A natural solution, isn't it?" Marvee asked.

"Not really," Brickman said. "The gel blocks the flow of water up from the roots to the leaves and fruit. It's like a person with blocked arteries. If blood can't flow through your body, you die. The same with grape vines. Without water or nutrients moving up the vine, the grapes whither and the leaves die, followed by the entire vine. It's already cost millions in lost production."

Dante scribbled down the quote and tapped his notebook with his pen as he thought.

"Once a vineyard is infected," Brickman continued, "the disease spreads quickly."

"How fast?" Dante asked.

"Well, in one typical case, a large vineyard had only a few infected vines. The next year, almost half the vines were infected. The year after, the entire vineyard was lost."

Dante pointed to the toxicology report he'd shown Brickman earlier. "What about this? Could this chemical spray stop the spread of the disease?"

"Yes, I suppose it would help," Brickman said. "It's an insecticide."

"So Morrison figured he had a spray to kill the insect and stop the disease," Dante said.

Brickman looked out the window and back at Dante. "It's not the ideal solution."

"Why not?"

"With any chemical spray, you're introducing a toxic substance into the environment," Brickman said. "These chemicals just don't just stop being toxic after they've been sprayed. They don't go away. The chemicals are around forever. The only reason they're less dangerous is because the chemicals are dispersed into the environment."

"Like this thiophanate-methyl," Dante said.

Brickman pulled off his glasses again and massaged the bridge of his nose before answering. "In its pure form, it's toxic, according to the letter. But if it's diluted, or combined with other compounds, it could be more dangerous or less dangerous. I'm not sure."

Dante glanced at Marvee.

"Think about it like this," Brickman said. "The active ingredient of many insecticides attacks the nervous system of the insect," Brickman said. "These chemicals are the most deadly substances on the planet."

Dante cleared his throat and sat forward, elbows on his knees. "So, if farm workers sprayed insecticides, they'd be exposed to high levels of it."

"Yes," Brickman said. "There's a reference in the letter to damage to the endocrine system. People who work around these chemicals are supposed to wear protective clothing."

"Like hazmat suits?" Marvee asked.

"Yes, like that," Brickman said.

"What about the wine?" Marvee asked. "Can it be contaminated?"

"If it was sprayed directly on the grapes, maybe yes, I suppose so," Brickman said. "The grapes would need to be washed. But it would be foolish to spray the grapes. There could be residual chemicals."

"You said killing the sharpshooter is not the best solution," Dante said. "What is?"

"The best solution is to grow vines resistant to the bacteria," Brickman said. "That way, the insects can't hurt the vines and you don't need to use any insecticides."

"Are there any disease-resistant vines now?" Dante asked.

"It seems the chardonnay grape and the pinot noir grape vines are the most vulnerable to the disease," Brickman said. "But the muscadine grape vines are resistant."

"Muscadine grapes?" Dante asked.

"Those are table grapes," Marvee said.

"Yes," Brickman said, taking a deep breath. "We think the muscadine grape vine developed a natural resistance long ago for some reason. The university here is working on disease-resistant vines now. But they won't be ready for planting for a few years."

"So the short-term fix is to attack the bugs and the disease?"

"That's the current tactic," Brickman said.

"If a product could kill the insects spreading the disease," Dante said, "it would be—"

"Huge!" Marvee said, sitting up.

"Tens of millions of dollars," Brickman said.

"Fruit growers in South America would want it, as would olive growers in Spain and Italy," Dante said.

Brickman nodded as Dante's mind churned.

CHAPTER 26

The sun was low in the western sky when Dante slipped into the newsroom. Jones was in his office talking with Ellsworth. Dante shed his sport coat and looked across the busy newsroom. Most reporters were at their desks, busily finishing and filing their stories. Dante felt a wave of anxiety as he glanced again at Jones, wanting to tell his boss what he'd come across.

Dante had feared the day might be a complete bust, but it had been the opposite. He'd unexpectedly encountered Marvee and made a trip to UC Davis and back with her. Meeting Marvee again, one-on-one, had been a major break. He tried to sort out pesticides, grape vine diseases, and how it affected his story. Dante took a deep breath as Jones waved for him to come to his office.

Yes! Dante's heart thumped. He grabbed his notebook and the toxicology report and headed to the office.

"We need to talk," Jones said as Dante stepped inside the doorway. Jones motioned to the only empty chair, came from around his desk, closed the door, and sat back down, a somber look clouding his face. The move made Dante suspicious. News stories were not normally discussed behind closed doors. Only personnel matters were.

Jones leaned forward on his desk and sighed. "Where the hell have you been?"

Dante hesitated, but said, "UC Davis, among other places. Doing research."

Jones looked at him, then glanced at Ellsworth, who was equally somber.

"A few developments you ought to know about," Dante said with some enthusiasm.

"Make this quick," Jones said.

Dante tossed the toxicology letter on Jones's desk.

"What the hell is it?" Jones asked, glancing at the letter and handing it to Ellsworth.

"What I told you about Morrison's motive for murder may not matter now."

"What?" Jones said.

"The shell game Morrison and his partner, Simon Grundy, played with all of those grapes. The mislabeling, the theft."

"You're kidding!" Jones said, sounding exasperated.

"No," Dante said. "I'm not."

"You're telling me after all this time, your investigation has fallen apart?"

Dante glanced at Ellsworth, then at Jones. "Not at all," he said. "Quite the opposite."

Jones looked at his watch, as if he were short on time. "Explain."

"Morrison and Grundy were developing an insecticide for grapes."

Jones leaned back and laced his fingers over his stomach. "An insecticide? What does it have to do with the murders?"

"You ever heard of Pierce's disease?"

"Vaguely," Jones said. "If I recall, it kills grape vines."

Dante explained how the disease spread, that the insect pest was poised for a major assault on California vineyards due to recent weather conditions, and no one had a cure.

"The glassy-winged sharpshooter?" Jones said with a laugh. "That's the name of the bug?"

Dante smiled. "The thousands of grape growers in this state don't think it's funny."

"I bet they don't." Ellsworth said. He pulled off his glasses and rubbed the bridge of his nose, looking tired of it all. Dante had a sinking feeling.

"So?" Jones said. "Connect the dots. What do you have there?"

Dante swallowed. "This disease and the cure, or lack thereof, could make or break the wine business in California. It's a big deal. Very big."

"You're working on a murder story, remember?" Jones said. "You're wandering around in the weeds."

Dante glanced at Ellsworth, then at Jones as it began to dawn on him this meeting had nothing to do with the story he was investigating.

Jones frowned, tilted back in his chair, and swiveled, irritation creeping across his face. "Well, what is it?" he said, motioning to the letter.

"The letter is from the State Office of Environmental Health Hazard Assessment."

"The what?" Jones asked.

"The agency that administers Proposition 65," Dante said, glancing again at Ellsworth. "It says the key ingredient to a pesticide is toxic."

"So this pesticide would do what?" Jones asked.

"Supposedly kill the bug spreading the disease," Dante said. "It's still experimental. But if it works, it would be incredibly valuable because the disease has become a global problem, not just for grape growers, but olive growers as well."

"You're saying it could stop a pest that's killing California vineyards and olive groves around the world?" Ellsworth asked.

"Yes, but the State of California says it's toxic," Dante said. "Causes birth defects."

Ellsworth's eyes narrowed. "If it was sprayed on the vines and grapes...."

"Yes. Toxic vines, and maybe even toxic wines."

"Tainted wine?" Ellsworth said, raising his eyebrows.

"Agricultural workers exposed to the insecticide have the highest risk," Dante said.

Jones and Ellsworth leaned back and sighed.

"Good work, Dante," Jones said. "But how does it connect to the murders and the shooting of Carelli?"

"If the pesticide is effective, it's worth millions, maybe billions of dollars."

"But not if it's toxic," Ellsworth said.

"Which is why some people would want to keep it quiet, maybe even kill to keep it quiet," Dante said.

"I don't get the connection," Jones said.

"Permission to use the pesticide was requested by a company called MG Enology," Dante said. "It's the company owned by Morrison and his partner, Simon Grundy."

Jones and Ellsworth look at each other.

"I need to talk with Grundy," Dante said. "He's the key to breaking open this story."

"I have some bad news for you," Jones said.

Dante glanced from Jones to Ellsworth and back, his stomach knotting.

"You're being taken off the story," Jones said. "I want you to give your notes to Hansen. She'll take the story from here."

Dante paled, his mouth went dry, his heart thumping. He clenched his jaw, sucked in a halting breath, and exhaled slowly. "Bullshit!" Dante started to stand, but Jones waved him back down.

"Sit down! We're not done," Jones said.

Dante settled back into his seat.

Jones looked at Ellsworth, who frowned.

"It's recently come to my attention you had some history with the late Bernie Morrison," Ellsworth said.

Dante looked defiantly at Jones and Ellsworth. "Yeah. So what?"

"Your late wife had a long-running affair with Morrison," Ellsworth said.

"How did you know?" Dante asked.

"My wife is very active with the Napa Valley Arts Council," Ellsworth said. "As was your late wife, Nicole. As was Morrison."

"Nicole's been dead for more than a year. Now Morrison's dead. It's all history. End of story."

"Not quite," Jones said. "Your trashing of Morrison's wines was your payback, pure and simple."

Dante clenched his jaw and glared at Jones.

"I thought you were over her," Jones said. "I really did."

"Some things you never forget," Dante said.

"It was an affair," Ellsworth said. "Nothing more, nothing less."

"You wouldn't say that if it was your wife," Dante replied.

"It happens," Ellsworth said.

Dante stared out across the newsroom, his mind churning with memories of Nicole. "After her accident, I found her phone in the car. It was full of text messages."

"From Morrison?" Jones asked.

Dante looked at him and nodded.

Jones waited. "You said she'd been drinking."

"She was driving herself to a rehab facility in Calistoga," Dante said. "She was pregnant. She wanted to clean herself up. Get straight. Dry out."

"I'm sorry," Jones said.

Dante looked at him, distraught.

"You blamed Morrison?" Ellsworth asked.

"Wouldn't you?" Dante asked.

"I'm disappointed in you, Dante," Jones said.

Dante drew a deep breath and leaned back. "But the fact is, Morrison's wines are cheap."

Ellsworth cleared his throat and sat up straight. "They're not. You're simply wrong."

"I'm not. But even if I was, it doesn't matter now. This story I'm working on is bigger, much bigger."

Jones and Ellsworth looked at each other.

"We're cutting staff," Ellsworth said.

"I'm your senior reporter," Dante said, swallowing hard. "I've given my heart and soul to this newspaper."

"We're prepared to offer you three months' severance pay," Ellsworth said. "It's a rather generous offer."

Dante looked at the floor, shook his head in disgust, stood and glared at Jones and Ellsworth, then walked out.

The drive from Santa Rosa to Sonoma went by in a blur. Even though he had known the job would end, Dante felt eviscerated, hollowed out, numb. He had figured he had another month left. A dull ache filled his head, leaving him in a fog, unsure of where he was driving and why. In the fading light of the evening, Dante began to smile at the irony. It was the sunset of his career. He could see the encroaching night.

He pulled to a stop at the ornate gate at the end of Carmen's driveway. *What am I doing here? She's got troubles of her own. The last thing she needs is me crying on her shoulder. But what else am I going to do? Go back to my condo, open a bottle of wine, drink it, and open another? Yes. Alone?*

Dante climbed out of this Mustang, walked to the gate, and extended a finger to the buzzer. He didn't feel like drinking alone. The buzzer sounded. After a minute, Carmen's voice came over the speaker. "It's me, Dante." The gate clicked and swung open.

Carmen stood in the open doorway dressed in shorts, flip-flops, and a loose burgundy 49ers football jersey. Her toenails were painted to match. The wound on her right thigh was wrapped in a flesh-colored elastic bandage. She leaned on an aluminum crutch. Her head was covered with her black beret.

"You're looking good. More or less healed," he said.

"You're full of compliments."

"I'm serious."

"So am I."

Dante looked her. "Are you going to let me in?"

"I'm thinking about it," Carmen said.

"What's your quandary?"

"My quandary is I'm hungry and I can't cook."

"But I can," Dante said. "Is Italian okay?"

Carmen smiled. "Better than okay." She retreated a couple of steps and swept her hand into the living room and toward the kitchen. "The kitchen is all yours."

"One condition," Dante said, stepping inside and pausing beside her. "A good Italian meal requires good Italian wine."

"Never a problem."

"And the cook requires a certain amount of affection."

"Hmmm. Okay. We have some of that, too." Carmen kissed his cheek.

CHAPTER 27

The next morning, the sun was shining brightly as Dante drove back to Santa Rosa. His mood had significantly improved from the day before. Carmen was in the seat beside him, her eyes hidden behind large sunglasses. Her crutch was wedged between the seat and the console. It was going to be her first day back to the office since the shooting and she'd dressed for the occasion, wearing gray, pinstriped slacks, a white blouse, and a red scarf tied loosely around her neck. With her head capped by a black beret, she looked like a 1930s French starlet.

Despite Dante's skepticism, Carmen insisted she was ready to return to work. There was too much to do for her to sit at home while casework continued to mount. She was scheduled for a doctor's visit later in the day and explained she'd simply take a taxi. Or her secretary would take her.

Dante didn't argue. He owed her a lot. Over wine and Dante's dinner of spaghetti carbonara, she'd convinced him the separation from the newspaper was an opportunity, not a tragedy. It had taken a while for him to agree with her, but he'd eventually come around. He still had to accept the offer of severance pay. Carmen convinced him to negotiate, explaining he didn't need to take Ellsworth's offer without a response.

"You're a known quantity, a marketable quantity," she said. "That's worth something. It's a starting point for negotiating your separation."

As she talked, Dante's anger was slowly replaced with a growing sense of self-worth, the hollowness in his soul replaced with a sense he still had a lot to do. Maybe it was the wine. They say in wine there is truth. *In vino veritas.* Maybe. He still had the story, after all. Two dead men in a Napa Valley vineyard, and the target of an attempted murder sitting in the Mustang beside him. By night's end, they'd come up with a plan.

Dante swung the Mustang from the street into the parking lot of her office building and came to a stop. He turned to her. "Are you ready for this?"

"More than ready," she said. "Call me later, and let me know how it goes."

Dante didn't want to say goodbye, not yet anyway. "What are you doing this coming weekend?" She glanced at him. "I…ah…don't know. Given my condition, probably not much." Carmen looked curious. "Why?"

"Ever been to the Russian River Valley?"

"Of course."

"I have a friend…actually, he's a friend of my mother's, who has a winery, and—"

"A friend of your mother's?"

"He owns an art gallery downtown. My mother's an artist, and, well—"

"You want me to meet your mother?"

"It's not like that." Dante's stomach churned with anxiety. *But what is it like?* Was he introducing her to his mother? He struggled to find the words. "It's…it's just a chance to get away from everything for a while. It's a big house overlooking a winery, vineyards."

"A big house overlooking vineyards? It's how I grew up. Why—"

"I thought you might enjoy it."

Carmen considered the offer. "You don't want to go by yourself?"

"The house overlooks the Alex Estates winery," Dante said, trying to be encouraging. "It's owned by Alex Tercero, who has a gallery near the Wharf. He sells my mother's work. I just thought…" Dante's voice trailed off.

"I know who he is. He produces some very good wines. Some of the best."

Dante glanced at her, then looked into the distance.

"Let me think about it," Carmen said.

Dante pulled into the newspaper parking lot and nosed into his usual space as if it was a regular day. He turned off the motor and sat. He was now an outsider, no longer part of the newsroom. He wondered if he would miss the camaraderie, but dismissed the thought. He'd been too much of a loner and was never one to hang out with his co-workers after hours.

Not that it mattered. Gone were the days of the dark and smoky bars across the street from newsrooms where reporters and editors huddled after deadline, talked about their stories, and drank their whiskey shots and beer. Gone also were the days when you'd find a good job with an established company and settle in, have your two-point-three children, work your way to retirement, and collect a gold watch at your going-away party.

Now it had become everyone for himself, or herself. Companies couldn't be trusted, not even the new high-tech companies with their perks and playpen ambiance. They too were periodically swallowed by bigger fish and scrubbed and rinsed of the dilettantes, slackers, and expendables.

Dante climbed out of his car and locked the door with a beep from his key chain. He drew a deep breath and opened the door the newsroom for what could be the last time. He expected a few stares from the remaining staff members in the newsroom, but no one seemed to notice. A solitary editor sat at the copy desk, a large cup of coffee beside his keyboard. Jones was in his office and glanced at Dante as he came through the open door.

As he'd done for the past few years, Dante settled into his chair, flicked on his computer, and pulled his notebook from his side drawer. He leaned back and flipped through the pages quickly, glancing at his jumbled notes and random quotes.

He mentally raked over the cooling embers of the Morrison-Ling story yet again. There was the ever-present threat of Pierce's disease, and now he'd learned it was present in the Southern California vineyards where it was attacking the most vulnerable grape vines: the pinot noirs and the chardonnays. He thought about Muñoz, who had lifted the lid on MG Enology. *What am I missing?*

Dante put the question to the back of his mind as he considered the chaos of paper on his desk. He had to sort through every scrap of paper, deciding to toss or keep it. One thing Dante knew for sure. He wasn't going to turn over his notes to Hansen, the crime reporter. Sure, they'd worked together, but no way was he going to give his story away.

Dante looked across the newsroom, and seeing Jones was alone, he navigated the newsroom desks and rapped his knuckles on the office door.

"Come in," Jones said, without turning from his computer screen.

Dante took a seat and waited as Jones swiveled and looked at him. "So, you considered the offer?"

Dante swallowed. "I'll take it, but with conditions."

Jones frowned, slowly shaking his head. "You're not in a position to bargain, you know. This is a take-it-or-leave-it deal."

"Maybe." Dante pulled a piece of paper from the inside pocket of his coat, unfolded it, and put it on Jones's desk.

"What's this?"

Dante leaned forward. "It's a letter of agreement giving me complete rights to my wine column."

Jones looked at the paper and lifted his eyes to Dante. "The column you so reluctantly write?"

"I started it," Dante said. "I built up a pretty good following. It gets hundreds of unique hits every week. And

it's got my name on it. The Grapes of Rath. It's worthless if
I'm not the one writing it."

Jones thought for a moment. "You have a point."

"Others can write wine reviews," Dante said. "There
are many self-styled wine experts around here who want to
show off their expertise. And they'll want their own name
on it."

"So what are you going to write about?"

"I'll continue to focus on insider stuff in the wine world.
Scandals, fraud, crime. The fun stuff."

"Jesus, Dante. You don't give up easily, do you?"

"Nope."

"Let me see what Ellsworth says," Jones said.

"There's more."

"Don't push your luck, pal."

"I keep the rights to my notes," Dante said. "Everything
I've collected so far on this story."

Jones sighed. "You know, all the research belongs to
the newspaper. You gathered it as an employee of the *Santa
Rosa Sun*. That's the law."

"I know. But it's my story, not Hansen's or anyone
else's."

Jones thought about it. "Considering Ellsworth's
nervousness about the material you've gathered, he might
agree." He looked at the paper Dante had put on the desk.
"Is it all in here?"

"In the best legal language I could afford."

"I'll run it by Ellsworth," Jones said.

"I'll be cleaning out my desk," Dante said.

He headed to the janitor's closet where he grabbed a large
rolling waste container for paper recycling and dragged it to
his desk. He grabbed a handful of paper, and dropped it to
the bottom of the container with a thud.

Thirty minutes later, his drawers were empty and the top
of his desktop was clean, save for the computer screen and
mouse. He stuffed his notebooks, each dated and labeled

with the stories inside, and bound them with thick rubber bands, into his briefcase. He was done.

Jones stood at his desk. "Well, well. A clean desk."

Dante looked up. "You know a clean desk is the sign of an empty mind."

"Whatever," Jones said. He tossed the release letter on the desk. "Ellsworth signed it. He must be in a good mood."

"Why?"

"He said if you want to freelance your column, we'd probably buy it."

Dante smiled. "Thanks."

"And I was right. Ellsworth prefers not to be associated with the story. It's all yours now." Jones smiled and extended his hand. Dante shook it with finality. "The severance check will be mailed to your house." He drew a deep breath and slowly exhaled. "It's been good working with you, Dante. Best of luck." They shook hands and Dante watched Jones walk back to his office.

Dante's stomach sank. He felt there was something else he should say or do. He'd worked with Jones for better than a decade. What's there to say, he thought, but goodbye? The rest was window dressing. With a shrug, he stuffed the notebooks into his briefcase. He sipped the last of the cold coffee from his paper cup. It tasted awful. He crossed the newsroom, emptied the cup into the drinking fountain, took a sip of water, and tossed the cup in the trashcan.

With the welcome drink of water, it came to him. The part of the story he'd missed. *The girl!* The seventeen-year-old who had died in one of Santos's sprawling vineyards in the Central Valley, supposedly because she hadn't been given enough water and food while she trudged up and down the rows of vines. It had been a big deal when it had happened, reviving criticism about working conditions for grape workers, which had improved only marginally since the days of Cesar Chavez and his United Farm Workers crusade.

Dante returned to his computer screen and typed in the search topic: vineyard worker deaths, California. He came up with a dozen stories he and others had written on the topic. Carmen had dismissed the fact Santos was liable because he'd hired a labor contractor who'd been accused of negligence. The man had failed to provide adequate water in the blistering summer heat. Carmen said the woman was in California illegally. Not that it mattered.

He scanned through the stories. There it was, plain as day. The contractor was Muñoz. *Of course!* The victim's name was Helena Hernandez. The cause of death listed was dehydration. He printed out a dozen stories on the large office printer, then picked up his phone and dialed. Muñoz answered on the second ring.

CHAPTER 28

Muñoz agreed to meet for lunch the next day, saying he had a couple of things to do in the morning. Dante declined Muñoz's offer to talk at his house again. He'd had enough of the Fruitvale vigilantes. They would rendezvous at a Mexican restaurant in Old Town Oakland.

Dante rolled across the Northern Bay on the San Rafael Bridge. The late morning sun was already hot and his windows were open, the salt air swirling as he realized there was life after the newspaper, and possibly a good life as an independent journalist and blogger.

Dante parked on the street fronting the restaurant, climbed out, and studied the sandwich-board menu scrawled with the day's specials. He glanced up the street to the Oakland Convention Center. He entered the open door and immediately liked the place. Muñoz was waiting near the entrance. He shook Dante's hand softly, the traditional Mexican style of greeting that avoids a firm and vigorous grip, which is considered aggressive.

The restaurant had a concrete floor and tile walls, and conversations caromed inside the open space. A handful of customers already made the place sound full. Dante followed Muñoz to the counter, where they ordered, then took their drinks to one of the smaller tables to wait for their food. The restaurant was nouveau Mexican, a fusion of what gringos imagined Mexican food should be. Dante sipped on an iced lime drink.

"Thanks for meeting with me," Dante said.

"What can I do for you?"

Dante could dance around the topic, but decided not to wait. "I learned recently Morrison and Grundy were working on a chemical spray to stop the spread of Pierce's disease. Do you know anything about it?"

Muñoz took a deep breath and exhaled, looking out to the street as the lunch crowd began to fill the place. A line had formed at the ordering counter. He looked at Dante. "I heard about that. But I'm not sure it was successful."

Dante waited for Muñoz to volunteer more. He didn't. Dante handed him the insecticide toxicology report he'd found at Morrison's house.

Muñoz looked worried and frowned as he tried to focus. "What is it?"

"A letter from the State of California. They tested the chemical spray."

Muñoz said nothing.

"The state says the pesticide is toxic," Dante said.

"It's poisonous?"

"It depends on the concentration," Dante said. "And the amount of exposure."

Fear spread across Muñoz's face.

"I know Morrison, Grundy, and possibly others, were working on such a product. But I'm not sure about the extent of the use, or how it was applied."

Muñoz continued to stare, his eyes wide. He looked away, lifted his ball cap from his head, and brushed his hand over his salt-and-pepper hair. "Mr. Santos is a good man. I help him with his vineyards."

Why is Muñoz talking about Santos? Of course! Santos is behind the product! "Would Santos have asked you to use the spray without telling you it was toxic?" Dante asked.

"*Es posible*. But I don't think so. " Muñoz smiled weakly.

They turned as a waiter arrived with their food, gourmet-styled tacos. Muñoz looked at his food as if trying to figure out what it was. He'd ordered *carne asada* tacos. He picked one up and bit into it. Dante did the same with his crispy fish tacos. They ate most of their tacos before either spoke again.

Dante took a breath and sipped from his iced drink. "Gilberto, please, don't worry. I don't want to cause you any trouble."

Muñoz looked up, confusion clouding his face.

"I'm just trying to get to the bottom of things. Wherever I look, there you are. You were there when the girl died working in Santos's vineyard. You were there when Morrison and Grundy were stealing grapes. You were there when Morrison shot and killed Chao Ling."

Muñoz shifted uncomfortably in his seat. "It was not my fault." He shifted and twitched, as if something was eating from inside.

"I didn't say anything was your fault," Dante said.

Muñoz glanced warily to the side, as if looking for an unwanted person to arrive.

Dante also looked where Muñoz's eyes had gone, but saw no one suspicious or threatening.

"They blamed me!" Muñoz said finally, his eyes flaring angrily as he thumped the table with two thick fingers. "But I did nothing!" he hissed.

The last mouthful of food stuck in Dante's throat. Muñoz glared angrily, his eyes glistening, his face flushed. Dante reached for his drink and sipped, not taking his eyes off Muñoz. He managed a swallow. *What the hell is he talking about?* His mind raced. But he knew. *The girl. The dead girl.*

"Helena Hernandez," Dante said.

Muñoz sat back, looked left and right, and leaned forward again. "They said I did not provide enough water *por los trabajadores!*" Muñoz shook his head. "Not true, my friend. It was a lie!"

"Water for the workers?"

Muñoz exhaled, still agitated. He leaned in close again and spoke quietly, but emphatically. "It was not the water. I had large coolers with ice. I had bottles of water. I had food."

"So what was it?" Dante asked.

Muñoz winced.

Dante looked at him, waiting for him to continue. But Muñoz was having a hard time getting it out. Dante picked up the remains of his last taco and took a bite. He needed Muñoz to calm down and talk. Dante sipped from his drink and cleared his throat. "What were the workers doing that day?"

Muñoz spoke softly again. "They were spraying."

Dante squinted, trying to process the information. "Spraying? Spraying the pesticide?"

"They were spraying it on the grape vines," Muñoz said.

"With the pesticide?"

"They said it was to control the disease," Muñoz said.

"Was it the product Grundy and Morrison were working on?"

"I don't know," Muñoz said. "It could have been. Santos said his vineyards were infected. The grapes were going bad. The vines were dying."

"Sounds like Pierce's disease."

"We got the spray in a couple of large drums," Muñoz said. "My people had been spraying it since the last harvest."

"That's six months," Dante said. "Most of the winter months."

Muñoz nodded.

"Did they wear protective clothing?" Dante asked.

"Just the *pañuelo*," Muñoz said, making a motion like wrapping a bandanna over his nose and tying it behind his head.

Dante looked at Muñoz, expecting more. "So what happened?"

"The girl, Helena, got sick. She was throwing up. She said her stomach hurt. She was crying in pain."

Muñoz's face crumpled, tears filling his eyes. "No one knew what was happening," he said, staring at his plate. "I took her to the emergency room. No one knew she was pregnant." He pulled a handkerchief from his pocket and wiped his eyes. "I'm sorry, but there was nothing I could do for her."

Dante felt Muñoz's agony and was stunned at the revelation. "Don't be sorry, Gilberto. It wasn't your fault."

Muñoz's eyes were wild with emotion. "Helena was *mi sobrina*."

A jolt passed through Dante. He sat up. "What? Your niece?"

Muñoz nodded, his eyes somber. "My cousin's niece."

"I was told she had no papers."

"I arranged for her to come," Muñoz said. "We got her a Social Security card. It's all she needed to work. We always have plenty of work. So why not?"

Muñoz had been a hero to hundreds of Mexicans desperate for work and a paycheck. For them it was a dream come true, a good paying job in *el Norte*. One of them had been Helena Hernandez. A distant relative, but to Muñoz, she was family. Dante reached for his drink and took a sip. He needed proof Santos had been using the spray. The autopsy report would tell.

"Can I talk to Helena's family?" Dante asked.

Muñoz sat upright. He had not expected the request. He puffed out his cheeks as he exhaled and looked to the street, then back at Dante. Muñoz nodded and said, "*Sí.*"

CHAPTER 29

The address was in East Salinas, a neighborhood of the California city made famous by John Steinbeck in *The Grapes of Wrath*. Riding in Muñoz's big gray pickup truck, Dante felt a twinge of guilt at having co-opted the author's book title for his wine column. He tried to focus on his upcoming interview as Muñoz slowed and exited US-101. At a stoplight, he turned left, drove under the interstate, and entered a sprawling neighborhood of aging ranch homes, driveways clogged with pickup trucks, panel vans, and older sedans, many with peeling paint and missing hubcaps.

Muñoz parked behind a black pickup truck in front of a modest house. A couple of older, well-kept pickup trucks sat in the driveway. Several young boys kicked a soccer ball in a front yard of patchy grass and dirt. Muñoz looked at Dante and motioned for him to follow.

Dante trailed Muñoz, who spoke in familiar, rapid Spanish to the boys, asking if their parents were home. The boys pointed to the door, saying they were waiting for him. Muñoz was about to knock on the front door when it opened. They were greeted by a thick-bodied woman with a coppery complexion, round face, dark eyes, and black hair tied behind her head. She and Muñoz exchanged a few words in clipped Spanish Dante couldn't decipher.

They stepped into a living room filled by a large sectional, faux-leather couch with cup holders and swing-up leg rests. A rectangular coffee table filled the center of the room and functioned as table for much more than coffee. The wall opposite the large couch was dominated by a flat-screen television on a wide console.

Two men and another woman rose from the couch and shook hands with Dante, as Muñoz introduced him in Spanish before they all took seats. "This is Ophelia," Muñoz said, motioning to the woman who had greeted them at the door. "She's Helena's aunt." The woman spoke to Muñoz, who turned to Dante and asked in Spanish what he'd like to drink.

"Is *horchata* okay?" Muñoz asked, sensing Dante hadn't understood.

Dante was thirsty and said anything wet was good. He scanned their faces. Everyone was grim. They were unaccustomed to having a gringo in the room—a gringo journalist, no less.

He understood their apprehension. The gringo world surrounded them, but was impenetrable. Their interactions with the gringo world were typified by *la migra*, the immigration agents, and a host of others best avoided like cartel enforcers and the police. There also was the inevitable, yet invisible "not welcome" sign hanging on the door of many restaurants and hotels. Mexicans migrants were to use the back door, stay quiet, and, when their work was done, disappear.

Ophelia returned with a large plastic pitcher of *horchata* and ice, and filled tall, plastic glasses before settling into a chair facing Dante. He took a sip of the milky sweetened drink. The aroma of cooking beans poured from the kitchen. Muñoz said one of the men in the room was his cousin, Raoul Perez, a man who looked much like him. Another was younger, his nephew, José Perez. The other woman was Ophelia's sister.

Dante pulled out his notebook, deciding against using his recorder. A notebook was less intrusive. He was not there to interview them and didn't really need their quotes. What he wanted was the medical examiner's report in the death of Helena Hernandez.

Ophelia was the wife of Raoul Perez, the owner of the house, Muñoz explained. Dante remembered how emotional Muñoz had been while describing the demise of Helena. The family ties were distant, but Muñoz was possessive, if not protective, of them all. They were his people who worked in the vineyards. Unlike some contractors, he cared about them.

"What can you tell me about Helena?" Dante asked Ophelia.

She responded in Spanish, Muñoz listening carefully as she rambled. Dante struggled to understand, picking up on a word here and there, worried he was missing critical details of the girl's death. Dante tapped Muñoz's shoulder. "I need to know what she's saying."

Ophelia stopped suddenly and sat back, having had a lot to get off her chest. Dante could see he and Muñoz, as well as the others, carried the burden of the girl's death. Watching the way the others listened respectfully to Ophelia told him she was the hub of family.

"Helena was from the state of Nayarit," Muñoz said. "She was the daughter of Ophelia's other sister. Helena wanted to come to America to make a new life for herself."

"How old was she?" Dante asked.

"She was only fifteen when she first came."

"She'd been working in the vineyards for two years?" Dante asked.

Ophelia nodded and Dante saw she understood English quite well.

"Did you know she had become pregnant?" he asked.

Ophelia glanced at the others and said, "*Si.*"

"Do you know who the father was?" Dante asked.

Her face darkened as she said, "No."

Dante turned to Muñoz, who listened intently, trying to remember it all.

When Ophelia fell silent again, Muñoz said, "The conditions for the farm workers and grape pickers are not always so good. For young girls like Helena…" His voice trailed off. "She was so beautiful."

Dante filled in the blanks. Helena was vulnerable. There were other women working in the fields, but the vast majority of the workers were men. Young men. Far from home and working long hours. "So, what happened?" Dante asked.

Muñoz looked at his hands, then glanced at Ophelia and the others. "It is impossible to know. She did not always work for me. If she had, I could have protected her."

"How long had she been working with the spray?" Dante asked.

"It was in the spring," Muñoz said. "The weather was very warm, and we were spraying the vines."

"For Santos?"

"Yes," Muñoz said.

"For how long?"

"We had been working in the vineyards for a month when she became sick."

Dante jotted notes.

"It was not my fault. I had plenty of water and food. They blamed me!" Muñoz said, his voice rising.

Dante raised a hand to calm him.

"It was not his fault," Ophelia blurted, speaking in heavily accented English.

Dante looked at her. "Do you have the medical examiner's report?"

Ophelia rose from the couch and disappeared down the hall to the bedrooms. Muñoz spoke to the others, shaking his head. Ophelia returned, leaned across the coffee table, and handed Dante a couple of sheets of paper.

Dante swallowed hard as he read. Helena had been diagnosed with an ectopic pregnancy. She had hemorrhaged badly and suffered significant blood loss. By the time she arrived in the emergency room, she was in cardiac arrest. But the toxicology report was more revealing. Subsequent blood analysis showed she died with high levels of thiophanate-methyl in her blood, among other pathogens. Dante looked up and saw fear and sadness in their faces.

"Maybe God wanted her to die," Ophelia, said, as she wiped tears from her cheeks. "She would never harm anyone or anything. She did nothing wrong."

His eyes glistening with emotion, Muñoz said, "Don't say that. It's not true. God loved her and took her to His home."

CHAPTER 30

The next day, Dante waited in Carmen's living room.

"What am I supposed to bring?" Carmen asked from her bedroom.

"Whatever you want," Dante said, still a little agitated from his visit with Muñoz the day before. It was Saturday morning, and he'd agreed to be at Tercero's winery and weekend house for lunch. "They have a pool. We'll eat well. Alex is something of a gourmand. Something casual, but nice for a dinner out. I don't know."

"A pool? A nice dinner?"

"C'mon," Dante said. "Let's go."

Carmen disappeared into her walk-in closet. Dante sighed, stepped into the bedroom, and sat on her bed, where Carmen had laid a bright pink and green overnight bag.

"Bring a swimsuit, if you want to sun yourself, shorts, a dress, and a nice blouse or two," he said.

"Really?"

"And whatever else you want." He watched as she carefully folded a couple of items and slipped them into the bag.

Finished, she turned to him with a worried look. "Are you sure about this?"

"What do you mean?"

"About this weekend."

Dante tried to decipher her question. "You mean us?"

"I'm not sure I'm ready to meet your mother and her longtime boyfriend."

Dante took her hand and leaned close for a kiss. Carmen turned away, giving him only a cheek. He kissed it lightly.

Dante held her hand as she sat on the bed. "Look at it like this. We've know each other for a short while, but we get along very well, don't we?"

Carmen dropped her gaze and pursed her lips in thought. "Yes."

"And with all that's happened lately, you don't want to be left alone in this house while I go away for the weekend."

"Yes, but…"

"So, we spend time together in a really nice place. It'll take your mind off all of the shooting and everything else."

"It's just that…."

"What?"

Carmen pursed her lips.

"Is it me?" Dante asked. "You're afraid it's too fast?"

"It's not you. Maybe I'm not ready to jump into this."

Dante looked at her, pondering. "Okay. The place isn't far. If at any time you feel uncomfortable and want to leave, just say so. We will. We'll jump in the car and go."

Carmen's eyes brightened, looking relieved. "Are you sure? Won't it be rude to just up and leave?"

"Don't worry," Dante said. "We can find an excuse. We'll say you're not feeling well. Whatever."

"You won't be mad at me?"

"Not at all."

Carmen leaned against him, slipping her an arm around his neck. "You're sweet." She kissed him. Dante pulled her close, but Carmen put her hands on his chest, resisting his embrace, and said, "I need to finish packing."

Dante smiled, pleased she'd acquiesced, and stepped into the kitchen where Carmen had left an opened bottle of cabernet. He pulled the stopper and poured himself a small glass.

"Starting a little early, aren't you?" she said from the middle of the living room. "Are you the one who's nervous now?"

Dante lowered his glass and ignored her remark. "It's the weekend. You want a glass?"

"I can wait," Carmen said. "We'll be at the winery in less than an hour."

Dante drank from his glass. "Have you been to Alex Estates?"

Carmen shook her head. "There're a lot of boutique wineries in the Russian River Valley. I haven't visited them all."

Dante gazed, admiring her figure. She wore tan pleated culottes extending just below her knee, covering the wide gauze and flesh-colored elastic bandage that encircled her thigh. Her ensemble was completed with a burgundy cotton blouse and gold sandals. Her beret sat tilted on her head, covering her scalp so you wouldn't know a bandage was under it. The dark stubble of her returning hair was now evident, and her brown eyes glowed like glassy chestnuts. The bag was at her feet.

"How do I look?"

"Great. Let's go."

Once in the car, they rode in silence, Dante's mind drifting back to his story. No suspects in Carmen's shooting had surfaced, according to Sonoma County sheriff, despite the man's insistence his department had cast a wide net, meaning he wasn't really sure where to look. The Ling murder was still an open case, the Napa district attorney had told him. Dante surmised the DA could not do much more with the Morrison-Ling case and had yet to make a decision about filing charges, if any. Against whom? Dante wondered.

Dante was having a hard time thinking of himself as an independent journalist, a lone ranger in the news business. His instincts were to go to the newsroom, meet with Jones, and decide what to do. But no more meetings with Jones. Forcing himself to take on his new role, he'd sent out a shotgun blast of emails, querying a host of Bay Area news outlets about carrying his column.

In the meantime, since Ellsworth had given him the rights, he'd created a new website and posted a couple of brief updates on the Ling-Morrison murder story. It was more fun than he'd thought. He realized he was free to write what he knew to be true, as well as what he thought about it all.

He'd written a speculative piece positing a connection between the two deaths and the shooting of Carmen Carelli, but stopped short of reaching a definitive conclusion, which could be suicide in the news business. By writing what he suspected to be true, but couldn't prove, he could later say he'd first speculated about the truth before anyone else. If it all played out like he thought, he could use his foresight to market his newly independent wine blog. He knew there was a connection, and the DA probably did as well, but Dante knew he was the only one who was writing about the connection publically.

Carmen had pushed her car seat back, placing her left foot on the dashboard and over the crutch she had wedged beside her seat. Dante glanced at her painted toenails and traced the line of her leg to the edge of her split skirt now hiked up over her knee. The beret sat tilted on her head, strategically covering the head wound. His attention was jarred back to the road when he hit the shoulder, the car rumbling and bouncing before he brought it back onto the pavement.

Carmen frowned. "Pay attention to the road. You have precious cargo."

Dante felt a knot growing in his stomach as the reality of the weekend loomed. He *was* nervous about bringing Carmen to Tercero's wine estate and tried to convince himself this was not a grand introduction of a new relationship. *So, what is it?* He still didn't have an answer. It had been a year since he'd been involved with anyone. Carmen was smart, aggressive, and voracious. Yes, it had been fast.

He was overdue for a relationship. *So, what's the big deal about this weekend? Why am I nervous?* Maybe he was more excited about Carmen than he cared to admit. She was a tiger in her own right, though she'd had a rough go of it lately. What was the attraction? She was not a stray, but a polished, reserved, educated woman like others who tended to populate the wine world. Maybe even a bit dangerous. He liked that.

Dante had convinced himself this weekend was a quick getaway, an overnighter with a friend. Nothing more. Still, the knot in his stomach tightened as he braked and turned onto the road at a carved wooden sign: Alex Estates. A tree-lined, paved road wound between vineyards and ended at a small parking lot where Dante stopped and turned off the engine. He drew a deep breath, trying to tamp down his anxiety.

"I still don't know if this is a good idea," Carmen said.

Dante frowned. It was too late to turn back. "Don't worry. It'll be fine. C'mon. Let's check out the winery."

They climbed out of the Mustang and into brilliant sunshine. The sky was clear, and the heat was softened by a light breeze. Dante shaded his eyes to survey the place. The vines looked strong and healthy, well maintained, the leaves wriggling in the wind.

This was the Russian River Valley viticulture area, Dante reminded himself, and Tercero's winery was in the Green Valley sub-district, perfect for its prized lighter wines. Tercero's winery looked perfect, almost too perfect.

A rectangular building rose across the parking lot, and beyond it were barnlike structures Dante guessed housed the working part of the winery. The winery was built in rustic Northern California style with pitched and shingled roofs. Dante eyed an asphalt drive curving past the tasting room and barns and up a hillside to where a two-story home provided a commanding view of the vineyards and the hills beyond. No wonder his mother loved to come to Tercero's estate to paint the vineyards.

Dante held Carmen's left hand as she leaned on the crutch under her right arm so she didn't put weight on her wounded right leg. They crossed the parking lot to the tasting room.

The floor inside was stone tile, the walls of decorative wood with thick varnished beams overhead. Paintings adorned the walls.

"My mother's work," Dante said, motioning to the unframed canvases. Beside each was white, hand-lettered price card, as if in a gallery. They stepped closer to a seascape, the beach cutting across the painting at an angle, waves pounding the sand, gulls gliding overhead. A solitary couple walked in the distance, hand-in-hand. The scene made him feel lonely.

"I like it," Carmen said.

Low tables and padded chairs made from finished barrel staves filled a corner of the tasting room, along with the obligatory racks of winery wear. Displays of the various Alex Estate vintages gleamed in the glow of overhead lights. Dante liked it. He liked it all.

Dante's phone rang. He pulled it from his back pocket and looked at the screen. "My mother," he said, placing the phone to his ear.

"Where are you?" Antonia asked.

"In the tasting room."

"Why?" she said. "We've got plenty of wine up here. And lunch. We're waiting."

CHAPTER 31

Tercero's multi-car garage had several open bays. Dante parked in one and climbed out. He took Carmen's bag in one hand and waited as she adjusted her beret and drew a deep breath. Doubt spread across her face, but she stepped forward unsteadily, yet with determination.

"Don't worry," he said, mustering as much confidence as he could. Even so, anxiety gripped his chest as he climbed the several steps to a varnished wooden front door, which opened just as he raised his hand to knock.

Antonia filled the doorway, greeting them with a wide smile, holding a glass of white wine in one hand and her vape in the other. "Oh, hello, dear," she said, leaning forward to peck Dante on the cheek. She slipped her vape into the pocket of her jeans and extended her hand. "This must be Carmen!" Antonia took her left hand. "So nice to meet you."

Antonia turned to Dante and smiled. "She's a sweetheart!" she said, then whispered to Dante, "and part of the Carelli family, no less," loud enough for Carmen to hear.

"Mama, please."

"Leave the bag there for now," Antonia instructed. "You can get settled later. Lunch awaits."

Dante glanced at Carmen, rolled his eyes, and followed Antonia down a short hall and into a gourmet kitchen with a broad granite-topped kitchen island topped by a built-in sink and stovetop. A couple of bottles of chilled chardonnay sat on the island, wet with beads of moisture.

A stout, dark-complexioned woman with a woven braid of black and white hair trailing down her back turned from the counter and smiled. She had a kind face, creased with age, and used the back of her hand to brush errant hair from her forehead. "This is Maria," Antonia said. "She helps us here on the weekends. She's a wonderful cook, as you will soon find out."

"*Hola*," she said, turning back to the counter and to mixing. Something struck Dante about the woman's appearance. He didn't know why, but he was having a moment of déjá vu. His gaze lingered as he searched his memory, following Antonia outside.

They passed through opened French doors to the patio where Tercero stood beside a table shaded with a large, rectangular canvas umbrella and covered with four place settings and a collection of covered serving dishes. Tercero wore pleated khakis shorts and a white polo with the Alex Estates logo embroidered in burgundy. He smiled broadly as he took Carmen's hand in his and gave her a peck on the cheek. "Carmen, it's so nice to see you again," he said, stepping back to take in her figure with a distinctly lustful gleam in his eye. "Please, have a seat." Tercero motioned to the empty chairs.

"I assume you like chardonnay," Antonia said, pulling a bottle from a chrome ice bucket and filling their glasses. After replenishing hers and Alex's as well, she shoved the bottle back into the ice as Dante and Carmen settled into the cushioned wooden chairs at the oval table, inset with granite.

"Well," Tercero said, lifting his glass, "let's toast to Carmen, a courageous survivor and shooter!"

"Thank you," Carmen said, a slight blush coloring her face. "I was just trying to stay alive." She lifted her glass and sipped.

"We're so glad you did," Tercero said.

"And to a relaxing weekend," Antonia chimed in, lifted her glass in the air, and took a long drink.

Tercero lifted the cover to a shallow metal platter filled with oysters on the half shell, arranged around a small bowl piled with lemon wedges, all sitting on a bed of crushed ice.

"Here we have a couple dozen of Tomales Bay oysters. The best there is around here." Tercero grabbed a couple of the lemon wedges, one in each hand, and squeezed juice over them.

Dante swirled his wine, sniffed and sipped, letting the chilled wine linger on his tongue. He looked at his glass thoughtfully. "Not bad. Not bad at all."

Tercero smiled. "That means you like it?"

"Yes, it does," Dante said. "A bit oaky, but it doesn't overpower the wine. I get flavors of vanilla, peach, and citrus. Nicely balanced."

"Please, Dante," Antonia said. "Are we going to hear wine talk all weekend?"

Tercero snorted. "Antonia! This is your son, and a newly independent wine critic. Let him talk!"

Antonia settled back, took a drag on her vape, and exhaled a small puff of white vapor.

"I age it in American oak for a couple of years," Tercero said. "Some people don't like the oak. But I do. It's a personal thing, I guess." He took a sip. "Help yourself to oysters," he said to Carmen.

Carmen smiled and placed several on her plate. "I love these," she said, "But of course, I don't have them often enough."

"I quite agree, you can never get enough as far as I'm concerned," Tercero said. "They're one of life's little pleasures."

"They're a notorious aphrodisiac, you know," Antonia said. "But Alex doesn't really need it," she added with a mischievous grin, glancing at Tercero.

"Ha!" Carmen said, an amused smile coming to her lips.

"It's an old wives' tale, as far as I'm concerned," Tercero said.

"No, it's true," Carmen said. "Researchers have found oysters contain amino acids that trigger the production of sex hormones."

"I wouldn't know," Dante said with a shrug.

"They're cold, slimy, and tasteless," Antonia said. "But they're no worse than other things I've had in my mouth."

"Antonia!" Tercero said. "Please."

Dante knew Antonia was on her way to getting high. As she had aged, the more she drank, the less restrained she had become. He'd grown accustomed to her crudities, but at times like this, her outbursts took him aback.

"I meant food," Antonia said, with a wry smile. "Actually, if I have to eat oysters, I prefer the barbecued oysters, the ones they roast on a grill and douse in barbecue sauce."

"We can have Maria grill them, if you want."

"Nope. I'm good with these slimy things as long as there's plenty of hot sauce around." Antonia put three glistening oyster shells on a small plate and doused each with hot sauce. She lifted a shell, and using a fork to ease one of the oysters into her mouth, chewed and swallowed. She followed it with a drink of wine and wiggled a finger at Carmen. "Go on! Your turn!"

Carmen smiled at Antonia. "Nicely done."

Carmen took an oyster from the tray, dashed each with a spot of hot sauce, and let one slide off the shell into her mouth. She chewed, swallowed, and blinked at Dante. "Not much to them, actually." Carmen glanced at Antonia. "You're right. It's no worse than other things I've swallowed."

"Ha!" Antonia said, slapping the table with a grin on her face. "I like her already. A kindred spirit!"

Tercero smiled weakly and with a quick shrug, tried to dismiss the comments. "So, how are you doing?" Tercero asked Carmen, trying to change the subject.

Carmen self-consciously patted the beret covering her head wound and gingerly adjusted her bandaged right leg under the table. "Much better. The doctors say they'll remove the bandages on my head in another few days. The bullet took a chunk of flesh from my thigh. So I'll be looking at a scar for the rest of my life."

"Will it be bad?" Antonia asked, taking a drag on her vape from the side of her mouth.

"Bullets tend to leave their mark," Carmen said.

"I think it'd be quite the conversation starter," Antonia said, a smile spread across her face.

"Mama, leave the poor woman alone," Dante said.

Tercero uncovered a bowl of creamy coleslaw and motioned for Carmen to help herself. "This is crab and coleslaw salad. You'll like it."

Carmen was about to speak when Antonia raised her hand. "Wait! I think I sense something."

Dante had a sinking feeling. Antonia was slipping into one of her routines: the psychic. She prided herself on being able read a person's aura, interpret dreams, and see past lives. He leaned back in his chair and caught Carmen's eye.

"The shooter." Antonia raised her hand, her eyes glazing. "It's coming into focus. I sense a dark force. Masculine. No, no." Antonia closed her eyes and tilted her head back. "No, it's distinctly feminine."

They all looked at Antonia in silence as she slowly opened her eyes.

"The threat is still out there," Antonia said.

"It's rather obvious," Tercero said. "The suspect hasn't been caught. Am I right?"

"Yes," Carmen said. "You're right."

"See!" Antonia said with self-satisfaction.

Carmen looked at Antonia. "I came here because I thought it would be good to get away from my house for a few days."

Dante put his hand on Carmen's. "We don't need to talk about the shooting." He scowled at Antonia.

"I'm sorry," Antonia said. "But I saw it so very clearly."

Maria bustled up to the table, placed a large serving bowl on it, and lifted the lid, revealing four large steamed artichokes.

"Ah yes," Tercero said. "Fresh artichokes from Half Moon Bay. You'll find none better anywhere on the planet. Help yourself." He pointed to two other containers. "Here we have real melted butter for dipping. I know it's bad for cholesterol, but in moderation…" Tercero used tongs to put one artichoke on each of their plates.

"Carmen represents your friend, Ricardo Santos," Antonia said to Tercero.

"I'm aware of that," Tercero said. "I know who to go to if I need legal help," he said, gazing at Carmen. "You're fearless. You're not afraid to take on tough cases."

Carmen smiled. "Well, actually—"

Dante said, "Carmen represented Chao Ling in a lawsuit against Bernie Morrison."

"He's the man who was shot by Morrison?" Tercero said.

"Yes," Dante said. "Morrison was shot by police when he refused to surrender."

"What is happening in wine country, for God's sake?" Antonia asked.

"I'm trying to figure that out," Dante said. He peeled a couple of leaves from his artichoke and chewed.

"It feels like things are spiraling out of control in the Napa Valley," Antonia said.

Tercero peeled a thick leaf off his steaming artichoke, dipped it in butter, and chewed the thick base. "From what I read," he said, "it looks like Morrison's death was a suicide. He wanted to die. No one in their right mind would point a gun at the police and not expect to die."

"A valid assumption," Dante said.

"With what you've uncovered about his and Morrison's dirty dealings, a murder/suicide is probably a good conclusion," Tercero said. "But why haven't we heard more about this stuff already?"

"Good question." Dante said. "The best answer is, no charges have been filed, so far."

"Why not?" Antonia asked.

Dante glanced at Tercero. "Any ideas?"

Tercero dabbed his lips with a cloth napkin. He reached for his glass, drank it down, and pulled the wine bottle from the bucket. The bottle was nearly empty. He poured the remainder into Carmen's glass and called out to Maria to bring another. He leaned back and gazed at Dante. "Maybe someone wants to keep things quiet."

Dante wondered how Tercero knew. But of course. He ran with some of the big dogs in the Bay Area.

Tercero turned as Maria handed him a freshly opened bottle of chardonnay. He stood and replenished the other glasses before plunging the bottle into the ice bucket. "The investigators may be giving the culprits plenty of rope to hang themselves." Tercero smiled.

"Could be," Dante said. "Morrison and Grundy's games forced a lot of wine to be quietly pulled from the shelves or not sold at all. It cost a lot of people a lot of money."

"Carmen, poor dear, seems to have been caught in the middle of it all," Antonia said. "My God! Weren't you terrified?"

"Of course," Carmen said. "Completely. But when you're in a situation like that, being shot at, you react."

"Did you think Morrison was capable of killing someone?" Antonia asked.

"I never had much direct contact with the man," Carmen said. "But what little I did gave me the creeps. I didn't know he was so unstable."

"Morrison made Carmen nervous enough that she carried a small pistol," Dante said.

Antonia frowned, as if surprised to hear it.

"After the lawsuit, I advised my client, Chao Ling, to not spend time at the winery," Carmen said. "I never really trusted Morrison after he refused to cooperate with a court order."

Tercero looked at Carmen. "But why would you become a target if Morrison is dead?"

"It's something I'd like to know, as would everyone else," Carmen said.

The conversation dropped as each finished their artichokes, leaving chewed leaves piled on plates Maria carried back to the kitchen. Dante squinted into bright afternoon sun, feeling lightheaded from the wine. He gazed absentmindedly at the sparkling pool water just a few feet away.

There was beguiling dreaminess to the valley. Wine country was an enchantress, Dante thought. Bewitching and dangerous. Maria reappeared with a platter of cheeses and a basket of crackers.

Tercero motioned for it to be placed in the middle of the table and pushed the ice bucket aside. "Can you now bring the bottle of pinot noir out here?" he asked Maria.

Maria dutifully turned back to the kitchen.

"This is a camembert, this is brie, and this is a lighter cheese," Tercero said, pointing to each. "They call it a breakfast cheese, but it can be eaten anytime."

"Marin County cheeses?" Carmen asked.

"I love them," Antonia said. "I've eaten them ever since I can remember." She cut a couple of wedges for her plate and grabbed a handful of crackers.

Maria arrived with the bottle of pinot noir and handed it to Tercero. He held the bottle up and showed the label to Dante. "This is my three-year-old pinot. I'm really happy with it." He stood slightly and leaned forward to fill Dante's glass.

Dante drank the last of his chardonnay and held out his glass as Tercero gurgled the wine into it. Dante swirled it, sniffed, and took a sip. "Nice. Very nice."

Tercero smiled. "Glad you like it." He filled the other glasses.

Dante cut a wedge of the soft cheese and pressed it onto a cracker. "I've found Morrison and Grundy were also working on another project."

They all turned to him. "Pray tell," Antonia said. "It can't be good."

"Let him talk," Tercero said, narrowing his eyes at Antonia.

"They were developing a pesticide," Dante said. "A treatment for Pierce's disease."

"What in God's name is that?" Antonia asked.

"It's a terrible thing," Tercero said with shake of his head.

"Well?" Antonia asked, waiting for an answer.

"It's a grape vine disease," Carmen said, her eyes on Antonia. "It kills them. It's been a big problem for the Southern California wineries, and it's spreading north."

Dante turned to Carmen, struck by the fact she'd never mentioned the disease before.

"Somehow I missed that," Antonia said. "It's not as if the wine shelves are empty anywhere in California."

"It's worse than you can imagine," Tercero said.

Dante looked at him intently, waiting for more. "How so?"

"The disease is up here as well, as Carmen says," Tercero said.

Dante sat upright, his heart pounding. "I'm told the state and local ag people have it under control. They even inspect and treat nursery plants coming into the area."

"The disease is endemic to this area," Tercero said. "The glassy winged sharpshooter is not the only carrier, by the way. This area is vulnerable. The disease is a real threat, I'm sorry to say."

Dante's mind buzzed. Professor Brickman had told him as much. Dante cleared his throat. "I'm told the chardonnay and pinot noir grapes varietals are especially vulnerable."

Tercero's eyes opened wide. "Yes. They are."

"And those grapes are primarily grown here in the Russian River Valley," Dante said.

"I'm afraid you're right again," Tercero said. "I've been battling the disease for the past several years."

"Here? In this vineyard?" Dante asked, surprised.

"For the most part, when the government people say it's under control, they're right," Tercero said. "But that doesn't mean it isn't here." He drank from his wine, pushed his chair back, and stood. "C'mon. Drink up. Let me show you something."

"Where are you going?" Antonia asked.

"To the vineyards," Tercero said. "You're welcome to come."

"I've seen them. I've been painting them for years," Antonia said, and looked at Carmen. "I'm going to nap in the sun, right over there, just like an old cat," she said, pointing to one of the lounge chairs. "Care to join me?"

"I think I will," Carmen said. "You boys go for a walk."

Dante turned to Tercero, who swallowed the last of his wine and turned toward the steps leading from the patio.

CHAPTER 32

Tercero pushed open the gate in the wrought iron fence surrounding the pool and Dante followed, hurrying down a graveled path through shrubs to the paved driveway. Tercero stopped at the road to survey his vineyards. Dante came beside him and scanned the outer perimeter of the estate where the dense green of redwood trees formed a natural barrier to the coastal winds.

"These are mostly new vines," he said, sweeping his hand toward several of the nearest vineyards. "We put them in three years ago. We should get good fruit from them this year, and certainly next."

"What are the grapes?"

"Pinot noir."

"Can I take a look?"

"This isn't what I want to show you."

Tercero turned and continued along the edge of the asphalt drive. They walked about half a mile, passing two more fenced vineyards.

The sun was high and hot, and Dante squinted in the bright light. A dull ache at the back of his neck had reached his forehead. Tercero knew about Pierce's disease as a matter of survival. Dante was convinced he'd been misled by officials who insisted the disease was not a problem in Northern California wine country. The prevalence of the disease was worse than they wanted to admit, certainly to the news media, which would sound the alarm. News of a deadly grape vine epidemic on the heels of unsolved wine country murders could be a yet another blow to the business.

They stopped at a metal fence gate that Tercero unfastened and pushed open. Stepping into the wide space between the rows of vines, they walked on sparse, dried grass to the middle of the vineyard. Tercero lifted a cluster of chardonnay grapes, yet to reach their full maturity.

"These are healthy grapes and vines," he said, letting the grapes hang freely before turning and walking to the far edge of the vineyard, nearly to the shadowy redwoods. Dante followed.

"This is the problem." Tercero lifted a few withered grape leaves, each with brown spots as if they'd been scorched. He grabbed a cluster of grapes. Half of them were dried and wrinkled.

Dante squinted in the sunlight. "Pierce's disease," he said.

"I'm afraid so." Tercero lifted his gaze and surveyed the rest of the vineyard, sweeping his hand toward the perimeter. "It's along this far edge now. It's moved from one section of vines to the next over the past few years. We try to stay ahead of it by eradicating the infected vines. But it's not easy."

"I see," Dante said. "How did you find this? Do you patrol the vineyards yourself?"

Tercero grunted. "No. I have a good man who helps me manage the vineyards. Gilberto Muñoz. He's one of the best."

Dante's stomach tightened. *Muñoz.* His mind raced. "I think I know him," Dante said. It was coming together. *Of course. Maria. The woman in the kitchen.* Now he knew why he recognized her. *Muñoz's wife.* She'd given him coffee the morning of the interview at his home.

"You do?" Tercero asked.

"He manages crews of migrant workers, grape pickers."

Tercero narrowed his eyes. "He's been invaluable to me."

"He works for other wineries as well."

"Of course," Tercero said. "His services are in high demand."

"I came across his name as part of the investigation into the Morrison and Ling murders."

"Really? Didn't know he was involved."

"He wasn't," Dante said. "He was at the winery when the shooting happened in the vineyard."

Tercero took a deep breath. "I hope the district attorney doesn't drag him into that mess. I don't want to lose him."

Dante massaged his temples, trying to push away the encroaching headache. "I don't think they will. He was only working at Morrison Creek. He ran when the shooting started."

"I hope he wasn't hurt."

"No, not at all. Morrison and Grundy were working on a pesticide to kill the insect carrier. It would supposedly stop the spread of Pierce's disease."

Tercero squinted into the distance as if he hadn't been listening.

"The pesticide might be useful to you," Dante said.

Tercero looked at him, as if the words had just registered. "I've heard about it."

"Would you use it?"

"I might," Tercero said. "But from what I know, it's experimental."

"The state says it's toxic," Dante said.

"My operation here is small," Tercero said. "Too small for experiments for an unapproved product. But I can't afford to lose any more grapes."

"Others might be willing to test it," Dante said.

"Maybe the big guys. They can afford to lose a vineyard or two. But people like me? No way."

Dante's mind raced. *The big guys. Like Santos, who has tens of thousands of acres of grapes.* "But if it was proven to be safe, you'd use it?"

"I'm losing grapes every year to the damned disease," Tercero said. "It's killing my bottom line. So, hell yes."

They looked out at the rows of vines stretching to the distant tree line in one direction and to the fermentation barns and tasting room in the other. A couple of cars pulled into the winery parking lot, disgorging eager wine tasters.

"Seen enough?" Tercero asked.

Dante followed Tercero out of the vineyard, along the road, and back up the drive to the house. *Tercero's not telling me everything he knows.* Dante knew where his search would take him next.

Like sunning seals on the California coastline, Antonia and Carmen lay sprawled on the padded lounge chairs. Antonia was asleep, her mouth agape, her head lolling to the side, her sunglasses on, looking comfortable under the overhead shade.

At the sound of the gate closing, Carmen raised her head, lifted her sunglasses to her forehead, and squinted at Dante from her similarly shaded lounge chair. "How was your adventure?" she asked.

"Good," Dante said, as he sat on the lounge beside her. "Alex showed me where disease is killing his vines."

"Is it bad?" she asked, pushing her sunglasses down her nose look at him.

"Yes and no," Dante said. "It's spreading through his vineyard, but he's staying ahead of it."

"That doesn't sound good."

"It's not. He's ripping out parts of his vineyard every year."

"Hmmm," Carmen said, closing her eyes and leaning her back.

"How's the sun?" Dante asked.

"Hot. We pulled the large umbrella over us."

"I see," Dante said. "Did you talk with Antonia?"

"She fell asleep not long after you left."

Dante glanced at his mother. She was quite browned, the result of successive weekends spent beside the pool. Dante was proud of how she'd taken care of herself, and despite her age, had maintained a modest figure. Still, Antonia's one-piece swimwear was a bit too revealing for a woman her age, he thought. And Antonia wasn't doing her skin any favors by sunbathing.

"Mother, put sun lotion on, for God's sake," Dante said, waving a lotion bottle.

Antonia lifted her sunglasses to her forehead and squinted. "I'd prefer a glass of chardonnay, actually. Be a dear," Antonia said, reaching for the lotion. "Get me a glass while I do this, okay?"

Dante handed the lotion to his mother.

"Anyone ready for refreshments?" Tercero said, appearing from the kitchen with an ice bucket, the neck of a wine bottle protruding from it, and four wine glasses. The bucket clunked on the table. He arranged glasses side-by-side and poured wine in each, saying, "I hear no nays. The motion passes by a unanimous vote."

CHAPTER 33

The singe and tingle of his sunburn didn't bother Dante as he sat that evening with Carmen, Antonia, and Tercero in a French-style bistro in downtown Sebastopol.

He'd changed into his swimsuit after the vineyard visit and joined the others on the chaise lounges at poolside. He had soon dozed due to a combination of the wine, the walk, and an overall exhaustion from his investigation. He'd slept for more than an hour and failed to use the sun lotion, despite his sharp rebuke of his mother for doing the same. Yet, the tingle made him feel alive, reminding him he was, after all, a physical being. Dante's mind drifted as he struggled to follow the table conversation amidst the cacophony of the restaurant dinner crowd.

After his nap, from which he'd awoken with a pounding headache, he'd swum in the pool, an activity he had loved since his days on the high school swim team. He hadn't bothered to work out in Tercero's personal gym, which he viewed with envy: a small room overlooking the pool and equipped with a treadmill, a padded and hinged weight-lifting bench, and a rack of free weights.

Tercero also had stripped down to his swimsuit, and after swimming several laps had toweled off. He had a barrel chest and a noticeable softness around the belly. Dante respected Tercero for the fact he kept himself relatively fit, despite his appetites. For a man in his late sixties, he looked at least ten years younger.

Dante wondered why Tercero spent so much time with his mother. He had money, and with his rugged, chiseled face, his thick mane of white hair, trimmed beard, and flashing dark eyes, could have just about any woman he wanted. Women half his age would welcome the chance to make and keep him happy. He watched with a pang of jealously as, more than once, Tercero studied Carmen, spellbound by her throaty voice, her olive skin, her sculpted lips.

Dante gazed at Carmen as the dinner conversation rolled on. She was limiting her wine consumption, only sipping and rarely emptying her glass. *Smart.* She was maintaining her composure, unsure of Dante's small family dynamics.

Tercero brought several bottles of his own wine to the restaurant. Since he no longer had a taste for craft beer, nor the stomach for mixed drinks, he explained, nor a desire to pay the inflated prices that restaurants charged for medium quality wine, he'd pay the corkage fee.

As the wine was poured, Antonia put her menu down and talked about sun signs, assuming Carmen was an interested audience. Dante was no longer embarrassed by it, though he placed very little credibility in the intricacies of astrology. Whenever he had scoffed at what he called her hocus-pocus, Antonia became irate and would point to vague astrological insights, forcing him reluctantly to concede she might be right after all.

"It's why Dante and I have such a good relationship," Antonia said, sipping from her freshly filled glass. "I'm an Aries, if you haven't guessed already, and Dante's an Aquarius... in the Age of Aquarius. He's perfectly situated in time and space."

Dante felt himself flush. Antonia's left eyelid was beginning to droop, a sign she was reaching her limit.

"You see, the way it works is we're both independent," Antonia continued. "Neither of us is willing to just sit back and let things take their course. You know what I mean?"

Carmen listened, not reacting.

"We both appreciate dynamic solutions to life's situations and problems," Antonia said. "We often disagree on what those solutions might be, but it keeps life lively, doesn't it dear?"

"I suppose," Dante said, glancing from Carmen to Tercero, who continued to gaze at Carmen, barely listening to Antonia.

"It's not like we don't appreciate tradition," Antonia continued. "It's just too many people are afraid to deviate from the past and try new things."

"I've heard an Aries can be very creative," Carmen said, "which is probably why you've spent a lifetime in art."

Antonia's face lit up. "You're right! See! I knew you would understand what I'm talking about. I couldn't imagine living my life any other way, frankly. I've always dreaded having a boss. I can't imagine such a thing!"

Dante rolled his eyes. "Bosses are a necessary evil for most of us mortals. They're not all evil."

Antonia squinted and took a furtive drag on her vape, exhaling a small puff of vapor.

"You'd better put the pipe away or you're going to get us tossed out of here for violating the smoking ordinance," Dante said.

"Why?" Antonia protested. "It's not smoke. It's vapor."

Dante sighed, wondering how long his mother could keep herself upright. She was an imposing figure, big-boned, a solid five-foot-eight, her skin browned from the sun, her dark eyes flashing. She was about the same height as Tercero but, when side-by-side, seemed to be taller.

"You're good for Dante," Antonia continued, as if she were in a private astrology session with Carmen. "As a Taurus, you're down-to earth, practical, not prone to Dante's flights of fantasy. He's so obvious about it. When his eyes go distant, you know he's out there."

Carmen grinned, looking embarrassed, and smiled sympathetically at Dante. He felt her hand slip onto his thigh, where she left it.

"Please, Mother," Dante said. "I'd like to remind you I'm not the only one at the table who's prone to flights of fantasy."

"It's an affliction of the creative, dear," Antonia said. "There's no getting around it." She took another sip of wine, cleared her throat, and refocused on Carmen. "I'm just thinking about all of the good things a Taurus brings to the table," she said, shifting her gaze to Dante. "You can only find your way in the world if your eyes are open, dear. That's what I'm talking about."

"Please go on," Carmen said with a polite smile.

Dante glanced at Carmen, suspecting she was amused at his increasing discomfort with Antonia's ramblings. Carmen squeezed his thigh once again, a gesture he took as reassurance.

"As I said," Antonia continued, "Aquarians can be very progressive and unconventional. This can lead to conflicts on politics and social issues, even taste in art, music, and literature. A Taurus likes to find what works and stick with it. This annoys an Aquarian. Oh, another thing, both signs can be stubborn."

"Speak of being stubborn," Tercero said. "I think you can claim the prize."

Antonia shot a fiery glance at Tercero, but her face softened into a smile. "I won't argue."

Tercero grinned, clearly pleased he'd landed a zinger.

Antonia sipped again from her wine. "Alex here is a Leo, which is why we have such a fiery relationship."

Tercero scowled at his wine glass, as if it displeased him.

"Fiery?" Carmen said.

"Oh, dear, you don't know the half of it." Antonia looked at Tercero, and reached out, placing her hand on his. "Poor Alex. You see we're also very independent, self-motivated people."

Tercero looked at her and smiled, his face softening.

"We both guard our own work and interests. Alex pursues his business interests and I my art. Neither of us could possibly possess the other," she said, making quote marks in the air. "We respect each other's right to do their own thing."

"It's true," Tercero said, putting his other hand on hers.

"That's not to say we haven't had our difficulties," Antonia said. "I embarrass Alex on occasion, since I always say what's on my mind."

"She's getting better," Tercero said.

"Alex actually *cares* what other people think," Antonia said with a derisive tone.

"You on the other hand…," Dante said.

"Guilty as charged!" Antonia shouted, grinning as she flung her arms out wide.

People around them turned to look.

Tercero sat back and shrank down, then looked up at the waiter who appeared at the table. "Now that all has been revealed," Tercero said, straightening up, "how about we order food?"

Back at the house later in the evening, Tercero and Antonia excused themselves for the night, citing an exhausting day. Tercero slipped his arm around Antonia's waist to guide her up the steps to the second-story bedroom. Dante was disappointed at the amount of wine Antonia had consumed. He knew she liked to sip throughout the day, whether or not she was painting. Watching her drink was becoming difficult.

Saying he wanted some fresh air and to sit by the pool, Dante took the opportunity for a night swim. It was a chance to move his body, sober up, and maybe work some of the alcohol out of his system. He slipped into his suit, grabbed a towel from the bathroom, and pattered barefoot down the hall and to poolside with Carmen, who sat and watched.

After several laps, Dante paddled about, and soon climbed out, his skin dimpling at the night chill. He grabbed a towel and began to dry himself, glancing up to the second-floor window where Tercero's figure was silhouetted. The bedroom light went dark.

"Let's go in," Dante said. Carmen had also seen the figure in the window.

It was a perfect Sunday for brunch by Tercero's pool. The sun was high and warm, softened by a slight breeze. A few puffy clouds drifted in the sky, as if placed for effect, a diversion from an otherwise empty blue sky.

Tercero had made huevos rancheros, with a side of roasted redskin potatoes, diced pork in a red chili sauce, and avocados. He ladled Maria's homemade chili sauce over the breakfast, and served it with warmed tortillas and a thermos of dark roasted coffee. He'd also mixed a pitcher of California champagne and orange juice chilled with ice.

Tercero gazed across his vineyards, sipped coffee, and turned to Carmen. "Aren't you worried about another attempt on your life?"

Carmen sipped her mimosa. "Of course. Who wouldn't be?"

"Do you have police protection?"

"I had it at the hospital for a few days," Carmen said. "But now, no. The thought of round-the-clock protection is unnerving. I'd rather take care of myself."

Tercero considered her response. "Take care of yourself? You're at quite a disadvantage now, I'd say."

"I can still use a gun," Carmen said.

Tercero looked dubious.

"Carmen's house is well-protected," Dante said. "It's just down the hill from the Carelli family mansion. It's surrounded by a vineyard and a sturdy fence."

"From the sound of it, a professional went after you. A fence and vineyard is only going to provide cover for such a person."

"But they missed," Dante said.

"They might not miss a second time," Tercero said.

Carmen looked from behind her wraparound sunglasses, saying nothing.

"You could stay here," Tercero offered. "No one knows you're here, and, well, the place is virtually unapproachable without being seen."

Carmen considered the offer. "I don't want to be a burden. Really, there's no need. Besides, I'd have to hire a guard, and, well, it's not cheap."

"What's your life worth?" Tercero asked.

Carmen pushed her eggs around her plate. "I'll keep it in mind."

Tercero smiled.

Antonia leaned back, stretched her arms above her head, and yawned noisily, as if having heard enough of Tercero's offers.

"Are you going to paint today?" Tercero asked Antonia. "It looks like the perfect day for it."

Antonia cleared her throat, her eyes obscured behind her sunglasses. "Every day's a good day to paint." She poured herself a tall glass of the bubbling spiked orange juice and drank half of it down. "But yes, dear. I am."

Dante's phone dinged, telling him he had a text message. He picked up the phone. It was from Marvee. The text read simply, "Simon is dead."

Dante's heart pounded, his mind racing. *What the hell?* He looked at the message and typed a response. "Where?"

The phone dinged with a reply. "Shady Oaks. You'd better get here fast."

Dante looked at Carmen, at Tercero, and then his mother. "Simon Grundy is dead. We've got to go."

Carmen frowned and lifted her sunglasses to her forehead. "What? How do you know?"

Dante showed her the phone.

"What happened?" Tercero asked.

"I don't know," Dante said. "But I need to get over there before they remove Grundy's body."

Antonia pushed her chair back and stood, dropping her cloth napkin onto her plate. She began to collect her dishes.

Their weekend was over.

CHAPTER 34

After saying hasty goodbyes, Dante sped back to Sonoma, dropped Carmen off, thanking her for joining him for the weekend, and promised to call her later. Carmen said she'd had more than enough involvement in the case, and quipped, "Don't get yourself arrested, okay?" He raced north to the Shady Oaks winery, his mind buzzing with this latest wine country death.

A sheriff's deputy motioned for Dante to stop, forcing him to brake hard at the entrance to the Shady Oaks winery parking lot. He lowered his car window and looked up at the deputy. "I'm with the news media, officer."

"You'll have to leave," the deputy said. "This is a crime scene."

Dante frowned, but pulled out his wallet to show the deputy his press pass, which identified him as a *Sun* reporter, even though he no longer was. "I'm a journalist."

The deputy was overweight with pink cheeks and a neck bulging over his buttoned collar. He took the pass in his fingers, examined it, and staring at Dante through the open window, handed it back. "You're the guy who's writing about the Morrison shooting, right?"

"That's me, alright," Dante said.

The deputy sucked in his gut, hitched up his pants, and adjusted the thick leather gun belt at his waist. He looked into the distance and back at Dante. "We got ourselves another one." The deputy scowled.

"Another one what?"

The deputy pointed a finger to the side of his head and mimed pulling a trigger.

A sinking feeling gripped Dante's stomach. He swallowed hard. "Suicide?"

The deputy frowned. "But I'm not authorized to talk to the press."

"Who is?"

The deputy shook his head, unwilling to answer the question. "You'll have to move your car, pal. We need to keep the lane clear for emergency vehicles."

"Move it where?"

The deputy pointed to an empty corner.

Dante pulled forward and parked. He climbed out and headed to the winery door, but the deputy had repositioned himself in front of it, waiting with thumbs jammed inside his belt, barring entry. Dante pulled out his phone and tapped in Marvee's number. She answered.

"Marvee? Are you inside?"

"It's terrible!" she said, her voice panicked. "They killed him!"

"Who did it?"

"I can't talk right now."

"I'm outside. Come see me."

"I'll try."

Dante turned to the deputy, who narrowed his eyes. They turned as an ambulance pulled into the parking lot, its lights flashing, and came to a sudden stop nearby. Three medical technicians jumped out, pulled a chrome-framed gurney from the back, and wheeled it into the winery.

Marvee came through the doorway and stepped outside. "He's a friend," she said to the deputy. "You can let him inside."

"Not without official permission," the deputy said.

Moments later, medical technicians wheeled a gurney loaded with a body draped with a sheet out the door and past them to the open back doors of an ambulance. Marvee and Dante watched as the gurney was hoisted into the back of the ambulance and the doors slam shut.

Marvee turned to Dante and hugged him, burying her face against his chest. "Simon didn't deserve to die. Not like that." She looked up at him. "What's going on, Dante?"

"You don't think it was suicide?"

Marvee pulled back and looked at him with watery eyes. "He has a wife and child. There was no reason for him to take his own life."

"You just never know, Marvee. People can be depressed or scared and never show it," Dante said. "Who found him?"

"I came to work early. I had things to do. I noticed the office door was open. When I looked into the office..."

"A suicide shot is usually to the side of head or in the mouth."

Marvee sucking in a halting breath. "Side of the head."

"But if he was murdered, the killers would want it to look like a suicide...."

"A gun was on the floor beside him," she said.

"Sounds like a suicide." Dante felt badly for her. "First Morrison and Ling. Someone tried to take out Carmen. Now Grundy's gone."

"Everyone liked him," she said.

"Not everyone. There could be plenty of people who wanted him dead."

"He was one of the nicest people I ever knew," she said.

"Maybe he knew too much?" Dante said.

Marvee wiped tears from her eyes and took a halting breath.

"C'mon, Marvee. We should talk. Let's get out of here."

"I can't just leave. I need to finish up here."

Dante's stomach churned. *Why Grundy? Who'd gotten to him? There are plenty of possibilities.* He mentally ran through some of the wineries defrauded by Grundy and Morrison. Even Sam Attica had said he wanted to kill the man. But it had been said in jest. Or had it? Dante regarded Marvee, and said, "You two must have been, well... very close friends."

"What are you asking?" she said.

"You know what I'm asking."

"He's married, Dante."

"You know his wife?"

"Of course. Her name's Sandy."

"Is she involved in the winery?" Dante asked.

"She runs the business end of things. Her family is pretty heavily invested in the winery."

"Where's she from?" he asked.

"LA. Her father's a movie producer. She and Simon met at wine school."

"So… you followed Grundy when he bought Shady Oaks with Morrison?"

"It was a job," Marvee said loudly. "I needed a… freakin'… job."

"All right. I get it." Dante looked at the highway. "You also know Santos?"

"Sort of. I never had much contact with him. I worked in the bottling plant for Santos's wines."

"Doing what?" Dante asked.

"I was what they called a quality assurance technician," she said. "There was a bunch of us. We unloaded the tanker trucks coming in. We had to make sure everything was sanitary, make sure the bottle-filling machines and corking machines and sealing machines worked. We had to move cases of wine around. It was tough work most days."

"I can imagine," Dante said.

"That's why I took up yoga. I hurt my back."

"What did Grundy do for him?" he asked.

"He was a winemaker, but he also worked with the guys in the microbiology department down in Modesto."

"Microbiology?" Dante asked. "Tell me about it."

"He never called himself a scientist," she said, "but you need to know about the microbiology of the vines and the chemistry of grapes and wine if you're going to be a winemaker and a consultant."

"So Grundy could be the brains behind a project to develop a spray to cure Pierce's disease."

"He could," Marvee said, sounding unsure of herself.

"Grundy knew all about wine and vine microbiology," Dante said. "Morrison knew about chemical treatments for molds and fungus. Then they teamed up to develop a spray to attack Pierce's disease."

"You're jumping to conclusions," Marvee said. "The pesticide was rejected by the state. Toxic. Remember? End of story." Marvee looked at him, eyes wide.

"Maybe," Dante said.

Dante turned to look as a couple of investigators emerged from inside the winery, one of whom was Jake Henshaw, dressed in his standard jeans, tan boots, and black fleece sheriff's vest. Dante waved, catching Henshaw's eye, but Henshaw frowned, not pleased to see Dante, and held up his hand for Dante to wait.

"Excuse me," Dante said to Marvee. "I need to talk to him."

"Whatever," Marvee said, and with a shake of her head, turned and walked back inside.

After Henshaw finished huddling with the other investigators, he walked over to Dante and said, "Why am I not surprised to see you here?"

"It's what I do," Dante said.

"I understand you're no longer with the *Sun*."

Dante drew a breath. "Word gets around fast." He suddenly feared Henshaw would cut him off since he was now independent. "So, what happened in there?"

Henshaw considered the question, but said nothing.

"It's still my story," Dante said.

"Okay," Henshaw said. "But off the record."

"Whatever," Dante said.

CHAPTER 35

The next morning, Dante awoke in his condo, his mind swirling with thoughts of Grundy and Marvee, Carmen and Tercero, and his mother.

Dante sat down at the makeshift desk he'd arranged in the second bedroom, opened his laptop, and scrolled through his emails. He had half-dozen congratulatory comments from a mass mailing announcing he would be writing independently from now forward. *But writing what?*

He unfolded the medical examiner's report and put it on his desk. *What do I have?* He looked it over, unsure of how to use it. What did it prove? The pesticide was being used extensively, despite being untested and unapproved, in a vineyard belonging to Ricardo Santos The spray was toxic. The Hernandez girl had died of complications due to exposure to it, not dehydration. He flipped open his notebook and flicked through the pages. It was time to talk to Santos. But first he had to talk to Carmen. She was the only person who understood what was at stake. And she could help.

Dante tapped the phone icon, found Carmen's number, and tapped again. The phone rang three times before she picked up.

"I need to talk to Santos," he said.

Carmen sighed into the phone, but didn't answer.

"Did you hear me?"

"Yes, I heard you." After a long pause, Carmen said, "You're still obsessed with the man."

"I have definitive proof he was using a toxic pesticide in his vineyards," Dante said. "It's what killed the Hernandez girl, not dehydration."

"The case is closed," she said.

"No, it's not."

"How do you know it wasn't dehydration?" Carmen asked.

"I have the medical examiner's report."

"You do?" she asked. "How'd you get it?"

"Sources, Carmen. Sources."

"So, what do you want from me?" she asked.

"Call him," Dante said. "Tell him he should talk to me."

"Or what?"

"I'm going to publish what I have online," he said. "It's in his best interests."

"Are you sure about this?" Carmen asked.

"Whose side are you on?" he said.

Carmen sighed noisily. "You're putting me in a bad situation. We've had some good times, you and I, but Santos is my client."

"It's why I called," Dante said. "He trusts you. He'll listen to you."

"If I call, he'll think I'm working with you," she said.

"No, he won't," Dane said. "And if I call him, he'll call you anyway."

"I don't want to be involved."

"You are already, Carmen."

She sighed again. "Okay. I'll call you back." The line went dead.

Dante went into the kitchen and poured himself another cup of coffee. Five minutes later, the phone rang.

"Okay. It's on. This morning," Carmen said. "But we have to hurry."

"Thanks," Dante said. "I'm on my way. I'll swing by your place and pick you up."

"He's not going to admit to anything, you know."

"Of course," Dante said. "But I need to lay out the evidence and let him respond."

Dante hung up, grabbed his notebook and his sport coat, and headed out the door. If the spray killed a worker, Dante knew the crime could be negligent homicide. Morrison, Grundy, and Santos were all working on the insecticide because they believed it could treat Pierce's disease. They hoped it would and could make them all millions of dollars. By the time the state figured out that it was toxic, Helena Hernandez was already dead. So there was a cover-up, Dante realized. *Did that explain the murders?* Even if it didn't, it was turning into one hell of a story. Dante's heart pounded as he slipped into the driver's seat and fired up his Mustang.

Rows of vines and fields of leafy vegetables spread across the San Joaquin Valley. Carmen was again slouched in the passenger seat, wearing her beret, her crutch wedged by the seat. "Are you sure you want to do this?" she asked.

"Yes. I'm sure."

The steady hum of the tires filled his car as Dante's thoughts returned to the day before. It had been a wild one. It had started at Tercero's place and ended at Shady Oaks. Grundy was dead of an apparent suicide. Marvee disagreed. Said Grundy had been murdered. But why?

If Grundy knew the pesticide had caused Helena Hernandez's death, he might have been riddled by guilt. *Enough guilt to take his own life?*

"So what are you going to ask him?" Carmen said.

Her question snapped Dante back from his thoughts. He glanced at her. "I want Santos to talk about the pesticide."

"You told me already. But do you seriously think he's going to tell you anything?"

"I need to give him a chance."

Carmen looked out her window. "A chance to do what? Incriminate himself?"

Dante caught her stare, telling him he was on a fool's mission. "The girl died on his land, working in one of his vineyards. She'd been spraying an illegal pesticide Santos helped develop. Ling, Morrison, and now Grundy are dead, and somehow they're all connected to it."

"I have a bad feeling about this, Dante."

"I don't like it either, but it's got to be done," Dante said. "It comes with the territory."

"He's going to deny any knowledge of it," Carmen said.

"Is that what you've advised him to do as his lawyer?"

"You think this is a circus act," Carmen said with a derisive tone. "You think you're a lion tamer who can put his head in the lion's mouth."

"Not really," Dante said. "Interesting image, though. You shouldn't worry so much. You know Santos. You've gotten him out of some tight situations. With you there, we're both better off."

"I've actually only met the man in person a couple of times."

"He's fond of women, especially ones who look as good as you," Dante said.

"That's why you brought met?" Carmen asked. "You're using me as a distraction?"

"Distraction? No. Protection? Yes. He'll pay attention to your advice and answer my questions, maybe without incriminating himself, maybe not. Regardless, he'll be more confident with you there."

"So I'm your protection," Carmen said.

"You don't need to say or do anything if you don't want to."

Carmen gazed at the passing vineyards. "You think Santos killed Grundy?"

"He may have hired someone to do it."

"A hit man?"

"Sure. Make it look like a suicide," Dante said.

"What kind of gun was it?"

"The cops told me it was a .22 pistol, probably a Walther."

Carmen asked, "Why would Santos want to kill Grundy?"

"Grundy may or may not have done himself in," Dante said. "Either way, he knew something that could bring Santos down."

"The pesticide?"

"Yes," Dante said.

Carmen gazed out the window, the sun blazing on the agricultural landscape. "A .22-caliber weapon is what they think was used on me."

Dante looked at her, then returned his gaze to the road. "You've known about the pesticide all along, haven't you?" Dante glanced at her again.

Carmen narrowed her eyes and frowned. "I'm not going to answer."

Dante smiled. "That's an admission."

"No, it's not," she said and fell silent. "But even if I did know about it, what does that prove? What does it have to do with Morrison's murder of Ling?"

"Morrison was a salesman," Dante said. "He also knew a little bit about chemical sprays from his previous business."

"I know."

"Morrison didn't know anything about grapes or wine."

"But Grundy did," Carmen said.

"Yes," Dante said. "Including the diseases that kill the vines and ruin grapes. So when Morrison learned about Pierce's disease. *Viola*! He came up an idea to create a pesticide to stop the spread of it."

"Okay," Carmen said. "It's pretty clear he could."

"But, Morrison needed a man with the technical knowledge of grapes and the pest."

"Grundy."

"Morrison knew if he could get a product that worked reasonably well, he could sell it."

"I know all of this," Carmen said.

"And who would be very interested in such a product?"

"Santos," she said.

"Of course," Dante said. "He owns thousands of acres of vineyards. Not only here, but in Spain and Italy. He also owns olive orchards. The disease can hit olive trees as well as grape vines. That's why they were testing the product on Santos's vines."

"So you've figured it out," Carmen said. "But the pesticide doesn't explain the killings."

"There's more."

"What?"

"Santos has the money and connections to take the pesticide global," Dante said.

"What exactly are you going to ask Santos, then?"

"Let me worry about that," Dante said. "The pesticide is the link. Somehow, Ling found out about it, probably from Morrison, possibly from Grundy."

"What does it prove?" she asked.

"You learned about the pesticide from Ling as well. The problem is the people who know about the pesticide are dead now, except for you."

"And you," Carmen said.

"That makes us both targets."

CHAPTER 36

Dante wheeled his Mustang onto a paved road and sped under an arched sign announcing the Santos Wine Company. He slowed as they approached a complex of concrete office buildings. Rolling to a stop at a gated checkpoint, he lowered his window. A Hispanic-looking security guard wearing opaque sunglasses and a dark brown uniform stepped out of a booth and leaned in.

"Who are you here to see?" the guard asked.

"Ricardo Santos," Dante said.

"Do you have an appointment?"

Dante looked up at the guard. "He's expecting us."

"Who's with you there?"

"Carmen Carelli. She's his attorney."

"Wait here," the guard said, retreating to the booth where he lifted a phone from a wall and made a call. Moments later, he waved them forward.

Tall cypress trees surrounded the parking lot and office complex, reminding Dante of the Italian countryside. It was Santos's attempt to soften the sterility of the concrete buildings and production complex, he thought, set in the midst of vineyards fading into the distant haze of the flat valley.

Dante parked near a building with the company name in red metal lettering affixed to the wall beside the entry door. Oak barrels were stacked to one side and large potted cactus plants lent a touch of prickly green to the bleak exterior.

Dante stepped out of the car and into the roiling sunlight. He adjusted his sunglasses and looked across the roof of the Mustang, catching Carmen's stare as anxiety gripped his gut.

"Are you sure you want to do this?" she asked again.

"Of course."

Carmen rested her crutch against the car and adjusted her black beret.

Ten minutes later, they sat on low modern couches in a spacious reception room where a couple of secretaries were at their desks, staring at computer screens. Dante wondered if they were working or surfing the Internet. Behind them, dozens of wine bottles were stacked in wrought-iron racks set against the walls. There were also several large photographs depicting Ricardo Santos with various men and women, none of whom Dante recognized, except for one with his mother's boyfriend, Alex Tercero. He gazed at the photo, which showed the two men smiling confidently, posed in front of fermentation tanks obscuring the vineyards in the background.

Dante pulled the notebook from his pocket and flipped through the pages. He'd jotted down a few questions, giving each a number. He had no grand scheme of questions to lead him to a climatic "aha!" moment. He'd been in too many interviews with paranoid, skeptical people to believe he could trick anyone into incriminating themselves. And, with Carmen there to protect him, it was nearly impossible for Santos to make a mistake. Dante preferred conversational interviews. He kept the endgame in mind and guided the subject to the goal. The precise route didn't matter.

Carmen sat beside him, a leather legal briefcase on the floor beside her feet.

Dante perused the extensive list of Santos's wine holdings posted on one wall in raised letters. His wineries included one in each of California's major wine regions, with products ranging from pricey, hand-crafted cabernets from the Napa Valley to box wines sold under his own name.

A leggy woman in a short, tight dress bustled around a corner and up to them. She extended her hand to Dante. "Hi. I'm Sofía Sokolova, Mr. Santos's executive assistant."

Dante stood to shake her hand. "I'm—"

"Dante Rath," she said, waving her hand to cut him off. "We've been expecting you."

Sokolova was a striking woman, with lightly tanned and smooth skin, ice-blue eyes, and long, straight dark hair. Dante guessed she was about five-foot-eight, and in her low-heeled shoes, stood nearly eye-to-eye with him. She shook Carmen's hand, saying, "Good to see you again, Carmen."

Sokolova turned to Dante. "Is this your first time to our facility?"

"Yes, first time," Dante said.

"Let me give you a short orientation." Sokolova moved with athletic grace and pointed to the wine rack with a slender, yet muscled arm. "Santos Wine Company is comprised of twenty-one individual brands, many here in California. These brands include a wide range of products, from champagnes to carefully aged port wines to boxed blends. Mr. Santos believes everyone deserves to enjoy a glass of wine. But he knows the wine-consuming public has very different tastes and budgets. So he's committed to providing a range of choices."

Dante clenched his teeth. "I'm quite familiar with Santos wines."

"Oh," Sokolova said, pausing. "Well, do have any questions?"

"There's a lot in the Santos world that's beyond the wine display."

"What are you interested in, specifically, Mr. Rath?"

"Well, Santos owns wineries and olive oil operations in Spain and Italy. I don't see them listed there."

Sokolova smiled politely. "Yes, of course. Those are part of our sister company. Santos International."

"And what about all of the other operations, such as the bottling and distributing plants, as well as your microbiology research?"

"Those operations are off-site," Sokolova said. "They're part of the organization we don't often talk about."

"Why's that?"

Sokolova narrowed her eyes. "Most people aren't interested."

"I'm curious about the microbiology," Dante said.

Sokolova gave him a quick shake of her head. "It part of the research department. I'm not sure what they're doing, and even if I did, I probably couldn't tell you. I'm not a scientist."

"Whatever," Dante said, frustrated.

"Come with me," Sokolova said, heading down the polished concrete hall, her heels clacking, her ponytail swishing. Dante and Carmen followed. "Mr. Santos is very busy," she said over her shoulder. "You didn't give us much advance notice, you know."

"I'm sorry, but this was urgent," Carmen said.

Sokolova grabbed the brass handles on a pair of tall, dark wood doors and tugged them open. "Here we are."

They entered a large office of gray carpeting, redwood paneled walls, and a view of vineyards shimmering in the heat, stretching into the distance. Massive fermentation and holding tanks connected by large pipes gave the winery the look of an oil refinery.

Ricardo Santos rose from behind his broad and polished desk. He had salt-and-pepper hair, rugged features, a confident smile, and piercing dark eyes at odds with a reserved, if not apprehensive demeanor. He wore a short-sleeved black shirt stitched with the Santos Wine Company logo in gold thread and loose-fitting jeans resting on tasseled loafers. He had adapted nicely to the casual California style. He came from around his desk and went straight to Carmen, held her hand, and kissed her on both cheeks.

"Oh, my dear," he said in a rich baritone voice, "I'm so glad you're here. Are you all right? You must still be in pain!"

Carmen flushed slightly. "I'm fine, Ricardo. I'm on the mend."

"I'm so, so sorry. Who could have done such a thing?"

He let go of Carmen's hand and turned to Dante, smiling weakly. "Well, this must be the journalist, Dante Rath?"

"Yes," Dante said, extending his hand to Santos.

"How very nice to meet you," Santos said, and shook Dante's hand briefly before glancing away and returning his attention to Carmen.

Santos motioned them to a square of leather couches surrounding a coffee table of thick and polished redwood. "Welcome to our offices," Santos said.

Sokolova stood nearby, her arms folded across her chest.

Santos looked from Sokolova to Dante, and again to Carmen. "Sofía will be here with us. I can't do anything without her."

Sokolova smiled weakly, unable to hide her distaste for Dante.

"She's a treasure. Her name comes from the Russian word *sokol*. It means falcon. We met in Italy where she was racing motorcycles." Santos leaned back in his chair and said, "She's my bird of prey." He smiled broadly at his comment. "Actually, she's an angel."

"Just pretend I'm not here," Sokolova said.

Dante smiled weakly at her.

"Let me first say I enjoy your wine column," Santos said. "It's why I agreed to meet with you. Very, ah, *insightful*," he said, emphasizing the last word.

"Well, thank you," Dante said, unsurprised at Santos's cynical tone. "It's always nice to get feedback."

"What can I do for you?" Santos asked with a forced smile.

Dante cleared his throat, looked at Santos, and glanced at Carmen, who gave Santos a knowing nod.

Sokolova circled behind Dante and Carmen, Santos tracking her movements.

"As you know," Dante continued, "there've been several unexplained deaths recently in Northern California wine country. People are wondering about the wine industry."

"Greed," Santos said.

"What?" Dante said.

"Greed," Santos repeated. "Winemakers have forgotten that the customer, not the winemaker, is the heart and soul of the business."

What the hell is he talking about? Dante was unsure how to respond, but said, "It should be obvious the customer comes first."

"Oh, but it's not," Santos said. "Look at some of those Napa and Sonoma winemakers. They think they're more important than the people who buy and drink the wine."

"Why do you say that?"

"The wine is overpriced," Santos said. "We here at Santos make wines people like to drink *and* can afford."

Dante exhaled slowly. He had not come to listen to Santos pitch his wines. "So you think greed was behind the recent killings in the Napa Valley?"

"Newcomers, really. Modern-day gold hunters," Santos said. "Neither of them knew what they were doing."

"You're talking about Bernie Morrison and Chao Ling at the Morrison Creek Winery?" Dante asked.

"Yes," Santos said. "That's what you came here to ask me, isn't it?"

"You were involved in Morrison's winery, as I understand it."

Santos thought about it and looked at Carmen, who nodded again for him to answer. "Morrison asked me for help from time to time. It was all quite informal," he said.

"Ling was an investor," Dante said. "Morrison shot him. Do you have any idea why?"

"Truthfully? No," Santos said. "But I do know Ling made a substantial investment in the winery. If I had to guess, I'd say it was over the money Ling had invested."

"As you know, someone also tried to kill your attorney here," Dante said, glancing at Carmen.

"Horrible!" Santos said, his eyes opening wide. "I was devastated when I heard the news. Carmen and I are… well, she's helped me through some difficult times."

"She was out jogging," Dante said.

Santos cleared his throat. "I'm very angry. The Sonoma police have done nothing! I've considered hiring a private investigator to look into the case."

"You don't trust the police?" Dante said.

"I expect them to do their job," Santos said. "But they're not. Why would anyone want to kill her? She worked with many other winery owners, and they're all people who love the business."

Dante jotted down the quote and waited for Santos to continue. "What do you expect your investigator will find?" he asked.

"I don't know who's behind the shooting, but I'd like to find out," Santos said, glaring at Dante. "Someone must pay for her injuries. It's only right."

Dante let Santos's words hang in the air. "Morrison and Ling aren't the only deaths," he said. "Simon Grundy, who used to work for you, was found dead yesterday."

Santos became animated again and waved his hands for emphasis. "I know. It seems they've ruled the death a suicide. But, who knows? It only drives home the point I made earlier. The police and sheriff's departments are not doing their job. What's going on? Why aren't the police making arrests? Why isn't anyone in jail?"

Dante jotted notes. "I'm sure you're aware Morrison and Grundy worked closely together?"

"Simon was a very good winemaker," Santos said. "He knew everything there was to know. I hired him right out of wine school. The only thing he lacked was experience."

"Grundy and Morrison formed a company called MG Enology," Dante said. "They consulted for and managed a number of wineries north of here."

"I used them on occasion," Santos said. "They helped me with my vineyards."

"Did you know they were developing a pesticide to control the spread of Pierce's disease?"

Santos looked at Dante, glanced at Carmen, and back at Dante. Santos drew a breath. "Pierce's disease is a big problem," he said, his eyes narrowing. "It could ruin the California wine business if it's not stopped. It's already devastated vineyards across Southern California."

"Temecula was especially hard hit," Dante said. "The grape growers had to rip out and replant vines. Did you work with Morrison and Grundy on their pesticide?"

Santos drew another slow breath and exhaled, lifting his hand as if to fend off Dante's question. "Let me explain something. Have you heard of *phylloxera vastatrix*?"

"Um, yes," Dante said. "The disease killed most the French vineyards in the late 1800s."

"It was spread by an insect, similar to the aphid," Santos said. "Once the insect began feeding on the vine, it became infected and eventually died. It's very much like the problem with Pierce's disease."

"Which is spread by the glassy-winged sharpshooter."

"I'm glad you're knowledgeable about these things," Santos said. "Anyway, there was, and still is, no known cure for *phylloxera*. The irony is the disease came from North America. The disease came to England with botanists who brought infected grape vines into their country to study the problem. But they didn't know what they were doing. Soon the disease had killed all of the English grape vines, and it quickly spread to Europe. Estimates were almost ninety percent of the grape vines in Europe died because of it."

"It's an amazing story," Dante said, wondering where Santos was going with it.

"The solution also came from North America, as you probably know."

"Yes," Dante said. "It's one of those stories the French wine makers don't like to repeat. The North American vines had developed a natural resistance to the *phylloxera* infection. As much as the French hated it, they were forced to graft their precious vines onto the root stock from America."

"Very true," Santos said. He glanced at Carmen, who smiled weakly.

"So, back to the pesticide," Dante said. "Morrison and Grundy believed they had a product to kill the insect that's spreading the disease. Did you help them with it?"

"You need to know how dangerous Pierce's disease is," Santos said, leaning back into his chair. "It's no trivial matter." He wagged his index finger. "The disease could do to the California wine industry what *phylloxera* did to the French more than a hundred years ago…"

"It would put a huge dent in the California economy," Dante said.

"It would be a catastrophe! Wine accounts for about $60 billion annually in California. There are more than 4,000 wineries in the state. Do you know how many people are employed in the wine business? More than 300,000," Santos said, his voice rising. "About $15 billion are paid to the state in taxes. That's just the industry. More than 20 million tourists come to wine country each year from all over the world."

Santos collected himself, cleared his throat, and glanced from Carmen to Sokolova, who pointed to her watch, as if time was running out. "So," Santos continued, "you can see if there's a viable product to stop or eliminate Pierce's disease, it would be very important."

Santos's words hung in the air.

"The disease has turned up in southern Italy in the olive groves," Dante said. "You have olive oil interests there and in Spain."

"Can you imagine what would happen in Spain and Italy if the disease is allowed to run its course?" Santos asked.

"The wine and olive oil industries in Spain and Italy would be devastated," Dante said.

"People just don't understand what it means," Santos said. "In Europe, growing grapes and olives is not just about economics. It's a way of life." Santos's face dropped, his shoulders were hunched, his eyes downcast. "My family has vineyards and groves of olives. It's our life. I can't imagine it being gone." He lifted his eyes to Dante and glared. "I won't let that happen."

"So you were part of the development of the insecticide spray for Pierce's disease?"

Santos took a deep breath and exhaled. "I am not going to be like many of my fellow Europeans."

"What are you saying?"

"Think back to the time when *phylloxera* hit Europe. The French waited until most of the vineyards were dead. When they realized they had a very serious problem, it was too late. Well, this is America. Neither I nor anyone else has to watch a disease destroy vineyards and olive groves before action is taken."

"The people I've talked to at the state agricultural department say the problem is under control."

"I wish it were true," Santos said. "But as you know, with more than 4,000 wineries, there's no way they can be on top of it all."

"I spent this past weekend with a friend of yours, Alex Tercero," Dante said.

Santos smiled. "Yes. Alex has been a good friend over the years. I'm sure you know he's been fighting the disease for several years."

"He showed me diseased vines," Dante said.

"I'm very fond of your mother's artwork, by the way," Santos said. "As is Alex. But I'm sure you know."

Dante's back stiffened at Santos's mention of his mother.

"I have several pieces of her art in these offices," Santos said.

"She's thrilled," Dante said.

"Did you know we met in Spain? My God. How times flies!"

Dante cleared his throat. "Did Morrison and Grundy approach you about their pesticide?"

"They did," Santos said, leaning forward and resting his forearms on his desk. "But the problem was it was untested." He again wagged his finger. "I told them I wasn't going to get involved until it was proven effective *and* safe."

Dante smiled to himself. *Santos is covering his tracks. He's distancing himself from the pesticide spray.* Dante drew a deep breath. "Morrison and Grundy needed an infected vineyard to test it."

"Yes, I suppose they did," Santos said.

"And you offered your vineyards when you found infected vines?"

"Oh, God, no," Santos said. "Not a chance."

Dante pulled the medical examiner's report from inside his sport coat pocket. He unfolded it and handed it to Santos. "This says Helena Hernandez, the woman who died working in a vineyard of yours, which is about fifty miles from here, had high levels of a toxic chemical called thiophanate-methyl in her system."

Santos raised a hand to stop Dante. "As far as I know, and I believe the state is in agreement, the girl died of dehydration. A lot has been written about the girl's death. It's a matter of public record."

Santos has his cover story prepared! Dante pressed on. "Actually, she died from hemorrhaging, loss of blood. It was a complication due to a malformed pregnancy."

"I didn't know," Santos said. "Thank you for informing me. But the poor girl's death was not my fault. I hired a contractor to provide the labor. He's the one who's responsible for the death."

"Are you aware the State of California has banned the pesticide Morrison and Grundy were developing, saying it's toxic?" Dante asked.

Santos looked at Sokolova, who smirked, her eyes narrow. He gazed back at Dante. "If that's the case," he said. "I'm glad I did not invest in their little venture."

Santos looked at Carmen, who maintained a weak smile.

"The pesticide's active ingredient, thiophanate-methyl, which I mentioned before, is the problem," Dante continued. "It interferes with human reproductive hormones."

"Well, it seems you've done your research. But what does it have to do with me?"

Dante handed him another sheet of paper. "This is the technical analysis of the spray Morrison and Grundy had developed. It was submitted to the state for review under the company name of MG Enology."

Santos held the paper in his hand, glanced at it, and handed it back to Dante. "I don't know anything about it."

"Hernandez and other workers were spraying insecticide in your vineyard."

"If they were, it was without my knowledge." Santos leaned forward, his elbows on his desk. "I believe Sofía explained to you we have thousands and thousands of acres of vines. I'm forced to hire people like Grundy to help me manage them. You don't think I actually keep track of thousands of acres of vines by myself, do you?"

Dante stared at Santos. *Plausible deniability.* "But you, of the few people who knew about this product, stood to benefit the most. Millions of dollars' worth of your vines and your wine are potentially at stake. If successful, the pesticide could mean millions of dollars in potential sales to grape and olive growers around the world."

"You're right. Absolutely right," Santos said. "I am very aware of the potential of such a product. But I would only get involved if it was safe!"

Dante sat back and asked, "You had no knowledge the spray was being tested on your vines?"

"None," Santos said. "Absolutely none." He glanced at Carmen, who sat motionless, and at Sokolova. "Did you, Sofía?"

Sokolova flung her arms wide, palms up.

"Vineyard workers have said they were using the spray for months," Dante said. "How could you have not known?"

"They can say what they want, but that doesn't make it true." Santos glared at Dante. "Let me say I hope you're not planning to print unsubstantiated accusations. Lies in newspapers or online blogs bring heavy penalties. False accusations can be costly. You're aware some online news organizations have been sued out of existence."

"There are workers who say they used the spray expensively in your vineyards."

"If they did, it was not with my knowledge," Santos said.

Dante jotted the comment in his notebook. He looked at Santos as he struggled to think of another question. He couldn't. They fell silent.

Santos looked at him. "Well, is there anything else I can help you with?"

Dante sucked in a breath. He glanced at Carmen and at Sokolova, whose smirk had not changed.

"Are you finished?" Sokolova asked.

Dante stood, folded his notebook, and slipped it into his pocket. "Thanks for your time," he said to Santos.

"My pleasure." Santos stood and motioned to his office door. "Sofía will show you out." He turned to Carmen. "Can I speak to you privately?"

Carmen had just pushed herself to her feet, and leaning on her crutch, motioned to Dante for him to wait outside.

CHAPTER 37

The interview tumbled in his mind as Dante drove north on California's Central Valley freeway, Route 99, on the way back to Sonoma with Carmen again in the passenger seat.

"What did you talk to Santos about after Sokolova ushered me out of the office?" Dante asked.

"Not much," Carmen said. "He thanked me for coming."

Dante looked at her. "Just curious."

"You were right. It was good for him and good for you that I was there."

They rode in silence.

"What are you thinking?" Carmen asked.

Dante glanced at her. "Santos lied. He knew everything about the pesticide."

"You don't know that. He could be telling the truth," Carmen said. "Did it ever occur to you Santos could have been the target? He may have been manipulated and used."

"You used the same argument to get his fine reduced," Dante said.

"Think about it," Carmen said. "Santos has everything Morrison needed to score big. Santos has money, a microbiology laboratory, and thousands of acres of vineyards. With Grundy's help, Morrison had access to Santos's vineyards where they could test and work with the insecticide. All the signs point to Santos being used by them."

"Do you seriously think Santos had no idea what Morrison and Grundy were testing the pesticide?" Dante asked.

Carmen looked at Dante. "It's very possible."

"Maybe, but I doubt it." Dante let the thought simmer. "Let's assume Santos knew all about the pesticide and was deeply involved in the development of it with Morrison and Grundy. Suppose Santos made a deal with them, but only if Morrison and Grundy could come up with development money. Along comes Chao Ling, who invests a million dollars into Morrison's winery. Only the money doesn't go into the winery. It is instead diverted into the development and testing of the pesticide by Santos's laboratory and vineyards."

"Go on," Carmen said, staring at Dante.

"Let's say the project falls apart for some reason," Dante said, "when the girl in the vineyard dies."

"Helena Hernandez," Carmen said. "But the official cause of death was ruled dehydration."

"But now we know the truth," Dante said. "Her death was due to a problem pregnancy caused by exposure to a toxic chemical spray."

Carmen fixed her gaze on the road ahead. "Santos seemed unaware of the real cause of death."

"But if he knew the truth, he also knew he could be liable," Dante said. "He could face criminal charges in connection with her death, maybe negligent homicide. He would also know if news about the toxic spray became public, he'd be ruined. Maybe deported. What if he couldn't pay his debts, which probably amount to tens of millions of dollars? He'd be ruined. His empire would crumble."

"They don't deport rich people," Carmen said. "Only poor ones."

"Only because people like Santos have the money to hire attorneys, like you."

"Ouch," Carmen said. "I didn't need that," her eyes flashing angrily. "I helped you by setting up this interview. Okay? Santos has been a client in the past. A good one. You put me in a bad position. So back off."

Dante swallowed. Yes, he was grateful to her. "I'm sorry. I don't mean to put you between a rock and a hard place. But hear me out."

"Okay, get to the point."

"If Santos was as deeply involved as I suspect, it would make sense he would want to get rid of anyone who could connect him to the pesticide and the girl's death, or the use of the pesticide in his vineyards. So he had reason to want Morrison and Grundy dead."

"But Santos didn't kill Ling or Morrison," Carmen said. "That's a huge problem with your theory."

"I know," Dante said.

"So you think Santos killed Grundy and tried to kill me," Carmen said, sounding more than a little skeptical.

"I'm not sure. Maybe Grundy's death was a suicide. We know Morrison and Grundy stole grapes from the vineyards they managed. They had a lot of enemies in the wine business. I had one vineyard owner tell me he wasn't sorry to hear Morrison was dead."

Carmen wrinkled her nose. "Since when do people kill over stolen grapes? No one's been charged, yet, in Grundy's death, and probably won't be." After pondering, she said, "Your theory means we could be targets."

"I said so earlier," Dante said. "Other than Santos and his assistant, we're possibly the only two people who know all about the toxic pesticide and the Hernandez girl. You're aware of Santos's business dealings, and so am I."

Carmen studied Dante. "What if someone was blackmailing Santos?"

"It's an interesting possibility. But who?" Dante asked. His question hung in the air. "Would Ling?"

"No," she said. "He wasn't that kind of guy. Morrison is my guess."

"Not Grundy?" Dante asked.

She shook her head. "He had too much to lose. Wife, family, winery."

"We'll probably never know."

"All of this speculation is giving me a headache. I need a drink," Carmen said, and gazed out the window at the passing vineyards. "You never really understand how many acres of grapes are produced in the Central Valley until you see it."

Dante swerved into the left lane and passed a gleaming silver metal tanker truck with tall exhaust pipes and the words, "Santos Wine Company," painted in red letters across the cab's side door. "That truck is filled with wine," he said.

"It's probably headed to Santos's bottling plant," Carmen said. "He doesn't waste any time getting his wine to market, does he?"

"They call it 'highway aging,'" Dante said.

The Mustang sped along the highway, passing more trucks before Dante settled into a gap in the traffic, letting his mind return to his theory about the deaths. After a few minutes, Dante glanced into his rear view mirror.

The massive cab of a tanker truck he'd passed earlier was on his tail, the truck's large, chrome front bumper moving closer. Dante stepped on the gas and put distance between the Mustang and the tanker, then checked his side mirror. The truck driver wore a straw cowboy hat and his face was shadowy, save for chromed sunglasses. Dante was puzzled, but dismissed it. Just another truck driver, he thought, returning his gaze to the road as the vegetable fields and vineyards flashed by.

When Dante looked into his rear view mirror again, he saw the large chromed front bumper of the tanker truck just a few yards from his trunk. "What is this guy's problem?"

"What?" Carmen twisted around and looked out the back window.

"This truck has been crowding me for the past five miles."

Carmen glanced at Dante as she settled back into her seat. "Truckers think they own this highway."

Dante sped up, glanced into his mirror again at the truck driver, and passed a couple of flatbed trucks piled high with crates of leafy vegetables. After putting distance between himself and the tanker again, he pulled back into the right lane and let his mind drift.

His eyes rose to the rear view mirror at the shifting of truck gears and the rumble of a powerful diesel engine. This time the tanker truck's massive chrome bumper banged against the back of the Mustang, making it lurch forward and swerve.

"What the fuck!" Dante shouted.

The tires screamed before Dante brought the swerving Mustang under control. He stomped on the gas, his heart pounding, fear surging through his body. The Mustang leapt forward and flew by a handful of trucks and cars.

"I'm calling 9-1-1!" Carmen yelled. "He's trying to kill us!"

Dante didn't ease up until he hit ninety miles per hour, then slowed and slipped back into the right lane. "He's probably high on meth," Dante said. "They get paid by the load, not the hour, so they drive like maniacs." But of course, Dante realized. *A Santos wine truck! He's trying to kill us and make it look like an accident!*

Carmen fished her phone out of her briefcase and began tapping the screen.

"We need to get off this highway," Dante said, checking his review mirror again "Shit! The exit for the road back to Napa is still ten miles ahead."

"We need to get this asshole's license plate," Carmen said.

"What? I don't want get that close again."

Dante wanted to punch the accelerator again, but was forced to slow as he came up behind a couple of lumbering vegetable trucks, one trying to overtake the other. Dante let the Mustang nose up to the rear of the truck on the right, impatient as a vegetable truck in the left lane tried to pass the one in the right.

Stuck behind the two trucks, Dante glanced at his driver's side rear view mirror, hoping to swerve into the left lane and trail the passing truck. Instead, his heart pounded as he saw only giant truck tires a couple of feet from his door. The gleaming metal tanker trailer was beside him, blocking the left lane.

"Holy shit!" Dante said, seeing the underbelly of the truck and its double rear axles, swinging toward him from the passing lane. The giant tires slammed against the side of his Mustang with an explosion of crunching metal, breaking glass, and screeching rubber.

Dante's left arm and shoulder slammed against the door as the Mustang lurched wildly to the right and hit the graveled shoulder, spinning sideways in a cloud of flying dirt and gravel. With a deafening *thunk,* the Mustang rose into the air as if launched. Dante felt the world rotate as the Mustang sailed through the air and crashed into the ground in an explosion of crunching metal and shattering glass.

"Hey! You okay in there?"

The man's voice sounded like it was from another planet, distant and tinny. Dante opened his eyes. He was hanging upside-down and staring at his shattered and caved-in windshield. Everything was covered with dust, dirt, and sparkling pieces of window glass. His shoulders burned, his neck ached, and a searing pain raged in his head.

The airbags, now limp and deflated, had deployed from the side and front, and the pungent scent of the exploded blasting caps mingled with the dusty air. But the bags had done their job. Otherwise he knew he'd be dead, his chest crushed against the steering wheel, his face shredded by the windshield.

"Hey! You okay in there?"

Dante tried to respond, but couldn't. He coughed and croaked, "Yeah." He turned his head stiffly to check on Carmen. Blood dripped from her face and soaked the fabric of the crumpled Mustang's roof. Her eyes were blank.

Shit!

He extended his right arm to her shoulder and touched it gently. "Carmen. Carmen."

She didn't respond.

"Oh, God," Dante groaned. *She can't be dead!* He closed his eyes in pain, refusing to accept the possibility.

"What?" the voice said.

"My passenger. She's hurt bad."

"It looks like it. But you're alive."

Dante turned and saw a bearded, chubby face staring at him. The man wore a baseball cap. Dante groaned.

"I saw it happen," the man said. "The fucker just knocked you off the road."

Dante groaned. The last thing he remembered was flying through the air.

"I called 9-1-1. The cops and an ambulance are on the way."

Dante's mind was beginning to clear, his eyes beginning to focus. "Thanks."

"You must'a really pissed him off," the man said.

"I guess."

"How bad are you hurt?" he asked.

"I don't know," Dante said. "My head hurts. My neck is sore. My shoulders ache."

"No broken bones?"

Dante did a quick mental scan of his body. Other than his overall ache, there were no sharp pains. Nothing felt broken. "Don't think so. Can you help get me out of here?"

"I can't," the man said. "If you're hurt worse than you think, I could be in deep shit. The paramedics need to get you out."

"Are you kidding me?" Dante said. "I can't hang like this much longer."

"Can you hit the seatbelt release?" the man asked.

Dante groaned.

"Put your hand against the roof. Break your fall. It'll protect your neck."

Dante extended his left hand over his head, pressing against the crushed metal of the padded roof.

"Now, reach up to your seat and find the release."

"How the hell do you know how to do this?" Dante asked.

"I used to work with search and rescue."

"Okay." Dante felt for the seatbelt stretched tight across his lap, chest, and shoulder, holding him in place. His fingers found the clasp. He squeezed. The clasp snapped free and Dante dropped, banging his head. "Ah!" Pain jolted through his neck and head.

"Now come to me," the man said.

Dante pushed himself sideways. A thick arm reached in and slipped around his neck and chest, grabbing him under the arm. Dante felt himself being pulled out the window.

"Watch your legs, now," the man said.

With his head and shoulders out, Dante twisted onto his back, and used his hands to snake himself the rest of the way through the opening. He lay panting in the sparse grass and weeds.

"Can you get up?" the man said.

Dante rolled to his side and onto his stomach, and pushed himself up onto his elbows. He grimaced at his rescuer. "Give me a hand."

The man grabbed Dante under the arms and helped him to his feet. Dante reached his arm around the man's shoulder to steady himself, fighting off a wave of nausea and dizziness. "I feel like shit," Dante said.

Slowly the spinning stopped and the scene came into focus. Back on the highway, cars and trucks rolled past, gawkers slowing to stare at the wreck. A king cab pickup truck with dual tires in the rear was off the road and sitting at an angle in the ditch. "That your truck?" Dante asked.

"It is," the man said. "You'd better sit down."

Dante traced his skid marks on the road and gravel shoulder where the Mustang had launched into the vineyard and wiped out a stretch of vines. He gazed at the mangled Mustang. It was totaled, the body crumpled, the glass shattered. In the distance he heard approaching sirens.

A couple of other cars had stopped on the side of the road. An elderly woman stood beside her passenger door, staring as if Dante was a ghost. *Maybe I am*, he thought. He gazed at the woman, finally dropping his eyes again to his smashed and upside-down car. *Oh, shit!* "Carmen!"

Dante listened for a response. "Carmen!" he shouted, and staggered around to the passenger window and dropped to his knees. Carmen's upside-down face was coated with dirt and drying blood. Her eyes blinked open. She turned her head and looked at him. He touched her dust-coated cheek.

"What the fuck?" she said, her voice craggy.

"We had an accident." Dante stroked her cheek with the back of his fingers. "Carmen. Stay with me, girl. We're going to get you to a hospital."

CHAPTER 38

Twelve hours later, bruised and aching, Dante inserted the key into the door of his condo. The lock clicked, and he pushed open the door. His neck was in a padded brace, and his arm was in a sling, both precautions against hairline fractures seen in the X-rays, the doctors told him, one in his neck vertebra and another his collarbone. A couple of small bandages decorated his face. Inside, he dropped his briefcase on the couch, and stepped into the kitchen where he debated making a pot of coffee or opening a bottle of wine. He went for the wine, filled a glass, and drank eagerly.

He'd spent the night in the hospital, mostly for observation, he was told. After breakfast and an examination by the on-duty physician early in the morning, he'd been released and told to do nothing for the next several days but rest and recover. He was to come back in week for a checkup.

Carmen was in the hospital—again. She'd be there for a few more days, they said, mostly for observation of a possible concussion and internal injuries. Luckily, the air bags had done their job. Carmen had suffered no new injuries except for bruises from the violent banging and jarring from the tumbling car. The accident had reopened her head and leg wounds, however, and had to be repaired with new sutures.

He felt terrible for her, much more so than for himself. After what she'd been through already, he had subjected her to even more pain. And for what? Because of the damned story he was chasing and still couldn't prove? Would she ever speak to him again? He wouldn't blame her if she didn't.

"Now what?" Dante said aloud, breaking the condo's unsettling silence.

Carmen would be laid up again for a week. It could've been worse, he thought. Much worse. You're both lucky to be alive, the doctors had said. Dante could only agree.

"He tried to kill us," Dante had told the state police. But his insistence had met blank stares from the investigators. "You could've been in the truck driver's blind spot," they said.

"That's bullshit," Dante replied. "It was deliberate."

"You need to let us handle this," the state police investigator had said.

"Look. I was there," Dante had said. "It was a Santos Wine Company truck. Before it ran me off the road, it rammed me from behind. I sped up and pulled into traffic, trying to evade the idiot."

The investigation could take weeks. Dante knew he didn't have time to wait for an arrest to prove what he knew to be true: Santos had tried to kill him and Carmen. *He wants to stop me from writing what I know. Santos tried to kill me once. He'll try again.*

Dante knew what he had to do.

The bus ride from Santa Rosa into the city could take hours sometimes, but it was what Dante wanted. Anonymous travel was safe travel. The ride gave him time to think and write. He had ditched his neck brace and slipped out of his arm sling. He swiveled his neck and listened to the crackling of cartilage. A jolt of pain shot though his neck, entering the back of his skull, but it quickly subsided.

His neck and shoulder muscles were tight as piano wires. He massaged and kneaded them best as he could, coaxing the muscles to relax. It felt good to be free of the choking neck brace. As the bus made stop after stop, people climbing on and off, he sat with his laptop open and began to outline his story.

Two hours later, Dante stepped down from the bus in the North Beach neighborhood he'd known since he was a child. It felt like home. He walked a couple of blocks to the Ling Dynasty restaurant and peered through the plate glass window. Mei Ling was again dressed in her red satin dress with gold embroidering.

Mei held a couple of large menus in the crook of her arm and, seeing Dante enter, waved. But her face fell at the sight of the small bandages on his face and forehead. "What happened to you?" she asked.

"I…ah... was in a car accident."

"You were hurt!" she said.

"Not as bad as my passenger."

"Who was… ?"

"Carmen Carelli."

"Carelli?" Mei's face fell in confusion. "What happened? Is she okay?"

"I was run off the road," Dante said. "And no, she's not okay. But she'll be fine, soon enough."

"Was this about something you wrote, again?" she said with a frown.

"Yes and no."

"Explain."

"I haven't written it yet," Dante said. "But I'm going to."

Mei led him to a booth along the wall and dropped a menu on the table. "Would you like tea?"

"How about some sake?" he asked.

"Sure."

His gaze followed her form-fitting dress as she disappeared into the kitchen. Dante glanced around. It was mid-afternoon, the dead time between lunch and dinner, yet the air was saturated with aromas of grilled vegetables and steamed rice.

Mei returned with the sake and slipped onto the bench seat across from him. After pouring two small cups full, she raised a slender arm, and they clicked cups. "Here's to survival," she said.

"I'll drink to that." Dante tossed the sake back, a sharp pain piercing his neck.

"So tell me what happened."

"Someone tried to kill me," Dante said.

"Who?"

"I don't know. We were driving back from an interview with Ricardo Santos. I was on State Route 99 when a tanker truck swerved into me and knocked us off the road. My car left the highway and flipped. It landed upside down."

Mei squinted. "You're lucky to be alive."

"I know," Dante said. "I should probably be in the hospital with Carelli."

"She was shot just a couple of weeks ago."

"I know. She was recovering. She agreed to set up the interview with Santos. She's represented him in the past. She came with me."

"Are you sure it wasn't just an accident?" Mei asked.

"That's what the cops say. But it wasn't random. The truck driver tried to kill me. It was a Santos Wine Company truck."

"Why would Santos want to kill you?"

"I've been looking into Santos's involvement with a toxic pesticide spray," Dante said. "Ricardo Santos runs Santos Wine Company."

"I know," Mei said. "He's one of the biggest winemakers in California. Why do you think he's responsible?"

Dante told her about Helena Hernandez and how she had died, not from dehydration, but from exposure to the toxic pesticide she'd been spraying in the vineyards.

"So you think Santos is afraid you'll link him to the girl's death?"

"Of course," Dante said. "He's already been in trouble with the state and the feds for mislabeling wine. This could shut him down, get him deported, or possibly put him in jail."

"I see," Mei said, refilling her cup and his.

"He kept the girl's death covered up by blaming it on the labor contractor."

"How did you find out about this?" she asked.

"A guy named Gilberto Muñoz. He was the contractor. Hired the grape pickers. But he didn't do it. The girl was a relative. He's angry he was blamed for causing his niece's death. "

"Santos should go after him, not you."

"He would if he knew how Muñoz has helped me."

"And you think Santos is trying to keep you from writing the story?" Mei asked again.

"Of course."

Mei weighed his words. "Why would Santos try to kill Carelli? She was his attorney, you said."

"She knows all of the players and has been helping me," Dante said. "Did you know Simon Grundy was found dead a couple days ago at Shady Oaks winery?"

"Of course," Mei said. "Marvee works for him. She's very upset."

"It's been ruled a suicide. Marvee says Grundy was killed," Dante said.

"She thinks it was made to look like a suicide," Mei said.

Dante sipped his sake. "Did Chao ever talk to you about Grundy?"

"Chao was upset with what Morrison was doing with Grundy and with Chao's money," she said. "But I never knew the details."

"Morrison and Grundy were stealing grapes from the vineyards they managed," Dante said. "They were buying and selling grapes they claimed were from the Napa Valley, but weren't."

"So that's why Chao was so angry at Morrison!" Mei said. "He was using Chao's money!"

"It's very possible," Dante said. "But that's not all."

"Did Carelli know about it?" Mei asked.

"I think so," Dante said. "She represented your brother. She had to know everything Chao knew."

Mei looked lost in thought. "My brother trusted her, so you're probably right. He said she knew everything and everyone in the wine business."

"It almost got her killed. Twice now." Dante dropped his eyes to his cup and took a sip as a wave of guilt swept over him.

Mei watched him. "So now what?"

"I need your help."

"It's not going to get me killed, is it?" she asked, forcing a smile.

Dante flushed, still feeling guilty about Carmen. "I need a place to hide for a while."

"Why are you asking me?"

"I thought your father might have an empty apartment I could rent here in Chinatown."

"To hide from Santos?"

"Yes. I need to lay low for a while."

"You really are afraid of him, aren't you?"

"I don't want to be visible for the next few days. And I need a quiet place to work."

"My father has a few apartments," Mei said, "but they're all long-term rentals."

Dante gazed at his empty cup of sake. "Hmm."

Mei's eyes brightened. "But I have something better. You can stay at Chao's house."

"Chao's house? Are you serious?"

"He has a place in the Sunset District. I've been staying there a lot. I'm sorting through his stuff. We're going to sell the place."

Dante liked the idea. It would be the last place anyone would look for him. "Are you sure?"

Mei smiled. "I use the house. Always have. I have my own room there. Chao let me stay there after my night classes at grad school."

It was perfect, more than perfect, Dante thought.

"Don't let my father find out you're there," Mei added quickly. "He'd kill me if he knew."

"Don't worry. It will only be for a short time. I can pay."

"Forget it."

CHAPTER 39

Fifteen minutes after saying goodbye to Mei, Dante stood at the street level door to his mother's apartment, his finger poised at the buzzer button. He'd grabbed a taxi on Grant Street and had the driver drop him off two blocks away from her Marina District flat. Dante glanced around the street, fighting off his paranoia.

Like the police, Mei was skeptical about his insistence Santos was after him. At least Mei had been polite about it, seemed to take him at his word, and agreed to help, if for nothing more than to unravel why her brother had died.

Dante didn't want to take any unnecessary chances, but he couldn't shake the sense of obligation drawing him to his mother's door. Antonia deserved to know what was happening since he was, after all, her only child.

He pressed the buzzer. The door clicked open and he bounded up the steps.

As Dante entered her flat, Antonia called out, "I'm in the kitchen, getting a refreshment." From the sound of her voice, he knew she'd been drinking. She was pouring a glass of wine and put a wine bottle on the counter with a clunk. When she turned to face him, her face dropped. "What the hell?" She cradled his face in her hands, touching his bandages, her dark eyes searching his face.

"A car accident. I'm fine, Mama." He removed her hands from his face.

Antonia stepped back, clinging to his sleeves. "You're *not* fine!"

Dante lifted a hand to stop her. "Pour me a glass and I'll tell you about it."

When he finished explaining what had happened, Antonia dropped her gaze to her now empty glass. "The poor girl."

"Which one? Hernandez or Carmen?"

Antonia blinked. "Well, both. But the Hernandez girl is dead, you said. I'm so sorry about Carmen. Bad karma, I guess. But she'll be okay?"

Guilt again gurgled up inside Dante. "The docs want to keep her in the hospital for a few days. She's been through a lot."

"I really like her, Dante. Are you serious about her?"

"I haven't really given it much thought," he said. "Haven't had time. Actually, I should be going."

"Going where?" she asked.

"I need to drop out of sight for a while."

Antonia scowled. "Because of the car accident?"

"It was no accident. It was one of Santos's trucks."

"I've driven on that road many times," Antonia said. "It's full of trucks roaring up and down, back and forth. It's always crowded, which makes it dangerous. It doesn't surprise me a truck driver would swerve into your lane, not seeing you."

"I could have died," Dante said.

"All the more reason for the idiot truck driver to run," she said. "He'll lose his job and go to jail. You'll never find him."

"He can be found," Dante said. "He was driving one of Santos's trucks. And he'll be charged, eventually."

Antonia took another drink, holding the glass in her hands. "Oh, by the way, Alex called here looking for you today."

Dante felt a surge of paranoia. "Alex called?"

"Yes. Why is it surprising?"

Dante swallowed hard. "What did he say?"

"He wanted to know if I'd seen you. He wanted to know if you'd been by."

Santos knows Carmen and I survived. Of course! Santos is tracking me, using his friend Alex. Dammit! I shouldn't have come. I've got to get out! Now.

"What's the matter?" his mother asked. "You look pale. Are you going to be sick?"

Dante drew in a deep breath. "It's Santos."

"You're making Santos into more of a crook than he is, *caro mio.*"

"You're only saying that because Alex is his friend and business partner," Dante said.

"Those two men move in the highest of circles in this state," she said. "They can't afford to act like thugs and criminals."

"Maybe that's who's in those circles."

Antonia's eyes flared. "Alex is an honorable man, Dante. He does right by me. Always has."

Dante dropped his gaze to his glass.

"You're still upset from the accident." Antonia's eyes softened. "It's a good idea you're going to lay low for a while. You should rest."

Dante drained the last of his wine and stood. "I've got to go."

Antonia came around the table and gave him a hug and a peck on the cheek. "Take care of yourself," she said.

"I will," Dante said. At the door he looked over his shoulder. Antonia was at the counter, pouring herself another glass of Tercero's chardonnay. "Don't tell anyone I was here, even Alex, okay?"

"Don't worry. I won't tell a soul. Just be careful, will you?"

Dante opened the door and hurried down the stairs.

On Lombard Street, Dante hailed a taxi and climbed in. The driver looked at him in the rear view mirror. "Where to?" the driver asked.

"Just drive," Dante said.

"Really?" the driver said. He was an older black man with a narrow face and who wore a frayed, stained Giants baseball cap with a tightly curled bill. It sat atop a closely cut head of speckled gray hair. He looked at Dante in the mirror with one milky and one clear eye set in a leathery face.

"Yes," Dante said, looking at the man's milky eye. *Can this guy even see?*

The driver put the car in gear and pulled into traffic heading east.

"Go downtown," Dante said.

"Anywhere specific?"

"No. And let me know if anyone is following us."

The driver looked again into the rear view mirror and smiled. "Are you serious?"

"Yes! Tell me if there's a car tracking us!"

"Okay. I've been driving in this city for most of my life."

"Make a lot of turns," Dante said.

"Are you all right, mister?" the driver asked, staring at him from the mirror. "Are you on the run?"

"Keep your eyes on the road, will you?"

The taxi made a right turn onto Van Ness Boulevard and sped up, weaving through traffic and hitting several lights. The driver turned left and bounced down California Street, his bulky Dodge Charger lifting off the steep drops and swerving around a cable car, the tires squealing. The driver wheeled the Charger sharply to the right at Grant Avenue and braked to a stop behind a line of cars waiting for the light to change at Pine Street.

"That was good," Dante said.

"Gets the heart pumpin', don't it?" The driver's eyes smiled in the mirror. "Just doing what you asked, boss."

"Thanks. I know you could lose your license for it. Did you see anyone?"

"No. If they was followin' us, they ain't now. No way. No how."

Dante twisted around to look out the back window, causing a sharp twinge in his neck. Cars crept up and stopped behind the taxi. He turned to the front. The soft chatter of the grainy television screen on the console filled the taxi.

Dante heard the revving of a motorcycle engine and turned to see a motorcyclist clad in black leather, a large black helmet, and reflective chrome visor weaving between cars until it pulled up behind the cab. *Could it be Marvee? But what would she be doing here in the city? Maybe Sokolova? Whoever it was certainly handled the motorcycle well.* He dismissed the thought. *Hell, it could be anybody.* Dante glanced at the rider, but couldn't tell if it was a man or woman, except the person seemed comfortable handling the motorcycle with its fiberglass screen flaring from the front and around the cyclist's knees.

As they sat at the light, the motorcyclist continued to rev the engine, higher and higher, until it was nearly screaming. This was no ordinary cyclist out for a ride—this guy was taunting. Dante's instincts told him not to take any chances. He turned back and sank into his seat, his breath becoming short. Dante glanced up and out of each side window, ready to jump if necessary.

The light changed and traffic began to move. At the corner, the taxi driver turned right and wheeled the Dodge around a couple of cars as he sped up Pine Street, stopping behind another line of cars at the intersection with Van Ness Avenue. There was nowhere to go.

As the sound of the revving motorcycle drew near again, Dante looked to his right. It had pulled alongside the taxi, the engine quietly purring. The cyclist leaned over and looked into the back seat, the chromed visor just inches from the window. *What the hell? What's going on?*

The rider placed booted feet on the pavement, sat up slightly and reached inside the black leather jacket, producing a pistol with a short silencer, pointed directly at him. Fear shot though his body. Dante grabbed the door handle and shoved it open against the motorcyclist.

The blow was enough to throw off the muffled shot, which slammed through the window glass, shattering it, but missing Dante. The rider leapt from the motorcycle as it banged to the pavement, the engine still running, and stumbled to the pavement between parked cars.

"What da fuck!" the taxi driver shouted, hitting his horn. "I had a feeling you was gonna be trouble." The driver looked around in panic. He was pinned in traffic.

Dante sprang out of the taxi, scrambled over the downed cycle, and leapt, his arms flailing, at the leather clad gunman, who held the gun high, trying to keep balance while staggering backward.

Dante's torso slammed into the shooter and they tumbled onto the sidewalk. Protected by the padded leathers, the shooter thrashed on the pavement, struggling to break free of Dante's grip. But Dante clutched the hand holding the gun, and jerked the weapon back and forth as he tried to wrest it away. The rider was strong and fast, but Dante felt he could hold his own.

Dante felt an explosion of pain as the shooter's knee found his groin. His stomach tightened and he gasped for breath, but maintained his grip, knowing that to lose it meant death. Tapping a reserve of strength, he swung the shooter's arms to the side and slammed the gun to the curb. There was a cry of pain as the gloved hand smacked against the concrete, the gun skittering along the pavement. The pained voice was higher than he expected, which made Dante pause. *What the hell?* "Who are you?" he shouted.

Dante looked for the weapon, which lay under a parked car. He went to grab it, but it was too far to reach. He scrambled to his feet and bolted up the sidewalk to the corner of Van Ness Avenue, wanting only to get away.

He looked around in panic and heard the insistent sound of a honking horn. It was the taxi driver, finally free of traffic, motioning for Dante to come. He jumped in and with a squeal of spinning tires, the Dodge tore off.

Dante twisted around to brush the shattered window glass from the seat, holding on as the taxi swerved in and out of traffic. *Who the hell is it?* Santos had sent someone. Of course. He survived the truck, and now this.

The traffic was too thick for the taxi to make it far. Dante was thrown against the front seat as the driver screeched to a stop, waiting to make a left turn onto lower Lombard Street.

"Thanks," Dante said as the taxi was suddenly silent.

"Had to get you outta there," the driver said, breathing hard from the confrontation. He looked over his shoulder to the missing rear door window and sighed. "Someone's gotta pay for the damned window!"

They both heard the sound of the motorcycle's engine revving behind them again. The taxi driver glanced in his rear view mirror, and Dante twisted around to look out the back window. The motorcycle was several car lengths back, snaking slowly between the idling cars, moving closer. The taxi driver gauged the cross traffic on Lombard, and seeing a break, stomped on the gas. The Dodge leapt through the red light at the intersection, barely avoiding a side-on collision and causing an eruption of squealing tires and honking horns. The taxi driver ignored the chaos and gunned the Dodge several blocks before making a sliding left turn onto Bay Street. The taxi raced along Bay Street, swerved right onto Marina Boulevard, entered the Marina District, and wove through traffic.

With the docks of yachts and sailboats whizzing by on their right, the driver looked again into the mirror and his eyes grew wide. The taxi driver said, "We got trouble again."

Dante twisted around, fear gripping his chest, and saw the motorcycle. He sank into his seat. "Holy shit."

"Who d' hell is that?" the driver shouted, glaring into the mirror.

"I don't know!" Dante yelled.

The taxi sailed past stop signs and under red traffic lights, and the sound of the motorcycle faded, but soon gained on them. The taxi driver sped on, guiding the Dodge under the Highway 101 overpass and into the Presidio, where the traffic was light, letting the taxi stay well ahead of the motorcycle. Reaching Lincoln Boulevard, which wound between the quiet buildings, the cycle was again on the taxi's tail.

A couple of bullets hit the back window, shattering it over the back seat and showering Dante with glass. The taxi driver stomped again on the accelerator, swerved along the winding road and through another underpass as the Golden Gate Bridge loomed nearby.

The taxi negotiated a long loop and sped toward the Pacific Ocean side of the peninsula, passing signs and cutoffs to Baker Beach as the vast blue-gray ocean came into view, spreading into the distant horizon.

Traffic thinned even more and the taxi raced along the winding cliff-top road, the cycle still on the taxi's tail. The taxi made a sliding left turn onto 25th Avenue overlooking the ocean at Lands End, and roared southward, entering the western edge of the Richmond District.

Without slowing, the taxi swerved right onto Point Lobos Avenue, and the taxi driver gunned the Dodge toward Seal Rock. The taxi sped around a cluster of tourists near a bus parked at the Cliff House. As the Dodge passed some cars, they both noticed a couple of San Francisco traffic cop cars parked at the edge of the road, the officers calmly writing parking tickets.

Dante felt like signaling for help, but there was no need. The cops lifted their heads as the taxi and cycle screamed past. The cops looked at each other, scrambled to their patrol cars, and gave chase, lights flashing.

The taxi raced south along the Great Highway as it dropped down from the cliffs and onto the wide and open double-lane road tracking the ocean's edge. The wide and straight road gave the cyclist an opportunity to pull out the gun again. Dante heard a couple more shots. With the back window already blown out, the bullets slammed into the front windshield, turning it into a spider web of cracks.

Dante carefully raised his head to look behind. The cops were in pursuit, closing in on the motorcycle. The cyclist looked back, then suddenly swerved left at a traffic light, leaning close to the pavement, and shot back toward the city, disappearing into traffic.

Unable to turn at that speed, the cops whizzed through the intersection and chased the taxi. Dante sank back into his seat. "It's over," he shouted. "You'd better stop."

The taxi driver looked at him in the rear view mirror, and seeing the motorcycle was gone and the flashing red lights of the squad cars on his tail, he hit his brakes pulled to the side of the highway.

CHAPTER 40

By the time Dante finished giving his statement to the San Francisco police, it was just after 6 p.m. He had endured several hours of questioning and quizzical looks from his interrogators as he tried to convince them the cyclist was an assassin chasing him because of a story he intended to write. The police had contacted the *Santa Rosa Sun* and spoken with Jones about his work there. That part of his story checked out.

The taxi driver, meanwhile, was none too happy about the impoundment of his vehicle or the police threats to charge him with reckless endangerment, being a public nuisance, and suspension of his driver's license and taxi permit. The driver had looked sullen and shook Dante's hand limply when he thanked the man for saving his life. Dante pulled out his wallet and gave the driver two twenties, which was all he had. Dante found an old business card. He scratched out his office phone number and circled his cell phone number. "Let me know what the window damage costs. I'm good for it."

The driver slipped his card into his shirt pocket. "You have an interesting life, man," he said. "Take care." He turned and walked down the street where he climbed into a waiting car.

Dante watched the car disappear into the city and walked a couple of blocks in the opposite direction, happy to be out of the stale air of the police station. He had a few hours to kill before he was to meet Mei. He was tired and hungry and needed a drink. He flagged down another taxi.

"Take me to the Mission," Dante said. He remembered a place where he could fade into the crowd, get something to eat, and have decent glass of wine or two.

When the taxi dropped him off, Dante stepped onto the sidewalk on Mission Street. It was a warm evening and the street was crowded, locals dodging gawking tourists. He scanned the crowd, fearful he might see a leather-clad motorcyclist. He took a deep breath, trying to stay calm, and walked a couple of blocks to Valencia Street where he ducked into a dark and crowded wine bar. It was a narrow place, with tables for two against the wall to his right. He navigated the bar, drinkers perched on and standing around bar stools, and found an empty one at the rear. The bartender dropped a menu in front of him.

The place had a global selection of wine, and he ordered a glass of a three-year-old Italian red, along with a plate of cheeses and cold cuts. His neck twinged again, sending a sharp pain up his skull and down his shoulder, adding to the ache he felt throughout his body. As he quickly drank a glass of wine and thought about the previous twenty-four hours, anger slowly replaced his paranoia—anger at everyone, including the cops, for suggesting he was losing his grip on reality. He drew a deep breath and exhaled, trying to settle himself. *You've got to calm down. Don't do anything stupid!*

Dante retraced the steps of the story: Morrison and Ling, Carmen, Pierce's disease, the spray, Grundy, Tercero's vineyard, Muñoz, and Hernandez. The trail had taken him to Santos. He knew he was right. The tanker truck accident was not random. God was not punishing him. He'd done nothing wrong. He'd done everything right. He was closing in on the answer, but needed one more confirmation to nail it down.

Twenty minutes after nine, Dante stepped onto an empty and dimly lit street in the Sunset District. The quiet was unnerving, his ears still ringing from the noisy chatter of the wine bar.

He walked a couple of blocks, clinging to the shadows. Like much of the district, this was a residential neighborhood of connected stucco houses, differentiated only by color. He walked a final half block and checked the address. He squinted in the darkness. There it was. He looked around. Not a soul.

A car crept down the street and turned into the short driveway. It was Mei. The garage door opened and the garage's interior light poured over the car and the driveway. He waved as he approached her car from behind.

The driver's window lowered. Mei looked up and smiled. "Have you been waiting long?"

"No. I was across the street."

"I saw. C'mon in." Mei pulled her car inside and Dante followed. She turned the car off. The garage door rumbled down and closed with a bang. Mei grabbed her bulky briefcase and purse and climbed out. Dante followed her upstairs.

It was a modestly furnished house with split bamboo floors, oriental rugs, and modern furniture. The place felt clean, the lines were pure and simple. Good *feng shui,* Dante thought, and tried to relax.

Mei tossed her designer jean jacket on the couch and let her briefcase and purse clunk to the floor beside a glass coffee table. Dressed in faded jeans and a beige T-shirt, she sighed and cocked her head to the side, her long hair falling over her shoulders. "I don't suppose you'd refuse a glass of wine?" she asked.

"No, I wouldn't. Thanks. It's been a hell of a day."

Mei scrunched her face with a confused look. "Again?" she asked.

Dante shrugged, then watched as Mei stepped into the kitchen, handily pulled the cork to a bottle of wine, poured, and handed him a glass. He compulsively sniffed as he swirled the wine. She did the same. "This is a bottle of Chao's private reserve stock from Morrison Creek," Mei said. "He has a dozen cases of it. I like it."

"A good nose," Dante said, somewhat surprised. He lifted his glass with a smile. "Better than I would expect from Morrison Creek."

Mei clinked her glass against his and took a deep drink.

"I appreciate you letting me stay here," Dante said.

"There's a spare bedroom and bath downstairs. It's yours as long as you need it."

"You're not afraid my being here could cause you problems?"

"I'll do anything if it helps me find out why my brother was killed," Mei said.

"Can I ask you a question?"

"Of course."

"Did Chao ever mention the pesticide to you?"

Mei looked lost in thought. "The pesticide? No. Why? What does it have to do with Chao's death?"

"I'm not sure," he said. "Can you check something for me?"

The glimmer faded from Mei's eyes, replaced by worry. "Sure," she said. "What can I do?"

"Show me Chao's desk."

She grabbed the wine bottle and led Dante into a room down the hall.

A low-backed office chair was pushed against a broad, heavy, glass-topped desk with curving chrome legs. The table's surface was uncluttered, save for the three computer screens arranged at the back. "I was hoping we might be able to get into his email, if it's not encrypted."

"Ahh… no problem," Mei said hesitantly, and sat.

Dante watched her fingers flick across the keyboard. "If you want to look through his emails, we can. But there's a lot. What do you want, specifically?"

"Any communications he might have had with the state of California."

"The state of California?" Mei said with surprise.

"Do a keyword search for insecticide or pesticide."

Mei's fingers flicked across the keyboard. A list of emails populated the screen. "There are dozens of emails between Morrison, Carelli, and Chao."

"About what?" Dante said, leaning close. "Let me read."

Mei read aloud. "'Multiple cases of exposure'...." She scrolled. "'Illegal testing of pesticide at the Santos vineyards'..." She looked up at Dante. "Here's one about a woman who died working at Santos vineyard. Must be the girl you mentioned."

"Yes. The cause was initially listed as dehydration."

Mei scanned through a lengthy email and looked up at Dante. "Chao writes here she died of complications due to exposure to the pesticide."

Dante's mind raced at the implications. "So, Chao knew," Dante said softly.

Mei looked back at the screen. "There's an attachment." She opened it.

"Looks like the medical examiner's report," Dante said. "Chao had a copy."

Mei read aloud. "'Helena Maria Hernandez… died due to complications caused by an ectopic pregnancy.' It says she had high levels of toxins in her blood."

"Exactly," he said. "That's the report I showed Santos just yesterday."

Mei looked up at him, searching his face.

"If your brother knew about the pesticide and the girl's death, there's no doubt now that's why he wanted his money back," Dante said. "If Morrison and his winery were linked to the toxic insecticide, the winery was as good as dead."

"But investors aren't liable," Mei said. "Limited liability corporations shield them."

"With a toxic pesticide killing a vineyard worker, and Morrison funding it with Chao's money? In the public's mind, the whole mess would be conflated, regardless of the legalities. Just the rumor would be enough to ruin a winery, big or small."

"That's why Morrison wanted Chao's money. In cash," Mei said, her face pale and drawn.

"When Chao learned about the problems with the pesticide, Morrison was afraid Chao would expose him, Grundy, and Santos," Dante said.

"Maybe my brother threatened them to get his money back," Mei said.

"Carmen knew about the pesticide as well," Dante said. "Shit. Santos or someone tried to kill her and maybe Grundy, too. To cover their tracks."

"Dead men don't talk," she said.

"I show up and throw the medical examiner's report in his face. Santos tries to kill me too. Twice."

"Twice?"

Fear grew in Mei's eyes as Dante gave her a brief version of the shooter on the motorcycle, the struggle on the street and the chase through the marina and to the coastline.

A soft thump sounded from downstairs. They fell silent. Dante froze, his heart pounding. He twitched, sending a shot of pain through his wrenched neck muscles.

"What the hell?" Mei said, pushing the keyboard away and slowly rising, her eyes wide with fear. "You were followed."

"How could anyone know I'm here?" Dante whispered. "I took a bus. I got off several blocks away." Dante glanced around. "We need to get out of here. What about the back? Can we get to it?" Dante stepped to the room's only window. It was two stories up, a straight drop to a concrete alley. He turned back to Mei.

Mei shook her head, held a finger to her lips, and pointed to the hallway. They stepped silently along the bamboo floor and turned the corner into the living room.

Dante gasped. Again he was face-to-face with a figure in black motorcycle leathers, head covered in a black ski mask this time, the silenced pistol in hand. *The same shooter!* Mei dove to the floor and tumbled toward the couch. The shooter glanced at Mei and pointed the gun at her. Dante impulsively twisted, leaned back, and kicked his leg out, like Marvee had shown him. His foot missed as the figure dodged and instead struck the shooter's right arm.

Dante's kick knocked the gun hand wildly into the air, making the shooter stagger backward. Seeing an opening, Dante charged and shouted, ramming his head and shoulder into his attacker's torso. They tumbled onto the living room floor.

The attacker struggled frantically and kicked, trying again to get a knee into Dante's groin, but mindful of his earlier encounter, Dante twisted so the angle was no good. He grabbed the arm and reached for the gun as an elbow slammed into his head. A jolt of pain stunned him, but he'd clutched the silencer and pushed the barrel away. He felt the gun jerk in his hands. *Thunk... thunk.* Two shots. The hot gun barrel slipped from his grip, with thoughts of singed fingers swiftly replaced by the painful crack of the gun grip against the left side of his head, once and twice.

Raising a hand to protect his head, he managed to grab the gun again, clasping his left hand over the pistol's trigger guard and grip. *Keep it anywhere but pointed at my head!* Another shot sounded… *thunk.* Dante thrashed harder, and the gun swung back and forth as each struggled to control it. The shooter jerked and yanked the gun wildly, but Dante refused to let go. Two more muffled shots… *thunk... thunk.*

"Drop it!" Mei shouted at the leather-clad figure, standing over the two thrashing bodies. Dante glanced up to see Mei holding a gun in her hands. *Where did that come from?* Dante and the shooter rolled back and forth, struggling for control of the weapon. With a great heave, Dante rolled onto his back, his arms extended above his head, both of his hands clasped over the shooter's grip.

Three deafening shots rang out—*Bam! Bam! Bam!*

Dante felt the jerks of the attacker's body as each bullet pierced the back of the leather jacket. The body went limp, legs twitching spasmodically.

His ears ringing, Dante groaned deeply from the dead weight on his chest and heard the wheeze of the attacker's final breath.

Mei stood over them, her gun still pointed at the body, as if it would suddenly spring back to life. Dante groaned, shoved the body off, and sat up. He looked at Mei, who slowly lowered the gun, her chest heaving, her eyes wide and glistening.

Dante pulled off the attacker's mask. He saw the face of Sofía Sokolova, Santos's bird of prey. It was a beautiful face, with neatly shaped eyebrows, her ice-blue eyes now lifeless and staring, her skin pallid. A spot of blood appeared at the edge of her mouth and slowly made its way across her cheek.

Dante felt the warm wetness of his own blood on the side of his head, dripping down his neck, soaking into his collar. The searing pain and burn of the wound flared, and the room began to swirl. He fell to the side as his world went dark.

CHAPTER 41

A few weeks later Dante wheeled his new Mustang into the parking lot of the Morrison Creek Winery. There was only one other car, and beside it was a sleek street motorcycle. The sight of it gave him pause, the chase through the city filling his mind until he pushed the thoughts away, remembering Sokolova was dead.

Dante parked, climbed out, and slowly closed the car door. A couple of workmen had attached a new sign over the tasting room entry. It read, "Chao Vineyards."

The workmen, still on their ladders, stopped as he approached. Dante ducked under the suspended sign, opened the door to the tasting room, and stepped inside.

The tasting room was silent. The wine bar was wiped clean, with new wine bottles clustered strategically, waiting for customers and tasters to arrive.

His eyes fell on the winery office door, slightly ajar, through which faint voices could be heard. He stepped close and listened. The voices stopped. He eased the door open.

Mei Ling and Marvee McGregor were locked in an embrace. Surprised, the women turned, mouths open, eyes wide. Marvee was dressed in her black motorcycle leathers and her arm was around Mei's shoulders, Mei's arm around Marvee's waist. "Dante?" Mei said with surprise. "What are you doing here?"

Dante forced a smile. "I wanted to congratulate you on getting the winery."

They both looked at him, neither moving nor speaking.

"I like the name change," he said. "Chao Vineyards. Good idea."

Mei and Marvee glanced at each other, broke their embrace, and looked back at Dante.

"It was Chao's dream," Mei said.

"Too bad he can't be here to enjoy it," Dante said.

They lapsed again into an awkward silence, broken as Marvee said, "I read the story on your blog about Santos and the pesticide. It's causing quite a stir."

"Santos fled the country," Dante said. He self-consciously touched the healing wound at the side of his head, now a bandaged scab. The hospital had shaved the left side of head, forcing him to get a Marine-style high-and-tight haircut all around.

"I see you're almost healed," Mei said.

"Thanks," Dante said. "You saved my life."

Mei shrugged as if it was nothing. "Both of our lives."

They fell into another awkward silence.

"There are several loose ends I wanted to tie up," Dante said.

Mei and Marvee glanced again at each other and back at him.

"Loose ends?" Mei asked. "What on earth are you talking about? It's all pretty clear."

"Maybe," Dante said.

"You read Chao's email," Mei continued. "Morrison killed my brother Chao when he threatened to expose Morrison, Grundy, and Santos and their poisonous pesticide."

"But," Dante said, "what I can't figure out is how Morrison learned the state had rejected his pesticide."

Mei and Marvee looked at him, but said nothing.

"Just like everyone else," Marvee said finally. "The letter you found at the house."

"Not really," Dante said. "Morrison never officially knew the state had rejected the pesticide."

"Of course he knew," Marvee said.

"The notice didn't come until after he and Chao were dead," Dante said. "He pulled the envelope from his coat pocket and held it out to them, pointing at the postmark. "It's postmarked the day after Morrison was killed. It was on his desk when I met you at his house," he said, giving Marvee a sharp glance.

Mei looked at Marvee, then at Dante.

"Snail mail," Mei said. "He was notified by email. Ever think of that?"

"You're right about email," Dante said. "But the email didn't come from the state."

"It didn't?" Mei said, her voice dripping with innocence.

"It came from you. You used Chao's email to make sure certain people, specifically Morrison, knew the pesticide was toxic."

"That's absurd," Mei said with a shake of her head.

Dante sighed, his stomach knotting. "Marvee, you knew last year the Hernandez girl didn't die of dehydration in the Santos vineyard. You knew she hemorrhaged from a problem pregnancy, caused by her exposure to the pesticide."

Marvee narrowed her eyes. "How would I know that?"

"Because you'd known Grundy from your days at UC Davis wine school. You'd worked with him for years. You knew everything he was doing."

"Yeah, so what?" Marvee said with a sneer.

"Grundy knew the pesticide was toxic, but not much else," Dante said. "When the girl died, he knew why. He confided in you." Dante exhaled slowly, tightness gripping his chest. "So you told Mei about it."

Mei scowled. "Why would I care about a Mexican girl dying in a vineyard?"

"You wouldn't," Dante said. "It's how she died that got you thinking."

"Thinking about what?" Mei asked.

"About how to get Chao's money back," Dante said.

"The fact Chao lost his money to the pesticide project was his problem, not mine," Mei said. "He might have been brilliant, but he could be very stupid."

"It was you who told Chao about the toxic pesticide," Dante said. "Like a good sister would."

"Of course," Mei said. "He needed to be told."

"But you also saw an opportunity," Dante said. "An opportunity to get your brother out of the way and get something you'd always wanted."

"Which was what?" Mei said.

Dante swept his arm widely. "This. Your own winery."

"Bullshit!" Marvee yelled.

Dante gauged Mei's reaction. "Using Chao's email, because he trusted you, you made sure Morrison knew that Chao knew about the pesticide, long before the state letter arrived to make it official."

Mei narrowed her eyes.

"When Morrison didn't respond," Dante said, "you pushed Chao to go see Carmen Carelli and file a lawsuit."

Mei continued to stare.

"Morrison panicked because he knew once the problems with the pesticide became public record as part of the lawsuit, it would be over for him and the winery, as well as Grundy and Santos," Dante said.

"You're bluffing," Mei said. "You don't know what you're talking about. You have no proof."

"Morrison was counting on the sale of the pesticide to repay Chao his money," Dante said. "But after Chao threatened to expose the toxic pesticide, Morrison murdered him, thinking no one would learn of the problems with the pesticide. And, conveniently, the sheriff's deputies killed Morrison, who'd all but lost his mind."

The two only stared.

Dante continued. "With both Chao and Morrison dead, it was an outcome you could only have dreamed about."

"Dreamed about?" Mei said, her eyes wide. "You're a bigger idiot than I thought. He was my brother! I loved him!"

"Your brother got all the praise and glory from your parents. You hated being an afterthought. When you saw how careless your brother was with his money, and how he was squandering his chance to have a prestigious Napa Valley winery—it drove you crazy. Owning a winery was your dream."

"You have no idea what you're talking about," Mei growled.

Dante drew a deep breath. "It was Marvee's dream too. You needed her knowledge and expertise in wine making. You promised if she'd help, you'd be partners."

"Shut the hell up and get out of here," Mei said.

"Your problem, Dante, is you never got over Morrison screwing your wife," Marvee said. "He got her pregnant. You hated Morrison. You wanted him dead as much as anyone. When you trashed his wines, it was like pouring gasoline on a fire. Now you're trying to ruin our dreams. You're a sick and vengeful man."

"I never wanted to kill Morrison," Dante said. "You're wrong."

"Get the hell out!" Mei yelled.

"Oh, I'm only getting started," Dante said.

Mei and Marvee glared.

"With Chao and Morrison dead, Carmen Carelli became the problem," he said. "She knew all about the toxic pesticide from your brother."

"This is ridiculous," Mei said.

"Carelli went to Ricardo Santos and told him what she knew about the pesticide. He offered her a huge amount of money if she would drop Chao's lawsuit against Morrison. She refused, since it was far less than the million dollars Ling was owed. So something had to be done about her."

"How do you know that?" Mei asked, her anger becoming obvious.

"Santos and his bitch, Sofía, tried to kill Carelli," Marvee blurted. "So why don't the police arrest them?"

"Santos fled to Mexico to distance himself from the investigation," Dante said. "And Mei killed Sokolova, remember?"

Mei's eyes opened wide. "In self-defense!"

Dante leveled his gaze at Mei. "You're right. And Santos and his hired gun tried to kill me, twice. But they weren't the only ones who wanted to get rid of Carelli. Because of what she knew, she could have easily prevented you from taking over Morrison's winery after the deaths in the vineyard." Dante shifted his gaze to Marvee. "So you tried to kill her on the jogging trail. Good thing for her you're a bad shot."

"You're out of your mind," Marvee said, her eyes angry and wild.

"Am I?" Dante asked. "This left Simon Grundy. Marvee, you worked with Grundy for years. You knew all about the pesticide and the problems with it. You also knew it was worth a fortune. But Grundy refused to make you a partner in the project."

"You don't know what you're talking about," Marvee said.

"You made good on your promise to Mei, and you killed him," Dante said.

"Bullshit!" Marvee shouted again, her eyes glistening with fear. "It was Sofía who killed Grundy, not me! He was the only one left who could tie Santos to the pesticide and the Hernandez girl. He and Morrison had been spraying it for months."

Dante glared at them. "Maybe."

Marvee twisted around, yanked open a drawer to Morrison's old desk, and pulled out an automatic pistol Dante recognized as the one Mei had used at Chao's house. She held it at arm's length with both hands and pointed it at Dante's face. Dante swallowed hard, his throat dry, his heart thumping. He lifted his hands in surrender.

"I say we waste him right now," Marvee said. "Get it over with."

Mei reached out and pushed the gun aside. But Marvee jerked her hands back and held the gun in Dante's face.

Mei looked steadily at Dante. "You're going to keep your mouth shut, if you want to live," she said, her voice low. "You're going to move on, forget about all of this, and find something new to write about. Is that clear?"

"Or what?" Dante said.

"Or we'll write the ending of your pathetic life story," Marvee said.

Dante's eyes darted from Marvee, to the gun, to Mei, and back to Marvee.

"Okay," Dante said, slowly lifting his hands, palms out. "I get it. Don't do anything stupid."

"Now get the fuck out," Marvee said.

Dante sucked in a halting breath and slowly backed out of the office.

Outside, Dante climbed in his car, his heart thumping, his head pounding. He fired up the engine, put the Mustang in gear, and peeled out of the parking lot and onto the road.

A mile from the winery, Dante pulled off the road and slid to a stop behind an unmarked panel van. Dante let his car engine idle. Investigator Henshaw flung open the rear doors to the van and jumped to the ground.

Dante saw the flicker of video screens inside the van and the electronic recording equipment affixed to metal racks, all monitored by other plain-clothes cops. Wearing his black fleece vest and jeans, Henshaw bent down to Dante's open window.

Dante unbuttoned his shirt and peeled off the tape holding a small microphone tightly against his chest. "I believe this is yours," he said, handing the tiny device to Henshaw.

Henshaw smiled. "We got good sound. With the micro-cameras we put inside, you nailed it."

Dante looked up at Henshaw. "I was almost killed."

"But you weren't. You should stick around. We're going in."

"McGregor is armed. She's got a pistol. Your ballistics experts may want to check if it's the same gun used on Carmen Carelli."

They turned as a tactical police van arrived.

"It's party time," Henshaw said. He pulled his pistol from his holster, checked the clip for ammo, and climbed into the passenger side, saying something to the driver. Henshaw gave a two-fingered salute to Dante, and the vans sped down the road to the winery.

Dante climbed out of his car, lifted his sunglasses, and squinted into the distance as SWAT team officers leapt out and took positions in the winery parking lot. He crossed his arms and waited. Shots erupted from the winery. Then silence. Dante looked at the ground, sighed, and shook his head in disgust.

EPILOGUE

Carmen sat on the porch of her house and looked at the vineyards surrounding her house. A soft breeze stirred the air, ruffling the leaves. She poked her fork into the bowl of cold pasta salad Dante had prepared.

"When are the doctors going to get you into rehab?" Dante asked.

She glanced at Dante across the rustic outdoor table. "As soon as everything stops hurting," she said, a scowl clouding her face.

"You'll feel better soon. You'll be aching to get some exercise."

"In time, I suppose." She lifted her fork and took a bite.

The beret was gone and her hair had grown out about half an inch, coming in thick and dark.

"Your hair's looking rather stylish," Dante said.

Carmen smiled weakly. "I still can't believe you agreed to wear a wire," she said.

"I had to. It was part of the deal I made with Henshaw. If he told me what I wanted to know, he said I had to help him. A fair exchange. It turned out fine."

"You were lucky."

"Yeah. Maybe. Strange how it all turned out."

"All because of a damned bug," Carmen said.

"The pesticide was Morrison's last stand."

"When Ling learned what Morrison had done with his money—"

"He wasn't happy," Dante said.

"It took time, but with Mei and Marvee playing puppet masters, Chao connected the young woman's death to the use of the pesticide."

"That's when the game changed," Dante said. He reached for his glass of chardonnay and sipped. "But Morrison didn't have Chao's money anymore. Marvee and Mei knew it. They also knew Chao would push Morrison off the cliff and into his personal abyss of madness by threatening to go public about the pesticide. Marvee knew how fragile Morrison's mental state was. She lived with him."

"Without the windfall from the pesticide, Morrison knew he was finished," Carmen said. "So he decided to take Chao with him."

"It almost fell apart when you went to Santos about the pesticide," Dante said. "Instead of getting angry, Santos offered you a bribe."

"Bribe? No. See? You're thinking like a journalist. It was an offer to settle the case."

"Same thing."

"No, it's not."

"When I confronted Santos about Helena Hernandez's death," Dante said, "he tried to distance himself from all of it. It almost worked. But Santos was involved from day one."

"Santos is a bastard," Carmen said. "I see that now. He used Morrison and Grundy to do the dirty work, and they used Chao Ling's money."

"It's ironic, though."

"Ironic?"

"Santos said greed was ruining the California wine industry," Dante said. "But greed is what got Santos and the others." He took a bite of the salad.

"Santos wanted the pesticide all to himself," Carmen said. "He planned to patent it."

"So what's going to become of Morrison's winery, now that Mei and Marvee are out of the picture?" Dante asked.

"I don't know," she said. "Legally, I still represent Chao Ling's estate."

"The family could sell it. They'll need the proceeds to pay for Mei Ling's defense."

"McGregor is the one who's in serious trouble," Carmen said.

"She tried to kill you, and maybe did in Grundy as well," Dante said.

"Thank God she's behind bars now. I don't have to look over my shoulder all the time. Mei can be charged as an accomplice, a co-conspirator, and an accessory to a murder and an attempted murder."

"Poor Grundy," Dante said. "A wine talent gone sour."

"Marvee could have killed him," Carmen said. "But his winery was struggling. Grundy knew he was somehow responsible for the Hernandez girl's death. With all he'd been stealing from Santos, he may have decided suicide was the best way out. Marvee hasn't been charged with Grundy's death. At least not yet."

"And Santos is in Mexico," Dante said. "He got away."

"There's no evidence directly connecting him to the murders. He didn't need to run."

"What about Santos Wine Company?" Dante asked.

"The wine is sold under many labels, and none of them mention the Santos Wine Company. The public won't connect the Santos name to any of the wine they drink." She looked at the vineyard for a long moment, then back at Dante. "What are you going to work on next?"

"I'm going to work on helping you heal. I think you should begin thinking about the next Bay-to-Breakers race through the city."

Carmen smiled and reached for her glass of chardonnay.

THE END

*For More News About Peter Eichstaedt,
Signup For Our Newsletter:*

http://wbp.bz/newsletter

Word-of-mouth is critical to an author's long-term success. If you appreciated this book please leave a review on the Amazon sales page:

http://wbp.bz/napanoira

CHAPTER ONE
Late July, 1996

Time passed in Winchester, Wyoming, at more or less the same rate as any other forgotten town on the edge of the high plains, but *The Bullet*'s newsroom clock appeared to be running backward.

The last time Jefferson Morgan had looked at the clock, just a few minutes before, it was almost eleven. Indeed, his wristwatch said it was eleven. Deadline.

But the clock on the wall now read ten-fifty. And four front-page stories were still unwritten.

Morgan thumped his watch. He had no way of knowing his two smart-ass reporters cranked the big hand back ten minutes at deadline time almost every Wednesday, stealing just a little more time to write stories that were, for the most part, already a week old.

Morgan watched as his impatient printer, Cal Nussbaum, whose own ink-smudged backshop clock was set *forward* ten minutes, prowled the jumbled newsroom. Anger stretched his long face even longer.

"Nobody gives a good goddamn about deadlines anymore," he mumbled.

The press was ready, if the news was not. The ink fountains filled, Cal rubbed his massive hands in a greasy black rag. He faced Morgan in the narrow space between the newsroom's prehistoric oak desks, dragging a vapor trail of oily ink, solvent and body odor.

Cal had worked for *The Bullet* since he was a kid back in the Forties, when he made fifty cents a day as a printer's devil.

Cal's veins ran inky black. He hated reporters. Their only virtue, in his mind, was their egotistic ambition to do less work for more pay: Few of them stayed more than a year.

The more Cal knew about young reporters, the more he preferred the company of pressroom rats. And for the reporters who dared trespass in his space, he displayed on his backshop wall several years worth of girlie calendars left by newsprint salesmen. It was a trifling rebellion, except that it asserted the sovereignty of Cal's borders.

Nonetheless, until the newsroom clock ticked past the eleven a.m. deadline, Cal restrained himself, barely.

"Wouldn't a happened when Old Bell was around," he complained.

"Old Bell" — Belleau Wood Cockins — had been the editor of *The Bullet* for more than fifty years. When he sold out to Jefferson Morgan a month before, he just cleaned out the deep drawers of his desk, packed up the only two reference books he ever needed — an annotated Shakespeare and a King James version of the Bible — and handed Morgan the keys. He never came back.

Since that day four weeks before, Morgan hadn't met a single deadline, and it pissed him off. The damned paper wouldn't even have been delivered on time if Cal Nussbaum hadn't bribed the boys at the Post Office with a twelve-pack of Coors every week.

In almost eighteen years at the *Chicago Tribune*, where the massive machinery of journalism churned every minute of every day in a near-perfect synchronicity, Morgan had never known anyone to challenge the consecrated institution of The Deadline. It existed as a kind of covenant between newspapermen and their deluded gods, and punishment would be swift and painful if it were ever violated. It was somehow sacrilegious that here, *in the very newsroom where Old Bell Cockins gave him his first byline*, the sin of missing a deadline could be atoned with twelve beers.

Morgan hovered over his two reporters, a pair of $250-a-week community college grads who'd been at *The Bullet* for less than a year. They bent their heads toward their ancient Macintoshes, pecking away at their late stories, always keeping the editor in the periphery of their sight.

The tiny brass bell above the front door jingled.

Morgan glanced up. Crystal Sandoval, the counter girl who took classified ads, renewed subscriptions, answered the phone and calmed all but the angriest readers with her friendly smile, was away from her chair.

The frail old man who shuffled through *The Bullet*'s door looked lost. He slouched across the foyer's checkered tile, as if gravity itself threatened to drag him under. His sharp face was hollow, almost cadaverous. A ragged thatch of white hair tangled at the sides of his bald head like dead weeds flattened under a weathered fence. The long sleeves of a stiff blue shirt hung past his wrists, its collar buttoned at his skinny throat, and his canvas belt was cinched so tight around his thin hips that the waistband of his brown trousers folded in a thick pleat at the front.

The old man looked around. His dark, sunken eyes were as sharp and serious as a worn sawtooth.

"Sorry. The paper's not out yet," Morgan apologized. Readers often visited *The Bullet* before noon on Wednesdays to snatch one of the first papers off the press. Over tuna melts and iced tea down at The Griddle, every word — from the police blotter to the Little League results to the editor's weekly column — would be cussed and discussed.

"Ain't here for no paper. You the editor?" the old man asked Morgan. His voice was a coarse scrape.

"That's me. What can I do for you?" Morgan asked, circling around the reporters' desks to the waist-high, swinging wooden gate that separated the tiny waiting area from the newsroom. He held a piece of copy paper with some scribbled notes in his left hand, as he extended his right courteously across the gate.

The old man's hand was knobby and dry, his wan grip as cold and blue as the paper-thin skin stretched across his arthritic knuckles. The inside of his knotted index and middle finger were stained brown, and his fingernails were cracked and yellow. Shaking his hand, Morgan smelled stale cigarettes and aging flesh.

"You don't know me," the old man said, lowering his voice to almost a whisper. "My name's Gilmartin. Neeley Gilmartin."

He waited for some recognition from Morgan, but Gilmartin wasn't a name he knew.

"Glad to meet you, Mr. Gilmartin. I'm Jeff Morgan. I've only got a minute. We're just finishing up the paper and I was just ..."

An impatient glower settled on Gilmartin's brow.

"I ain't got no time for fuckin' around here either," he rasped, suddenly less brittle than he'd first appeared.

"Mr. Gilmartin, I understand, but this is a bad time for me. Can you come back in an hour or two, after we put out the paper? Then we can talk."

The old man waved him off, as if he were brushing away a fly. The cracked corners of his mouth turned down in disgust.

"I'll wait right here. No place else I gotta be. Go sell your goddam papers," Gilmartin said, shuffling toward the three spindle-backed Windsor chairs lining one wall of the cramped foyer. He eased his bony hips into the farthest from the window.

"And don't make me wait all fuckin' day," Gilmartin sniped. His face twinged in discomfort as he fished a crumpled pack of Camels from his shirt pocket. He knocked one out of the squarish package and wedged it between his thin, crooked lips. Then he took it out again, stiffening momentarily, his eyes closed so tight his face seemed to fold at the middle.

There was pain in this old man.

The stories were an hour late.

Cal Nussbaum was so angry he wouldn't even speak as he sliced long slicks of type into precise blocks, carving off wasted margins of white paper like a butcher cuts fat off a good steak. The pages fell together under Cal's knife, and he finished his work long past the time he'd normally go to lunch. The old four-unit Goss Community press waited, its hungry black belly rumbling.

Morgan was angry, too. He jammed a pica pole in his back pocket and felt his jaw tighten as he left the backshop, preparing to reprimand his reporters for their insouciance about deadlines. He composed his come-to-Jesus sermon in his head as he threaded his way down the narrow hallway, past the pungent bathroom that doubled as a darkroom, toward the newsroom.

But the reporters were gone. They'd sneaked out to lunch like scared, hungry fugitives. The newsroom was quiet except for the metallic ticking of the ceiling fan that droned incessantly all summer, occasionally sailing a stray sheet of paper off the litter-strewn archipelago of desks.

But Gilmartin hadn't left.

For two hours, he'd squirmed his aching hips in the hard-pan wooden chair, chain-smoking and watching townfolk pass *The Bullet*'s gold-lettered front window. If a passerby looked in, Gilmartin turned away.

From time to time, he'd get up and read the yellowing front-pages Old Bell had hung on the foyer wall. Five decades worth of the town's biggest stories, banner headlines tall and thick, lined up across the wall in earnest black frames. "SLURRY BOMBER DOUSES THEATER FIRE," said one. "BASEBALL PARK NAMED FOR BIG-LEAGUER," said another.

The old man lingered in front of one in particular: "GIRL'S KILLER CONFESSES."

The swinging gate into the front foyer squealed as Morgan stepped through. The checkered floor around the old man's shoes was dusted with cigarette ashes.

"Mr. Gilmartin, I'm very sorry it took me so long. I guess we're going to have to get better at this newspaper stuff," he said. He smiled but wasn't in the mood to make excuses for his indolent reporters. "Anyway, can I get you anything? Coffee? Water?"

The old man turned around and glared at him. If his body was slowly decaying, the fire in his eyes was not. He ignored Morgan's offer.

"Where's the old guy who used to be here?" Gilmartin asked.

"Bell Cockins? He retired about a month ago. You know him?"

"Yeah, a long time ago. I been away."

"Things change pretty quick, even here, I guess," Morgan said.

Gilmartin pointed at the newspaper on the wall.

"You read this shit?"

"Some of it," Morgan said. "There's a lot of local history up there."

"Fuck that," Gilmartin scoffed. "Some of it is bullshit."

Morgan was a little surprised.

"How's that?"

Gilmartin put his finger on one of the front-page photos, the one he'd studied so long. In it, a young man, an accused killer, glared banefully at the camera over his tattooed shoulder. The look was malignant and cold.

"That's me," Gilmartin said.

Morgan didn't believe it, or couldn't. *This old man, a killer?*

He studied the photo and looked at the old man. The body had wasted away, but the eyes were the same. The old man wasn't lying.

Gilmartin patted down a pack of Camels, searching for one more. It was empty.

"You got a smoke?" he asked. Morgan shook his head. Exasperated, Gilmartin tossed the crumpled pack on the pile of unfiltered butts in the ashtray beside him.

"I need a smoke bad," the old man said, scowling. He sidled stiffly past Morgan to the front door. Hot air boiled off the sidewalk as he held it open.

"I gotta get outta here. The place stinks," he said impatiently. "You comin' or just breathin' hard?"

Morgan looked around the empty newsroom. Cal Nussbaum leaned against a doorway, watching them. When Morgan caught his eye, Cal shook his head in disgust and disappeared into the back.

They walked a block down Main Street to the Conoco, the nearest cigarette machine. It was midday in late July, hot enough to curdle the asphalt were the street met the gutter. Gilmartin shuffled along, sweating. Morgan could hear him breathing hard before they'd taken a dozen steps, but he persisted.

"I ain't got no silver," the old man said, patting his pockets. Morgan had just enough change for two packs. Gilmartin hastily stripped off the cellophane, peeled back the top of one pack and whacked it against the heel of his palm. He clamped his lips around the cigarette that stuck out farthest, then lit up.

Gilmartin took a long drag and exhaled slowly, letting the smoke seep out of him in devilish blue curls. He stuffed both packs safely in his breast pocket, which now bulged against his cratered chest.

"I been smokin' all my life and it ain't killed me yet. Ain't gonna get a chance to kill me neither," Gilmartin said, then paused while he took another long draw at his cigarette. "You ever come close to dyin'?"

"Maybe once," Morgan answered. He shoved his hands deep in the empty pockets of his khaki slacks and studied Gilmartin's face. He was reluctant to share personal information with the old man, but it sounded to him as if a door might be opened.

"I was just a kid, maybe seven or eight. I was playing alone on an inflatable raft out at Rochelle Lake. The wind came up and blew me out farther and farther into the deep water. Nobody heard me screaming. I was afraid the raft would spring a leak or tip over and I'd drown. I held on for dear life until a fisherman came by and pulled me out."

Gilmartin looked even paler and more pinched in the harsh sunlight. He avoided looking at Morgan as he spoke, just peered down into the gutter, where a thin drool of muddy water trickled almost imperceptibly toward the storm drain. He flipped an ash into the tiny stream, where it floated a few feet then dissolved.

"You make any deals when you was out there? You promise your god that you'd be a good little boy if he'd just blow your scared little ass back to shore? Did you lie to Him just to save yourself?"

The sun was hot and the smell of gasoline overpowering as they stood there on the corner by the gas station. Morgan scuffed the sole of his worn leather Oxford across the sidewalk as if he were trying to scrape something off, but he was trying to remember what it felt like to encounter death. The skin on his back prickled in the heat as he imagined, all over again, cold water spilling into his lungs, weighing him down, clamping his throat closed.

"Not any I remember. I was just scared. I didn't want to die."

"You do dumb shit when you think you might die," the old man said, smoking and watching the empty street in front of them.

The air was dead calm. Smoke hovered around Gilmartin. He tilted his head back and breathed deeply through the cigarette, his cheeks sucking slowly inward. His hand trembled. Then from nowhere, a cough wracked his whole body, distorting his face as it erupted from deep inside.

"Let's find someplace cool to sit, Mr. Gilmartin," Morgan suggested, touching the old man's elbow.

"Yeah, sure, paper boy."

Across the street and up past a few storefronts was Winchester Park, a patch of sprinkled green near the center of town. They sat on a concrete bench in the cool shade beneath the towering cottonwoods. Birds bickered unseen in the branches above them. The playground thirty yards away was crawling with children on summer vacation.

"I'm not sure what you need from me, Mr. Gilmartin," Morgan said, his leg bent across the park bench as he faced the old man.

"I need your help to do something I can't do for myself. I'm seventy-three fuckin' years old and I can hardly wipe my ass without help. If I could do this thing on my own, I would," Gilmartin said. He fumbled in his lumpy shirt pocket for another cigarette. "I hate reporters, but I ain't got no other choice. I need *you*."

Morgan learned one good lesson on the cop beat: Don't waste time being indignant. Only the amateurs stay mad, his city editor once told him.

"Okay, fair enough. But let's cut to the chase here. Why me and what for?" Morgan asked coolly.

Gilmartin scratched his skeletal fingers through the thin mat of his white hair and stared between his knees at the thick grass. His trousers draped across his emaciated thighs and the muscles at the back of his bent neck bowed out like the slack cords on a marionette. He sat unmoving for a while, elbows on his knees, cupping a lighted cigarette in his palm.

"I ain't proud of what I am, but I ain't no killer," Gilmartin said. "I been almost fifty years in prison for a crime I never done. That's the fuckin' truth. When I was your age, I already done thirteen years of hard time and I was lookin' at a lifetime still to go. It was like dyin' real slow. Back then, I made some choices to save my life, and maybe they was the wrong choices. Now I'm seventy-three and I'm dyin' fast. Got cancer all through me. Hurts like a motherfucker and I'd just as soon be six feet under where it don't hurt no more. But I don't wanna go without clearin' up my name."

Morgan's lips thinned. It was all just a con. He'd heard crooks deny their crimes since his first day on the beat at the *Chicago Tribune*. After a while, he stopped believing prisoners altogether. Reporters were easy marks for sociopathic inmates who were always screwing with the system, exploiting every soft spot. Young reporters, hungry for a big story or in a hurry to change the world, yearned to believe they could ferret out injustice, tip the scales back into equilibrium, and clear an innocent man's name. Even Jefferson Morgan had that crusading spirit once, but he soon found out it never really happened that way. Cons had too much time to think up new ways to manipulate honest people.

Gilmartin was lying, too. Morgan didn't know why, but it didn't matter.

Except the cancer.

Only that part seemed true. Gilmartin's body was decaying in front of his eyes. Morgan recognized the surrender that follows every jolt of pain. He'd seen how it consumed the flesh, then snuffed out the light inside.

Bridger's face flickered across Morgan's memory. His only child was just eight years old when he died of leukemia, two years before. Morgan found no comfort in death except that his little boy's pain had finally ended.

The old man tossed his cigarette on the grass and smothered it with a cheap shoe. Then Gilmartin turned to Morgan and looked deep into him. The severe old man, rough as a cob, had tears in his eyes.

"The state docs said I only got another few weeks, a month maybe, before I die. They just opened the gate and turned me out like a sick animal they didn't have no guts to shoot. That was a couple weeks ago. I'll be feedin' worms long before the first snow, but ... you're the only guy what can save my name. You gotta believe me."

But Morgan didn't.

The high Wyoming sky was the color of worn denim, rendering Gilmartin's pale features more sickly, more desperate. Morgan said nothing, but the old man must have seen misgiving in his eyes.

Children giggled as they teetered and tottered, and Gilmartin's gaze drifted toward them. A pain from somewhere deep inside him crawled across his brow like a poisonous black bug. His jaw tightened and his bottom lip quavered.

When he finally spoke, the old man's voice had softened, the words almost stuck in his raspy craw.

"I never done killed that little girl ..."

www.ingramcontent.com/pod-product-compliance
Lightning Source LLC
Chambersburg PA
CBHW070828190726
48292CB00006B/2149